BLOODLINES

Written

By

J.A. Pettis

Copyright © 2013 of J. A. Pettis
All Rights Reserved

Cover Illustrated by J.A. Pettis

ISBN-13: 978-1481927598
ISBN-10: 1481927590

For additional copies, please contact Createspace
www.createspace.com

BLOODLINES

J A PETTIS

*THIS SERIES is DEDICATED to my grandparents,
Wayde and Ruth Ann Henderson*

RIP

You both are truly missed!

LOVE YOU

TABLE OF CONTENTS

PROLOGUE • 2

CHAPTER 1
The Descendants • 14

CHAPTER 2
Meeting • 30

CHAPTER 3
The House On Manor Avenue • 56

CHAPTER 4
Do You Believe In Magic • 71

CHAPTER 5
Night of the Full Moon • 84

CHAPTER 6
A New Beginning • 101

CHAPTER 7
Life As Witches • 123

CHAPTER 8
Take Their Powers Thrice • 159

CHAPTER 9
Evil Rising • 185

CHAPTER 10
Protection • 207

CHAPTER 11
The Last Stand • 238

TABLE OF CONTENTS

CHAPTER 12
The Finale • 252

CHAPTER 13
A Magical Life • 266

ACKNOWLEDGEMENTS

First and foremost, thank you to my Lord and savior in heaven. If it wasn't for your grace, mercy, and blessings, this book would not have been created. I have been through so much with this book, but you have helped me pull through and finish it to completion. Thank you.

To my Family: To Mom, for being the head of this project (besides me), teaching me how to write, reading every draft, helping me with editing and structure, and everything else you do. I love you so much! ***To Dad***, for being a hard worker. You have worked so hard over the years and haven't complained once. You're perseverance was an inspiration to help me keep going on. Love you dad. ***To Quinisha** (sissy)*, for telling me to write in the first place. If you hadn't, this would've never happened. Love you and miss you Navy girl. ***To Misha** (little sis and my #1 fan)*, you are the best! You've always liked my work, even when I've hated. And if there's a #1 fan out there, they can't beat you. P.S. thanks for editing my cover!

***To Erin D** (my friend, like a second mother)*, thank you so much for your help with this book. You helped me find my writing voice, you read most of the story for plot, and helped me add depth. You are the greatest!

To Linda B, thank you for helping with reading and editing. You helped so much with your feedback, I truly appreciate it.

To Chad Savage, for making and allowing me to use the font that is scattered throughout this work, NOSFEROTICA. You rock man!

To My Friends, those I didn't name, I didn't forget about you! Thank you for your ongoing support of me; I have truly been blessed with such an encouraging group of people in my life!

To the reader, thank you so much for purchasing my book! I hope you enjoy every page!

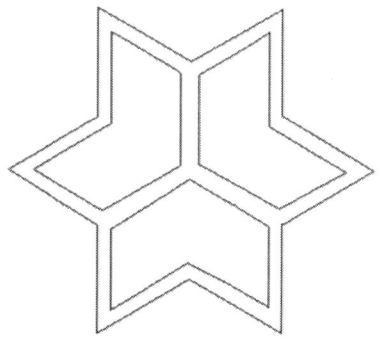

PROLOGUE

FOR CENTURIES, the powerful world of magic was kept unknown to mortals, unless you considered card tricks, pulling a rabbit out of a hat, or cutting someone in half without killing them, "powerful magic." Because of the witch trials of 1692 in Salem, Massachusetts, it was important to keep the magical world between magical beings only. This was maintained by a group of witches and wizards known as the Wizards of the Wise. This group changed over time, with some retiring and no longer performing magic. But their morals and values remained the same. Along with keeping magic a secret from mortals, there were laws within the magical community that were mandatory. One of the main laws enforced was the Forbidden Law.

The Forbidden Law was created to keep mortals and magical beings from having intimate relationships, where a mortal could become involved in the magical world. It was also forbidden to conceive with a mortal. Mortals had untouchable powers within themselves; but if a mortal was half magical being, their magical half could connect to the untouchable powers, which would make them extremely powerful. To the Wizards of the Wise, this posed as a threat to the magical community. Therefore, if a magical/mortal being was created, the punishment was death to the entire line of magical beings that created the child, the mortal involved, and the child itself.

Though most magical beings feared this law, it was broken by a witch named Angelika from the Weltrinch line of witches. The Weltrinch witches were well known in the magical community for their reputation of saving innocents and bringing peace to the world. They had been around for decades and were the most powerful family for the unbreakable bonds. This changed however, when Angelika fell in love with Samson Blackwood, a mortal with whom she had a son, Samuel. Over time, Samuel began to come into his powers, exhibiting extraordinary abilities that most magical infants didn't possess. Her family was very displeased with her, but she felt that no one should be told who they can and can't fall in love with. To Angelika, her love for Samson and their son was much stronger than the wrath of the Wizards.

Learning of Angelika's treason, the Wizards of the Wise became infuriated and set out to kill her and the Weltrinch line. Knowing what the Wizards were going to do, Angelika took matters into her own hands to protect the future of her family line. So, she cast a protection spell on Samson and Samuel to protect them from the Wizards. The only downfall of the spell was if either of them were to break the Forbidden Law three times, the spell would be broken. After doing this, she left Samson and took Samuel away to protect Samson from any magical harm. Angelika then placed Samuel under the care of a friend who was close to the Weltrinchs to raise him until he turned eighteen.

Before leaving her son for the last time, Angelika gave Samuel an amulet shaped like a six-pointed star that was gold and had a blue rectangular gemstone in the middle of it. The amulet's gemstone held a powerful force field inside of it that would protect Samuel until he was old enough to properly use his powers. Once she protected her son and husband, the Wizards of the Wise ambushed Angelika and the Weltrinchs, and killed them. Many years followed after this and the Wizards searched diligently for Samson and Samuel, having no luck at all. The Wizards assumed that the two were killed, because demons and warlocks could sense newborn magical beings and would kill them for their powers, but that wasn't the case. Samuel was alive and well, learning the craft with his care giver and accelerating in his powers at an unusual rate.

At a young age, Samuel felt a connection with mortals that couldn't be explained. Naturally, his mortal half was drawn to them, which helped him fit in with society well. Muscular and 6 foot 2 with dark – almost black – eyes, his ivory skin tone contrasted with his jet black hair, making him appear older than he was at fifteen.

Being half witch and half mortal had its advantages, but it did cause him to have a double life. With his witch side, Samuel was victorious against all of his opponents when it came to magical encounters. His powers were extremely advanced for his age – as he was sixteen when they reached their full potential – and he was feared among evildoers. His powers included: the ability to move things with his mind (telekinesis), foresight and the power of knowing (seer), and he had strength above the natural level of human strength (super strength). With his mortal side, his looks were usually what got him the attention he wanted from women, who he couldn't seem to get enough of. He was aware of the Forbidden Law, but his mortal half was so drawn to mortals that his mind was clouded by what he knew was right. Though he had been in various relationships, Samuel got involved intimately with three women.

The first was a young woman named Fiona Carson. Fiona was slim and stood a foot shorter than Samuel, having fair-skin with baby blue eyes and curly brown locks. Born and raised in a small town near Philadelphia, Fiona was a high-spirited and loving young woman. She was always looking to help those less fortunate or those in need, but at times would keep to herself when it came to personal issues. Fiona's childhood wasn't the greatest, having to live with passive father and a verbally abusive mother. Though her father was a quiet man, Fiona got most of her helpful and loving qualities from him. Her mother on the other hand, was a very hateful and malicious woman, and seemed to have a strong loathing toward Fiona, which she kept throughout Fiona's childhood and teenage years.

Despite her rough beginnings, Fiona had always been a big dreamer. It was in her interest to be a fashion designer, seeing that she loved to sew and make garments so much. But her mother shot that down every chance she got and suggested she just continue to work at the diner she owned. But that wasn't the life Fiona wanted. And when her father passed away due to kidney failure caused by diabetes, her mother developed a horrible smoking and drinking habit, which forced Fiona to leave her home at seventeen.

Fiona started her new life attending a university in Brooklyn, New York, where she met Samuel. Fiona was very awkward around Samuel at first, seeing that he was an aggressive young man, which wasn't what she was used to because her father never showed aggressiveness. Because of that, it was difficult to for Fiona to open up to Samuel.

Samuel was immediately attracted to Fiona because of her looks, but he wasn't sure if the feeling was mutual. Once she opened herself to him, Fiona became just as mesmerized by Samuel as he was with her. In due time, the two began to date during their second year at the university. Samuel did everything he could to make sure Fiona was happy, wanting her to have all her hearts desires. He wanted nothing more than to protect her and be there for her forever. Fiona felt the same way as Samuel did, and she dreamed of having children with him and growing old together. Though their love for each other was strong, Samuel never disclosed his secret to Fiona about being a witch.

Fiona's mother became aware of her relationship with Samuel, which she strongly disapproved of, and was disgusted by their love for each other. But she became more appalled when the two married in the beginning of 1990 and relocated to Paterson, New Jersey, shortly after they graduated. Because her mother continued with the verbal abuse and crass remarks about her and Samuel, Fiona disconnected herself completely from her mother and continued on with her life.

Samuel and Fiona were happy together during their marriage, rarely ever having disagreements or arguments. That was until Fiona got pregnant. After realizing she was with child, Samuel started feeling that something wasn't right. Because he couldn't figure out why he felt that way, Samuel became slightly tense and depressed, which affected his relationship with Fiona. Eventually, Samuel had a vision that showed the Wizards of the Wise destroying him, reminding him of the Forbidden Law. The vision caused Samuel to be more tense and fearful than previously. Though he wanted to stay with Fiona and see their child, he knew he had to leave for Fiona's protection. Subsequently, Samuel abandoned Fiona when she was seven months pregnant and magically separated himself from her, so that their marriage bond would be broken. Two months later, Fiona gave birth to Samuel's first son.

Samuel felt horrible for what he had done to Fiona. Anytime he thought of her, he felt the pain and sorrow that she had every day. Samuel knew he had to do something to get his mind off her, to continue on with his life. No later than two months after their separation, Samuel moved back to Brooklyn, New York, where he met his second future wife, Rachel Lesling.

Short and curvy in build, Rachel had a medium caramel skin tone with wavy dark brown hair and brown eyes. Rachel could strike up a conversation with anyone she came in contact with and felt others pain, helping them deal with their issues positively. With that, she was also aggressive when it came to getting what she wanted and was a believer of preventing major issues in life before they occurred. Rachel had a privileged life, growing up in a wealthy and Christian based home. Her father and mother were both successful physicians on the Upper East Side of New York City, were Rachel lived all her life. High society events and gatherings were what she had been used to, indulging herself into medicine and public health issues at the early age of eleven. Because of this, Rachel was always more advanced than her peers, who she ridiculed for their lack of maturity.

With the influence of her parents, Rachel strived to be a physician and start her own practice, attending a local university to become a physician. Upon her starting college, Rachel's parents were seriously injured in a fatal car accident, which left them both brain dead. For three painful weeks, Rachel learned what was most important in life and humbled herself in the sight of God, right before her parents passed. The death of her parents left a void in Rachel's heart, but she continued to strive on and heal.

After her parents' death, Rachel felt the need to escape from her high society lifestyle. On a regular basis, she visited a café near Brooklyn, New York, and on one occasion she met Samuel for the first time. Samuel and Rachel were both dealing with loss, and Samuel felt they had that in common. Once again, Samuel's mortal side took over his emotions and he feel deeply in love with Rachel. He admired her compassion and love for people, feeling that he had a similar care for them. Rachel felt when she was with Samuel, the void in her heart was complete again.

By early May of 1991, Samuel and Rachel married in New York City, planning to relocate to Atlantic City, New Jersey. After finding an apartment in the heart of the city, Samuel and Rachel traveled to Amelia Island in Florida for their honeymoon. The two had a romantic time their first night, but an alarming dream that Samuel had of the Wizards of the Wise spoiled the honeymoon. Samuel couldn't believe he had been so selfish and foolish again, knowing that what he had done could possibly put him and Rachel in danger. In an urgent attempt to protect Rachel, Samuel left her alone on the Island, without a trace.

A year had passed after his marriages with Fiona and Rachel had ended. At age twenty-four, Samuel had become depressed and was slowly weakening, while he continued to have visions of his two sons growing up. Once again, his mortal side took over and he subjected himself to mortal ways of sulking, thus he began to drink often at bars in Brooklyn. One evening outside of a bar, he encountered a young woman who looked to be in her early twenties. She had an ivory skin tone and was short but slender. Her chocolate eyes stood out, but went well with her cascading light brown hair. He never knew her name, being intoxicated at the time of their meeting.

Samuel had drunken a little too much that night, and his body began to reject it. The young woman saw Samuel passed out on the side of the street and felt sorry for him. In an attempt to help him, she took Samuel to her apartment to get him sobered up. While he was with her, Samuel told the young woman everything; from his past wives and sons, and even about him being a witch. She promised she would keep everything he had told her a secret. Samuel felt that the young woman really cared about his feelings and knew that he meant well. Their quick connection led to a kiss of passion and an intimate night together. When Samuel awakened the next morning, he wasn't sure what had happened, but he knew that he had once again broken the Forbidden Law. Samuel left the young woman in her apartment, later realizing he had left her with child.

Breaking the Forbidden Law for the third time broke the spell Angelika cast on him. Samuel knew that he had to protect his sons and their mothers from the wrath of the Wizard, even if that meant letting them destroy him.

Outside of Brooklyn, New York, it was a quarter to midnight and the streets seemed to be quieting down. The tall buildings in the area were dimmed and dark clouds hovered over the skies, while a cool breeze whisked through the air. On the sideways, Samuel was walking in a black hooded jacket with his hands in his pockets. He knew that his end was coming, he could feel it. After breaking the Forbidden Law, he wasn't sure if he would surrender or fight. It was never his intention to break the law, nor hurt the women he had been with. Because he hurt them, he felt that he should be punished. On the other hand, he knew if he were killed that the Wizards would go after his sons and they would be killed, along with their mothers. He was torn.

Samuel turned down a dark alley and walked on, hearing a swooshing noise behind him. Stopping where he was, Samuel looked back and saw five figures wearing black cloaks with red trimming standing at the entrance of the alley. One stood firmly in front of the other four, while they stood side by side. Samuel turned around completely and stared at them. He couldn't make out their faces, but he knew who they were. It was the Wizards of the Wise.

"Can I help you?" he asked. The figures continued to stare at him, not responding to his question. Getting frustrated, Samuel crossed his arms looking at them, frowning up his face with his eyes squinted.

"I said, can I help you?!"

Without warning, one of the wizards waved their hand and Samuel flew back, hitting a nearby building and falling to the ground. Struggling to get up, Samuel got on his hands and knees when the wizard standing in front of the others spoke.

"Who are you?" he countered.

"Really? That's what you want to know?" Samuel laughed under his breath.

"ANSWER HIM!" one of the wizards in the back demanded. Samuel got up and looked at the five wizards, taking off his hood. He dropped his hands back to his sides and continued to stare back at them.

"Who's asking?" he said, delaying his response.

"The Wizards of the Wise," proclaimed another. Samuel took a silent deep breath and his heart began to beat faster than a car speeding on a freeway.

"Samuel Weltrinch," he said firmly.

The wizards gasped and continued staring at Samuel. It couldn't be. A Weltrinch was still alive? The thought was outrageous. The wizard that stood in front took two steps forward, while Samuel tightened his fists.

"We eliminated the Weltrinchs…you're lying!" the lead wizard snapped.

"Actually, you didn't," Samuel taunted them. "My mother was smarter than you think. She was able to save me at the last minute."

Samuel gave off a cocky smirk and crossed his arms, while the wizards stared at him in awe.

"And who was your mother?!" commanded the lead wizard.

"Angelika Weltrinch."

Angered, the lead wizard thrust his arms out in front of him and Samuel flew back into the middle of the alley on to the ground. The wizard walked over to where Samuel was, when he pushed himself up with his arms, still on his knees.

"Not only are you an ABOMINATION, but you had the nerve to break the Forbidden Law yourself. You fool! You will feel the wrath of the Wizards…and so will your descendants!"

His head hung down, Samuel began to laugh, shaking his head before he looked back up at the wizards.

"You're never going to find them," he said.

"And why is that?" the wizard questioned.

Samuel looked down again and his palms began to glow blue, as debris whirled around in the alley.

"That's for me to know...and for you to never know!"

Suddenly, Samuel thrust his hands forward and a wave of wind hit the wizard and he flew back into the others. Samuel jumped to his feet and ran in the opposite direction of the wizards. The wizards got up and stared off in the direction Samuel had gone in, when the lead wizard looked back at all of them with a frown.

"Follow him and kill him," exclaimed the lead wizard. With a nod, the four wizards rushed off through the alley after Samuel.

Samuel ran through the alley and arrived in a fenced off area, stopping to see which direction he would go in next. As he made his way to the middle of the area, the Wizards of the Wise entered the area and stopped, seeing him standing still. Samuel glanced back at them and the lead wizard rushed in behind them, pointing at him.

"Get him...NOW!!!!" he shouted. The four wizards charged at Samuel and he turned toward them with a smirk. Samuel grabbed on to his amulet and it began to glow dark blue, while he closed his eyes. *Feel the power of the mind,* he thought, when the area began to shake uncontrollably. The four wizards stopped running toward Samuel and stared at him, watching debris lift from the ground. Suddenly, Samuel opened his eyes and the pavement bulged under the wizards, sending them flying back away from him.

"Argh!!" they exclaimed. The lead wizard stared at Samuel in shock. Then, he walked toward Samuel with a frown on his face, when Samuel stopped glowing, along with his amulet.

"You will not defy us. We are the Wizards of the Wise!" he exclaimed and thrust his hands out in front of himself. Immediately, shock waves shot from his palms toward Samuel, while he placed his hands out. The shock waves stopped midway of reaching Samuel and the wizard stared at him in shock, while he smirked back at him.

"This is...impossible!!" he yelled with disbelief. Samuel and the wizard continued holding the shock waves, when one of the wizards got up and thrust his arm out, shooting a shock wave at Samuel. The shock wave hit Samuel and threw him back.

"Ahh!!!" Samuel cried, slamming into the ground. While the other wizards stood to their feet, Samuel struggled to get up, finally lifting up on one bent knee. He looked up at the wizards, while they walked toward him slowly. Samuel tightened up his left fist and his hand started glowing bright blue. He lowered his head back down and raised his left hand in the air. Without warning, Samuel slammed his fist into the pavement, causing it to create a cracking split that shot toward the wizards. When the split reached the wizards, they were thrown into the air once more, flying back into the building behind them. Samuel stood up quickly and ran off down the path behind him, as the lead wizard stood up and followed him.

Samuel continued down the path, while he heard the wizard running behind him and getting closer. Samuel glanced back for a moment, holding his right hand out. Suddenly, a blue aura appeared in Samuel's palm and he threw it back at the wizard. The wizard managed to dodge his attack, quickly throwing a shock wave in Samuel's direction. Samuel dropped down and slid on the ground, turning the next corner and dashing off. He ran down the path and two wizards appeared at the end of the alley way with their palms out toward him. Shock waves expelled from their palms, charging toward Samuel. At that point, Samuel knew he couldn't dodge their attack; he only had one other option. Coming to an abrupt stop, Samuel's amulet began to glow blue, the shocks hit him, and shocked his entire body. The lead wizard arrived behind him, witnessing him being shocked. Samuel soon vanished with a blue light, but his amulet remained in place for a moment, only to disappear seconds later. Hearing a noise behind them, the two wizards looked back and saw Samuel standing there with his arms crossed.

"Boo," Samuel teased with a smirk. The wizards jumped in surprise. Angered, the two gathered shock waves in their palms and prepared to attack Samuel again, but he threw his hands out toward them and sent them flying back into the lead wizard. The other two wizards came around the corner and helped the others stand. Samuel placed his left hand out in the air and the top of the buildings around them shattered, crashing down. Samuel back flipped out of the way and executed a three point landing. The wreckage from the buildings blocked the path of the wizards, while they stared at the rubble with frowns on their faces. Placing their hands out, shock waves shot from their palms and hit the rubble, gradually breaking it down. Seeing this, Samuel stood upright and dashed off down the path behind him. Soon after, the rubble erupted, creating a path for the wizards once more.

"We can't let him escape!" the lead wizard yelled. The wizards came together and ran down the path after Samuel.

Samuel continued to run through the alley, turning each corner as quickly as he could. When he turned the next corner, Samuel tripped over a bump in the pavement.

"Ugh!" he exclaimed. Samuel fell on his side and rolled over on the ground, getting covered in dirt. Samuel sat up on his hands and knees, thinking about his sons. Tears slowly built up in his eyes and he looked up into the sky. He realized he wasn't fighting for them, he was fighting for himself. He was being selfish, showing the wizards what he was capable of and that they couldn't stop him. He had the power to defeat them if he wanted, but that wouldn't keep his sons safe from the other Wizards of the Wise. He had to do something to protect what was most important.

"I can't end it like this…I have to save them."

Tears fell down Samuel's face and he thought up a spell in his mind. He took off his amulet and put one of its pointed edges to his left forearm. Samuel drug the amulet from his forearm to the palm and blood seeped from his split skin.

"With this blood…I shed tonight; bless my three sons in this fight."

Tears continued to fall down his face, while the blood from his arm dripped on the ground.

"All my power I give to thee–"

Samuel held the amulet in his right hand, watching the gold turn to pewter and the blue gemstone darkened.

"–and they will be the Trinity."

Samuel began to glow blue and the amulet broke into three pieces shaped like arrows. The blue glow left Samuel and went inside the pieces of the amulet, as he dropped them on the ground. Without warning, the wizards came around the corner and saw Samuel on his knees, putting their arms out toward him. Samuel began to feel pain like someone was crushing his entire body with thousands of boulders. The wizards lifted him up in the air while he groaned and hollered in pain, when the lead wizard came around the corner and walked between the others, staring at Samuel.

"Your end is here," declared the lead wizard. Then, he placed his arms out toward Samuel and white electric shock waves shot out of his palms hitting him.

"Aaaaahhhhh!!!" cried Samuel, while the shock waves consumed him. The shocks continued to jolt Samuel until he burst into flames, becoming specks of dust that dropped to the ground. All the wizards lowered their hands to their sides, vanishing with a bright white light. Suddenly, the amulet pieces began to glow three different shades of blue, lifting up into the air, disappearing shortly afterward.

Samuel gave up his powers and met his demise at the hands of the Wizards to protect his sons. After their hunt for a few years, the Wizards of the Wise stopped their search and waited to see if Samuel's sons would surface. But when they didn't, the Wizards of the Wise began to wonder why they couldn't find them. The only person who knew that was Samuel, and this secret wouldn't be revealed for many, many years to come.

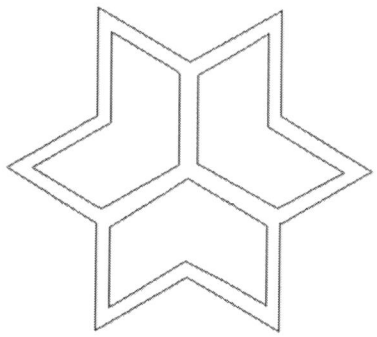

THE DESCENDANTS

NINETEEN YEARS LATER, the Wizards still hadn't heard or seen any activity that indicated Samuel's sons were still alive. Though they were pleased to rid the magical community of one abomination, the idea that three of them were roaming around was unsettling.

It was about ten minutes until four o'clock in New York City. The sun was still shining brightly, while it slowly set. A young man stood in the living area of an empty condo, staring out a large window. A look of annoyance was across his face, while he watched the city below him. He knew this would be his last time to glance at the beautiful big apple.

He was Jacob Blackwood, Rachel's son, Samuel's second child. Slim and about 5 foot 11 inches, Jacob had a medium caramel complexion with brown eyes and dark hair. Jacob talked to most people and was always helpful to others. He was quick to tell a person about themselves, whether they wanted to hear it or not, which made his peers perceive him as stuck up.

Jacob was moving back to his hometown in Paterson, New Jersey. That was the last thing he wanted to do. He knew he wouldn't hear the end of it from old friends and acquaintances, who had disclosed their dislike for him leaving, saying he wouldn't make it. He wanted to prove them wrong, but that wasn't the case. Jacob took a deep breath and his cellphone vibrated in his jacket pocket. He took out his phone, unlocking it, and saw that he received a text, which read:

Hey honey! I know you're upset,
but it'll get better! I believe that you
have a gift and you will be blessed with
it. It doesn't matter where you live,
if you are meant to be an amazing
writer, it's gonna happen wherever you are!
Call me when you make it to the station!
kisses Love Mom

"Mom," Jacob said shaking his head and looking at his phone. He put his phone back in his pocket, walked over to the front door of the condo, and grabbed his luggage bag. Looking back, Jacob glanced at the condo one last time before opening the door and leaving.

Jacob had lived in Paterson his whole life with his mother Rachel. After Samuel left her, Rachel decided she didn't want stay in the apartment she and Samuel had rented together in Atlantic City, due to all the memories she had there. Then, she met James Hatcher, a commercial real estate agent who traveled around the area. He was muscular and about 6 foot 2, having a caramel skin tone with brown eyes and a shaved head. James showed Rachel property in Paterson for an office space and apartment, which she bought and relocated. Since then, the two began an intimate relationship and Rachel had a son with him, James Jr. (who they called Jay J). They hadn't married, mostly because Rachel feared he would leave her, since that was what happened in her previous marriage.

Being in another relationship had its complications, mainly because

Jacob and Jay J didn't get along. Jacob wasn't happy about his mother's relationship with another man, not being too fond of James. Over the years James and Jacob appeared to get better, but he continually pushed him away because he "wasn't his real father." Jacob envied the fact that Jay J's father was around and his wasn't, which was part of the reason he didn't care for him either. Jay J was always spoiled, since by the time he was born Rachel had become a successful physician in the Paterson area. He was envious of Jacob, feeling that no matter what he did Rachel would love Jacob more because he was her first child. The two always clashed after being around each other for too long, much to Rachel's displeasure.

Because of his bittersweet feelings about home, when Jacob turned nineteen he moved to New York with his friend Andrew. Jacob wanted to pursue a writing career, while Andrew wanted to be an actor on Broadway. Jacob was very skilled in writing and poetry, and it was his dream to be an author and poet someday. He self-published his first poetry book, *Poetry for the Soul*, but after months of no success, he was ready to give up on his dream. Then, it seemed things were falling into place for Jacob, but his hopes where shattered when Andrew was killed in a fatal car crash. It became difficult for Jacob to keep up with the condo alone, making every dollar stretch. But after a year of struggling, it was proven ineffective.

Jacob arrived at the Metro-North train station, dragging his luggage across the ground, while passengers began to form a line to board the train. Jacob looked up and saw a large train pulling up to the boarding area. Jacob ran over to the line with his bag, feeling his phone vibrating in his pocket again. Once he reached the end of the line, he stopped to take his cellphone out and saw it was his mother calling.

"Really Mom?!"

Jacob rolled his eyes and answered his phone, following closely behind the line to the train.

"I thought you told me to call you when I got here?" Jacob reprimanded her.

"I was waiting," Rachel started with a worried tone. "But I knew your train left at a 5:45 PM and its five minutes 'til...so I–"

"Mom, calm down please. I was going to call you when I got on the train. It took forever to get a taxi and traffic was ridiculous on top of that."

"Okay, just making sure you didn't miss your train. What time will it arrive in Paterson?"

"In about an hour and thirty minutes or so…I think."

"Good! I'll be off work, so Jay J and I will come get you."

"Oh, great," said Jacob, rolling his eyes once more.

"I don't appreciate the sarcasm, besides your little brother misses you."

"Yeah, okay…mom gotta go. Love you, bye."

Jacob quickly hung up his cellphone and stepped on to the train, as the doors closed behind him. He walked over to a booth and sat down, putting his luggage under the seat. Then, Jacob sat back and stared out the window. Within moments, the train pulled off and left the station, in route to Paterson.

In Paterson, a black pick-up truck drove through the small neighborhood of Lakeside Valley, arriving at number 7223. The driver's door of the truck opened and a young man stepped out. It was Isaac Blackwood, Fiona's son, Samuel's first son. He was four inches taller than his mother and slightly muscular, having fair-skin with brown eyes and dark shoulder length hair.

After Samuel left, Fiona never remarried or dated, feeling that no one could replace the love she had for Samuel. For the first few years, Fiona struggled as a single parent, working at a local breakfast diner to supply for her and Isaac. But it wasn't enough to take care of everything Isaac needed. Even with her struggle, Fiona's love for Isaac was what kept her sane. But eventually she became so depressed that she considered giving Isaac up for adoption, feeling he deserved a life she couldn't give him. Before reaching her breaking point, Fiona met an older woman named Agnes Klein, an evangelist at a local church. Agnes was a short woman with ivory skin, blue eyes, and short brown hair. Fiona first encountered Agnes in a store near her home, where Agnes witnessed to her about God. Fiona converted to Christianity at twenty-six and Agnes took her under her wing as a daughter, helping her develop a close relationship with God.

Once Fiona became mature in Christ, things started to pick up for her and blessings began to manifest in her life. She was able to start her business as a seamstress and became very successful. After this, she opened her own store where she sold many of her pieces to the public. After developing her connection with God, Fiona made sure that she brought Isaac up with the same values that Agnes shared with her.

Because of the morals Fiona taught him, Isaac matured very quickly for his age like Fiona did, but personality wise, he was the opposite of her. He typically kept to himself unless he knew you, or if you struck up the conversation and he was very selective with who he helped. It didn't take much to upset him either, and when you did, he made sure you knew it. Isaac was always a bookworm, indulging himself in historical works and being eager for knowledge early on. His intellectual skills were way above average, which allowed Isaac to graduate from high school a year early, with plans to enroll at a college outside of New York. But instead, he moved out of his mother's home and into a small apartment right outside the city, starting work at a local coffee shop, Ray's Café.

In spite of the hardships that Fiona and Isaac faced, the two had a strong, loving relationship. But Fiona felt like Isaac was holding himself back to stay near her, since she didn't have anyone else. She wanted him to feel free and go his own way, but every time the topic was brought up, Isaac would deny any desire to leave.

Isaac closed his door and Fiona stepped out of the passenger's side, still looking like she did years ago but more mature. Isaac walked to the bed of the truck and took out bags full of groceries. Fiona walked over to the truck bed and smiled at Isaac, as he looked over at her.

"Sweetie, thanks for helping me grocery shop again," Fiona said smiling.

"That's what I'm here for mom; somebody's gotta help take care of you in this big house," Isaac responded. Fiona grabbed three grocery bags out from the truck and walked over to Isaac.

"I appreciate it hon," Fiona said, kissing Isaac on his cheek. The two walked up to the house, Fiona unlocked the door, and they entered the living room. The two stepped through the living area and entered the kitchen, when Fiona turned on the lights. She placed her bags on the island and Isaac placed his on the counter top near the refrigerator.

"So how was work today?" Fiona asked smiling at Isaac.

"It was okay…I guess," said Isaac. "It got really busy around lunch time."

Isaac began to pull frozen products out of the bags, placing them in the freezer.

"Did you hear Valerie Skyes moved back in town today?" Fiona asked.

Isaac closed the freezer door and froze in place. Isaac didn't have many friends, but one of them was Valerie Skyes. His heart started pounding rapidly; the memories of him and Valerie together rushing through his head. She was the same height as Isaac, slender with fair-skin, baby blue eyes, and long light brown hair. Isaac and Valerie had been in the same school district since preschool, with the two developing a close friendship at a young age.

Valerie was a lot more open than Isaac, but when he was around her, he seemed more talkative and pleasant. Throughout their friendship, they appeared to have a liking for each other, though neither of them would admit it. Isaac and Valerie even planned to go to the same college in New York City. But when they graduated from high school, Valerie left without him to attend a university in Baltimore, Maryland, feeling the art program they offered was more promising. Because of that, Isaac cancelled his plans of moving to New York and stayed in Paterson, claiming that he just "changed his mind," when really it was because of Valerie. The two lost contact after that, but that didn't stop Isaac from thinking of her, even after four years. Isaac turned around toward Fiona with a look of surprise on his face.

"No I hadn't heard," he said with a slightly cold tone.

"Yeah, I ran into her mom at the mall last week and told me she was coming back to finish her program at a local university," Fiona continued, putting spices in the cabinets.

"Oh okay," Isaac said, brushing off the subject. He opened the refrigerator and started to fill the drawers with refrigerated items, when Fiona looked back at him.

"So that's all you have to say?" She wondered, staring at Isaac.

"Yeah, that's it," he said.

"Aren't you to good friends? I thought you'd be a little more excited about it."

"Mom! Just leave it alone, okay?" Isaac snapped.

"Okay…just saying," Fiona said, throwing her hands up. Isaac rolled his eyes and continued to put items in the refrigerator. Fiona finished putting the spices in the cabinets and picked up the empty bags, throwing them in a recycle bin near her. Isaac closed the refrigerator and walked over to the island, grasping its edges and taking a deep breath. Fiona looked at Isaac and stepped over by the island.

"I wasn't trying to upset you," Fiona mentioned. "I just thought you'd want to know that your best friend was coming home."

"I know…I'm not mad," Isaac admitted, placing his hands over his face. "I'm just a little exhausted, that's all."

Fiona smiled at Isaac and walked over to him, placing her hand on his back.

"Why don't you try and take it easy for a while?" Fiona suggested. Isaac took his hands off his face and stared at his mother, while she continued smiling at him.

"That's easier said than done," he said.

"Just try it, for me."

Isaac looked at Fiona and smiled, when she kissed him on his cheek again and held him from the side. Isaac placed his arm around her and leaned his head over her shoulder.

"You know what, how about I make you dinner before you go. Does that sound good?" Fiona asked. Isaac stood up straight and let go of her, nodding in agreement.

"How does pasta and meatballs sound?" she asked.

"Sounds good to me," Isaac said with a smile.

"Good! Do you mind lending me a hand?"

"Not at all," said Isaac. Fiona and Isaac walked over to the cabinets and took out boxes of pasta, preparing to make supper.

In an apartment complex near downtown Paterson, a young man was sitting on a futon in the left corner of the room. It was a very small apartment, with the main room serving as the bedroom, living room, and the kitchen, having a small bathroom toward the back. It wasn't the best, but it had fit his current budget. He sat silently, looking at the job listing section in the local newspaper diligently.

He was Cameron Evans, Samuel's third child. Cameron looked the most like Samuel, having dark hair and being very muscular and tall, with the only differences being his tanned ivory skin and chocolate eyes. Cameron wasn't a people person, but if the person seemed friendly he would be open with them. He could also be overly emotional at times, which was usually when things didn't go his way.

Cameron had a troubled childhood. Because his mother abandoned him, he was placed in a Catholic orphanage when he was a boy. During his earlier years, Cameron always felt unwanted. It was difficult to watch other children get adopted, while he remained in the orphanage and continued getting older. Over time, no one even considered him; they didn't want to adopt a troubled teen. On his sixteenth birthday, Cameron became fed up with his "pitiful life" and wanted to put an end to it. Taking matters into his hands, Cameron slit his wrist and attempted to drown himself in a tube. When he did this, he encountered the face of God. God told Cameron his time wasn't up yet, and that he had much more to offer. Cameron woke up in a hospital with a new outlook on life, beginning his gradual recovery. With worry he may attempt suicide again, the orphanage placed Cameron under psychiatric care for his protection. No one believed him when he said, "God saved me; I saw his face." It ultimately forced them to keep Cameron institutionalized for a longer period.

After two years, Cameron was released from psychiatric care, still believing what he saw was real, though he suppressed it. Feeling embarrassed of his suicide attempt, Cameron started wearing a wrist band to cover his scar. But he felt that he needed to share his story somehow, wanting his voice to be heard. So he took it upon himself to enter a creative writing contest, where he wrote a fictionalized synopsis of his life, which won him a scholarship and got him enrolled in Victor's University.

Everything seemed to be getting better for Cameron. He got a job as a busboy in a local restaurant, he excelled in all his subjects at school, and he was even able to purchase a car and apartment near the university. It all was too good to be true. Soon, the restaurant filed for bankruptcy and had to lay off several employees, including Cameron. This put him in a tight bind and he started paying bills later than he should've, which made keeping up with his apartment difficult.

The more frustrating part was that none of the bill collectors were being considerate of his situation, leaving Cameron with a load of stress on his shoulders. Cameron continued reading the newspaper silently, until finally he threw it on the floor and crossed his arms.

"This is a waste of time," he said with a frown, putting his hands over his face. Suddenly, he heard a knock at his door and he looked up, standing to his feet. Cameron walked over to the door to open it, seeing a short, bald chubby man with brown eyes and ivory skin standing in the door way. It was the landlord, Mr. Stevens. He had been coming to Cameron's apartment every other day for the past two weeks, demanding he pay his rent. Cameron continued to ask for extensions, but Mr. Stevens was growing tired of that.

"Where's my money Cameron?" Mr. Stevens asked. Cameron rolled his eyes and slightly stepped back. He lifted his left arm up, placing his hand over his forehead.

"I–I'm working on it," Cameron stuttered. Mr. Stevens shook his head, still frowning at Cameron.

"You've been saying that for the past two weeks now," Mr. Stevens continued, "and I'm getting *very* impatient."

Cameron placed both his hands over his face and slowly pulled them down, lifting his head up.

"Look, just–just give me some more time…I'll get you your money."

"No! I'm not waiting for you anymore. You got three days to pack up and get out."

Cameron stared at Mr. Stevens in shock, when he stormed off. Cameron followed closely behind him and grabbed him by his shoulder, when Mr. Stevens turned around quickly and brushed him off.

"Wait! You're kicking me out!?!" Cameron exclaimed. "Where am

I supposed to go?!"

"Not my problem kid. You should've thought about that," Mr. Stevens rebuked Cameron, shaking his head. "Tsk, so pathetic."

Cameron stopped following Mr. Stevens and watched him storm out of the apartment building. He stood still in the cold hallway and his mouth slightly dropped open, while tears slowly fell down his face.

That evening at Paterson's train station, it was cold and windy, with a shimmering darkish orange hue in the sky. Rachel stood by the arrival area patiently. She looked older in appearance, but kept many of her youthful qualities. She was still dressed in a blazer and pencil skirt, since she had just left her office twenty minutes prior. While she stood still, a tall and muscular young man with a light caramel tone and brown eyes walked over to her, holding a pair of car keys. It was her other son and Jacob's half-brother, Jay J. Rachel looked at Jay J and he handed her the car keys with a smile.

"The attendant said his train should be here in a little while, they had a couple of delays," said Jay J.

"Oh good! I can't wait to see him. I missed him so much," Rachel exclaimed, placing her hands in front of her chest and smiling with excitement. Then, a train pulled up to the station and sounded its horn, coming to a complete stop.

"I think that's his train," said Jay J. Rachel's face lit up, when the door to the train slowly opened and passengers began to get off. The two peered around other passengers to see where Jacob was, while the station became crowded. To their excitement, Jacob got off of the train with his luggage in hand, looking around.

"I see him," Jay J said, as he and Rachel quickly rushed over where Jacob was. Seeing them coming, Jacob took a deep breath and began to walk toward them slowly, when Jay J got up to him and wrapped his arms around him.

"Hey big bro," Jay J exclaimed, squeezing Jacob tightly. Jacob grunted and looked at Jay J, patting him on his back.

"Hi," Jacob said reluctantly. Jay J let go of Jacob and backed away from him. Jacob placed his luggage on the ground, when Rachel walked up to him and opened her arms wide. Then, she embraced Jacob and kissed him on his forehead.

"Oh sweetie I missed you so much," she said. Jacob held his mother back and closed his eyes.

"Yeah...I missed you too."

Rachel, Jacob, and Jay J were in Rachel's silver 2012 Lexus ES 350, on their way back to their house. The neighborhood they were going through consisted of all two story homes. This was her third time moving in the last five years, but she felt an upgrade was needed since everyone was getting older. Rachel looked over at Jacob, while he continued to stare out his window.

"So you moved...again?" Jacob said, looking at Rachel with one eyebrow raised.

"Yes. We had the other one for two years...but the neighborhood was getting a little out of hand," said Rachel.

"Yeah, I'm glad we moved into this neighborhood, it's a lot more peaceful here," Jay J added. Jacob stared at the dashboard and rolled his eyes, chuckling under his breath.

"Why is it more peaceful? You're not in everybody's business?" Jacob sneered, when Jay J glared at him with a frown.

"No...it's 'cause you aren't there to start any bull with anybody," Jay J retorted. Rachel stared at him from her rearview mirror and glared at Jacob from the corner of her eyes.

"Don't you two start," she said. Jacob cleared his throat and rolled his eyes staring out his window, shaking his head.

"Wouldn't have if somebody would keep their mouth shut," said Jacob.

"Please, you're the one who instigates everything," Jay J exclaimed.

"BOYS! That's enough," Rachel snapped, shaking her head and focusing back on the road. Rachel turned on to Lily Estates Place and drove down the street, until she reached a three story mini mansion on her right. Jacob looked up at the house and Rachel pulled the car into the driveway. The three got out of the car, while Jacob continued staring at the house. Rachel went to the trunk of the car and got out Jacob's bag. Jacob looked back at her and she rolled it over to him.

"So…do you like it?" she asked. Jacob looked back up at the house, as Rachel stepped beside him.

"It's really big," said Jacob.

"Just wait until you see the inside," Rachel said.

Jay J rolled his eyes and rushed into the house, while Jacob stared at him. Rachel and Jacob walked up to the house and went inside, entering the foyer. Jay J went up the spiral staircase and Jacob looked to the left in the living room, where a flat screen TV was playing a football game. Then, James came around the corner of the main hallway and into the foyer with a smile on his face.

"Hey Jake," he said with a grin and open arms.

James and Jacob shared a brief one arm hug and stepped back from each other.

"How are you feeling? How have you been?"

"Yeah, I'm fine; I just need to lay down…I have a really bad migraine."

"Oh, well your room is on the third floor in the back," Rachel said rubbing Jacob on the back of his neck. Jacob nodded walked over to the stairs, dragging his bag up to the third floor. Rachel exhaled and looked over at James, who was staring at her.

"You must've told him already," James said, crossing his arms. Rachel shook her head and placed her hand over her forehead.

"No, I didn't," said Rachel. "He's been annoyed since he stepped off the train. I haven't said too much of anything to him."

"I'd like him to know sometime soon," said James.

"I know, just give it some time," Rachel said, walking off from James up the stairs.

"Okay," James said. He walked back into the living room and sat down on a love seat, continuing to watch the game.

That night, Jacob was in a room on the third floor of the house. The sky had gotten dark, whilst a cool breeze filled the air and came in the room through the cracked window. He had boxes with his things in them stacked on top of each other on the right side of the room, unopened. Jacob was sitting on the bed with his luggage bag wide open, staring off into space. He couldn't think of anything at the moment other than how he just didn't want to be there. And the more he thought about it, the more aggravated he became. While he continued to sit on his bed, he heard a knock on the door, as Rachel stepped in the room.

"Hey," Rachel said. She looked at Jacob and walked over to the bed, sitting down on the edge. "Is your migraine better?"

"A little bit," said Jacob. "I took a Tylenol…so that should help."

"Good," Rachel said with a smile. She put her hands together in her lap and Jacob looked up at her. Rachel began to think over her conversation she had earlier with James, knowing she had something to needed to tell Jacob. But she wasn't sure how he would react. Rachel looked up at Jacob and cleared her throat, while he continued to stare at her confused.

"What?" he asked.

"I have something I'd like to tell you," Rachel said.

"Okay…what is it?"

"It's about me and James," she started again, "I was going to surprise you but he insisted I tell you now."

"Oh God," Jacob exclaimed. He began to fumble through his open suit case, while Rachel stared at him with her arms crossed.

"Okay, you know James and I have been together for a while, right?"

"You mean eighteen years?" Jacob commented, continuing to search through his bag. Rachel frowned at Jacob and sighed.

"Anyway, I said that because he proposed to me a month ago–"

Jacob stopped looking through his bag and slowly glared at Rachel, with a blank stare on his face.

"–and I said yes."

Looking back down in the bag, Jacob slightly shook his head in annoyance.

"Great, congratulations," he muttered sarcastically.

"Look, I know you haven't always been fond of James, but he loves me and I'm happy with him. I told you because he wants you to be in the wedding, and so do I."

"Mom you don't have to keep telling me, I get it. You love him, he loves you. But that doesn't mean I have to like it."

"But we still want you to be in the wedding."

"I'll think about it," Jacob said with a cold tone. Rachel was taken aback by Jacob's comment and crossed her arms in disbelief. Instead of being happy for her, he was being snappy and crude. Jacob stopped what he was doing and looked up at Rachel, exhaling and placing his head over his forehead.

"Sorry, I just...I'm really not in the mood right now."

"Why not?" Rachel asked. Jacob paused for a moment after he zipped up his bag. He looked up at Rachel with a serious look on his face.

"You know why I'm not."

"Actually Jacob I don't," Rachel said, raising her voice. "You've had an attitude since you got off the train and I have no idea what your problem is. So please enlighten me."

Jacob rolled his eyes and put his luggage bag on the floor next to the bed.

"You know I didn't want to come back here. I was tired of Paterson, the people...everything."

"Then why did you come back?"

I didn't have a choice!" Jacob snapped, staring at Rachel. She uncrossed her arms and closed her eyes for a moment, as Jacob looked away from her and balled up his fists on the bed.

"You know Jacob...maybe that's why it didn't work out," Rachel said. Jacob glared over at her with a frown, his eyes getting glassy.

"You left for all the wrong reasons. You were trying to escape your problems instead of trying to fix them."

"Maybe fixing them is too hard," said Jacob. "Maybe it's easier to just leave everything behind."

Rachel moved closer to Jacob and placed her hand over his, while he loosened up his tight grasp.

"Look, I know it's hard, but God doesn't want us to just sweep our issues under a rug and pretend like they don't exist. He wants us to deal with them and grow from them."

"What if we can't?" Jacob asked, while tears fell down his cheeks.

"We can, in his strength...not our own."

Rachel opened her arms and held Jacob. Jacob wrapped his arms around Rachel and she kissed Jacob on his forehead, while they held on to each other.

"I love you Jacob," she said.

"Love you too mom," he said.

At New Shore's apartment complex outside downtown, Isaac pulled up in his truck and parked it near an apartment building in the back of the complex. The moon shone bright over the area and Isaac got out of his truck, walking up to the door and entering the apartment building.

Inside, Isaac was in an open area that had four apartments on each side. He went up the staircase in the middle of the hall and he arrived in another area similar to the first floor. He walked over to the left, reaching the third apartment door. Isaac took his keys out of his pocket and unlocked the door, entering the apartment.

Isaac turned on the light switch near the front door, closing it behind himself. He walked past the kitchen counter on his right and placed the keys down on it, walking into the hallway. Isaac walked into the bedroom at the end of the hall and took off his jacket, stepping over to his closet and hanging it up. He stepped back over to his bed and flopped down, exhaling deeply. Isaac began to undress himself down to his shorts and undershirt, pulling his comforter back and rolling over in the bed. He turned out the light on the lampstand near the bed and placed the cover over himself, closing his eyes.

Later that night, Isaac tossed and turned in his bed anxiously throughout the night, until eventually he opened his eyes and looked around the room. He saw the bedroom door was closed, although it hadn't been before he fell asleep. Isaac threw the comforter off himself and sat up on the bed. He stood up on the floor, realizing that it was colder than usual. Isaac began to walk toward the door slowly with his right hand out, grabbing the door knob and opening the door. He looked at himself and realized that he was wearing the clothes he had on before he went to bed.

"What the heck," he exclaimed. Isaac looked up and widened his eyes, seeing that he wasn't in his apartment anymore. The room was dark and consisted of wooden floors, walls and shelves, somewhat like an attic. Isaac walked into the middle of the floor and heard the door slam behind him. He jumped and looked back at the door, watching it lock itself. Turning back around, Isaac saw a glass podium that held a large brown book.

"What is that," he mumbled to himself, moving toward the podium slowly. He raised his eyebrows confused, stepping in front of the book. The front cover was blank, but after a few moments, words began to write themselves on the cover, spelling out: *The Book of Magic*. Isaac narrowed his eyes and focused on the book. He picked up the book and examined it, gazing at its cosmetic wear and tear. Isaac put the book back down on the podium and looked up, seeing Jacob and Cameron standing on the other side of the room. Jacob and Cameron looked at each other muddled. Then, they glared at Isaac, while he stared back at them. None of them knew who the other was, staring at each other unsteadily.

Suddenly, a piece of Samuel's amulet appeared around Cameron's neck. Cameron looked at the amulet in shock and grabbed it, looking up at Isaac and Jacob with worry in his eyes. Jacob stepped back from Cameron in awe, when a piece of the amulet appeared around his neck. Jacob jumped in shock and stared at the amulet muddled.

"What the heck is going on?!" Isaac exclaimed. He backed away from the podium hesitantly, when the last piece of the amulet appeared around his neck. Isaac gazed at the amulet with widened eyes, while he shook nervously.

Isaac opened his eyes abruptly, realizing he had been dreaming the entire time. He rolled over on his back and took a deep breath, placing his hand on his chest. When he did this, he felt something strange on himself. Isaac quickly leaned over and turned on his lamp, throwing the comforter off. He looked down and saw that he was wearing the amulet that appeared around his neck in the dream. Isaac sat up and stared at the amulet, while he held it in his hand.

"What is this?" said Isaac, staring at the amulet confused.

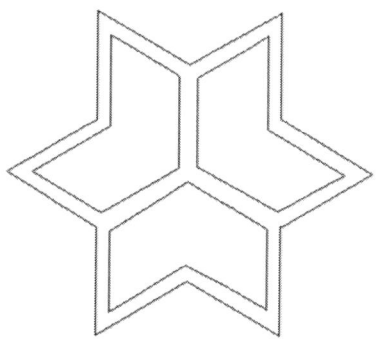

MEETING

IN AN UNDERGROUND CAVE, a male figure wearing a black hooded cloak was moved swiftly through the cold caverns. The cave was dark and damp, with small stalactites hanging from the ceiling. He seemed about 5 foot 10 and slightly muscular, but his other features were cloaked. He continued down the path, until he arrived in an open area were several cloaked figures stood. The area was large like a throne room. He stopped near the entrance and the cloaked figures looked back at him.

"Let him through," a raspy masculine voice muttered in front of the cloaked figures. They stepped aside, leaving an open path that led to a rock-like throne. A dark shadowy figure sat at the throne, staring at the cloaked figure. The cloaked figure walked between the others and stopped a few feet away from the throne.

"Leave us," The shadowy figure order, as the others vanished one by one. The cloaked figure smirked and removed his cloak, revealing himself to be a young man. He was the younger brother of the shadowy figure on the throne. They were known as Baine and Liem.

Baine was the one that sat on the throne. He was the same height as Liem but more muscular, having a tanned ivory skin tone and bluish green eyes with shoulder length brown hair. Liem looked like Baine, but a few years younger with greenish blue eyes and spiked brown hair. Baine was the type of person who didn't care about what people thought about him and he often acted on instinct instead of thinking it over. Liem on the other hand was very concerned about others opinions, but it didn't stop him from doing things his way.

Baine and Liem came from a long line of warlocks known as the Xaviors. The Xaviors were notorious power thieves who stole magical beings abilities. The Xaviors remained anonymous over time, but were eventually exposed and eradicated, leaving the two as the last of their coven. They continued their family's legacy and formed a new coven with fellow warlocks, being feared among magical creatures and remaining unknown to the Wizards of the Wise.

"That didn't take long at all," said Baine, looking at Liem. He stood from the throne and walked up to Liem with a smirk on his face.

"What did you find?" he asked.

"There are three new witches rising," Liem started, staring back at Baine. "They haven't come into their powers just yet, but they will in the next twenty-four hours... I can feel it."

Liem looked at Baine with a smile, when he turned away from Liem.

"What else do you know?" asked Baine.

"Not much, I wasn't able to sense a lot about them," said Liem.

Baine turned back toward Liem, continuing to frown, when suddenly his eyes became pure white. Then, Isaac, Jacob, and Cameron's faces flashed before him quickly. Liem stared at Baine with worry, when his eyes changed back to normal.

"What did you see?" Liem asked. Baine looked over at Liem slowly.

"Baine what did you see?" Liem asked.

"Isaac, Jacob, and Cameron," said Baine with a grimace. Liem stared at Baine, stepping back over to him.

"You saw them…didn't you?" Liem wondered, widening his eyes.

"Yes. I saw them…and all their power," Baine exclaimed. He grabbed Liem by his shoulders, while they continued to stare at each other.

"If we take their powers Liem, we will be unstoppable!" Baine went on.

"What are you talking about?" Liem asked, while he looked at Baine confused.

"These are very powerful witches brother," Baine informed him. "If we take their powers, we'll be the most powerful warlocks in history. We'll be able to overthrow the Wizards of the Wise. All the laws will be ours, and we'll be able to rule the entire magical community. That's what I saw."

Liem stared at Baine in shock for a moment. Then, a smirk came across his face.

"So, what are we waiting for?" Liem asked.

"That's more like it," said Baine.

In Rachel's home, Jacob was in bed sleeping, covered up with his comforter. Then, Rachel burst into the room.

"Good morning sweetie!" she exclaimed. Jacob jumped and fell out of his bed with his comforter wrapped around him.

"It's time for breakfast in the dining room!"

Jacob took a deep breath and threw the comforter off of his face, rubbing his eyes.

"Really mom? It's seven forty-five in the morning," Jacob fussed.

"Yes it is, on a Monday morning. Now come on Jacob, you'll miss my delicious breakfast I made for everybody."

"Oh my God…fine," Jacob whined, as Rachel began to clap and smile at Jacob.

"Okay! It'll be ready in about forty-five minutes, all right?"

Rachel left the room and closed the door behind her. Jacob flipped over on his hands and knees, when he felt something rocking against his chest. He looked down and took the comforter off himself, seeing the amulet from his dream. Isaac and Cameron's faces rushed into his mind, while he recalled the dream. He tried tugging at the amulet to get it off, but it wouldn't budge. Eventually, Jacob stopped pulling at it and stood to his feet, staring at the amulet confused.

Jacob was dressed for the day and went down to the dining room about an hour later. He entered the foyer, when Jay J stepped out of the living room and stared at him. They didn't say a word to each other, trying to avoid conversation. Then, Rachel popped her head around the corner of the foyer and the two glanced at her.

"Good morning you two," said Rachel with a smile. Jacob and Jay J stared at her expressionless.

"Morning," they said together vapidly.

"Breakfast is ready," she told them, going into the dining room.

Jay J turned around and went into the dining room, while Jacob stood in the foyer. Jacob slowly walked into the dining room and saw James and Jay J sitting at the table, pulling out a chair and sitting down. Rachel placed a bowl of fruit and a breakfast plate near Jacob with a smile, sliding silverware over to him.

"Since it's your first day back home, I won't make you do your own plate," she said. Jacob looked up at Rachel and raised his eyebrows, smiling back at her awkwardly.

"Thanks mom," he said, picking up his fork. Jay J looked over at him with jealous eyes, shoving pancakes in his mouth. After saying a prayer to himself, Jacob opened his eyes and picked up his fork, watching Rachel pour him a glass of orange juice. She placed it near him and sat down in the chair on the other side of the table. Rachel looked around the table at the three of them, smiling happily.

"Look at all of us; all my family is here," said Rachel. James looked up and smiled, continuing to eat his food. Then, he looked over at Jacob, noticing his amulet. James finished chewing his food and watched Jacob, when he realized James was staring at him.

"What?" Jacob asked, lowering his fork down.

"Where'd you get that?" James wondered. Jacob stared at James and cleared his throat, realizing he was referring to his amulet. He didn't even know what it was, how could he tell him? Jacob swallowed his food and smiled at James nervously, trying to figure out what to say.

"Huh?" he responded, playing dumb.

"That amulet you're wearing, where'd you get it?"

Rachel and Jay J looked at him and noticed the amulet, while Rachel gazed at it. For some reason, it seemed oddly familiar to her. Jacob kept trying to come up with an explanation in his head, but none of them sounded appropriate. Eventually, Jacob shrugged his shoulders and shook his head, still looking at James.

"Ya know…it's been so long since I got it, I don't even remember," he lied. "It was from some antique shop me and Andrew visited frequently in New York."

"Really? I love antiques like that, it's gorgeous," James complemented.

"Thanks."

"Yes…it is," Rachel added. "I almost feel like I've seen it before."

"Hmm, must be a déjà vu," Jacob said, brushing her off. Rachel continued to stare at the amulet, while pondering over where she had seen it before. Jacob smiled nervously and started eating again. Rachel shook her head and took a sip of her water, glancing over at Jacob again.

"On another note, what are your plans for today?" Rachel asked. Jacob looked up at Rachel, taking a drink of orange juice before answering her.

"There's a university near downtown I wanted to check out," he replied.

"Oh okay…which one?" Rachel inquired.

"It's called Victor's University," said Jacob. "I made an appointment with admissions at 9:20 AM."

Rachel lit up and sat upright in her chair with a smile.

"I know exactly where that is," she exclaimed. Rachel jumped from her seat and picked up her plate, while Jacob stared at her in shock.

"Let me put this away and we can go," she said.

"Whoa, whoa, whoa… wait," said Jacob. "I was going to go by myself."

Rachel placed her hand on her hip, when Jacob threw his hands up.

"Besides, don't you have to work today?" he continued, crossing his arms.

"I took the week off because you came home," said Rachel.

"Mom!? What about your patients?"

"They can see my nurse practitioner, that's what she's there for."

"But–"

"I'll go get my purse and I'll be ready," Rachel interrupted, walking out of dining room into the kitchen, while Jacob sat still in his chair.

"Great," he said, getting up from the table and heading for his room. James looked at Jay J, who was stuffing himself, with his eyebrows raised.

"All righty," said James, as he went back to eating his food.

In Cameron's apartment, Cameron was in his shower standing under the shower head. He ran his hands through his hair and closed his eyes, sighing deeply. Cameron turned the water off and took his towel off the top of the shower door, wrapping it around his body. He stepped out of the shower and walked over to the sink, grabbing a small towel to wipe the steam off the mirror. While wiping the mirror down, Cameron noticed something on his reflection's chest. In a panic, he rubbed the mirror off quickly, realizing he was wearing the amulet from his dream. Cameron dropped the towel on the counter and saw the dream playing through his head, seeing Isaac and Jacob's faces in his head. Cameron stared at his reflection and grabbed the amulet, feeling his heart beating out of his chest. *What the heck is this*, he wondered, staring back down at the amulet. Then, the amulet started glowing bright blue and Cameron's eyes widened in shock, while his mouth dropped and he stared on in awe.

After realizing the amulet wouldn't come off, Cameron got himself dressed and began to pack up his things in trash bags, clearing out his apartment out. He tied up the last bag and stood to his feet, glancing around the apartment one more time. Taking a deep breath, Cameron walked out of the apartment, bags in hand, and closed the door. He made his way outside near his black 1996 Buick Skylark and threw the bags in the backseat. Closing the door, he looked to his right at a small building near two apartment buildings, which was the leasing office. Cameron walked over to the building quickly and opened the front door. Once inside, Cameron glanced over at the lobby for a split second, walking up to the front desk. He looked around the office, seeing no one around to assist him.

"Really," he complained. Cameron looked at his watch and realized it was 8:47 AM, almost ten minutes before his class started. He knew he'd probably be late, but he didn't want to be later than he needed to. Cameron skimmed the counter top for something to get someone's attention, seeing a bell near him. He slammed his palm on the bell repeatedly, when Mr. Stevens burst out of back office behind the counter annoyed.

"What?!" he screamed, realizing it was Cameron. Mr. Stevens calmed himself and walked up to the counter, crossing his arms with a smirk on his face.

"I see you've finally come to pay your past due rent," he sneered. Cameron stared at Mr. Stevens and didn't say a word, his nostrils flaring in annoyance and his face turning red.

"I knew you weren't as lousy as I thought," Mr. Stevens went on, chuckling while holding his belly. Then, Cameron's amulet started glowing again, with neither of them noticing it. Mr. Stevens continued to laugh at Cameron maliciously, placing out his hand toward him. Cameron reached into his jacket and took out his apartment key, slamming it into Mr. Stevens' palm when the amulet dimmed. Mr. Stevens stopped laughing and looked at Cameron in disbelief, staring down at the key.

"What is this?" he asked with a tremble.

"Looks like an apartment key to me," Cameron said with an attitude. Mr. Stevens glared back up at Cameron, his face swollen. With an anger huff, Mr. Stevens flipped his hand over and slammed the key on the counter.

"I tried to be nice to you kid, I gave you extra time, and this is what you do? I was trying to be merciful!"

"I don't need your mercy…I'm too *pathetic* for it anyway," Cameron retorted, turning away from Mr. Stevens. Without looking back, Cameron made his way toward the exit, when Mr. Stevens bashed his fist on the countertop.

"You little brat," he snapped. "You're useless, STUPID BASTARD!"

Cameron reached the exit door and began to breathe heavily. His amulet started glowing again, but this time, the glow radiated from the amulet to his right palm, as he grabbed the door knob. When he pushed the door open, it ripped off its hinges and flew into the middle of parking lot. Mr. Stevens jumped in shock and stared Cameron, his eyes widened with fear. Cameron glanced down at his hand, watching electric shocks vanishing into the creases of his palm. Cameron rushed out of the leasing office and got in his car, leaving the apartment complex.

Cameron wasn't sure what had happened, but he was still shaken up from the incident that took place at the apartment. He kept replaying it in his head over and over, trying to justify it. Unfortunately, that wasn't possible.

Cameron eventually pulled into the parking lot of Victor's University. He glanced back and forth through the lot, seeing most of the parking spaces were taken. Cameron continued driving, until he saw an available space he slightly passed.

"Ugh, darn it," he said. Cameron put the car in reverse and started backing into the space when a black Corvette sped into the space and turned off.

"Oh, come on! Really?" he exclaimed. A tall muscular guy stepped out of the car and a slim blonde girl followed shortly after him. The guy threw his arm around the girl's neck and she giggled, while they both stared at Cameron.

"Really dude? I had that space," Cameron argued.

"Yeah, now you lost it," the guy said, flipping Cameron off. The girl giggled again and the two walked toward the university. Cameron hit the steering wheel with his palm and put the car back in drive, pulling off to find another parking space.

Near the university, Jacob and Rachel walked along the side walk by green yards and stopped to gaze at the university's main buildings. There was an arch in front of the buildings that had **VICTOR'S UNIVERSITY** across it in bold letters. Jacob and Rachel started walking again, seeing a white water fountain in the main court just under the arch. A larger building could be seen behind the fountain, connected to the buildings beside it with **Main Office** across the top.

"Wow, I always forget how great this place is!" Rachel said with excitement. Jacob rolled his eyes, when the two heard a female voice call out, "Hey, Rachel!"

Rachel and Jacob glanced over and saw a woman wearing a black suit coming toward them out of the grass. It was Tracey, an old friend of Rachel's and a professor at the university. Tracey was a little taller than Rachel, with a light tan skin tone, hazel eyes, and long dark brown hair. She and Rachel went to college together and were roommates during their bachelor's programs. After graduating, they went their separate ways and got their doctorates, but they remained in touch.

"Hey Tracey," Rachel exclaimed. Rachel and Jacob walked up to Tracey and she hugged Rachel tightly. The two backed away from each other with a smile, when Tracey looked over at Jacob.

"Hello Jacob," she said.

"Hi Mrs. Tracey," Jacob replied. Tracey hugged Jacob briefly, glancing back at Rachel with a smile.

"What are you doing here? Don't you have to work?" she wondered while laughing.

"No, I took the week off because Jacob moved back home," Rachel responded with a smile, pulling Jacob close to her. Jacob rolled his eyes in embarrassment, looking down at his phone. Then, he saw that it was 9:17 AM and his eyes widened.

"Mom...I'm gonna be late!" Jacob yelled, throwing his arms up.

"Oh, go ahead without me I'll meet you there," she said softly.

"Sure," said Jacob, running off from Rachel and Tracey, while they giggled playfully. Jacob got back on the path heading toward the school and started staring at his phone, looking through his schedule.

After finally finding a parking space, Cameron jumped out of his car and threw his back pack over his shoulder, rushing toward the school. Looking at his watch, Cameron realized it was 9:19 AM and widened his eyes.

"Oh my God, I'm going to be so late!" Cameron exclaimed with worry.

Jacob continued to walk toward the main office, staring down at his phone and–

BAM! Jacob and Cameron collided and fell on to the ground, when

Jacob's phone flew out of his hand and Cameron's glasses flew off his face. They looked up and watched Jacob's phone and Cameron's glasses crash on the concrete.

"NOOOO!!!" the two cried in unison.

"My glasses," said Cameron.

"My phone," said Jacob. The two tried to get up, not realizing their arms were wrapped around each other's, falling over again. Unlinking their arms, Jacob and Cameron stood up and walked over to their broken items. Jacob picked up Cameron's glasses and Cameron picked up Jacob's phone. The two turned toward each other and held out the items for the other to take, looking into each other's eyes. They hesitated. For some odd reason they felt they had seen one another before, but they couldn't remember where. They stared at each other and took their items back, wrinkling up their foreheads.

"Do I know you from somewhere?" They asked one another.

"I don't think so," Cameron answered.

"But you look–" Jacob started.

"Familiar," they finished together. Suddenly, their amulets began to glow and they stared at them surprised. Jacob backed away from Cameron and he stared back at Jacob. Jacob dropped his mouth open, when their amulets stopped glowing.

"Okay, I'm going to pretend like that didn't happen," said Jacob. He turned away from Cameron and started walking toward the main office again. Cameron looked down at his amulet and back at Jacob. He felt a strange tugging at his spirit to do something, his heart beating hastily. Without hesitation, Cameron ran after Jacob and placed his hand on Jacob's shoulder, as Jacob stopped and looked back at him.

"I'm sorry; I feel I know you from somewhere. I just can't remember where," Cameron said, while Jacob stared at him.

"I don't think you do," said Jacob, pulling away from Cameron. Cameron reached out and grabbed Jacob's arm, stopping him again.

"Don't you feel it?" Cameron wondered. Jacob looked at Cameron, feeling the same strange tugging at his spirit that Cameron felt. He continued to stare at Cameron, remaining silent, as Cameron stepped back from him slowly.

"I'm Cameron," he said, holding out his hand toward Jacob. Though Jacob wavered for a moment, he put out his hand to Cameron with a smile.

"I'm Jacob."

The two exchanged a handshake, while Cameron smiled at Jacob. Then, Jacob flinched and his eyes twitched, seeing himself in the room from his dream. He looked to his right and saw several blurred wooden structures, not sure where he was. Looking to his left, Jacob jumped and saw Cameron staring at him with worry in his eyes.

"Are you okay?" Cameron asked him. Jacob's eyes twitched again and he snapped back, realizing he was at the school, still shaking Cameron's hand.

"You okay?" asked Cameron, while he watched Jacob's eyes. Jacob looked at Cameron and they let go of each other's hands. Jacob stepped back from him and tried to ignore what had just happened. It was obvious he was the only one who had just seen that.

"Yeah, I'm fine," said Jacob, brushing it off. Cameron looked down at Jacob's phone and saw that the entire screen was shattered.

"I'm sorry about your phone," he said sincerely. Jacob looked at his phone and shook his head, staring up at Cameron.

"It's not that big of a deal," said Jacob. He looked down at Cameron's glasses while he held them tightly, seeing they were crumbled.

"I'm sorry about your glasses though," Jacob said. Cameron smiled at him, lifting the glasses up to his chest.

"I have a spare pair, it's okay," he said. Jacob nodded and looked down at his watch, realizing it was 9:28 AM. Jacob threw his arms in the air and smacked his hand on his forehead.

"Great, now I'm late," he exclaimed. Cameron bucked his eyes and began to panic, forgetting about his tardiness from his class.

"Oh shoot!" he shouted. Cameron darted off toward four buildings to the right, while Jacob watched him confused. Looking to his left, Jacob saw Rachel coming up to him.

"You're done already?" said Rachel. Jacob stared at her straight-faced and crossed his arms.

"Very funny mom, very...funny," said Jacob

"What?" Rachel asked, looking confused.

"I guess I should go in and set up another appointment," Jacob grunted. Jacob walked into the court area while Rachel followed behind him, entering the main office.

The inside of the lobby was a descent size, having a waiting area on the right with two couches and university's program brochures on a table to the left. In front of them was the desk were a young woman sat by a computer. Her hair was pulled back in a bun and she was dressed in business attire. Once Jacob and Rachel reached the front counter, the young woman looked up at them with a smile.

"Hello, welcome to Victor's University," she said cheerfully.

"Hi," Jacob started with a nervous smile. "I had a meeting with an admission's rep about ten minutes ago and I wanted to reschedule, since I'm late."

"What's the name?" asked the receptionist.

"Jacob Blackwood."

The receptionist began to type Jacob's name into the computer, while Jacob tapped his fingers on the counter. The receptionist sat back in her chair and looked up at Jacob.

"It looks like we can still see you today, let me double check."

"Okay," Jacob replied. The receptionist picked up her phone and dialed an extension, waiting for the other end to pick up. Rachel stepped closer to Jacob, when he glanced back at her.

"What did she say?" Rachel asked.

"They might be able to squeeze me in today," said Jacob. The receptionist hung up the phone and looked at Jacob again with a smile.

"If you both can have a seat, Josh will be with you both in a moment," the receptionist informed them.

"Thanks," Jacob replied. He and Rachel walked over to the couches and sat down next to each other, waiting for the rep to meet them in the lobby. Eventually, a young man came out of a door on the left, wearing a white dress shirt and dark blue dress pants, with a matching tie. He was a little shorter than Jacob, having an ivory tone with blonde hair and blue eyes.

"Hi, you must be Jacob?" he asked.

"Yes I am," Jacob answered, standing up with Rachel. The young man got over to them and shook Jacob's hand.

"I'm Josh, I'll be taking you on your tour today," he said. "Are you ready?"

"Yeah, I'm ready," said Jacob.

"Okay, let's go."

Josh led Jacob and Rachel out of the Main Office and they began their tour of the campus.

After about an hour, Josh had taken Jacob and Rachel around the entire university, making their last stop in one of the classroom buildings. The three walked down the hallway, until Josh took them over to window, showcasing a class in progress.

"This is what the classroom looks like during second session," said Josh. "This session is the most appealing to students, especially those who work in the evening."

Jacob and Rachel stepped by the window and saw students sitting in rows of seats, while the professor lectured. Jacob watched the students take notes, while the professor wrote on the board.

"But that's pretty much the whole campus, besides the dorms of course," Josh continued. "Do you guys have any questions for me?"

Jacob looked at Rachel and crossed his arms, leaning back on the wall.

"What are my tuition options?" asked Jacob.

"If you'd like I can see if someone in financial aid can talk with you," said Josh. "Is that all right?"

"That's fine," Jacob answered.

"Okay, follow me."

Later, Jacob and Rachel were sitting in a small office by a desk, waiting for someone to come in. Eventually, an older man wearing a black suit walked into the room and stepped behind the desk. Though he was tall, he was slightly chubby. He had an olive skin tone with green eyes and was bald.

"You must be Jacob?" he asked reaching his hand out to Jacob. With a smile, Jacob held out his hand toward the man.

"Yes, I am," said Jacob.

"I'm Rob, director of financial aid."

The two shook hands and Rob turned to Rachel, putting his hand out to greet her.

"And you must be Dr. Blackwood, yes?"

"Yes, it's a pleasure," Rachel responded, shaking Rob's hand. Rob sat down in his chair and put his spectacles on, flipping through a folder he held in his hand.

"So you wanted to know your loan options, right?" asked Rob, glancing up at Jacob.

"Yes, I was," said Jacob.

"Okay. Well you already have an associate's degree, so your credits will transfer. You'll only have to complete two years to receive a bachelor's."

"Right, so what are my options for funding?" Jacob pressed. Rob looked down at the folder again, reading on.

"You have several," he started, "we can see if you're eligible for a Pell grant; or we can see what student loans best fit your budget."

"How much is tuition?" Rachel jumped in. Rob glared over his spectacles at Rachel, clearing his throat.

"For a four year student you're looking at roughly thirty thousand, but since he's only going for two years, it will be about half. So, the amount you're looking at for Jacob is somewhere around sixteen thousand."

"Oh that's nothing!" Rachel exclaimed, fumbling through her purse. Jacob stared at her embarrassed, shifty his eyes back and forth at her and Rob.

"Um...mom, what are you doing?" he asked, his eyes broadened. Ignoring Jacob, Rachel pulled out her check book and placed it on her lap, taking her pen to the check.

"Do you all take checks?" she asked boldly.

"MOM!" Jacob exclaimed, dropping his mouth open and blinking his eyes at Rachel. Rob stared at them, raising his eyebrows, not sure how to respond.

"What?" Rachel wondered.

"I don't want you to pay for my schooling; I can get a loan," Jacob responded.

"Jacob, I got it," said Rachel. Rachel looked back at Rob, while his eyes focused on her.

"So, do you?" Rachel asked again.

"Uh...yes–yes we do," Rob responded hesitantly.

"All right; I'll take care of that now."

"Uh, no you won't," Jacob argued, staring at Rachel.

"Jacob, I am going to take care of it. Why get a student loan if you don't need one?"

"Mom, I want to do this by myself!"

"Jacob–"

"Mom–"

"Jacob–"

"Mom–"

"Jacob–"

"Mom–"

Rob watched the two go back and forth for fifteen seconds, until he finally decided to interrupt them.

"You can pay half with a check and get student loans if you'd like," he suggested.

"No!" Rachel and Jacob snapped, glaring over at Rob. He jumped back in his chair and swallowed, his eyes widened in shock.

After a long debate with his mother, Jacob decided that Victor's University wasn't the right place for him. He and Rachel stepped out of the main office, glancing back at Josh while he waved them off. Returning the gesture briefly, Jacob turned back around and walked with Rachel toward the parking lot.

"That could have ended a little smoother," Rachel mentioned, crossing her arms. "At least they didn't kick us out for yelling at each other."

Jacob glanced over at Rachel with a frown, not saying a word. He rolled his and looked forward, seeing a tall and fair-skinned brunette male walking up toward them. Jacob immediately recognized him and realized it was an old classmate of his from college, Kurt Dean.

Jacob and Kurt weren't ever friends, but remained acquaintances after their time in school. Kurt was one of the people who expressed their dislike for Jacob going to New York, also being one of the few who told him his dream of being a writer was "irrational." And the fact Jacob was back in Paterson was the perfect ammunition for an unwanted earful. Kurt looked up at Jacob and smiled with a look of surprise, when Jacob tried to pretend he was pleased to see him.

"Jacob Blackwood," said Kurt.

"Kurt," said Jacob blandly. Kurt stepped up to Jacob and the two exchanged a one arm hug, stepping back from each other quickly. Slightly annoyed with Kurt's untimely arrival, Jacob crossed his arms and cleared his throat.

"Why are you here?" Jacob asked, not really caring.

"I'm attending the university, gotta finish up that nurses degree. What brings you to back to Paterson?"

"Didn't you see my Facebook status?" said Jacob with a cold tone. Rachel glared at him, as Kurt laughed under his breath.

"Oh yeah... that's right, it didn't work out in New York. I figured it wouldn't."

Jacob exhaled and stared at Kurt, while he babbled on, "I've always felt that goals should remain realistic and not extraordinary. That leads to nothing but disappointment and wasted potential. Don't you agree?"

"No goals are unrealistic...as long as you strive for what you want, you can achieve your goal."

"I beg to differ," Kurt started with a shrug, "I'd rather do something normal than something that I'm going to fail at. Don't wanna fall flat on my face for the whole world to see. Any who, later!"

Kurt waved at Jacob and walked off toward the school, while Jacob stood in place with a look of disbelief on his face. With a grunt, Jacob continued toward Rachel's car and got in quickly. Rachel followed behind him, stepping into the car and starting it up. She looked over at Jacob, seeing his face was red with rage.

"Are you all right?" Rachel asked.

"You know he's lucky I didn't grab him by his scarf and hang him right there in the middle of the court yard," Jacob finally blurted out. Rachel bucked her eyes at him, while he took heavy breaths and flared his nostrils.

"I don't think hanging him would have done you any good," said Rachel.

"This is why I didn't wanna come back," Jacob started again, "I hate these people."

"You don't mean that."

"Yes I do!"

Rachel crossed her arms and frowned at Jacob, while he stared out the front window. She knew exactly what his issue was, but she knew he wasn't going to talk.

"Is that what's wrong with you?" Rachel asked. "You're worried about what people think?"

"I don't need people to tell me I failed," Jacob started, "I know that. I already took forever to even finish the darn poetry book; I don't need everybody reminding of my misfortunes."

"First of all," Rachel exclaimed, "you did not fail. Just because things didn't go like you thought they would, doesn't mean you failed."

Jacob shook his head and rolled his eyes. "Then, why do I feel like I did? I had these big dreams, I go to New York, and now come back? I'm a laughing-stock."

Rachel grabbed Jacob's hand, while he stared off in the car.

"You can't worry about the naysayers, their opinion doesn't matter," said Rachel. "The only opinion that matters is the one that gave you that dream in the first place."

Jacob closed his eyes, knowing what Rachel said was right. He was too focused on what others were saying, instead of believing in himself and being proud of his accomplishments. Jacob opened his eyes and looked at Rachel, nodding in agreement.

"All right mom, I'll try not to," said Jacob.

"Good."

Rachel leaned over and kissed Jacob on his forehead. Sitting back in her seat, Rachel put the car in reverse and pulled out of the parking lot, leaving the university.

Near downtown Paterson, Isaac was behind the front counter in Ray's Café counting down a register, while the customers were sitting at their tables and enjoying their coffee, while soft music played.

Ray's Café was one of the smallest coffee shops in the area, with six serving tables, the front counter, and a small kitchen behind the counter. Though it wasn't very spacious, customers continued to come back because the employees strived for excellent customer service. The shop was run by Jeff Manning. Jeff was very muscular in build and 6 foot, with ivory skin, green eyes, and short cut hair. Jeff's great grandfather founded the café, and since then, his family continued to keep the café up and running. Jeff worked at the café since he was 20 years old, and now at age 32, he had been managing it for the past five years. He made sure that his staff continually provided their guests with the best customer service, and because of that, the café remained popular among the public.

Isaac completed counting down the register, when a young man came out of the kitchen. He was four inches taller than Isaac and had a medium ivory skin tone. He was slim with short dark blonde hair and his eyes were bright blue. His name was Kyle Phillips, one of the café employees. The two worked well together and always knew how to get things done quickly and efficiently. Because of that, Jeff gave Isaac and Kyle more responsibilities than their peers, although Isaac was the most trustworthy.

Kyle walked over to Isaac and leaned over on the counter, watching him close the register drawer.

"So how'd I do?" asked Kyle.

"It's even," said Isaac.

"Sweet! I'm out," Kyle exclaimed, snatching off his apron. Kyle handed his apron to Isaac and he tied it around himself. When he did this, Kyle noticed his amulet and chuckled.

"Ah dude," Kyle started, "you know Jeff's gonna kill you if he sees that necklace on you while you're working."

Isaac looked at Kyle confused, soon realizing he was referring to his amulet. Isaac looked down at the amulet and back at Kyle, his eyebrows raised.

"Yeah...about that, I'm probably not gonna be able to take it off."

"Really? Isaac, you're so weird sometimes," Kyle laughed.

"I'm serious," Isaac said sternly, when Kyle's facial expression dropped. Jeff had a strict dress code for the employees, and a part of it was they couldn't wear necklaces or chains. This was put into effect after a customer found one in their beverage, which most likely happened during the production process. Kyle knew if Jeff saw Isaac's amulet, he'd be livid. Kyle walked up to Isaac and tucked the amulet behind Isaac's apron with a shrug, feeling it wouldn't be visible that way.

"There you go…I'm leaving now," said Kyle.

"See ya," said Isaac. Kyle went into the cabinet behind the counter and grabbed his jacket, throwing it over his shoulders. With a wave, Kyle walked out of the café. Once Kyle left, the amulet started shaking under Isaac's apron, flipping itself in front of it. Isaac looked down in shock and his forehead wrinkled up, while he stared at the amulet angrily.

"Really!?" he exclaimed, "Great…just great."

Hearing the kitchen door open behind him, Isaac turned back and saw Jeff coming out the kitchen, holding a tray of beverages in his hand.

"Hey Isaac, take this to table three," said Jeff. "Kyle made these before he left, but was obviously too quick to get off today."

"Sure, I'll take them over," said Isaac, taking the tray from Jeff.

"Thanks, it's a caramel latte and a black coffee decaf, two sugars."

"Got it."

Isaac held the tray up and walked over to the table closest to the front window, where two middle aged women sat. One of them was fair-skinned with green eyes and short curly brown hair, while the other was a little darker in skin tone with brown eyes and shoulder length black hair. The brown haired one was rather plump and short, and the black haired woman was tall with a medium build. Isaac smiled at the women and cleared his throat, when they looked up at him.

"Hello ladies. I have a caramel latte–"

The black haired woman put out her hands and Isaac handed her the caramel latte on a saucer.

"–and I have a black coffee decaf, two sugars."

Isaac sat the coffee down near the other woman and she twisted up her face with a frown.

"What is this?!" she complained, staring at the coffee with her arms spread out. Isaac looked down at the woman's coffee confused, scratching his head.

"Um, it's a black coffee decaf with two sugars ma'am," he said, raising his eyebrows. The woman looked up at Isaac and rolled her eyes, crossing her arms thereafter.

"Don't sass me boy," she snapped. "That's what it's supposed to be, but this has a cream in it, it's not dark enough."

Isaac cleared his throat, preparing an apology for the woman.

"Ma'am I do apologize. We can remake it for you," he sympathized.

"Tsk! Please, who's to say you won't mess it up again?" the woman fussed.

"If you give us a chance ma'am, we can definitely fix it for you," Isaac continued. The woman rolled her eyes at Isaac again and crossed her legs, staring out the window, her face becoming swollen with rage.

"This is ridiculous! This is the third time I've come here and you've messed up my order, I am getting tired of it!"

Suddenly, Isaac's amulet began to glow dark blue and he became frustrated with the customer. Neither he nor anyone else noticed it glowing, but the woman continued to complain.

"If it weren't for us customers, you wouldn't have a job!"

"Okay, that's not the issue, but–"

"I don't wanna hear you're excuses anymore!"

The woman became very loud and irate, causing other customers to look their way. Hearing the ruckus, Jeff stepped out of the kitchen and saw Isaac speaking to the customer, while she yelled at him.

"I have had it with your horrible service!"

Isaac's amulet continued glowing and his face turned red. He saw himself in his mind knocking the mug over in the woman's lap, while she shrieked in horror. Isaac remained silent and the woman kept scolding him, when her coffee mug began to shake on its saucer.

"I will tell all of my friends that your service is not worth their time! We'll all just go to Starbucks!!"

Without warning, the mug fell over and spilled in the woman's lap.

"Aaahhh!!!!" she screamed, jumping out of her seat. Isaac stepped back in shock, while the customers looked over at the table again, watching the woman pat herself down. Isaac's mouth dropped open and his eyes widened. The woman continued to yell and scream, as her friend got up and helped her clean off. Isaac wasn't sure what happened. He didn't touch the cup and the woman didn't spill it on herself. What was going on?

"Oohhh!!! You little brat!" the woman hollered, grabbing her purse. She swung it at Isaac and smacked him in his side, knocking him back.

"Ouch!" he exclaimed, staring at the woman.

"I am going to report you all to the Better Business Bureau and you *will* get shut down!!"

In an angered rush, the two women stormed out of the restaurant and Isaac turned around, seeing all of the customers watching him. They weren't sure what happened and they didn't seem appalled by Isaac either. Isaac looked up in embarrassment, while Jeff crossed his arms and made a head gesture to get Isaac to come over. As Isaac walked over to Jeff, he backed into the kitchen and Isaac slowly followed. Isaac walked into the kitchen and saw Jeff standing by the sink on the right side of the kitchen frowning, his arms still crossed. Isaac walked over to the counter on the left near a cabinet of ingredients and put the tray down, when the kitchen door closed.

"What was that?" Jeff asked angrily.

"Look, I know what you think, but I swear I didn't do anything," said Isaac.

"So, it just spilled itself on the woman?!" Jeff exclaimed.

"No Jeff. I don't know what happened, it wasn't me," Isaac pleaded.

Jeff stared at Isaac and exhaled deeply. Isaac knew his story was unbelievable, but he didn't know how to prove he didn't do anything. He saw himself in his mind knocking the coffee over on the woman, but he knew he couldn't and didn't actually do it. But for some odd reason, he felt he did do it. Isaac put his head down and Jeff uncrossed his arms, rolling his eyes.

"Look I believe you," Jeff said, when Isaac looked up at him shocked. "I know you're not like that…but you need to watch it in the future, all right?"

"Okay, I will," Isaac promised. Isaac turned around to leave the kitchen, when Jeff called him.

"Hey," he said. Isaac looked back at Jeff and he threw a wet towel toward him. Isaac caught it in his hand and glanced at Jeff.

"Clean up that mess," said Jeff. With a quick salute, Isaac walked out of the kitchen and the door shut behind him.

Meanwhile, Jacob and Rachel were walking down the streets in the downtown area. After grabbing lunch, the two spent the rest of their afternoon relaxing and enjoying the early summer weather. Rachel watched Jacob, while he stared at the buildings in the area, seeming entranced.

"Are you all right, Jacob?" Rachel asked. Jacob looked up at her and smiled, placing his hands behind his back.

"Yeah, I'm fine…it's just so nostalgic walking down these streets," he said. "I feel like it's been forever since I've been down here."

"Oh, well it has been a few years since you've been here," Rachel mentioned.

"Yeah, it's just kind of weird."

Rachel began to look at her watch, sighing under her breath.

"What's wrong?" Jacob wondered.

"Oh nothing…I was just thinking about the office."

"Mom, the office is literally like two minutes away," said Jacob. "If you want to check things out, feel free too."

"No," said Rachel, "the only reason we came out here was so we could chill together...and get you a new phone."

"Which you didn't have to do," Jacob said. "All I'm saying is you're off the entire week. You have plenty of time to spend with me."

Jacob and Rachel stopped walking and stood in front of Ray's Café. He stared at Rachel and raised his eyebrows, crossing his arms. Jacob looked into the café window and saw Isaac come out of the kitchen. He watched Isaac walk over to the table the irate customer sat, and he began to wipe it down. Jacob recognized him slightly, but wasn't sure where he had seen him before. Jacob continued to stare at Isaac, until he walked away from the table and went back into the kitchen.

"I think I'm gonna stop by for a little bit, ya know," Rachel said, catching Jacob's attention. "I'm sure there are some messages I can take care of."

Jacob looked back at Rachel and she pulled out her car keys, smiling at him.

"Do you wanna go with me or will you meet me back here?"

"I can just chill out in this café 'til you get back, I guess," he said.

"Okay, I'll be back."

"All right."

Rachel walked off from Jacob toward a parking lot and he entered into the café. Jacob stepped inside and looked around, seeing the table Isaac had cleaned was available. Jacob stepped over to the table and sat down, pulling his cellphone out of his jacket pocket.

Isaac came back out of the kitchen and saw Jacob sitting at the table. He stood still by the back counter, slightly recognizing him. Suddenly, his amulet began to glow dark blue again. Isaac saw it glowing and quickly grabbed it before anyone noticed. He turned his back toward the customers and continued holding his amulet, seeing Jeff standing behind him.

"Gah!" Isaac exclaimed, jumping in shock.

"What are you doing?" Jeff asked.

"I uh–uh…um, I was about to go, um, greet the customer," said Isaac, still holding the amulet tightly. Jeff noticed him doing this and stared into Isaac's eyes.

"Move your hand," he said.

"Uh about that, you might not want to–"

"Move your hand, Isaac," Jeff grunted through his teeth. Isaac moved his hand from the amulet and Jeff stared at it, though it had stopped glowing.

"Okay Jeff, please don't get mad at me," said Isaac, "but I can't take it off."

"Why'd you put it on?" said Jeff.

"I didn't put it on, it–"

"So it put itself on?"

"Yeah, pretty much," Isaac responded with a shrug. Jeff continued to stare at Isaac, uncrossing his arms.

"You're treading on ice Isaac," Jeff warned him.

"I know Jeff," said Isaac, "and I know that it's against the rules to wear anything, but I promise it won't come off."

Jeff placed his hand over his forehead and shook it back and forth, blowing out a breath.

"It can't come off?" he asked.

"Not at all," said Isaac.

"And you can promise me there won't be any accidents?"

"I promise," Isaac assured him. Shaking his head again, Jeff waved Isaac off, giving him the okay to continue on.

"He's lucky I like him," Jeff mumbled, walking back into the kitchen. Isaac turned back around toward the customers, looking back over at Jacob. After little hesitation, Isaac walked over to Jacob to greet him properly.

"Hi, welcome to Ray's Café," said Isaac, as Jacob looked up at him. Jacob placed his phone on the table and smiled back at him.

"Hi," he said.

"Can I get you anything?"

"No, I'm actually just waiting for someone."

"Okay, well just let me know if you'd like something. I'm Isaac."

"Thank you," Jacob responded.

Jacob's eyes twitched again and he was back in the attic from his dream. This time, he was still looking at Cameron, who asked again, "Are you okay Jacob?"

Jacob shook his head and stepped back from Cameron.

"He'll be okay…we all will, once this is over," a voice said in front of him. Jacob looked up and saw Isaac standing by the glass podium reading a large brown book. Snapping out of his hallucination, Jacob's eyes twitched again and he was back in the café.

"Like I said, if you need anything just let me know," Isaac repeated, when Jacob looked up at him and nodded. With a smile, Isaac walked away from Jacob and went back behind the front counter, entering the kitchen. Jacob stared in the direction Isaac had gone in, feeling what he sensed when he met Cameron. He wasn't sure what it meant, but something was unusual.

Jacob's phone suddenly started vibrating on the table and startled him, catching his attention. Glancing down, he realized it was his mother calling. Jacob picked up the phone and answered, clearing his throat.

"Hey mom," he said.

"Hey hon, I just wanted to tell you that I am pulling up to the café as we speak," said Rachel.

"That was fast," said Jacob.

"Yeah, I still had a lot to take care of."

"I'm sure; you probably had a lot of messages from your patients."

"No, that's not what I meant."

"Then, what did you mean?" Jacob asked, throwing his free hand in the air, when he heard a car from outside. He looked over his shoulder out the window and saw his mother waving hard from the driver's seat of a red 2013 Chrysler 300 AWD.

"Oh dear," he said, hanging up his phone and getting up from the table. Jacob left out of the café and walked over to the, as Rachel stepped out of it with her arms in the air.

"Surprise!" exclaimed Rachel.

"Is this what you were doing?" Jacob wondered, staring at the car in awe. Rachel lowered her arms, still smiling at Jacob.

"I know that you love Chryslers, so I bought this for you on Saturday," she confessed.

"What a surprise," Jacob said with a smile.

"You like it don't you?" Rachel asked. Jacob looked up at Rachel and nodded.

"Yes…I love it mom."

Jacob walked over to Rachel and gave her a hug, while the two embraced tightly.

"Thank you, mom," said Jacob.

"You're welcome sweetie," she replied.

Ending their hug, Rachel walked over to the passenger's side of the car, when Jacob looked around for her car.

"Hey mom, where's your car?"

"Oh, it's at the dealership," she said. "I figured you'd want to take your new car for a ride. Can you take me to it?"

Jacob smiled at Rachel and they stepped into the car. Jacob looked around and put the car in drive, pulling off down the street.

Back in the café, Isaac was still in the kitchen when Jeff walked over to him with a tray of fresh scones.

"Can you take these out and put 'em in the case?"

"On it," he said.

Isaac took the tray and walked out of the kitchen, seeing that Jacob was no longer in the café. Isaac placed the tray on the counter and began to feel the strange feeling he felt when he first saw Jacob. He still couldn't fathom what the cause of it was, and he couldn't stop it either. Isaac opened the case and placed the scones inside, locking it back afterwards. Isaac stood up and exhaled, going back into the kitchen and closing the door behind him.

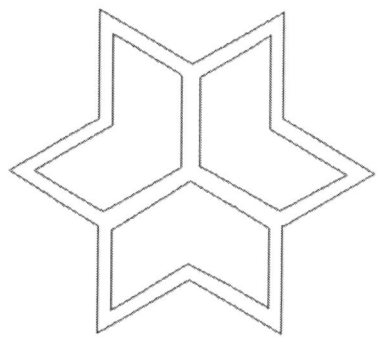

THE HOUSE ON MANOR AVENUE

BY NOW, Isaac and Cameron had both met Jacob, but they hadn't met each other. They had three things in common: strange amulets that weren't removable, the feeling they knew each other, and an experience of supernatural power. To add to that, the visions Jacob had when he encountered Isaac and Cameron made it worse. And as the days went on, things seemed to get stranger.

The sky was cloudy and gray that Friday morning. It was most likely going to storm later on in the day, since thunder and lightning had been striking periodically. Cameron was asleep in his car on the side of the road downtown. He had been doing this all week after being evicted. He tried to get housing on campus, but they wouldn't have any rooms available in the dormitory until the next semester. He wanted to stay in a hotel, but all the hotels were too expensive for his budget, since he had forty dollars left to spend.

Still asleep, Cameron leaned his head over toward the window, snoring loudly. The windows of the car were slightly rolled down, letting in a cool breeze that went through the air. Then, Cameron's amulet began to glow bright blue, when thunder crackled in the sky. With a flinch, Cameron woke from his sleep and wiped his eyes, observing his surroundings. He looked up outside the car and saw an envelope appear in midair with a white aura around it. It swirled around in the air, until it slid through the cracked window on the passenger's side of the car. Cameron grabbed his glasses from the dashboard and put them on, seeing the glowing envelope in the seat.

"Whoa! What is that?"

Cameron slowly reached his hand over and picked up the envelope, which stopped it from glowing. He turned it over and saw that it was addressed to him. He felt something small and metal-like inside the envelope and opened it, seeing it was a handwritten letter.

Dear Cameron,

I am sorry I wasn't there for you. I wanted to be in your life...but I couldn't. I was taken away from this world before you were even born. But I want you to know that despite that, I have always held a place for you in my heart. I have left a key for you to your new home with this letter. I hope once you're there you will fully understand the truth and embrace it. I love you so much.

Sincerely,

Dad

Cameron stared at the letter in shock. How could he be getting a letter from his father? And from the way he spoke, it was though he knew he would be dead when Cameron received the letter. Cameron put the letter in his lap and pulled a small silver key from the envelope that was taped to a small note. Separating them, he saw the note had *13 Manor Avenue* written on it.

"I gotta find this place," he said. Cameron started his car and placed the letter in the passenger's seat, driving down the road in a hurry.

Later that morning, Cameron walked up to the door of the computer lab in Victor's University and slowly entered the room. He held his backpack on his shoulder, while he stared at the letter in his right hand. Cameron looked around the lab and walked over to an available desk with a computer, sitting down in the chair. He dropped his backpack on the floor and placed the letter down, logging into the system. He immediately clicked on the internet browser and the window popped up. He searched for a webpage to give him directions and looked over at the piece of paper with the address on it.

"Okay, 13 Manor Avenue," he muttered. Cameron typed in the address and directions from the university to Manor Avenue populated, showing the address was thirty five minutes away.

"That's not too far from here."

Cameron printed the directions and logged off, picking up his backpack and letter. After logging off the computer, Cameron rushed over to the printer and picked up the directions. He folded them up and exited the computer lab with haste.

Isaac was in the kitchen of Ray's Café, making a Frappuccino for a customer. He originally didn't work until later that evening, but Jeff asked him to open for a couple hours because he was running late due to a family emergency. After topping the Frappuccino with wiped cream, Isaac put a plastic top on it and walked out of the kitchen. He took a straw from the front counter drawer and stepped out on the floor, walking over to a table where a young woman sat reading a book. Isaac placed the Frappuccino down and the young woman looked up at him with a smile.

"Here you go," he said.

"Thank you so much," the young woman exclaimed.

"You're welcome."

Standing upright, Isaac heard the door chime ring. He glanced over and saw a young woman walk into the café. She looked around for a moment, when her eyes met with Isaac's. After gazing at her for a while, Isaac realized who she was…it Valerie Skyes. His heart started pounding swiftly and his palms became clammy, when Valerie's face lit up.

"Isaac?" she said, continuing to look at him with a smile.

"Valerie," he said. A smile slowly appeared on Isaac's face and Valerie walked over to him quickly. She threw her arms out wide and wrapped them around Isaac, while he hesitantly held her back.

"It's been so long, I missed you," she said, still holding him tight.

"I know, I missed you too," Isaac agreed, keeping his composure. The two let go of each other and stepped back. Valerie continued smiling at Isaac, while he stared into her eyes.

"So, how have you been?" she asked him.

"I've been all right," he said, "just working here at the café. It helps with bills and my apartment isn't too far from here."

"That's convenient," Valerie exclaimed.

"Yeah, it is," Isaac replied. With a serious tone, he looked at Valerie and put his hands in his pockets. "I didn't realize you were coming back today."

"Yeah, I figured it would be best to come home now," she said. "I've already started registering for classes."

"Cool."

The two paused for a moment. They began to look around, trying to figure out what to say. Then, Isaac looked back at Valerie and took a deep breath.

"Do you want something to drink?" Isaac wondered, while Valerie stared at him.

"Sure," she answered with a shrug. "What do you have?"

Isaac smirked and politely put his arm behind Valerie, walking her over to an empty table.

"I have something you're gonna love. I'll be right back."

"Okay," she replied nervously. Isaac stepped away from Valerie and went back behind the counter. He grabbed a cup and filled it to the rim with coffee. Valerie watched Isaac with a nervous smile, when he entered into the kitchen.

Isaac walked over to the counter top on the left and placed the cup down. He took various ingredients out of the cabinet and mixed them into the coffee, making a ginger bread latte, Valerie's favor cookie. With a smirk, Isaac opened the refrigerator and took out the whip cream, topping off the latte with a quick swirl.

Back on the floor, Valerie waited quietly, when Isaac came out of the kitchen with the latte in hand. He walked over to the table and placed the latte down with a grin.

"What is it?" Valerie asked.

"Take a sip," he pressured, still grinning. Valerie picked up the latte and took a sip, widening her eyes in surprise. She placed the cup back on the table and looked up at Isaac with a smile.

"It tastes like gingerbread!" she said with excitement in her voice.

"Your favorite cookie," said Isaac. "I remember I used to get gingerbread cookies and give them to you in kindergarten. And I continued to do it throughout middle school."

Valerie looked up at Isaac in surprise, while he smiled at her.

"I've been trying to perfect the recipe for quite some time, and I finally got it right…just for you."

"I can't believe you remembered that after all this time," said Valerie, gazing at Isaac.

"Some things you don't forget," he said. Then, Jeff came into the café quickly and rushed behind the back counter, clocking into the computer system.

"Uh…I gotta get back to work," Isaac said, turning away from Valerie.

"How much do I owe you?" she asked, as he glanced back at her and smirked, shaking his head.

"It's on the house," said Isaac. Then, he quickly walked back to the counter and looked at Jeff after he clocked in.

"Hey Jeff," Isaac exclaimed. Jeff grabbed the kitchen door and glanced back at Isaac.

"Thanks for coming in for me," he said.

"Oh no problem, I'll just go clean up the kitchen before you start your shift."

"I got it; you can go ahead and head out."

"But, um–" before Isaac could finish, Jeff opened the kitchen door and saw various ingredients out on the counter top. Jeff paused and glared back at Isaac, while he smiled nervously.

"Were you making stuff not on the menu again?" Jeff asked with a frown.

Isaac shrugged his shoulders. "Whoops."

Jeff shook his head at Isaac and rolled his eyes, entering the kitchen. Isaac heard the doorbell chime again and glanced back, seeing the mail man enter the café. The mail man walked up to Isaac and handed him a stack of mail with a smile.

"Hello," he exclaimed with glee.

"Hey," Isaac replied, taking the mail.

"It's going to be a magical day today isn't it?" said the mail man.

"What?" Isaac wondered, raising his eyebrows. He stared at the mail man confused, while the mail man kept a smile on his face. Looking at the mail, Isaac ignored what the mail man had said, sifting through the mail briefly. Suddenly, something in the middle of the mail began to glow white. Isaac bucked his eyes and quickly placed the mail on the back counter before the mail man noticed.

"Uh…yeah, I guess so," Isaac stuttered.

"Have a great day!" said the mail man, saluting Isaac and leaving the café. Isaac turned back toward the mail and quickly fumbled through it to find what was glowing. Eventually, he saw an envelope that was addressed to him.

"What the heck," he said, staring at the envelope in awe. Isaac bent down behind the counter and opened the letter, when a small key fell out on the floor. He picked up the key and stared at it, taking the letter out shortly afterward.

Dear Isaac,

It's me, your father. I know you never knew me, but I knew you. I saw you in my dreams and visions. I am sorry that I couldn't be in your life like I wanted to, but things had to be this way in order for you to live in peace. I have much to tell you my son, and I hope you find all the answers when you arrive at 13 Manor Avenue. I love you son.

Sincerely,

Dad

Isaac stared at the letter slightly muddled and worried. *A letter from my dad?* Isaac thought, while he stood up and continued to look at the letter. Then, Jeff came out of the kitchen with his apron on, staring at Isaac confused.

"What are you still doing here?" he asked. Isaac glanced back at Jeff and folded up the letter, placing the key in his pocket.

"I was just getting the mail," he answered.

"All right...well you can head out. I'll see you later this evening."

"Okay."

Isaac took off his apron and placed it in the cabinet under the counter, grabbing his jacket. Isaac threw his jacket over his shoulders and looked out on the floor for Valerie. She had already left, but she left a folded piece of paper on the table.

"Don't forget your tip," Jeff said, when Isaac looked at him. He nodded and walked over to the table, picking up the paper. Stepping outside, Isaac opened the paper and saw it had *"Call me sometime 973-443-5656"* on it. Isaac blushed and walked down the side walk to the parking lot, getting into his car. He pulled up the GPS on his cellphone and entered in the address from the letter. Directions came up immediately, showing it was about fifty five minutes away.

"I guess I have time to take a little trip," he said. Isaac started his car and pulled out of the parking lot, taking off down the road.

Jacob was on his cellphone, pacing in the foyer of Rachel's home, while she and Jay J watched him from the dining room. Jacob was doing a phone screen for a job at a local magazine company called Paterson Life. They were looking for local writers, and since that was what he loved doing, he figured he should give it a try.

"Okay...thank you...bye."

Jacob hung up the phone and looked at Rachel and Jay J, who were still staring at him.

"So, what did they say?" Rachel wondered, on the edge of her seat.

"Well," Jacob started, sitting down at the table, "they said the head of the magazine is interested in meeting me, and he wants me to come in for an interview on Monday."

Rachel grinned and clapped her hands with excitement.

"Oh Jacob, that's great!" she exclaimed. "This just could be your break."

"I know," said Jacob. "I really want to get back into my writing like I did before."

"Well for all you know, things could be falling into place," Rachel mentioned, when Jacob looked at her with a smile. Jay J rolled his eyes and his facial expression changed to a frown. Abruptly, Jay J got up from the table and stormed out of the dining room, rushing into the kitchen. Jacob and Rachel looked over at the kitchen door, as it slammed shut. Rachel got up and went into the kitchen after Jay J, when Jacob sat down. Suddenly, his amulet began to glow and he stared down at it in annoyance.

"What now," he wondered aloud. Then, Jacob began to hear Rachel and Jay J's conversation from the kitchen, as if he was in there with them.

"What's the problem?!" Rachel snapped.

"I'm tired of hearing about how Jacob!" Jay J exclaimed. Jacob looked over at the kitchen door with a frown, continuing to listen in.

"What are you talking about?" Rachel asked, slightly confused.

"Ever since he came home, all I've been hearing about is Jacob!" Jay J yelled angrily. "You keep spending time with him and you're just leaving me high and dry!"

"I've been spending time with Jacob because I'm helping him pick himself up."

"Yeah, I see he's always been your favorite."

"Now don't you even go there with me, I have never shown favoritism," Rachel defended herself.

Jacob's amulet stopped glowing and he could no longer hear Rachel and Jay J's conversation. He looked away from the kitchen door and crossed his arms, staring off in the dining room. He began to feel annoyed with how childish Jay J was acting. Moments later, Rachel walked out of the kitchen and sat back down in her seat, as Jay J came out shortly after her. He sat back down in his seat and crossed his arms, still frowning.

"So I was thinking," Rachel started, "maybe tomorrow we can all have a family outing, since James is off. I think it would be nice for us to spend some quality time together. Sound good?"

There was a strong tension between Jacob and Jay J. And currently, none of Rachel's tactics were breaking it. Jacob shook his head, when Jay J glared at him.

"No it doesn't," Jacob said abruptly. Rachel looked over at him in shock, while Jay J tightened his fists, frowning at Jacob.

"Jacob!" Rachel exclaimed.

"No mom, I'm done dealing with this," said Jacob. "Until Jay J can act like an adult, I'm not doing anything with him."

Jacob pushed his chair away from the table and left out of the dining room, rushing up the stairs to his room. Jacob closed his door and locked it, flopping down on his bed and crossing his arms. Then, he heard a knock at the door and stared at it with irritation.

"I don't feel like talking right now," he said, not knowing who was at the door.

"Jacob, we need to deal with this," Rachel's voice was heard on the other side of the door. "It's an issue and I'm tired of the bickering,"

Jacob didn't say another word. He didn't care if it was an issue that needed to be dealt with; he was tired of it too. Realizing Jacob wasn't going to come out, Rachel exhaled and stepped away from the door. Jacob continued sitting on the bed, when he saw a bright white light reflecting on the wall in front of him. He looked behind himself and saw a glowing white envelope on his lampstand near the bed. Jacob got up and walked over to the lampstand, picking up the envelope and breaking the seal. He flipped the envelope over and a key fell into his hand. Jacob stared at the key and took a letter out of the envelope.

Dear Jacob,

I know by now you've grown so much. I wish that I could've been there to see you take your first steps, and to hear your first words, but I wasn't able to be. I know a lot of things about you my son, though I would have liked to have been there for you in person. I'm sure these last few days have been hard, but I know that you are starting to understand things now. I want to show you the truth, so that you can understand everything completely. This key enclosed will give you access to 13 Manor

Avenue, the place where I hope all of your questions can be answered. I love you son.
   Sincerely,
   Dad

Jacob stared at the letter silently. He wasn't sure how he could be getting a letter from his father, and he didn't know how it got in his room. Jacob placed the letter on his bed and looked out the curtains, watching the rain come down. He walked over to his closet and took out his jacket, throwing it on and grabbing the letter from the bed. Jacob picked up his messenger bag from the floor and threw it over his shoulder, walking out of his room quietly. Jacob went down the stairs and crept past the living room, where he saw Jay J lying down on the couch, watching TV. Jacob walked up to the door and left out of the house, closing the door behind him. Rachel heard the front door from her room and looked out her window, seeing Jacob walk toward his car. Rachel shook her head with disappointment and closed her curtains. Jacob got in his car and placed his bag in the passenger's seat, blowing out a breath. He took the letter out of his pocket and looked at the address again. Then, Jacob started his car and pulled off, driving out of the neighborhood.

That afternoon, the rain was coming down harder than earlier. Cameron was driving down a dark road when he saw the street sign *Manor Avenue* on his left at the end of the intersection. He stopped at the sign and turned down the street, looking around for the correct address. He saw several manors aligned on both sides of the streets, while they were fairly spaced out from each other. Eventually, Cameron looked to his left and saw a large black and brown manor. It was manor 13. Cameron slowed down and made a U-turn in the street, pulling up by the side walk near the manor.

   Cameron stared at the manor for a second. Then, he got out and pulled his hood over his head, holding the key in his hand. He closed his car door and began to walk toward the house. He walked up the stairs that led to the front door, seeing gold metal plates of the house number near it. Cameron stopped near the door and stared at the key, when a strange feeling of worry came over. *What if this key doesn't work, what am I gonna do?* Cameron thought, as he put the key in the door and turned it. The door clicked and slowly swung open, while he stood motionless in the doorway. He stared into the manor nervously, stepping inside with hesitation and closing the door behind him. Then, the door locked itself and Cameron stepped away from it, looking around in the hall.

"Hello...hello," he said, thinking someone would answer. He didn't hear a response. Cameron stared up and saw three mini chandelier lights aligned along the ceiling. He looked to his left, seeing an entryway to the living room area. It was completely furnished with a couch and love seat near the outer walls in front of a window and had a coffee table in the middle of the floor. Cameron stepped into the area and saw a bookshelf and a large TV stand on the opposite side of the room. He walked through the room and went through another entryway that led back to the main hall. He looked to his right and saw a staircase that led to the second floor, across from the living room. He made his way over to it, slowly walking up the staircase.

Once he arrived in the main hall of the second floor, Cameron saw a room in front of him with the door open. He stepped into the hall and glanced around, realizing that it led to other rooms and a staircase to another floor. He paused in the middle of the hallway and raised his eyebrows, gawking at the manor's size.

"Wow, this place is huge," he exclaimed to himself. Then, Cameron looked at the staircase and walked over to it, following them to the next floor.

Outside, Jacob turned on to Manor Avenue and stared at the house, seeing manor 13 on his left. Jacob parked on the opposite side of the street and got out of his car, staring up at the manor. He walked across the street, went up the stairs, and reached the front door of the manor. He stared at the door and dug in his pocket for the key. Jacob placed the key in the door and opened it, stepping into the house. He closed the door and walked into the middle of the hall, examining it thoroughly.

"Wow, this is really nice," he said. Jacob stared at the dining table at the end of the hall, seeing an entrance to another room on the right.

Jacob walked over to the door and opened it, walking through a short hall and entering the kitchen. An island stood in the middle of the floor, while cabinets and a countertop surrounded it on the opposite side of the room. Jacob looked over to the right and saw a staircase that led to the second floor, seeming to be a back entry. He walked into the middle of the kitchen and saw a door on the left that led to the basement. Jacob stepped over to the door and hesitantly walked down the steps to the lower level.

Back on the upper level, Cameron reached the third floor of the manor and entered a condensed hallway. He walked down the hallway quickly, seeing a door that was closed at the end. Cameron stepped up to the door and placed his hand on the knob, entering the room. He looked around the room and realized he was in the attic. Cameron recognized the room from the dream he had earlier that week. He walked across the wooden floor, staring at two wooden book shelves that had a large chest next to it on the right. Then, he walked into the middle of the room and glanced to his left, seeing two cabinets that were closed. Near him was a small table surrounded by three chairs, while glass podium stood a couple feet away.

"I've been here before," he said to himself. *CLICK!* Cameron jumped, looking to his right. He saw that the chest had opened up and cautiously walked over to it. Cameron bent down on his knees and threw the chest cover back, looking at the various items in the chest. One item that stood out in particular was a small black book. Cameron took the book out and examined it, staring at the faded letters on it the read, *Samuel Blackwood.*

"Samuel Blackwood?" he said, rubbing his hand across the book. Cameron opened the book and a small picture fell on the floor. He picked the picture up and stared at it, seeing it was a picture of a young man. He looked like Cameron, but his skin was paler and his eyes were much darker. Cameron widened his eyes, realizing it was his father.

Back outside, Isaac arrived at the manor and parked his car on the street. He got out and stared at the manor, his eyes squinted. He took the key out of his pocket and walked up to the front door slowly. He held the key out toward the door and froze up. *What am I doing?* Isaac thought to himself, stepping back from the door. He shook his head and put the key back in his pocket, turning away from the house. Suddenly, Isaac heard the door knob turn and the door came opened, as he glared back at the manor. Isaac stopped and looked into the main hall of the manor, looking to see if anyone had opened the door.

With a deep breath, Isaac walked into the hall and stopped near the staircase. Out of nowhere, a gust of wind blew through the air and slammed the front door closed. Isaac flinched and looked back at the door, his heart beating rapidly. He walked back toward the door and locked it, holding his hand on his chest.

Isaac stepped away from the door and turned around, when Jacob came back into the hall after hearing the door slam. Oddly enough, the two recognized each other from their meeting in the café. Jacob stared at Isaac and walked toward him slowly, while Isaac stood still.

"Isaac?" said Jacob, remembering his name. He stared at Isaac confused while he looked back at him, not knowing what to say.

"You're the guy in the café, right?" Jacob continued.

"Y–Yeah that's me," Isaac stuttered, stepping back.

"This isn't your house, is it?" Jacob wondered. Isaac stopped and didn't say anything. Jacob swallowed and continued to stare at Isaac, feeling slightly awkward.

"Um, not exactly. I, ah…got a–a letter from my…uh, my dad," Isaac stuttered on again, while Jacob widened his eyes. "It told me to come here."

Jacob stopped a few feet away from Isaac, the two staring at each other with similar expressions of confusion.

"You…you got a letter from your dad?" Jacob asked. Isaac nodded. Jacob placed his hand over his forehead and blew out a breath, looking back at Isaac while shaking his head.

"That's impossible, my dad left me a letter telling me to come here," he said. Isaac stared at Jacob, reaching into his pants pocket and taking out his letter. He showed it to Jacob and after a quick look at it, he realized it was the exact same handwriting in his letter.

"Oh my," Jacob exclaimed, as Isaac pulled his letter away from Jacob.

"What?" Isaac asked, while he stared at Jacob confused. Jacob looked up at Isaac, took his letter out of his jacket, and handed it to him. Isaac compared the letters, seeing the handwriting was identical. He looked back at Jacob, when the two heard footsteps coming from the upper level of the manor. Isaac and Jacob turned toward the staircase, when Cameron came down the steps and saw them. He heard the door slam from the attic and came down to see what happened. Jacob remembered him from their encounter at the college, while Cameron stared at the two confused.

"Who are you?" Isaac asked him.

"I could ask you guys the same thing," said Cameron.

"You don't remember me? I'm the guy you bumped into at Victor's?" Jacob wondered. Cameron stopped to look at Jacob, recognizing him.

"Oh, yeah," said Cameron. "What are you doing here?"

"I got a letter telling me to come here," said Jacob, "and so did he."

Cameron chuckled and walked toward Isaac and Jacob with a frown, reaching into his back pants pocket.

"Well, this must be some kind of sick joke or something," he started, "because so did I."

Cameron pulled out his letter and showed it to Isaac and Jacob, seeing the same handwriting on Cameron's letter as theirs. Isaac shook his head and stepped back from the two.

"What does this mean?" said Isaac.

Before Jacob or Cameron could answer, an aura of light appeared over their heads and the three looked up. The aura turned into an envelope and it drifted to the floor, while the three stared at it. Jacob picked the envelope up and opened it quickly, as Isaac and Cameron stepped behind him to see what it said.

My sons,
Now you know the truth. Embrace it.

Dad

Isaac, Jacob, and Cameron looked at each other in shock, when suddenly lightning and thunder struck and all the lights in the manor came on. The three stepped back and stared at each other, recalling the dream they all had four nights before.

"I remember where I first saw you guys now," said Isaac.

"In our dream; we all had the same dream that night," said Jacob.

"And we connected," said Cameron.

"Like brothers," the three finished together.

BOOM! Isaac, Jacob, and Cameron were startled by the noise and glanced back at the front door. Jacob walked over toward the door, while Isaac and Cameron followed behind him. He opened the door and looked around, seeing no one nearby who could have knocked or banged on the door. Closing the door back, Jacob looked down and saw a large leather book that had a faded six-pointed star on the front. Jacob grabbed the Book and turned toward Isaac and Cameron, staring at the Book.

"What is that?" Cameron asked, staring at the Book.

"The Book of Magic," Isaac answered, as Jacob and Cameron stared at him.

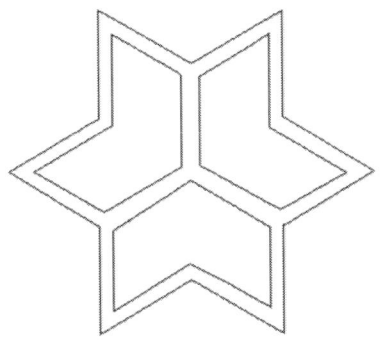

DO YOU BELIEVE IN MAGIC

NOW THEY KNEW THE TRUTH. They were brothers, by the same father. Samuel knew that it would probably be a struggle for them to accept at first, though eventually, they would have to. But that wasn't the only revelation that Isaac, Jacob, and Cameron would encounter. There were things they had yet to discover.

After a couple of hours, the rain had stopped and the sun was shining over Manor Avenue. Isaac was sitting on the couch in the living area, staring at the Book Jacob had found. He had been pondering over several ways to open the Book, but he continued to dismiss them all. Isaac, Jacob, and Cameron had spent most of their time trying to get the Book open, having no luck. The thing that made it stranger was that the Book didn't have a lock or key hole on it anywhere. So why couldn't they open it? Jacob came into the living area and sat next to Isaac, who was still staring at the Book sternly.

"Have you thought of a way to open it yet?" Jacob asked. Isaac continued staring at the Book, shaking his head.

"Nope; and I'm starting to get really frustrated," said Isaac. "The more ideas I come up with, I just throw them out."

Jacob looked down at the Book, when Cameron came into the living area. He stood in the doorway, staring at Isaac and Jacob.

"Any luck?" he asked. Jacob looked up at Cameron and shook his head. Cameron walked into the room and stood near the coffee table, glaring at the Book.

"It's like the Book is sealed or something…and there's no way to open it," said Jacob. With a cocky smirk, Cameron picked up the Book and stared at it for a moment. Then, he threw it at the floor. The Book hit the floor and bounced back into Cameron's face. Cameron fell over and the Book bounced out of the living area into the hall.

"Ow," Cameron cried. Isaac and Jacob got up and went over to Cameron to help him up, while he rubbed his nose.

"That was brilliant," Isaac said sarcastically. "Now the Book has gone off somewhere."

"Do you have a better idea?" Cameron retorted, crossing his arms. Jacob began to look around for the Book, when he looked in the hall and saw the Book resting on the edge of the dining room table.

"Uh…guys, I think I found the Book," said Jacob. Isaac and Cameron looked back and widened their eyes, seeing the Book on the table. The three walked into the main hall and rushed to the table, staring at it together.

"How the heck are we supposed to open this thing?" Jacob asked.

"And how did it get all the way over here?" Cameron added.

"It's possessed," said Isaac. Jacob and Cameron stared at Isaac.

"Really?" said Jacob.

"I'm just saying," said Isaac. The three stared at the Book again, still clueless with how to open it. Then, Isaac's amulet began to glow dark blue. Jacob and Cameron stared at Isaac, when Jacob's amulet began to glow blue.

"What's going on?" Cameron panicked. Cameron looked down at his amulet and it began to glow bright blue. Isaac, Jacob, and Cameron looked at each other and felt the amulets loosing up, when clasps appeared on their bands. Jacob felt the clasp against his neck and reached behind himself, taking the amulet off.

"We can remove them now?" Isaac asked, staring at Jacob.

"Why now," Cameron added, glaring at Isaac confused. Jacob continued to stare at his amulet, realizing the shape of it looked like a piece of the six-pointed star on the Book.

"I get it now," said Jacob. He looked at Isaac and Cameron, removing his amulet from its band. Jacob walked up to the Book and placed his amulet in one of the spots of the six-pointed star. When he did this, the amulet stopped glowing. Jacob looked at Isaac and nodded, hinting that he should do the same. Hesitantly, Isaac removed his amulet and placed it in one of the spots on the Book. Isaac's amulet stopped glowing and sealed itself with Jacob's. Isaac and Jacob looked over at Cameron, while he stared at them confused. Cameron took a deep breath and took his amulet off, staring at it calmly.

"Here goes nothing," said Cameron. He placed his amulet in the last open space of the six-pointed star and the amulet sealed with Isaac and Jacob's amulets. Without warning, the Book began to shake, the gems on their amulets turned white, and the entire Book started glowing. The Book swung open and the three covered their eyes, being engulfed by a bright white light.

Uncovering their eyes, Isaac, Jacob, and Cameron looked around and realized they were no longer in the manor. It seemed as if they were in a city, but it wasn't familiar to them. They stood in front of an alley, surrounded by dull skies and tall buildings. Isaac walked in front of Jacob and Cameron into the streets, looking for other civilians.

"Where the heck are we?" Isaac asked. Jacob walked up behind him and glanced around, shaking his head.

"I don't know…this place doesn't look familiar to me," said Jacob

BOOM! The three looked back abruptly, hearing the noise come from the alley. Then, Cameron began to hear voices coming from the same direction.

"Get him!"

"Don't let him get away!"

"You will be punished!"

Cameron turned toward the alley, frowning up his face. Without informing Isaac or Jacob, Cameron darted off into the alley.

"Cam–Cameron wait!" Jacob hollered. He and Isaac ran into the alley after Cameron. Cameron ran through the alley swiftly, continuing to hear the voices shouting out.

"We will stop you!"

"Give up fool!"

Cameron reached the end of the path and looked around the corner, seeing a man on his knees, his back facing Cameron. Then, Cameron began to hear footsteps behind him. Looking back, he saw Isaac and Jacob coming up to him. Isaac and Jacob stopped and bent over, breathing heavily and staring at Cameron.

"Hey! You can't just run off like that," Isaac snapped.

"I'm sorry," Cameron responded, "but I heard something and I came to see what it was."

Then, the man began to speak. "I have to save them."

Isaac, Jacob, and Cameron peaked around the corner, watching the man take off a six-pointed star amulet. He put one of the pointed edges to his arm and ran it from his forearm to the palm of his hand, as blood seeped from his skin.

"What is he doing?" Cameron wondered.

"I don't know," said Isaac, "but I feel like I know him."

The man began to speak again, but this time, he said everything in a rhyme.

"With this blood…I shed tonight; bless my three sons in this fight."

Isaac, Jacob, and Cameron continued to watch the man, listening to the shakiness in his voice, while blood dripped on the ground.

"What is he talking about?" Isaac asked, looking over Cameron's shoulder.

"How should I know," Cameron snapped, staring back at Isaac angrily.

"Hey, chill out," Jacob said.

The man continued chanting, holding the amulet in his right hand.

"All my power I give to thee – and they will be the Trinity."

Suddenly, the man began to glow blue and the amulet broke into three pieces. The blue light left the man and went inside the amulet pieces, dropping to the ground. Without warning, four black cloaked figures came around the corner in front of the man, putting their arms out toward him. The man began to squirm in pain and the cloaked figures lifted him up in the air while he groaned and hollered.

"What are they doing?!" Cameron grunted, tightening his fists. He began to walk around the corner, when Isaac and Jacob grabbed him by his arms.

"What are you doing? Are you trying to get killed?!" Isaac exclaimed, frowning at Cameron.

"I'm trying to stop them from hurting that man!"

"I don't think you can," Jacob responded. The three looked back over at the man, listening to his wails of pain worsen. Then, another cloaked figure came around the corner were the others stood and walked between them, staring at the man.

"Your end is here," said the cloaked figure. He put his arms out toward the man and white electric shock waves shot out of his palms, hitting the man.

"Aaaaahhhhh!!!" the man cried.

"No!" Cameron hollered, running around the corner.

"Cameron stop!" Jacob yelled, as he and Isaac ran after Cameron. The shock waves shocked the man until he burst into flames, becoming specks of dust that dropped to the ground. The cloaked figures dropped their hands to their sides, vanishing with a bright white light.

"No! Stop!" Cameron cried, reaching the man's burnt ashes. Suddenly, the amulet pieces that were on the ground began to glow three different shades of blue, lifting up into the air. Isaac and Jacob stopped behind Cameron, staring at the amulets while they suspended in the air.

"What in the world," Isaac exclaimed. To their surprise, the amulets dashed toward them and the three closed their eyes, being engulfed in a bright light again.

Opening their eyes, the three realized they were back in the manor. They looked at each other confused, when the Book shot out three auras of light that went inside of them. Isaac, Jacob, and Cameron flew back into the hallway and slid across the floor, when their amulets came off the Book and hovered over the floor. The amulets stayed connected, while the star turned gold and the gemstone lightened up. Isaac, Jacob, and Cameron looked up and saw the amulet, as bright white lights began to swirl around in the air above the amulet.

"Oh my God," said Jacob. The three continued to watch the bright lights swirling around, when they eventually formed the shape of an adult male. The lights quickly dispersed and revealed a spirit that looked like an older version of Samuel. Their hearts began to beat rapidly, while they watched the spirit stare at them firmly.

"Dad," Cameron exclaimed. Jacob and Isaac looked at Cameron confused, slowly looking back at the spirit of Samuel. The spirit of Samuel walked closer to Isaac, Jacob, and Cameron, while they stared at him in shock.

"Now, my sons, you know who you really are," he said. Isaac, Jacob, and Cameron backed up from the spirit into the front door of the manor.

"Don't be afraid…I'm not here to hurt you," he said softly. "I have come to inform you of the battle you are about to encounter. There is much I need to tell you, but so little time."

Isaac, Jacob, and Cameron sat up against the door, while still looking into their father's eyes.

"You three are my sons, descendants of a powerful line of witches known as the Weltrinchs."

Isaac, Jacob, and Cameron widened their eyes, confused and surprised, while Samuel's spirit continued.

"But with this name, we all hold a curse that is punishable by death. We have broken a law that forbids the creation of children between a mortal and a magical being, me being the first, and you three being from me and your mortal mothers. The three of you are the last descendants of the Weltrinch line."

"So…we're witches?" Jacob asked hesitantly.

"Yes. And you mustn't tell any other magical beings that you are from the Weltrinch line, or that I am your father. I referred to myself as a Weltrinch when the Wizards of the Wise came for me to protect your namesake. Refer to yourselves as the Blackwoods, which was my father's surname, for the Wizards have no knowledge of it. Together you must form a new coven and fight for your freedom, and change the ways of the magical world before it's too late."

Then, Samuel's spirit put out his hands toward Isaac, Jacob, and Cameron, as three different colored blue auras came out of his hands and went inside of them.

"I give you three my powers," Samuel started again, "which you have already exhibited in your recent days. To Isaac, I give the power to control things with your mind."

Isaac began to glow dark blue and he looked up at Samuel's spirit, his mouth slightly dropped open.

"To Jacob, I give you the power of foresight and the power of wisdom and knowing," he said, watching Jacob glow blue, while he stared at him. "Use these powers wisely, as they go hand and hand."

Samuel's spirit turned to Cameron, and he began to glow bright blue, looking up at his father's spirit.

"And to Cameron, I give you the power of superhuman strength. You are strong, but with your new found strength, you will become even stronger."

Samuel's spirit lowered his arms and stared at Isaac, Jacob, and Cameron. The three stopped glowing and stood up slowly. With a smile, Samuel's spirit continued.

"These powers will bind you three together, and they will protect you. But until you truly bond, your full potential will not be achieved."

The three began to look at each other, watching Samuel's spirit slowly fade away.

"Be safe my sons, and may you be blessed."

With his final words, Samuel's spirit vanished, the amulet turned pewter, and the gemstone darkened. The amulet separated into three pieces once more and they stopped hovering, falling to the floor. Cameron walked over to the amulet pieces and stared at them, watching them shimmer in the sunlight. He looked up at Isaac and Jacob, who seemed to be stuck on what they were told. They were witches? They couldn't be witches. Witchcraft was not something tolerable. How were they supposed to accept that? Cameron stared at them, while they stood in the hall silently.

"Well," Cameron started, "what are you guys thinking?"

Isaac looked up at Cameron and his face turned red. He was infuriated.

"What am I thinking?" he asked. "I'm thinking: what the heck have I gotten myself into!"

Cameron looked at Isaac seriously. He couldn't respond. He knew they didn't want any of this, though he felt it happened because it was meant to be. He was open to accepting his new destiny, but he could see that wasn't the case for Isaac and Jacob. Cameron put his head down, clearing his throat.

"I don't know what we've gotten ourselves into either," said Cameron. "But I don't think there's a reason we shouldn't try to figure this thing out...we are brothers after all."

Isaac laughed under his breath. "Twenty-four hours ago I didn't have any brothers...so why should I just start acting like I do just because some spirit said so?"

"That spirit was our father!" Cameron snapped, stepping toward Isaac.

"Oh, well excuse me if I'm not all gung ho about it. I was living a perfectly normal life before I met the both of you."

Jacob looked over at Isaac in disbelief, aggravated by his comment.

"You act like we all weren't," Jacob finally broke his silence. Isaac shot an angered glare at Jacob. Then, he looked back over at Cameron.

"Well, I don't care what you say. I'm not a witch, and I never will be."

Isaac opened the front door and was about to walk out when Cameron hollered out, "Where are you going?!"

Isaac looked back at him with a frown, breathing heavily.

"Away from here," said Isaac.

"So that's it...you're just gonna run away from it?" Cameron asked. "This is a part of who you are. You can't just dismiss it!"

"I can do what I want!" Isaac shouted. Isaac turned around and stormed out of the manor, rushing over to his truck. He got in quickly and started it up, driving off down Manor Avenue. Cameron looked back at Jacob, staring at him slightly worried.

"How are we supposed to do this without him?" Cameron wondered. Jacob looked over at Cameron with doubt in his eyes.

Cameron shrugged his shoulders, and his demeanor became saddened.

"Jacob, you can't go too," he said. Jacob looked down at the floor, pondering his thoughts. He couldn't accept it either.

"Cameron, I don't think I can do this," said Jacob.

"But we're supposed to do it together. Didn't you hear what dad said? Our powers bind us together, we need each other."

Jacob shook his head, having a different feeling about it all.

"Well, I can't do it," said Jacob. He went into the living room and picked up his bag, throwing it over his shoulder. Walking toward the manor's exit, Jacob stepped out of the doorway, when Cameron grabbed his arm. Jacob glanced back at Cameron and saw tears in his eyes.

"Jacob, you can't go," he said. "You guys are all I have left."

Cameron had nothing else. He had nowhere to live, no food to eat, and no money to supply for himself. He was empty. Jacob sighed softly and his eyes began to tear up. Jacob turned away from Cameron and pulled his arm away slowly.

"I'm really sorry Cameron," he said. Jacob walked out of the manor and Cameron fell to his knees. Jacob walked across the street to his car and got in. He sat inside his car and cleared his throat, whipping his eyes. Then, he started his car and drove off, leaving Manor Avenue. Cameron sat back on the floor and tears fell down his face, while he sat alone in the manor. Then, their amulets began to glow white on the floor. Two of them disappeared and the one that was left appeared around Cameron's neck. Cameron hung his head down and placed his hands over his face, when his amulet stopped glowing.

Jacob returned to his mother's home and parked his car on the street, stepping out. He walked up to the house and went through the front door, hearing noise from the television in the living room. Stepping into the foyer, Rachel came from the dining area. Her arms were crossed and a frown was on her face. Jacob was slightly startled, not realizing she was going to be there waiting for him to return.

"Where have you been?" she said. Jacob stood still. He didn't want to tell her. He wasn't sure how, "I was at a manor this letter told me to go to, and while I was there, I found out I have two brothers and that we're witches," would sound. He stood in silence, watching Rachel tap her foot on the floor.

"Did you hear me?" she pressured

Jacob stared at Rachel. "I've just been driving around."

"For five hours!" Rachel exclaimed. Jacob stepped back a little and exhaled, staring at Rachel.

"Yeah, I just had to clear my head," he said.

"You didn't call, you didn't let me know you were going out," Rachel went on, "I didn't know what was going on."

"Well, I'm sorry; I didn't feel like talking about it. I've been a little overwhelmed lately."

Rachel rolled her eyes and uncrossed her arms, shaking her head.

"All right, I forgive you, but don't do it again."

Jacob nodded, walking around Rachel and heading up the stairs. Once he made it to his room, Jacob blew out a breath and his amulet suddenly appeared around his neck with a white glow. Jacob jumped in surprise and stared the amulet angrily.

"Great," said Jacob, flopping down on his bed and covering his face.

After a long drive back, Isaac had returned to his apartment complex. He entered his apartment and walked over to the kitchen counter, flipping on the light switch. Isaac took off his jacket and threw it on to the counter, leaning over it. He continued to think about what had happened earlier that day, and what had happened the other days, over and over again. He couldn't accept something that was against his spiritual beliefs, nor his morals and values. It wasn't happening. Isaac began to feel his cellphone vibrating in his pocket. Reaching in his pocket, Isaac saw it was Fiona calling him.

"Hey mom," he said.

"Hi precious," said Fiona, "I called you earlier, but you didn't answer, so I figured I'd call again."

"Oh yeah, sorry about that," said Isaac. "I had a lot on my mind."

"Oh honey, is everything all right? What's going on?"

Isaac took a deep breath and his eyes became glassy. He couldn't bring himself to telling his mother what he found out. He wasn't certain what her reaction would be. And to be quite honest, he didn't want to know.

"You know mom...I don't wanna talk about it," Isaac answered, his voice sounding slightly raspy and scratchy.

"Okay...well, you know I'm here if you need me," said Fiona.

"I know."

There was a pause in the conversation. Then, Isaac spoke again.

"Look mom, I gotta go...I have to work in thirty minutes," he said.

"Okay sweetie, I'll let you go," she said. "Take care of yourself."

"I will," Isaac responded.

"Bye honey."

Isaac hung up his phone, placing it on the kitchen counter. Without warning, a small white glow formed near his chest and his amulet appeared around his neck. Isaac stepped away from the counter and looked down at the amulet angrily, grabbing it with his right hand. He tightened his fist around the amulet, staring at it furiously.

"Why me?! WHY!!" he hollered, looking up in the air. Isaac fell back on the floor, while he held his legs close to him, weeping sorrowfully.

Liem stormed through the dark caverns of the Xavior's cave, covered by his cloak. Since Isaac, Jacob, and Cameron had received their powers and became aware of who they were, it would be much harder to acquire their powers. This bothered Liem, though he sensed no changes in his brother's mood. He went through a dark tunnel and entered a large open area. Candles were lit to keep the room from seeming completely dark, while several dark cloaked figures stood in a circle chanting together. Liem walked past them slowly, entering a dark hallway that led to the throne room. Stepping into the throne room, Liem saw Baine standing in the middle of the floor, his back turned toward him.

"Brother, I have news," said Liem. Baine opened his eyes and they were pure white. They soon changed back to their natural color, when he turned toward Liem.

"What news do you have for me...that I haven't already seen Liem?" Baine asked. Liem swallowed, glaring at Baine firmly.

"Then, you know?" Liem asked. Baine stared at Liem and turned back away from him, walking toward the other side of the room.

"I do," Baine replied. Liem walked up to Baine and stopped where he stood. Liem stared at Baine angrily, while Baine remained calm and composed.

"Why are you so relaxed?!" Liem shouted. "They know they're witches now. There's no way we will be able to take their powers now!"

The thought of that frustrated Liem, but Baine was in no way concerned. Baine chuckled under his breath, turning toward Liem once more.

"In case you have forgotten brother, I predicted this would happen," Baine said boastfully.

"We should just leave them alone then, am I right?" said Liem. "There is no point in getting ourselves killed over these witches."

Baine shook his head and continued looking at Liem.

"You're missing the bigger picture Liem. They may have knowledge of who they are, but we can still take their powers before they are fully developed."

Liem crossed his arms and looked down at the ground. He looked back up at Baine and began to shake his head.

"No, it's not worth it," Liem argued. "I'm sure there are other powerful witches out there whose powers we can take, that will allow us to over throw the Wizards of the Wise."

"Not like these witches Liem," Baine reassured him. "We cannot let this opportunity pass us by when it's being presented to us on a silver platter. We are power thieves; it's what we do best. Taking others abilities and using them to destroy them is what we live for."

"Well, I don't think we should push it. I felt their connection. It's stronger than any I've ever felt before."

Baine put up his right first finger and shook it back and forth, chuckling and shaking his head again.

"Tsk, tsk, tsk...Liem, you really don't see it do you?"

Liem stared at his brother confused, uncrossing his arms.

"You see, their connection is very weak and fragile. What you felt was what they could possibly become. They have the potential to be very powerful, but until they truly connect, this will be very hard for them to accomplish."

Liem continued to stare at Baine with doubt.

"So, what is your plan then?" Liem asked. Baine smirked, walking up to Liem and placing his hand on his shoulder.

"Right now, they aren't accepting their destiny to be witches; they are toiling with what to do. This is the perfect time for us to take advantage of them."

"In what way?" Liem questioned.

"By leading them straight into their demises, one by one," Baine replied. Liem smirked at Baine, finally realizing they still had a chance to get the brother's powers.

"We can end them now, and take over the magical world," Baine added.

"How will we do it?" Liem asked, staring at Baine, eager to hear the rest of his plan.

"It's simple brother," said Baine. Baine let go of Liem's shoulder and stepped back from him a little, putting his arms out. Suddenly, a dark gray aura appeared between Liem and Baine, when electric shocks sparked around it, lighting up the room. With a thunderous boom, the aura flattened and a black skeletal beast with glowing red eyes appeared over the aura. Liem smirked, watching Baine lower his hands and stare on at his masterpiece.

"I call them, the Annihilators," he said. "They will take care of them for us."

Liem looked on in amazement, when Baine clapped his hands together. With an electric spark, the aura and beast turned into a lightning bolt and shot up, bursting out of the cave. The bolt of lightning shot into the sky and exploded in midair with another thunderous boom. Then, three lightning bolts dispersed from the explosion, shooting across the city of Paterson.

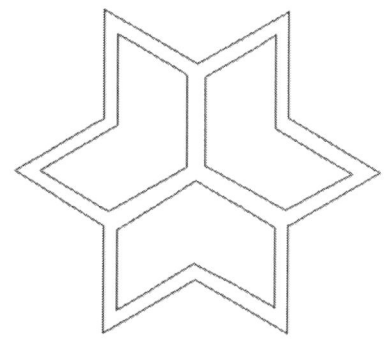

NIGHT OF THE FULL MOON

NOT MUCH TIME HAD PASSED since Isaac, Jacob, and Cameron found out they were brothers and witches. All of it was too unbelievable. But what struck them the most was the part about being witches. They didn't sign up for that, they didn't ask to be cursed with anything, and they weren't going to accept it or be happy about. Why should they let a spirit, who claimed to be their father, tell them who they were? These things kept the three away from each other for the remainder of the day, until midnight came.

Jacob sat in his room near his window. His lights were off, and the window curtains were open. The skies had darkened quickly that evening. It was raining and the moon was full, though dark clouds covered it occasionally. Jacob continued to contemplate what had happened. He was uneasy about everything because of his spiritual beliefs and upbringing. He kept wondering how he could be open to something that was against his beliefs. Jacob began to stare out his window, hearing a knock at his bedroom door.

"Who is it?" Jacob said dully. Rachel opened the door and observed the room, seeing Jacob by his window.

"What in the world are you doing in the dark?" Rachel asked, closing the door and reaching for the light switch.

"Please don't turn the light on…I have a horrible migraine," he said. Rachel put her hand down and walked over to Jacob's bed and sat down. She knew that Jacob wasn't acting himself, but she wasn't sure why.

"So, what's going on?" Rachel asked. "You've haven't come out of your room since you came back."

"It's nothing," he lied, not wanting to tell his mother what was going on. Rachel could be very critical at times, and he didn't need that. Rachel moved closer to Jacob and grabbed his left hand, leaning over and holding his hand between hers.

"Is it about what was said earlier?"

Jacob shook his head, still looking out the window. He hadn't looked at Rachel yet, which was starting to frustrate her.

"Then what is it?" Rachel asked again, still not getting a response. "Jacob!"

Jacob finally looked over at her, while she kept staring at him.

"Talk to me," she pleaded.

"I can't," he said, staring into Rachel's eyes. Rachel took a deep breath and put her head down.

"I already know what you're going to say," he added.

"No you don't," Rachel said sternly. "You can't assume what I'm going to say just because you feel a certain way."

Eventually, Jacob glanced back over at Rachel.

"What would you do…if you found out something about yourself, that you couldn't change, and it was against your beliefs?"

Rachel sat up on the bed. She wasn't expecting him to ask her a question.

"Well, it depends on what we're talking about," she answered, looking at Jacob. "I mean, is it a good thing or a bad thing?"

Jacob puffed up his cheeks and blew out, looking at Rachel.

"Um…well, it's pretty bad."

Rachel widened her eyes and swallowed, staring at Jacob and clearing her throat.

"Okay, is there anything good that will come of you accepting it?"

Jacob paused. He hadn't thought of it that way. Despite what he was, his powers could be used for good. He could use them to help people.

"I think so," said Jacob. Rachel smiled at him.

"Well, I hope that one day…you'll be comfortable enough to tell me what's going on," said Rachel. Jacob looked at Rachel and smiled.

"I do too."

Jacob and Rachel leaned toward each other and embraced. Then, Jacob's eyes twitched and he saw Cameron running down a dark alley, while a large beast chased after him. He couldn't quite make out the beast, seeing a large black blur. Cameron tripped and fell on the ground, while the beast crawled over him. The beast began to run its claws across Cameron's chest and face, and he hollered in pain while blood seeped from his wounds. With a white flash, Jacob then saw Isaac walking through a parking lot, when a similar beast jumped down on him and began to run its claws across his body. Isaac hollered in pain, bleeding on to the ground. Jacob's eyes twitched again and he was back in his room. Rachel let go of him and saw a look of shock in Jacob's eyes.

"What is it hon?" she asked concerned. "Jacob, what is it?"

Jacob looked at Rachel, his mouth dropped open.

"I–I have to go," he said. Jacob jumped up and grabbed his jacket off his bed.

"Where are you going!?!" shouted Rachel, standing to her feet. Jacob stopped in the doorway and glanced back at Rachel.

"To accept a new part of who I am," Jacob said firmly.

"Okay," said Rachel reluctantly. Jacob opened the door to his room and was about to exit, when Rachel called out to him.

"Be careful, all right?" she said, holding her chest. Jacob nodded and left out of the room quickly.

In Ray's Café, Isaac and Kyle were working the night shift together.

Despite how they usually worked together well, Isaac had been in a bad mood the entire shift. Considering the circumstances, he felt he was entitled to be aggravated. He hadn't left out of the kitchen the entire shift; he just kept himself and made orders. Isaac was near the ingredient cabinet making a latte, when Kyle came bursting into the kitchen with his arms crossed.

"So what's been your problem tonight?" Kyle fussed. Isaac put a lid on the latte and paused. He glared at Kyle with a frown on his face.

"Well?" Kyle continued to pressure him.

"Don't you have customers to be helping or something?" Isaac snapped. Kyle rolled his eyes and shook his head.

"Really Isaac? We close in like a minute," he said. "You know there's only one person in here."

Without responding, Isaac handed Kyle the latte. With a grunt, Kyle went out of the kitchen, while Isaac began to put up supplies and lock up the cabinets. He walked over to the storage closet in the back of the kitchen and took out a broom and dustpan. Closing the storage closet, Isaac turned back around and saw Kyle standing back in the kitchen by the sink.

"All right, we're closed now. What's your deal?"

"Look, I obviously don't wanna talk about it," said Isaac. "So, I don't understand why you keep asking me."

"Well, I thought we were friends Isaac," said Kyle. Isaac stared at Kyle, with a less angered face than earlier. He wasn't trying to shut anyone out. But he couldn't even understand what was going on, let alone explain it.

"Even if I told you, you wouldn't get it," Isaac responded, walking out of the kitchen. Kyle uncrossed his arms and began to tap his fingers on the sink with his eyes squinted. Kyle eventually walked out of the kitchen and saw Isaac sweeping the floor.

"Try me," he said.

"Just leave it alone Kyle," Isaac snapped, while he continued to sweep. Then, Isaac saw himself flipping a table across the room in his mind, while Kyle continued to annoy him.

"No, I'm not," Kyle argued. "You need to learn how to deal with your issues."

Isaac stopped sweeping and eyed Kyle angrily.

"Kyle! Would you just shut up?!" shouted Isaac. Without warning, a table lifted off the floor and flew into the wall, shattering to pieces. Kyle ducked down, while pieces of the table flew across the café. Isaac stood in shock, when Kyle stood up and gazed at Isaac with his mouth wide open. Isaac swallowed and scratched the back of his neck, feeling embarrassed.

"Uh Isaac," Kyle started, "is that what you were talking about?"

Isaac put his head down and exhaled, nodding briefly.

"'Cause that was awesome!" Kyle exclaimed, jumping up and rushing over to Isaac. Isaac stared at Kyle, raising his eyebrows.

"How did you do that?" Kyle asked.

"I don't know…it's been happening when I get angry or frustrated," said Isaac.

"Wow!" Kyle went on. "Just think of how it will be when you learn to control it!"

"No!" shouted Isaac. "I'm not learning how to control anything!"

"Are you crazy!?! That is an amazing gift," Kyle argued. "And you're telling me you're not going to use it?"

"For what? I don't need an *amazing gift*; my life was perfectly fine before–"

Kyle stared at Isaac, looking at his necklace. Then, he realized that it must have something to do with it.

"That necklace," Kyle started, "it has something to do with this…doesn't it?"

Isaac began to breathe heavily, staring off in the café. He didn't want to use anything that would remind him he was a witch, nor learn how to control it.

"You do realize if you don't learn how to control the power, it will be out of control?" Kyle mentioned. "That was clearly demonstrated here."

Isaac stared back at Kyle and shook his head.

"What if it goes against everything I believe in? What if it's something evil?"

"Yeah right," Kyle laughed. "You may be a douche sometimes, but there is nothing evil about you."

"Thanks, that makes me feel better," Isaac commented sarcastically, rolling his eyes.

"Look, I'm just saying...do what you want with it. It's your power."

Isaac hadn't thought of it that way, he had just shut it all out. He could use his power, but he could also be different.

"You're right," Isaac agreed.

"I know," Kyle said with a smile. Isaac stared at him and shook his head, holding the broom in his hand.

"Now, we should probably fix this up so we don't get chewed out by Jeff," said Kyle.

With a nod, Isaac smiled at Kyle.

"Yeah, we should," he said.

Cameron was leaving out of a downtown restaurant, after finishing his last meal for a while. He walked over to his car in the parking lot and started it up. After a few seconds, he pulled out of parking area, taking off down the street. While Cameron was driving, he seemed distracted, not really paying attention to his surroundings. He couldn't stop thinking about Isaac and Jacob. For so long, Cameron wanted to find a part of his family, a part of himself. He felt he had finally done that, but it was taken away by the fact they were witches. He knew that kept Isaac and Jacob away.

Cameron continued driving down the road, when the front of his car started smoking.

"What the heck?" Cameron exclaimed. The car began to gradually slow down, until it came to a complete stop in the middle of the road. Cameron stared at the car angrily, slamming his fists on the steering wheel.

"Ugh!!!" he groaned. Putting his forehead down on the wheel, Cameron began to softly whimper, running his hands through his hair. Calming himself, Cameron unbuckled his seat belt and got out of the car. He stepped out and saw anti-freeze all over the ground, showing the car had overheated.

"Great," he complained, walking over to the hood of the car and opening it. Smoke shot up from the engine and Cameron slammed the hood back down. Then, lightning struck in the air with a roar of thunder, as Cameron looked up in the air, watching the clouds get darker. Cameron walked away from his car, looking around for someone who could help him. Suddenly, lightning struck a power line and it fell over, crashing into Cameron's car, causing it to explode and burst into flames. Cameron was knocked over by the blast and fell on his back. He got up from the ground, watching sparks fly around, seeing his car engulfed in flames.

"Are you serious?!" he shouted. The rain slowly calmed down the flames on his car, but the car – including all of his things – was destroyed.

"Aah!!!" Cameron cried, swinging his fist in the air. Breathing heavily, he walked off from his car, making his way down the street.

Arriving downtown, Jacob pulled into a parking lot near an office building. The parking lot was close to the alley he saw Cameron get attacked in his vision. His plan was to find Cameron and prevent the attack; then, he would find Isaac before he was attacked. Though his plan seemed simple, he had no idea how to execute it. Jacob glanced down at his watch and saw it was almost midnight. Jacob glanced back up and looked around the area, waiting to spot Cameron.

"Where is he?" Jacob wondered. "If it wasn't raining, I might be able to see him."

Jacob's anxiety level was rising. He could feel his heart beating swiftly and his palms becoming clammy. Bouncing impatiently, Jacob looked to his left and finally saw Cameron walking down the street. Cameron looked around before he entered the alley, pulling his hood over his head. Jacob sat up in his seat and turned the car off, quickly getting out. Jacob ran across the parking lot, entering the alley after Cameron.

Cameron moved along the alley's path, looking back and forth for shelter. When he turned a corner, lightning struck the ground behind him. Cameron was startled. He looked back, not seeing anything, and continued on through the alley. On the ground where the lightning struck, a black blob formed slowly. Suddenly, the moon came from behind the clouds and shone brightly over the blob. Soon after, it turned into a large black skeletal beast with an oval shaped head and pointed chin. It was an Annihilator, the beast Baine created. The Annihilator stood in place, its eyes closed shut. Flaring its nostrils, the beast started slowly creeping after Cameron. A moment later, Jacob ran into the alley and stopped, looking around for Cameron. With no sign of him, Jacob dashed off, trying to prevent his vision.

Cameron continued on, while the Annihilator crept behind him quietly. Eventually, he reached an area that went in three different directions and stopped. Looking around, Cameron saw a large dark shadow gradually covering him from behind, feeling heavy breaths against his neck. His heart pounded rapidly and he slowly turned his head, looking back. To his shock, Cameron saw the Annihilator behind him with its head down.

"Oh my God!" shouted Cameron, falling back on the ground. Unexpectedly, the Annihilator lifted its head up, revealing its glowing red eyes.

"RAAWWWRRR!!!" growled the Annihilator. Cameron backed up on the ground and stumbled to his feet, running off. The Annihilator slammed its claws on the ground and dashed after Cameron. Cameron ran as fast as he could, but the Annihilator was gaining on him. He ran to his right, which led to a high fence that blocked off a nearby parking lot. Stopping, Cameron turned back and saw the Annihilator standing behind him. The Annihilator raised its right claw and knocked Cameron to the ground.

"Ugh!" he cried, rolling over on his back.

Rushing through the alley, Jacob looked around for Cameron, running with haste. He took a turn down a darker path, when a lightning bolt struck the ground near Jacob's feet, knocking him over.

"Ugh!" Jacob groaned, stumbling to the ground. Jacob looked up, seeing a black blob on the ground, watching it turn into an Annihilator. The Annihilator turned its head toward Jacob, opening its eyes. Jacob leaped to his feet and widened his eyes, staring at the Annihilator.

"RAAAAAAWWWRRRR!!!" the creature growled. Jacob dashed off to escape and the Annihilator chased after him. Then, the Annihilator hit Jacob, knocking him into a wall, as he tumbled by a fenced area. The Annihilator stood above Jacob and continued to breathe heavily. Jacob turned over, watching the Annihilator arch its claw to attack him. Jacob rolled himself out of the Annihilator's way, causing it to gash a hole in the lower part of the fence.

"RAAWWWWRRRRR!!!!" the Annihilator cried furiously. Jacob quickly crawled through the fence, when the Annihilator reached for him, not realizing its claw was too big. Angered, the Annihilator tried to rush through the hole, but got stuck, watching Jacob stand up and run off.

"RAAWWWWRRRRR!!!!!!!" the Annihilator screamed.

Meanwhile, Cameron continued to struggle against the Annihilator, when it clawed into his hoodie and snatched it off. Cameron pulled away toward the fence, but the Annihilator snatched him back, slamming him on his back.

"Ngh!" he grunted, while the Annihilator stood over him.

"RAAWWWRRR!!!" the Annihilator grumbled, breathing heavily over Cameron. Cameron squirmed frightfully and his eyes teared up, when the Annihilator came down on him with its claw, using full force.

"Nooo!!!!" Cameron cried. Suddenly, his amulet began to glow when the Annihilator struck his chest, and its attack was blocked by a bright blue force field. Then, a shock wave shot from the force field, throwing the Annihilator away from Cameron.

"ARHM ARHM!!!!!" the Annihilator whimpered, hitting the ground. Cameron jumped up, making his way toward the fence, climbing it quickly. The Annihilator struggled to its feet and saw Cameron escaping.

"RAAAWWWWRRRRR!!!"

The Annihilator charged at Cameron and hit the fence, causing him to lose his grip. Cameron dangled on the fence with his right hand and the Annihilator swung its claw at him, slashing his free arm.

"Ahh!!!" Cameron yelled. The Annihilator reached for Cameron's leg and tried to pull him off the fence, while Cameron tried to shake it off. Eventually, Cameron kicked the Annihilator in the face and knocked it back. Cameron reached for the top of the fence with his other hand and pulled himself over the fence. He fell over on the other side and hit the ground on his back, while the Annihilator got up slowly. Seeing the Annihilator, Cameron stood to his feet and held his wounded arm, darting off in the parking. Suddenly, Cameron ran into Jacob, they both fell on the ground, and Cameron's glasses flew off his face, shattering on the ground. Jacob sat up and looked at Cameron, watching him struggle to get up. Then, Jacob rushed over to Cameron, seeing his arm wound.

"Cameron, are you okay?" Jacob worried. Cameron shook his head and the two stood to their feet, hearing a loud crash come from behind them. Jacob and Cameron glanced back and saw that the Annihilator had burst through the fence, walking toward them slowly.

"Oh my God! Another one," Jacob exclaimed. He and Cameron backed away from the beast hesitantly, when they heard a thud coming from the left. The two looked over, seeing the Annihilator that was chasing Jacob stumble into the area. Jacob and Cameron jumped back and the two Annihilators came to each other's sides, staring at them. Jacob and Cameron stepped away from the Annihilators, watching them closely.

"RAAAWWRRRRRR!!!" the Annihilators screeched.

"Run!" Jacob yelled. Jacob and Cameron ran off down the street, with the Annihilators rushing after them.

Back at Ray's Café, Isaac and Kyle had finished cleaning up and were about to leave. Isaac shut all of the lights off, while Kyle waited by the entrance door. After Isaac set the alarm, Kyle opened the front door and the two left out of the café. Isaac took out his key to the café, when a black SUV pulled up near them. Locking the door, Isaac turned to Kyle and exhaled.

"Well, here's my roommate," Kyle said. "Have you decided what to do?"

Isaac shook his head, placing his hands in his pockets. He still wasn't sure what he wanted to do yet. But now, he was trying to be more open minded.

"I'm still thinking it over...I'm not sure yet," he said. Kyle placed his hand on Isaac's shoulder with a smile.

"I'm sure you'll figure it out," said Kyle. "When you're ready, you'll know what to do."

Kyle let go of Isaac's shoulder and walked over to the SUV, hopping in on the passenger's side. Once the SUV pulled off, Isaac stared up in the sky. Then, he walked down the street to the parking lot behind the café. Reaching the parking lot, Isaac looked up at his truck and saw a bolt of lightning strike the ground in front of him, which heaved him back on the ground. Isaac struggled to sit up, seeing a black blob appear on the ground. Isaac backed away from the blob, watching it turn into an Annihilator. The Annihilator began to crawl toward Isaac, as he got up of the ground and ran off.

"AAARRRRRAAAAAWWWRRR!!!" The Annihilator squealed. Isaac ran down the street, reaching path that led to an open area. Isaac rushed down the path, but the Annihilator grabbed him by his ankle, knocking him down. The Annihilator pulled Isaac closer to itself and arched its claw into the air. Then, Isaac's amulet began to glow and he threw out his arms to block himself. When he did this, the Annihilator flew off of him. Staring at his hands in shock, Isaac jumped up and ran off. When Isaac reached the open area, he ran into Jacob and Cameron, causing the three to tumble to the ground.

"Does no one know how to run and watch where they're going at the same time?!" Jacob exclaimed. Isaac sat up and realized who they were, while they stared at each other.

"What are you guys doing here?" Isaac asked confused. Before they could answer, an Annihilator came into the area slowly from the opening on the right. The three stood up and stared at the Annihilator, hearing a growl come from the left. Isaac, Jacob, and Cameron looked to their left and saw another Annihilator crawling into the area, grumbling under its breath. Isaac glanced back where he came from, seeing the Annihilator that was chasing him. The three started backing away from the Annihilators, as they closed in on them. Then, Jacob looked back and saw another path behind them.

"I'd love to answer your question," Jacob started, "but I feel it absolutely necessary that we run."

Grabbing Isaac and Cameron by their arms, Jacob pulled the two with him and the three ran off. With an angered growl, the Annihilators came together and galloped after them.

Isaac, Jacob, and Cameron ran down the dark path, hearing the Annihilators following close behind them. The three continued running through the alley, until they reached a dead end. Turning back, they saw the Annihilators standing a few feet away. The Annihilators slowed down, creeping toward them, knowing they had no way out.

"Uh oh," said Jacob.

"This is it…we're not getting out," said Cameron, staring at the Annihilators. The three backed into the wall and the Annihilators stood over them. Isaac, Jacob, and Cameron moved closer together, their hands slightly touching. Then, their amulets began to glow and the Annihilators stared at them confused. Suddenly, a divided six-pointed star appeared on the wall behind them. The Annihilators backed away, when the three looked at the wall, seeing the symbol. Without warning, blue shock waves shot out of the symbol and attacked the Annihilators, lifting them into the air.

"ARHM ARHM!!! ARHM ARHM!!!" The Annihilators whimpered. The shock waves disintegrated the Annihilators and they dropped to the ground, turning into a large black puddle of gunk. The symbol vanished from the wall and the three stepped away, standing over the puddle. The Annihilators' eyes were still visible, eventually sinking into the puddle. The three stepped back and looked at each other. Staying close, the three made their way out of the alley.

Isaac, Jacob, and Cameron arrived back at the manor, later that morning. Cameron rode with Jacob, while Isaac drove himself. The entire ride, Jacob and Cameron didn't speak. And after arriving at the manor, the three remained quiet. They were still in shock from everything that happened, not completely dealing with it. One thing they knew for sure, after that night, was that they would not be able to do this alone. Regardless whether they liked it or not, being together and using their powers was their only means for survival.

Cameron sat at the dining room table, resting his wounded and still bleeding arm on a towel. Looking up at the front door, Cameron saw Jacob coming back inside with a first aid kit in his hand. Jacob walked over to the dining room table and sat in front of Cameron, opening the kit. Jacob took a container of peroxide, cotton balls, gauze, and coban wrap out of the kit. Jacob exhaled and looked at Cameron, while they stared at each other. Eventually, Jacob broke the silence.

"Can I…uh, see your arm," he asked.

"Oh...yeah, sorry," said Cameron, unbuttoning his shirt. He pulled his shirt off and moved closer to Jacob, while he put on a pair of gloves. Jacob picked up some cotton balls and poured peroxide on them, wiping Cameron's arm.

"Hssh, ah that burns," said Cameron.

"It shouldn't, it's only peroxide," said Jacob. Cameron stared at Jacob, watching him wipe his arm down.

"I guess I'm just baby," Cameron laughed. Jacob looked at Cameron and chuckled, placing gauze over his wound. Jacob began to wrap up Cameron's arm, while he continued to stare at Jacob. Jacob looked at Cameron again, laughing under his breath.

"What?" he said.

"So, you just keep a first aid kit in your car?" Cameron said smirking. Jacob finished wrapping Cameron's arm, pulled of his gloves, and dropped them in a small biohazard bag inside the kit.

"I used to be a nurse. I just like to keep these kinds of things handy," he said.

"So, you do keep one in your car?" Cameron laughed.

"Yes, I like to be prepared," Jacob responded with a laugh. After the laughing stopped, Cameron looked at Jacob again, this time with a more serious stare.

"Were you going to be a doctor?" he asked. Jacob shook his head.

"No...I wanted to be a writer, but that hasn't worked out for me yet," said Jacob. He began to put everything back inside the kit, taking out the biohazard bag and tying it up.

"Well, thanks for bandaging me," said Cameron. Jacob closed the kit and looked at Cameron with a smile.

"You're welcome."

The two began to hear footsteps from the second level of the floor, coming down the staircase. Jacob and Cameron looked over at the stairs, seeing Isaac come down slowly. He stopped after reaching the main hall and stood in place. Then, Isaac turned toward Jacob and Cameron, walked over to the table, and sat across from Cameron. Jacob and Cameron looked at each other, not speaking again. For a moment, they had forgotten all about what brought them together in the first place, which also kept them apart. Isaac brought the silence back with him, while he stared at the table. Jacob and Cameron could see the frustration in Isaac's eyes, but he wouldn't look up at them. Then, to their surprise, Isaac looked up at them and exhaled.

"Why did this happen?" he asked. Jacob and Cameron looked at each other again, not sure how to respond.

"What do you mean?" Jacob asked. Isaac pushed away from the table and stepped back into the hall. Jacob and Cameron stared at Isaac, watching him put his hands on his hips, breathing heavily.

"I mean, why do we have to be witches?" Isaac answered. "Why were we given these powers? I'd just like to know why."

Jacob and Cameron lowered their heads down, thinking over what Isaac said. They didn't know why they were witches, and they couldn't answer Isaac.

"I just…I don't understand, why we have to deal with this," Isaac added.

"Because we can handle it," said Jacob. Isaac and Cameron looked over at him. Isaac walked back over to the table, slamming his palms down on its edges.

"What do you mean, because we can handle it?" Isaac questioned Jacob. Jacob took a breath and swallowed, preparing his response.

"God doesn't give us more than we can bear," Jacob responded. "We live in this world that's full of sin…we were born into this, but it doesn't mean we have to like it."

"So what are you saying?" Cameron asked. Jacob looked over at him, clearing his throat.

"I'm saying we have two options," said Jacob.

"Which are?" asked Isaac.

"We do this, but we do it differently, and we don't have to accept it like it's okay, but we deal with it."

"Or," Cameron pressured.

"Or we ignore all this and we'll probably die," said Jacob. Isaac and Cameron looked at each other for a moment. This was a difficult decision to make. Living in sin was wrong, regardless what it was. But they knew that something had to be done, and ignoring that they were witches would only make things worse. The two looked back at Jacob, while he continued.

"I think after tonight it's clear that if we ignore this, the end result won't be good," he said. "It's going to be hard, but I think we can eventually find a way."

Isaac and Cameron looked at each other again. Then, they looked at Jacob and nodded in agreement with him.

"Okay," said Jacob.

Baine's wrath was imminent. His plan of killing the brothers before their connection had been foiled, his creatures were destroyed, and his pride was crushed. Baine's anger grew, while he stood still in the cave's throne room. Liem appeared with a puff of black smoke, seeing his brother stand stiffly in front of him.

"Baine," said Liem, walking toward Baine slowly.

"This…this is impossible!" Baine exclaimed. Electric shocks appeared in the palm of his right hand. Baine threw an electric ball at the wall in front of him, which caused an explosion and the cave rumbled.

"Uhhhh!!! How did this happen?!" Baine hollered, his voice echoing throughout the cave. Liem stood in front of Baine.

"Brother," Liem tried to interrupt Baine's rampage, but he continued.

"I had all of this planned out. There is no way they were able to defeat my creatures!"

"I told you Baine, you underestimated them," said Liem. Baine looked over at Liem and his eyes began to glow bright red.

"I–DID–NOT!!!" Baine shouted, causing the cave to shake uncontrollably. Liem stared at Baine and backed away from him.

"Baine calm down. I was just making a point," said Liem. Without warning, Baine charged at Liem and slammed him up against the wall.

"You were trying to make a point?!" Baine snapped, grinding his teeth together.

"I was just saying they're stronger than you thought," said Liem, shaking in his brother's grip. "I thought you would've seen this coming."

"You know my visions aren't always accurate!" Baine shouted. "How was I supposed to know Jacob would see the Annihilators and rush to his brothers' rescue?! Huh!?! Answer that Liem!"

Liem stared at Baine, while he tightened his grip and kept him against the wall.

"Baine," Liem cried, "What are you mad at me for?! I'm not the enemy here."

Baine's expression of anger quickly changed to a stare of regret, when his eyes changed to their normal color and he lowered Liem to the ground. Baine backed away from Liem, while he held his throat and tried to catch his breath.

"I'm so sorry brother," said Baine. "I don't–I don't know what came over me."

Liem walked over to Baine, placing his hand over his shoulder.

"Baine, let's just forget about them," said Liem. "Look what it's doing to us, turning us against each other. We will end ourselves if we continue on like this."

Baine stared at Liem. What he was saying was true. It was changing him. He had become so consumed with killing the brothers and taking their powers that it was affecting his demeanor. Baine nodded in agreement with Liem, when suddenly Baine's eyes turned pure white. He saw himself and Liem standing over the balcony of a mansion near a dark forest. Then, Cameron came out on the balcony, wearing all black clothes like the two of them.

"Welcome Cameron, to the Xaviors," said Baine. Cameron looked over at him with a smirk, his eyes turning bright red. Baine's eyes changed back to their normal color and he realized he was back in the cave with Liem.

"What is it brother?" Liem asked with concern. Baine didn't answer. Then, he began to chuckle under his breath, while Liem stared at him disturbed.

"Baine, what did you see?" he pressured.

Baine glanced back up at Liem with a smirk on his face.

"Cameron, the youngest brother, is going to join us," he said. Liem stepped back from Baine in shock. Liem put his head down and began to shake it in disbelief.

"H–how is that possible?" Liem questioned.

"He is the most impressionable of them all," said Baine. "He wants to experience a different side of magic than his brothers, which he will soon realize. That's when we will approach him, become his 'friend,' and bring him closer to the dark side."

Liem's face lit up. He could tell that Baine felt this plan would work, though he was still skeptical of it.

"And how will we keep his brothers from stopping us?" Liem asked.

"I haven't gotten that far yet, but this plan is only secondary. I still believe that we can take their powers, but we have to go at a different approach. Besides, the vision will only come to pass if Cameron doesn't change his feelings about magic. And if he doesn't, we'll have him on our side."

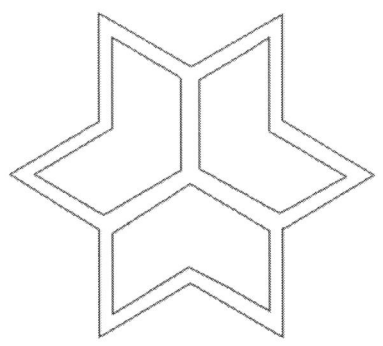

A NEW BEGINNING

ISAAC SAT SILENTLY at the dining room table later that morning. He had a horrible headache, hanging his head over the table. He hadn't gotten a minute of sleep, and to his knowledge, Jacob or Cameron hadn't either. Everything was still a bit overwhelming for them, though it all happened so fast. Isaac kept thinking over everything, but the more he thought about it, the worse his headache got. His hands covered his face, while his head throbbed in pain. Slamming his hands down on the table, Isaac saw Cameron coming down the steps into the hall. Cameron walked over to the table and stood by a chair, when Isaac glanced up at him.

"Hi," said Cameron.

"Hey," Isaac replied. Cameron pulled out the chair and sat down at the end of the table. He put his hands together, still looking at Isaac.

"Couldn't sleep?" asked Cameron. Isaac shook his head, looking down at the table.

"No...not at all."

"Yeah, me neither," Cameron agreed with a sigh. The two sat in silence. Isaac closed his eyes and exhaled, while Cameron stared at him.

"What's on your mind?" Cameron wondered. Isaac shook his head again, opening his eyes.

"Well," Isaac started, "I'm thinking about how extremely weird all of this is; and how much it goes against my morals and values."

Isaac paused, staring off into space. Cameron stared at Isaac, waiting for him to continued, but he remained silent and dazed.

"Maybe...I should get over it, right?" Isaac wondered, looking back at Cameron.

"Not necessarily," Isaac and Cameron heard behind them. The two looked back at the staircase and saw Jacob standing at the end of the steps. He walked over to the table and sat down, opposite of Isaac.

"We're still adapting to it," Jacob finished. The three began to look around at each other, gradually hanging their heads down. Despite being together, there was one thing they hadn't talked about yet...their powers. They were attacked by beasts they'd never seen before, and they stopped them just by standing near each other. Of course they knew that wouldn't always be the scenario. Isaac lifted his head back up and glanced at Jacob and Cameron.

"So, what are we going to do about our powers?" Cameron asked, looking at Isaac and Jacob. "I'm sure that last night isn't the last time we're going to encounter supernatural creatures."

Isaac and Jacob looked at each other, then over at Cameron again.

"You're right, last night isn't the last time," a voice echoed through the house, when Isaac, Jacob, and Cameron began to look around. "There are many more battles to come."

The three glanced back, seeing white lights swirl around in the hall. They stood from the table and walked into the hall, when the lights formed a male figure. Suddenly, the figure turned into an elderly man with ivory skin and green eyes. He had short gray hair and wore a cascading white cloak with red trimming. He stood in front of Isaac, Jacob, and Cameron calmly, while he smiled at them. The man walked toward them slowly and the three backed away from him, staring into his eyes.

"You have nothing to fear, I'm not here to harm you."

"Who are you?" Jacob asked.

"I am Lester, a Wizard of the Wise," he said. Isaac stepped in front of Jacob and Cameron, staring at Lester firmly. They were skeptical. From what the spirit of their father told them, they were to stay as far away from the Wizards of the Wise as possible.

"What do you want?" Isaac demanded.

"I am here to formally welcome you all to the magical community," said Lester. The three looked at each other confused, glancing back at Lester.

"Oh, well thanks...I guess," said Isaac. Lester nodded and placed his hands together, walking closer to Isaac, Jacob, and Cameron.

"I am also very curious of your origins," Lester added. The three froze in place, staring at Lester slightly perplexed.

"Surely you know it is not common for witches to come into their powers later in life."

They didn't know what to say. They were warned by their father not to reveal who they were, and they had no idea how to explain their origins. Isaac and Cameron looked at Jacob, assuming since he was omniscient, he would have a clue. Jacob stared at them shortly, looking back at Lester.

"We're from the Blackwood line and we're brothers...half–brothers from the same father," said Jacob. "I'm Jacob Blackwood, this is my older brother Isaac Blackwood, and this is our younger brother Cameron Evans."

"I see...I've never heard of the Blackwoods before," Lester replied.

"Our family kept to themselves...they weren't really noticed," Jacob continued on with his story.

"Intriguing. What is of your mothers?"

"We don't know about our mothers," Isaac chimed in. Jacob glanced at Isaac, quickly glaring back at Lester.

"So, they were killed then?" Lester asked, inquiring more of the brothers' back story.

"We're assuming so," Cameron added.

"I apologize," said Lester. "I am sure that this isn't easy for you three, but at least you have each other."

"Yes, we do," Jacob agreed. "If it weren't for these amulets our father left us while we were young, we wouldn't have connected."

Lester nodded with understanding.

"I understand this is all fresh to you three," Lester started, "but I come to inform you of a battle that is at hand."

Isaac stepped toward Lester and crossed his arms. "What battle?"

"The world of magic is not all that it seems. There is a very powerful darkness that we cannot yet detect, that is quickly rising up among us."

"What does that have to do with us?" Jacob asked.

"The magical community is not about one being for themselves only. We work together in keeping the balance between good and evil, by protecting the world from dark forces."

"Dark forces?" asked Isaac.

"Yes. There have been several incidents…incidents of these forces stealing powers from others for their own. They are devouring us…using beasts of great power. Similar to the creatures you battled last night."

Isaac, Jacob, and Cameron looked at each other, and then back to Lester.

"They are targeting young witches and warlocks, as well as other magical beings, absorbing their powers and killing them off. This kind of treachery is not acceptable amongst our kind."

"Why are you telling us this?" Jacob asked.

"You three are gifted individuals. You have the power to stop the dark forces if you join the battle in protecting our world and the earthly realm."

"And how would you know that?" Cameron probed, crossing his arms and glaring at Lester.

"I believe that was clearly demonstrated last night, am I right?" Lester countered. Cameron uncrossed his arms, looking at Isaac and Jacob.

"If any of us want peace again," Lester continued, "we must work together to put an end to these forces of evil."

They were pressured. The three felt as though Lester was trying to manipulate them into fighting alongside the magical community. Still, they weren't easily persuaded. The three agreed that they could be a great help, however, they remained leery of the thought.

"Please consider it," Lester went on. "This is for the greater good and it will make things better for all of us."

Isaac, Jacob, and Cameron looked at each other, while Lester stared on at them.

"We'll think about it," said Isaac. Lester put his head down and slowly backed away from them.

"Well then," said Lester, "if you choose to consider...be safe."

White lights swirled around Lester until they consumed him. Then, he vanished into thin air. Isaac stepped where Lester stood and turned toward Jacob and Cameron. Jacob crossed his arms and looked up at Isaac concerned.

"At least he believed our story," Cameron said with a shrug, looking at Isaac and Jacob.

"Yeah, and now they're trying to get us to fight with them," Jacob mentioned, shaking his head.

"So what are we gonna do?" Cameron asked. The three stood still, considering what Lester had told them. Suddenly, a loud thud from behind startled the three, when they glanced back. The Book of Magic had appeared on the dining room table. The three walked over to the table near the book, when it opened up to a blank page and words appeared in their father's handwriting:

$$Do\ It$$

The three stared at the Book in shock. Then they looked at each other, realizing that their father was instructing them to go along with Lester's request.

"Okay then, that solves that issue," said Cameron.

With the strange conformation from their father in the Book of Magic, the three made their decision to help the in the battle against the dark forces. Though they agreed, they still had one problem remaining…how where they going to enhance their powers? It was a topic that continued to be brought up over and over again, with no resolve. It was starting to become frustrating to them because they had no idea how to fight the dark forces. Nonetheless, with this frustration, they had to carry on.

Jacob and Cameron arrived at Victor's University in Jacob's car, while the sun rose near the clouds that Monday morning. Jacob slowed the car down, pulling into a parking spot near the university's main entrance. Jacob put the car in park and sat back, while he and Cameron stared out the front window. They hadn't spoken to each other the entire ride, since they had engaged in a heated argument the night before amongst the three of them. Eventually, Jacob exhaled and looked at Cameron.

"So, I'm going to call my mom today…to ask her for some help," Jacob broke the silence. Cameron looked over at Jacob confused.

"With what?" he wondered.

"With you," said Jacob. "I know your car got destroyed in the storm that night, and all your stuff was in it. Plus, I'm sure you're getting tired of wearing clothes that are too small for you."

"That's better that than wearing the same thing every day. Besides, there not *that* small, just a little tight."

"That would be too small," said Jacob sarcastically. Cameron rolled his eyes and crossed his arms.

"What are you gonna tell her?" Cameron asked. "That you have two brothers and one of them needs a whole new wardrobe 'cause it all blew up in his car?"

Jacob stared at Cameron seriously, blinking his eyes and twisting up his mouth.

"You're funny," he said.

"I'm just saying…I don't think she'll be too open to giving you money for a total stranger."

"That's why I'm not telling her what it's for," Jacob confessed. Cameron shrugged and looked out the window. While Cameron continued to sit there, he began to think on their conversation the night before about their powers. He was tired of talking about it, but it was an issue that affected all of them. He was ready to find some resolve, and not continue to blow it off.

"Have you figured out what we're gonna do about our powers yet?" he asked. Jacob looked over at Cameron muddled. *Why is he bringing that up again?* Jacob thought. He cleared his throat and swallowed, staring back out the front window.

"Why?" asked Jacob.

"Well, yesterday we got into a pretty intense argument about it, which got us nowhere. So I wondered if you had gotten any ideas."

"That's pretty random…but no, I didn't. And the only reason we didn't get anywhere is because we all obviously have different opinions."

Cameron and Jacob looked away from each other, as Cameron shrugged.

"It's not like we have a whole bunch of time to be procrastinating," he said. "We need a resolution."

"I get that…but it isn't like there's some quick fix for all this," said Jacob.

"I guess we'll have to call on the spirits," Cameron commented. Jacob looked back at Cameron with his eyes widened in shock.

"What!?!" Jacob exclaimed.

"What?" said Cameron. "I don't see you coming up with any ideas."

"We're not doing that. And how would we do that anyway…use a Ouija board?"

"That's what they do in the movies."

Jacob stared at with disgust, when Cameron eyed him from the corner of his eye, and looked at him with a smirk.

"Would you relax already," he said. "It was a darn joke."

Jacob shook his head and looked off, chuckling under his breath.

"Okay…I'm going to pretend this conversation didn't happen," said Jacob.

"Of course," said Cameron, "just keep blowing it off…like it doesn't matter."

"Look this not the time or the place to be getting into this again," Jacob mentioned. Then, he glanced at the dashboard and saw it was five minutes until nine o' clock.

"You should get going, you'll be late. And I have my interview in thirty minutes."

"Yeah, whatever."

Cameron got out of Jacob's car and he walked toward the school. Jacob was slightly shocked by Cameron's comment. But to some extent, he understood Cameron's frustration. Nothing was being dealt with, just thrown around and shut back down. With a deep sigh, Jacob pulled out of the parking space, heading for the university's exit. Cameron stopped and glanced back, watching Jacob pulling off. Cameron shook his head and continued walking toward the classroom buildings, when Liem appeared with a dark smoke behind one of them. Liem peeked around the building and saw Cameron walking into the third classroom building, while students walked around the other buildings. Liem stepped back behind the building and smirked, grabbing the collar of his shirt. He popped his collar and his black attire changed to a black hoodie, denim jeans, and sneakers. Liem ran his left hand through his hair, stepping from behind the building with a smirk.

"Time to introduce myself," he said. Liem snapped his fingers and a backpack appeared on his back, walking into the building Cameron entered.

Jacob arrived in downtown Paterson around a quarter after nine. While making his way to his interview, he couldn't help but ponder over his and Cameron's heated conversation. Not that thinking over it now would do him any good, but it seemed to distract him from his interview nerves. Jacob continued down the road, arriving near a four story office building. He pulled into the parking lot and stared at the building, which had a large **PATERSON LIFE** border across the top. Parking his car, Jacob turned it off and stepped out, still staring at the building. Now his nerves were kicking in.

"Wow…it's much bigger than I thought it would be," he said. Jacob walked away from his car and stepped toward the building hesitantly. He walked up to the buildings revolving doors and pushed his way through, stepping into the lobby.

Jacob looked back and forth in the lobby, watching the workers walk by, dressed in their business suits and dresses. Jacob softly cleared his throat and rubbed his hands together, feeling slightly intimidated. From the looks of it, everyone seemed to be in their late thirties. He was only twenty one. How could he possibly get a job somewhere like that? Jacob focused his sights on a large desk in the middle of the area, where a thin, pale skinned brunette woman sat, also dressed in business attire. Jacob walked up to the desk and stopped near the woman, who was sitting at a computer with a head set on. She stopped typing and looked over at Jacob sternly, when cleared his throat again.

"Can I help you?" she asked. Jacob blinked at her a couple of times, cautiously responded.

"Um…yes I have an interview with Tyler Donnelly at 9:30 AM," he said.

"What's the name?" she asked, looking away from him.

"Jacob Blackwood."

The woman looked back at Jacob quickly, widening her eyes with surprise.

"You're Jacob Blackwood?" she gaped. Slightly confused, Jacob raised his right eyebrow and nodded slowly.

"Oh my goodness," she exclaimed. "I swear when I spoke with you I thought you were older!"

Embarrassed, Jacob began to scratch his head, laughing quietly to himself.

"Yeah, I get that a lot," said Jacob, looking off and rubbing his neck nervously. The woman hit a button on her head set and began dialing an extension on her phone.

"Mr. Donnelly, I have Mr. Blackwood for you. Okay sir…I'll send him up."

Jacob looked back over at the woman, when she looked back at him with a smile.

"He is actually ready for you now. If you head down the hallway ahead, take the elevator to the fourth floor, he will meet in the lobby upstairs."

"Okay, thanks."

Jacob walked away from the desk and headed down the hallway, reaching the elevator. Hitting the button on the wall, the elevator doors opened and Jacob entered the elevator. Arriving on the fourth floor, Jacob walked into a waiting area that was similar to the lobby of the first floor, being tad smaller. He looked in front of himself and saw the receptionist desk, where another woman sat on a computer with a head set on. Behind the desk on both sides were hallways that led to offices and cubicles. Jacob looked over to left, where he saw a tall, slightly muscular man in a black suit walking toward him. He had ivory skin and brown eyes with short, dark blonde hair. Surprisingly, he looked younger than most of the workers in the office, which was a slight relief to Jacob.

"You must be Jacob," he said with a smile. He walked up to Jacob and put his hand out to him.

"Yes, I am," said Jacob, shaking the young man's hand.

"Nice to meet you, I'm Tyler Donnelly," the young man replied.

Jacob slightly widened his eyes in surprise. *This is Tyler Donnelly? The head of the magazine?* Jacob thought, trying to keep his composure. He was shocked that the magazine's owner looked so young, but it made him feel he had chance. Tyler placed his hands together at his waist line, looking off behind.

"If you don't mind, we take this into my office," said Tyler. With a nod, Jacob followed Tyler down the hallway to his office. Later, Jacob was in Tyler's office sitting across from him at his desk. Tyler had asked Jacob most of the questions he had already answered during his phone screen, but he did his best to reiterate them. The entire time, Jacob rubbed his hands together nervously, while staying calm and professional.

"I know I've asked you a lot already," Tyler started, "but I'm interested in your intentions with Paterson Life."

"Well, I believe I can bring freshness to the magazine," said Jacob. "I'm a very creative person, so I always have new ideas."

"I see…what entry do you think you'd best fit in?" Tyler asked, staring at Jacob seriously.

"I think I'd fit in best with the new entry for young adults," Jacob specified. "Being a young adult myself, I kind of have a feel for what my generation is in to."

Tyler nodded, keeping a serious look on his face. Jacob tried to sense if Tyler liked any of his answers, but his nerves were over powering everything. Tyler sat forward in his chair and placed his hands on the desk in front of himself, looking at Jacob.

"I have one more question for you," Tyler said, while Jacob nodded slowly. "I understand you lived in New York and published a book. I was just curious to know if you'd be interested in publishing again."

Jacob sat still in his chair. He pondered over this thought before, but was slightly discouraged because of his low level of success.

"I have considered it…but I'm not sure right now," he admitted. Tyler nodded and stood up from his seat, when Jacob stood up after him.

"Well Jacob, it was a pleasure to meet," said Tyler. "I will have someone call you once I've made a decision."

"Okay, thank you so much for this opportunity," said Jacob, shaking Tyler's hand again. Jacob turned away from Tyler and walked out of his office, leaving out of the building.

It was a steady day of business at Ray's Café, while Isaac and Kyle worked together in the kitchen. Since Kyle was Isaac's only friend to confide in, he told him about their encounter with Lester, including him asking them to help them fight the dark forces. To Isaac's surprise, Kyle was opposed to the whole thing.

"What?!" Kyle exclaimed, staring at Isaac. "No way! They've lost their minds!"

"Keep your voice down Kyle," Isaac snapped, when Jeff burst through the kitchen door, staring at them.

"What's going on in here?" he asked. Isaac and Kyle stared at Jeff nervously.

"Nothing," said Isaac. "Kyle's just being loud."

"Well, hold it down," Jeff demanded. "The customers can here you from the floor."

Jeff walked out of the kitchen and Isaac rolled his eyes, going back to making the cappuccino.

"So, are you guys gonna do it?" Kyle asked with concern.

"I don't think we really have a choice," Isaac said.

"Uh, yeah you do," Kyle laughed. "Tell those old kooks you don't owe them anything."

"Yeah right, I'm sure that'll go over well."

Isaac shook his head and rolled his eyes, placing a cover on the cappuccino and handing it to Kyle. Kyle took the cup and walked out of the kitchen, while Isaac took a wet towel and wiped the counter down. Kyle came back into the kitchen and walked back over near Isaac, when he blew out a deep breath.

"Look, all I'm saying is if you guys really don't wanna do it, I don't see why you're gonna just 'cause a book said so."

"It's a lot more complicated than you think," Isaac warned.

"Obviously," said Kyle. Then, Jeff came into the kitchen and knocked on the counter by the door, as Isaac and Kyle looked back.

"Isaac, you've got somebody here for you," he said. Jeff backed out of the kitchen, while Isaac raised his eyebrows. Isaac walked out of the kitchen and saw Jacob near the front counter. Jacob looked over his shoulder at Isaac sternly and turned around, when Isaac stepped from behind the counter.

"Hey, what are you doing here?" Isaac wondered.

"Can you talk for a minute?" Jacob asked. Isaac's facial expression dropped to serious stare, hearing the solemn tone in Jacob's voice. Isaac looked back at Jeff, who nodded him on, allowing him to go out. Isaac nodded back; then, he and Jacob stepped out of the café. A little later, Isaac and Jacob were outside in the downtown area, walking and talking.

"So how'd your interview go?" Isaac inquired.

"Eh–well, uh…it–it went okay," Jacob stuttered with an uncertain shrug.

"Wow…that sounds promising," Isaac replied sarcastically. Jacob stared at Isaac and crossed his arms.

"Look, I was too nervous to sense if he liked me or not," he defended himself. "I have no idea if it was a good or bad interview."

"I'm sure it couldn't have been that bad," said Isaac. "I mean I know I've only known you for a couple days, but you're really good at carrying yourself in a professional manner…when you need to."

"Thanks Isaac, I feel so much better now that you said that," Jacob said sarcastically. Isaac glanced at Jacob, while they continued walking down the street. Isaac crossed his arms, looking forward again.

"So why did you come over? Is something wrong?" he asked. Jacob looked at Isaac, remembering he had originally gone to talk to him about Cameron's comment, though he already knew Isaac's response.

"Um, no reason really," Jacob lied.

"Yeah right," said Isaac. "So you were all monotone for no reason?"

"Even if I tell you, I already know how you're gonna react."

"It's too late for that excuse don't you think? Spill it."

The two stared at each other, when Jacob put his head down and cleared his throat.

"Well, we obviously have an issue that hasn't been addressed yet," Jacob started. Isaac rolled his eyes and shook his head, letting out an aggravated sigh.

"Oh God…is this about the whole power thing?" Isaac grunted.

"Cameron and I had a short conversation about it before he went to class."

"I am so tired of hearing about that and talking about it. It's brought up in every conversation now."

"I'm sorry you feel that way, but it's a part of us now. And it's not like they're gonna figure themselves out overnight."

"Why does he keep bringing it up?"

"Because he's concerned, just like I am, and I'm sure you are too…you just won't admit it."

"I'm not," Isaac snapped. "If it were up to me, we wouldn't be doing this."

"But we are," Jacob retorted. "So to keep saying that is irrelevant."

Isaac glared at Jacob angrily, while he stared at him mutually.

"What's the point of talking about it? We never get anywhere," Isaac mentioned.

"It went somewhere today," said Jacob. Isaac glared at Jacob confused, uncrossing his arms.

"What are you talking about?"

Jacob looked at Isaac, rolling his eyes and breathing out of his nose.

"Cameron made a suggestion of connecting to spirits using a Ouija board."

Isaac stopped walking and Jacob stumbled, realizing Isaac halted.

"What?" Jacob asked.

"What do you mean, what?!" Isaac snapped. "You just told me that Cameron suggested using a Ouija board to learn about our powers. What kind of response were you expecting me to have?"

Jacob walked back to where Isaac stood and placed his hands on his hips.

"Well, it's not like I agreed with him," Jacob said. "Besides, I think it was just a bad joke anyway."

"Oh, so he's joking now?" Isaac chuckled. "I think it's a little premature to start making magic jokes, especially considering all of us still don't agree with this 100 percent."

"I really don't think you need to get all bent out of shape about it," said Jacob.

"Then what did you tell me for?"

Jacob looked off from Isaac, shaking his head. Isaac rolled his eyes at Jacob and started walking along the sidewalk again. Eventually, Jacob followed after Isaac, and the two made their way back to the café.

"Well, I need to get back," Isaac said, turning toward the door.

"Isaac," Jacob called out, when Isaac looked over his shoulder at him. "We really should be trying to figure out what to do."

Isaac paused and put his hand on his forehead, turning back toward Isaac.

"Well, have you thought of any ideas yet?" Isaac asked. "'Cause unfortunately, Cameron is the only one who has; and his idea is outta the question."

"Not really," Jacob started. "At first I thought the Book would have something in it, but that was incorrect."

"That doesn't mean there couldn't be another book or something out there that could help," Isaac pointed out.

"Like what though?" Jacob questioned. "I'm sure there isn't an encyclopedia for this kind of stuff."

Isaac stared at Jacob with widened eyes and his face lit up. What Jacob said sparked him. An encyclopedia was exactly what they needed to help them. Isaac was ecstatic, they had reached a breakthrough.

"Jacob that's brilliant!" he exclaimed, while Jacob stared at him confused.

"What did I say?" Jacob wondered.

"An encyclopedia, that's exactly what we need," Isaac went on. "I can't believe we hadn't thought of that before."

"Okay…one problem: how do we even know one exists for what we need?" Jacob asked.

"I don't see why one wouldn't," Isaac assumed. Jacob stared at Isaac, blinking at him repeatedly while frowning.

"All right, I appreciate your optimism…but let's get real," Jacob said. "There's no way we'll be able to find something like that in time for all this. Plus, where would we look?"

Isaac crossed his arms and sighed deeply, lowering his head down. Figuring out where to find what they need would be a challenging task, but the more he thought it over, the more simple it all seemed.

"Maybe…maybe a library would have something like that," said Isaac. "Library's usually have tons of encyclopedias."

"Yeah, okay…that can still take forever to find the right library to go to Isaac," Jacob said, continuing to mention their lack of time.

"Not necessarily. We really only need to check the biggest one, and there's a library right outside the city that I'm sure it has a pretty vast selection of encyclopedias."

"Okay, well good luck with that," Jacob commented, turning away from Isaac.

"Oh I'm not going," said Isaac, "I have to get back to work."

Jacob turned back toward Isaac with his mouth twisted up, squinting his eyes.

"So, who do you think is supposed to go?" Jacob asked.

"Well, I have to work and Cameron's at school…but you don't have anything to do," Isaac said with a smile, as Jacob dropped his mouth open.

"Excuse me?!" Jacob exclaimed. "I don't recall volunteering for that."

"Yep, good luck bud. Text me what you find," Isaac said. With a wave, Isaac went back into the café and rushed behind the front counter to help a customer. Jacob's mouth was still dropped open, in awe of what just happen. With an angered grunt, Jacob stormed away from the café, heading for the parking lot.

Back at Victor's University, Cameron was in his biology class, taking notes while a tall, scrawny and ivory toned man lecture in front of a black board.

"I believe that's enough for today," said the professor. "I'll see you all Thursday; please be ready for the quiz."

The students began to gather their things quickly, leaping from their seats. The students rushed out of the classroom, when Cameron stood up and followed the crowd out of the room. Stepping into the hallway, Cameron bumped into Liem and dropped his books and notes on the floor.

"Uh, great," Cameron exclaimed with frustration, bending down to pick up his things.

"Oh man, I'm sorry about that," Liem apologized. "I wasn't paying attention at all."

Liem bent down and pick up one of Cameron's books, holding it out to him with a smile.

"It's not a big deal," said Cameron, taking his book from Liem. He stood up quickly and began to walk down the hallway, when Liem stood up and stared at him. Feeling that Cameron was shutting himself off, Liem pointed his hand toward Cameron, and a transparent wave went through the hall and passed through him, causing him to stop. It was a spell that forces an individual to open up to the caster. Liem put his hand in his pocket and walked toward Cameron. Cameron didn't realize what had happened, but felt that something wasn't right. He looked back at Liem, as he got up to him and stopped.

"Lecture was pretty boring today wasn't it?" Liem asked. "I swear, usually Professor Dean is much more entertaining."

Cameron stared at Liem confused, wondering why he was talking to him.

"Uh–uh, yeah, I–I guess," he struggled with his words. Liem nodded with a smirk, looking down at Cameron's amulet.

"Wow, that's a cool looking amulet you're wearing…what does it stand for?" Liem asked. Cameron glanced at his amulet, looking back at Liem.

"It's just something my father left me," he responded. "I'm not really sure."

"Really," said Liem. "It almost looks like something a *witch* would wear."

Cameron widened his eyes and swallowed nervously, staring at Liem in shock. Then, Cameron slowly backed away from Liem and walked down the hallway toward the exit. Liem placed his hand over his face and shook his head, growling under his breath.

"Dang it," Liem exclaimed, balling up his fist. Dropping his hand to his side, Liem looked around at the other students in the hallway, rushing out after Cameron.

Outside, Cameron was moving quickly toward the parking lot, but he didn't see Jacob's car anywhere. Then, another transparent wave passed through him, and he stopped where he was. Cameron looked around to see what was going on, but didn't see anything suspicious. He looked over his shoulder and saw Liem running toward him. Cameron turned around, when Liem reached him and started catching his breath.

"I'm sorry; I wasn't trying to scare you off," said Liem. "I just–"

Liem stopped himself and stared at Cameron. Cameron looked at Liem with concern, wondering why he cut himself off.

"What?" Cameron asked. Liem blew out a breath, looking around to see if anyone was near them.

"I just…I sensed that you were…a witch," he said. Cameron widened his eyes, staring at Liem. How could he have sensed that?

"What?" Cameron exclaimed.

"Don't worry, I'm a witch too," Liem told him. "Well…actually, we consider ourselves warlocks."

"We?" asked Cameron.

"Yeah, my brother and I," said Liem. Cameron calmed his expression down, still staring at Liem with caution. Then, Liem chuckled, placing his hand on his forehead.

"My bad...I'm Liem," he said, holding his hand out toward Cameron. Cameron slowly put out his hand and the two exchanged a handshake, while Liem smiled.

"I'm Cameron," he said. Liem and Cameron ended their handshake, staring at each other.

"I really wasn't trying to startle you," Liem went on, "it's not every day you meet others who have magical powers."

"Yeah, it is pretty farfetched," said Cameron.

"So you're a witch, not a warlock...right?" Liem asked Cameron.

"Yeah, that's right."

"That's interesting, your family must have been mostly been women."

"We're not sure."

"We're? There's more? You have siblings?" Liem exclaimed, apparently excited, though he already knew this. Cameron nodded again, when Liem's face lit up.

"Wow, this is amazing! It's like we were meant to meet or something," said Liem.

"Yeah, I guess so," Cameron agreed. Liem looked at his watch and glanced around for a moment, looking back at Cameron.

"You need a ride?" Liem asked Cameron. Cameron shook his head, looking around the parking lot for Jacob's car again.

"You do realize we got out of class an hour early right?" Liem said. Cameron stared at Liem again, taking a deep breath. He figured there'd be no point in waiting for Jacob to arrive in an hour, when he had an offer for a ride back. Cameron cleared his throat and nodded.

"Yeah, actually I do," he said.

"Come on," said Liem. Liem and Cameron walked toward the parking lot near a dark blue 2013 Maserati GranTurismo. The two got in the car and Liem started it up, zooming out of the parking lot and down the street.

Jacob arrived at the library Isaac had told him about, pulling into the parking lot. He got out of his car and stared at the building. It was large, similar to that of a museum or a court house, with the words **Union Library** across the top. Jacob walked up to the staircase that led to the entrance slowly, continuing to gaze at the building. Then, he felt his cellphone vibrate in his pocket. Jacob took out his phone and saw it was a text message from Cameron:

> *Hey, I don't need you to pick*
> *me up. I got a ride home already.*
> *Thanks anyway.*

Jacob shook his head and shrugged, putting his phone back in his pocket. Eventually, Jacob made his way up the stairs and up to the door, pulling it open and entering the library.

Jacob walked into the brightly lit hallways, stepping across the refined wooden floors, passing a computer lab to his right. Jacob continued down the hallway and made his way to the librarian's desk on his left. He stopped by the counter and saw a plump older woman, sitting behind the counter on a computer. The librarian looked up at him with a smile, when he smiled back at her.

"Hello dear, welcome to Union Library," she said. "Can I help you with something?"

"Uh, hi…I was wondering, do you have a section for encyclopedias?"

"Why yes we do," the librarian replied, pointing behind Jacob. "Go up those stairs behind you and in the room up there, that whole section is encyclopedias."

"Thanks."

Jacob looked behind himself and saw a staircase leading to a room on the second level. He walked away from the librarian's desk and went up the staircase, entering the room of encyclopedias. The room was the smallest in the library, but it still had several bookshelves throughout it. Jacob made his way to the right side of the room, looking along the shelves for books on magic. Jacob looked back and forth, not seeing anything that caught his attention in particular.

"God, this is ridiculous," Jacob grunted. He stopped in the middle of the isles, browsing through the encyclopedias.

"The encyclopedia of language, the encyclopedia of the world–"

THUD! Jacob was startled by the noise beside him, glancing over to the isle next to him. Looking on the floor, he saw a large blue book on its face. Jacob stared at the book and walked toward it slowly. Once he got up to the book, Jacob picked it up and flipped it over, seeing the cover title:

A Guide for Supernatural Gifts
Telekinesis, Premonition, and Superhuman Strength

Jacob looked to see if anyone else was around; then, he glanced down at the book.

"A Guide for Supernatural Gifts," Jacob read. "How ironic."

Jacob looked at the back of the book, seeing it had no barcode on it. Jacob looked around again, seeing no one was nearby, shoving the book into his bag. Jacob moved swiftly out of the room and rushed down the steps, when the librarian called out to him.

"Did you find anything good?" she asked, causing Jacob to stop.

"No…not what I was looking for," he told her.

"All right then. Have a good day," said the librarian, as Jacob waved at her and left out of the library.

Isaac returned to the Manor at a quarter 'til four. He hung his jacket up on the door hook and walked toward the dining room table, sitting down and putting his hands on his face. Then, the front door flew open and Jacob stepped into the manor, when Isaac glanced over at him. Jacob saw Isaac at the table and walked over to him, holding his messenger bag on his shoulder.

"Hey, wasn't expecting you to be here today," said Jacob.

"Yeah, I wanted to see if you found anything at the library," Isaac said.

"Actually, I did find something," Jacob started, fumbling through his bag. "It's very odd how I did though."

"What do you mean?" Isaac wondered.

"Well, I was in the encyclopedia section, looking for book on magic, when I found this–" Jacob took the book out of his bag and placed it in front of Isaac, "–on the floor in the isle next to me."

Isaac picked up the book and examined it, glaring back up at Jacob.

"A Guide for Supernatural Gifts?" he said.

"Yeah, and what's even stranger is that it's specifically for all three of our abilities," Jacob mentioned, when Isaac chuckled under his breath.

"How'd you get out of the library without anyone giving you the crazy eyes checking this out?" he asked. Jacob swallowed and cleared his throat, blinking his eyes at Isaac.

"Well, I didn't exactly check it out," Jacob admitted. Isaac stared at Jacob in disbelief, placing the book on the table.

"So…you stole it?" Isaac concluded, when Jacob rolled his eyes.

"No, it has no barcode on it."

"So, if an item doesn't have a price tag…you can just take it?"

Jacob crossed his arms and stared at Isaac angrily.

"First of all, what library do you think actually carries books like this?" Jacob asked. "Second, the book appeared in the isle, most likely by magic. So I'm positive that the library doesn't have this book on file."

"But do you know that for a fact?" Isaac antagonized Jacob.

"I'm going to punch you…in the face," Jacob snarled. Then, the two heard the front door open behind them. They glanced back and saw Cameron coming into the house. He took his backpack off his shoulder and placed it behind the door, seeing Isaac and Jacob at the dining room table. Confused to what was going on, Cameron walked over to the table hesitantly.

"Your home late," said Jacob.

"Haven't been consulting with any spirits or playing with Ouija boards have you?" Isaac scorned him. Cameron stared at Isaac angrily, flaring his nostrils.

"No," said Cameron. "One of my classmates offered me a ride home and a bite to eat. Can I do that?"

"Nothing's wrong with that," said Jacob. Cameron rolled his eyes and turned back away from them, heading toward the upper level.

Then, Jacob remembered what he was going to tell Isaac, deciding to include Cameron.

"Hey Cameron," he said, when Cameron stopped at the edge of the steps. "I found out what we can do to improve our powers."

Cameron paused, looking over his shoulder at Isaac and Jacob. Jacob waved his hand at him to come back to the table, when Cameron grunted with annoyance. Cameron walked over to the table and sat across from Isaac, balling his fists together.

"Okay, so this book appeared to at the library," Jacob started. "It covers all our powers: telekinesis, premonition, and superhuman strength. And it even shows you ways to evolve your powers and develop similar abilities."

"Okay, what kind of stuff is in there?" Cameron wondered. Jacob opened the book and flipped through it. Then, he stopped and looked up at Isaac and Cameron.

"It has information on the abilities and exercises that can be done to advance them."

"Sounds like this will be pretty beneficial in the end," said Isaac.

"I think it will be," Jacob agreed. "And the sooner we get started, the sooner we can defend ourselves properly and help others."

"And we can help with the dark forces Lester was talking about. This is genius," Cameron exclaimed. Jacob closed the book and looked up at Isaac and Cameron with a smile.

"I say we get started," Jacob suggested. Isaac and Cameron nodded in agreement, and the three prepared for their intensive training.

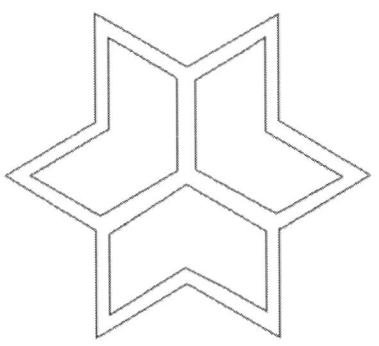

LIFE AS WITCHES

OVER THE NEXT FEW MONTHS, Isaac, Jacob, and Cameron trained diligently on a daily basis to progress their abilities and help against the dark forces. During the process, the three learned new forms of their powers that were advanced compared to how their father used them. Isaac was able to enhance his power of telekinesis, using it by physical movement and psychological control. Jacob had clearer premonitions, and as a result, he developed a strong sense of wisdom and discernment. Cameron was able to increase control of his superhuman strength and discovered the power of superhuman agility, which allowed him rapid impulse and reaction. With their improved and new found abilities, the three had been fighting off demons that were spawning in town and near New York, while trying to maintain their daily lives at the same time.

Isaac continued working at the café, still being the only one who had a job. He maintained his time at home by continuing to learn more about the craft, discovering many things involving the laws and limitations that were to be withheld by magical beings. Even with his busy work and magic schedules, Isaac was able to renew his friendship with Valerie Skyes. But many times when they did try to hang out, magic seemed to get in the way.

Jacob stayed persistent with his job hunt, while being Cameron's ride to school. It was frustrating because he thought he would have heard from Paterson Life Magazine by now. He didn't mind the alone time he got during the day, although, it was sometimes boring. With his alone time, Jacob was able to focus on searching for potential threats that could be connected to the dark forces, which were the assumed causes of recent deaths and disappearances of magical beings.

Cameron started back at Victor's after having a short time off for summer. He used that time to pick himself back up after losing everything. He kept his friendship with Liem, though he remained unaware of Liem's true intentions with him. With his brothers indulging themselves in the craft, Cameron felt he wasn't doing anything that involved magic. So he joined the wrestling team at the university to keep himself occupied, not realizing that he was stimulating his super strength, making him an unbeatable contender.

Though they had their individual things, the three would come together at the end of the day and read the Weltrinch line's histories, written by their father in the Book of Magic. This gave them a better understanding of their destiny and some insight on their father's past. With few chronicles they had discovered, however, they knew there was more to their family's past that they didn't understand. But they also knew that things would eventually reveal themselves overtime. In the midst of everything, the three tried their hardest not to tell anyone they were witches or that they were from the Weltrinch line, which was becoming more and more difficult. It was even harder for Isaac and Jacob, since they had to keep everything a secret from their mothers. Having to leave town unexpectedly to help magical beings being attacked wasn't the easy thing to explain. Having the best of both worlds was not proving to be very beneficial.

It was a dark and cold night in the downtown area of Binghamton, New York. The wind brushed through the air and the stars shone the sky, while the moon hid behind the dark clouds. The lights in buildings were dimmed, but the streets were lit by numerous light poles in the area. Isaac, Jacob, and Cameron were walking down the sidewalk, looking around for any suspicious activity. Jacob got a lead from scrying, which showed him a witch being murdered by the dark forces. None of them really wanted to be there, which was plastered plain as day on their faces with frustration and annoyance. Isaac exhaled and stopped walking, when Jacob and Cameron glanced back at him, their eyebrows raised.

"What?" Jacob asked, while he and Cameron stood in place. Isaac shook his head and looked down, grunting with a sigh.

"I'm tired of this," he said.

"Join the club," said Jacob.

"You're not the only one," Cameron added. Isaac chuckled under his breath and shook his head again.

"Why did we agree to do this anyway?" Isaac questioned. "It's not like learning how to use our powers wasn't gonna be hard enough for us."

"If I recall correctly," Jacob started, "we did this because dad told us to through the book."

"And, because it's the right thing to do," Cameron jumped in. Isaac stared at the two and crossed his arms, frowning angrily.

"Well, I wish we would've thought things through a little, 'cause this is really interfering with my life."

Jacob laughed to himself, placing both hands on his hips. "Really?"

"Yeah, really," Isaac continued. "I can't even make plans anymore without having to cancel them at the last minute. I've had to cancel on Valerie two nights in a row."

Cameron frowned at Isaac and crossed his arms, staring at him with his eyes narrowed.

"You act like it's not interfering with all of our lives," he said. "I have a test tomorrow I should be studying for, but I'm here instead."

"Yeah, okay," Isaac blew him off. "But it isn't interfering with you guys' lives as much as mine. I'm the one who's been working forty plus hours a week to pay the bills and make sure other things are taken care of at the manor, and I'm not even living there yet. I'd like to have some kind of break since I'm doing everything on my own here."

"Wait a minute," Jacob snapped, rolling his eyes and pointing his finger. "You aren't the only one who's taking care of the manor. Because if I'm not mistaken, I'm the one who's been borrowing money from his mom to help out here and there, and I hate doing that. And I'm the one who has been working my butt off trying to find these magical beings so we can save them, which is interfering with me finding a job. And unfortunately, we kind of signed up for all this when we agreed to work this whole 'magic' thing out. So don't even start with your complaining."

"Are you done now?" Isaac asked sarcastically, staring at Jacob.

"Barely," said Jacob.

Then, Cameron heard a whooshing noise behind him, when a cool breeze ran over him. He glanced back quickly, looking back and forth, seeing a dark shadow entering into an alley to his right. Cameron began to walk toward the alley, ignoring Isaac and Jacob while they continued to bicker. Cameron stepped in front of the alley's entrance, when he saw a dark figure standing in the middle of the path.

"Hey!" he hollered, when the figure looked back at him with glowing yellow eyes. The figure dashed off down the path and Cameron rushed after it, when Isaac and Jacob heard him and saw him darting off.

"Hey! Cameron, hold on!" Jacob hollered out. Isaac and Jacob ran into the alley and followed after Cameron. Cameron reached the end of the path and stopped, when Isaac and Jacob caught up to him, slightly out of breath.

"Why did you run off like that?!" Isaac yelled.

"Maybe if you and Jacob wouldn't have been arguing, you would've seen what was behind me," Cameron snapped. Isaac stared at Cameron with a frown, while Jacob examined around the area briefly. Then, Jacob looked at Cameron confused.

"Something was behind you?" he asked. Suddenly, the dark figure brushed past them, knocking them on to ground. Looking up, the three saw the figure standing in front of them, when it turned into a large beast with sharp pointed fangs and claws. The beast continued to stare at the three with its piercing eyes, while it smirked and laughed under its breath. Isaac, Jacob, and Cameron stood up, staring directly at the beast.

"That's it!" Cameron exclaimed, charging at the beast. The beast growled at Cameron and swung its right arm at him, hitting him in his side.

"Ugh!!" Cameron cried, flying into Isaac and Jacob. The three fell back into the building behind, when the beast dashed off into the night. The three struggled to their feet quickly; then, Cameron stared in the direction the beast rushed off in.

"Dang it!" he hollered.

"Cameron, track that bastard," said Jacob. "We can't let that one slide!"

"Definitely not, this one is a little cocky," Cameron agreed. Looking off into the night, Cameron's sight zoomed in the direction following the beast, catching up to it quickly. Then, his vision passed by the beast, reaching Confluence Park near the Susquehanna and Chenango rivers. There, he saw a short and petite ivory toned young woman standing by the river, looking off into the night. He could see she was wearing a silver round-shaped amulet with a purple jewel in the middle of it. She was the witch Jacob had seen when scrying for the dark forces. Cameron blinked and he was back by Isaac and Jacob.

"We need to get to Confluence Park," Cameron exclaimed, zooming off into the night, with a gust of wind blowing behind him. Isaac and Jacob covered their faces, while debris swirled around from Cameron's turbulence.

"Hey!!!" Jacob screamed.

"What is he Superman now?" Isaac commented.

"I know right?" said Jacob, shaking his head. The two looked around; then, Isaac tapped Jacob on his shoulder.

"Come on, we can follow him with my truck," he said. Isaac and Jacob ran out of the alley, heading for Confluence Park.

At the park, the witch was staring across the river, while the light posts shined behind her. A cool breeze picked up from the coolness of the lake, while the area remained quiet and sound. The beast arrived on

Memorial Bridge and stared down at her. Feeling something watching her, the witch glanced back at the bridge, but the beast had already moved. She looked to her sides frantically, seeing nothing near her. Without warning, she was knocked over on the ground and she struggled to get up. She looked around frantically to see what had knocked her over.

"Who's there?!" the witch cried. She stood up and looked around in a panic again. Hearing no answer, the witch walked off the river's overlook and on to the sidewalk, continuing to look for her attacker.

"What do you want?!" she yelled, when the beast appeared behind her. Sensing its presence, the witch looked behind herself and saw the beast standing there.

"Aaaahhh–Ugh!" The witch screamed, but was interrupted when the beast grabbed her by her throat and lifted her into the air. She grabbed the beast's hand and tried to pull away, but she wasn't strong enough to fight it off. Tears feel down her cheeks, while the beast smirked and stared into her eyes.

"Don't worry...it will be over soon," said the beast with a deep raspy voice. The witch continued to struggle against the beast, choking in its grasp.

"It's no use, you're no match for me!" it sneered. Then, the witch's amulet began to glow purple, when the beast covered its eyes and loosened its grasp on the witch.

"Ugh!!! You stupid girl," cried the beast, dropping the witch on the ground. She quickly recovered and jumped up, running off in the park. The beast saw the witch escaping and charged at her, knocking her on to the ground. The beast flipped her over on her back and crawled over her, arching its claw behind itself.

"Nooo!!! Please don't kill me!" she pleaded, when the beast eyes started glowing brighter than before.

"Nighty night witch!" the beast exclaimed. As the beast came down toward her, out of nowhere, Cameron flew toward the beast with a side kick, knocking it away from the witch. Cameron landed on the ground and the beast flew on to the overlook near the river. Cameron helped the witch to her feet and looked at her, while the beast stumbled to its feet.

"Are you all right?" Cameron asked her.

"Yes, I am," she said. Then, the beast growled loudly, when Cameron and the witch stared at it shocked.

"You foolish boy!" the beast hollered. "I will rip you to shreds!!!"

The beast charged at Cameron, when he pushed the witch behind him and dashed toward the beast head on. Cameron and the beast clashed, grasping each other's palms tightly. The two struggled on, until Cameron thrust the beast into a nearby tree.

"RAAWWRRRR!!!" the beast cried. Then, Isaac and Jacob pulled up on the side of Memorial Bridge, jumping out of Jacob's car, staring down at Cameron and the witch. The two looked over and watched the beast lift itself up rapidly, gasping in shock.

"Oh no," Jacob exclaimed. "We need to get down there quick."

Isaac and Jacob leaped over the side of the bridge, landing on the sidewalk. Then, the beast charged at Cameron furiously.

"Cameron, watch out!" Jacob hollered. Cameron looked back, seeing Isaac and Jacob rushing toward him, when he was caught off guard by the beast and knocked back. Cameron flew into Isaac and Jacob, and the three fell over on the ground. The beast stared at the witch with a smirk, walking toward her slowly, when Cameron looked up and saw it heading for her.

"No!!" he cried, leaping from the ground and charging at the beast. Cameron head butted the beast in its stomach, forcing it away from the witch. Isaac and Jacob ran over to them, stopping behind Cameron. The beast slammed its fists on the ground, scrambling to its feet.

"Jacob, get her away from here," said Cameron, blocking him and the witch from the beasts view.

"Sounds like a plan," said Jacob, grabbing a hold of the witch's arm, pulling her down sidewalk toward the bridge. Isaac stepped beside Cameron and he looked at him, when the beast growled at them.

"RAAAWWWRRRR! I will crush your bones into tiny pieces!"

The beast hurried toward Isaac and Cameron, when Isaac waved his hand at it, but nothing happened. Isaac waved his hand for a second time, but it didn't work.

"Why isn't this working!?!" Isaac exclaimed. Without warning, the beast smacked Isaac and Cameron in their sides, knocking them into a tree far off.

"Ugh!" the two cried, rolling over on the ground. Isaac looked up and struggled to get up, huffing angrily.

"Why the heck wasn't my power working?" he said again, while Cameron sat up, rubbing his forehead.

"Maybe your powers aren't strong enough against large beasts like that yet," Cameron suggested.

"Then what's the point of having them?!" Isaac snapped. The two heard the beast growl, looking toward the bridge, watching it go in the direction that Jacob had gone in with the witch.

"Come on," said Cameron, pulling Isaac up. The beast went under the bridge and saw Jacob and the witch running off, reaching the other side of the park. The beast started running after them, when Isaac and Cameron rushed after it. The beast caught up with Jacob and the witch, knocking them on the ground. Jacob and the witch stared at the beast, when it crawled over them, holding its claw over them. Then, Jacob's amulet started glowing. He looked around the beast and saw Isaac and Cameron running toward them, seeing their amulets glowing. Jacob looked up at the beast, watching it arch its arm back to attack them. Jacob and the witch rolled out of the beast's way, causing it to slam its claw into the ground. Jacob and the witch ran toward Isaac and Cameron, the witch rushing behind them, while Jacob stood by their sides. When the beast looked back, Isaac, Jacob, and Cameron held their palms out toward it, and a blue wave shot from them and hit the beast, causing it to glow bright red.

"RAAAWWRRRRR!!! This can't be the end!!!" the beast cried. The beast exploded, which knocked the four over on the ground. Lifting themselves up slowly, the witch looked at Isaac, Jacob, and Cameron with a smile.

"Oh thank you, thank you for saving me!" she said.

"No problem," Jacob replied with a smile, when Isaac crossed his arms. Isaac looked over at the witch and she noticed him frowning and staring at her angrily.

"I apologize for making you come out here like this," said the witch, holding her head down. "You must have scried for me."

"We did," Jacob confirmed. "We've been tracking the dark forces for the past two months."

"Oh yes, as we all have. But not many are as brave as you three; you defeated that beast with ease!"

"Nah, it was nothing…we've fought worse," Cameron commented with a cocky smirk. Jacob looked at Cameron with a serious stare, smacking him in his arm.

"Ouch," Cameron whined. Isaac continued to stare at the witch, until she looked back at him with a slight smile.

"What were you doing out here anyway?" he asked, when she widened her eyes. "I mean, it's the middle of the night, and you're out here by yourself. I would think one would know better than to do something as careless as that."

"You're right, it was careless," she admitted. "But I come out here every once in a while, this is where my boyfriend was murdered. He was a wizard, but he was ambushed by a swarm of demons. It's the only place I can still sense him."

Muddled, Isaac looked off and cleared his throat, feeling bad for asking her that without knowing her reason. Jacob crossed his arms in disbelief, when the witch smiled at them again.

"Well, I guess I should be going," she said.

"Yeah, we should get going too," Jacob agreed, looking at Isaac and Cameron.

"Thank you again, so long."

Waving goodbye, the witch turned around and walked away from them, fading into the night. Then, Jacob looked at Isaac with a serious stare.

"What?" Isaac wondered.

"When you have the opportunity, you don't take a moment's hesitation to be rude do you?" Jacob asked. Isaac rolled his eyes and started walking away from Jacob and Cameron, shaking his head.

"You can't tell me you weren't wondering the same thing," said Isaac.

"So what if I was," Jacob retorted. "I didn't say anything to her about it."

"Well at least we managed to stop another creature from killing someone," Cameron tried to change the subject, when Isaac and Jacob glared at him.

"Yeah, whatever," Isaac sneered. "I just don't understand why we have to risk our lives to save everybody...I haven't seen anyone trying to rescue us."

"We're always together...and we haven't been attacked like this," Jacob pointed out.

"Except for that first night we used our powers together...but that was before we became super witches," Cameron added, when Isaac stared at him. "Besides, if we wouldn't have arrived when we did, that witch would've been killed."

"That's not my point...my point is, I'm tired of doing this. It's becoming very draining."

"How can you be drained already?" Jacob asked. "We've only been doing this for two months."

"Exactly, two months too long," Isaac snapped back, walking off from Jacob and Cameron again. The two looked at each other and began to follow after Isaac, catching up to him.

"Look, your complaining is getting really old," said Jacob. "No one wants to do this, but I'm sure we can't just stop because we're tired."

"Who says we can't?" Isaac asked, stopping abruptly.

"I'm saying it wouldn't make sense to."

"Yes, because you know all things, right?" Isaac commented.

"No," Jacob disputed, "I think it would be stupid to do that. That's an opening for everything to come after us while we're off guard."

"Oh, well excuse me for coming up with a stupid idea...as if you haven't ever."

"When did I say that?"

"Didn't have to, it's how you act, because you're *so* omniscient."

"You're just mad because your power didn't work against the beast. Not my problem."

"Do you guys always have to argue?" Cameron intervened again. Isaac and Jacob stared at Cameron angrily, when he bucked his eyes at them and backed up.

"No, we wouldn't have to if Jacob would shut up sometimes."

"Well Isaac, if you would stop complaining I would shut up, 'cause I wouldn't have to try and shut you up."

"Well guess what, I'm sick and tired of putting my life on hold for magic," Isaac snapped. "And I'm not doing…it anymore!"

Jacob and Cameron looked at Isaac confused. From his serious undertone, they could tell he wasn't backing down this time. As crazy as it seemed, he wasn't going to give up on having a normal life, no matter how difficult it became. To him, he felt he deserved one. Jacob stared at Isaac with disbelief, throwing his arms in the air.

"What is that supposed to mean?!" Jacob exclaimed staring at Isaac.

"It means when tomorrow comes and you feel the need to go scrying for more beasts to kill and innocents to save, count me out."

"Wait, so that's it? You're just not gonna help?" Cameron asked.

"Don't know what else to tell you," Isaac said. Isaac turned away from them and started walking down the path, when Jacob laughed under his breath.

"Well, I don't know what tell you Isaac," said Jacob. "We all have to deal with this now. That's just the bottom line. You can't just quit when you don't feel like doing it anymore."

"Watch me," Isaac retorted, continuing to walk without looking back. Jacob looked at Cameron and pointed at Isaac, dropping his mouth open in shock.

"Do you hear him? Do you hear him?!" he asked. In a hurry, Jacob grunted angrily and stormed after Isaac, while Cameron watched him. Cameron stared at Isaac and Jacob, while exited the park arguing.

"Lord, give me strength to deal with them tonight," Cameron said, his head held up in the air.

"ISAAC!" Jacob screamed. "You get your butt back here! I will hound you until we get back to the manor."

"Oh God," Cameron whined. With a hesitant trot, Cameron followed after Isaac and Jacob, as they left out of the area to return to the manor.

With another failed attempt, it seemed that the Xavior's plan wasn't working in their favor. Isaac, Jacob, and Cameron had defeated every beast and creature Baine had conjured, and they had saved most of the victims that were being attacked in their area. Baine stood still in the throne room of the cave, while he held his chin and groaned under his breath. Then, a dark smoke rose at the entrance and Baine looked up, seeing Liem appear. Liem walked toward Baine and stood in front of him, crossing his arms. Baine put his head down, continuing to hold his chin.

"What's the matter?" Liem asked. Baine sighed and dropped his hands to his sides, turning away from Liem.

"It's not working," he said.

"What's not working?" asked Liem.

"The beasts aren't strong enough to defeat them," he said.

"Isn't that what we wanted?" Liem mentioned. "For them to be unbeatable...until that very last moment?"

Baine looked back at Liem, his eyes piercing with frustration. Though they had a second plan to stop the brothers, by turning Cameron evil, Baine didn't want that to be their primary goal. But Liem seemed to be too fond of Cameron.

"You're too infatuated with Cameron," said Baine.

"But you saw it," Liem said. "Isn't that why you had me get to know him in the first place?"

"Yes, but my intentions with him once his brothers are killed are opposite of yours."

"And how is that?" Liem asked, crossing his arms and frowning at Baine.

"You want him to be with us, and I...well...I want to kill him."

Liem uncrossed his arms and stared at Baine slightly shocked and confused. He didn't understand the point of coercing Cameron to their side was, if he just wanted to kill him in the end. Liem stared at Baine.

"That doesn't make any sense...and you know it," Liem told him. "If that's all you want to do, why are we wasting our time?!"

Baine didn't say anything, his mind was already clearly made up, and he didn't care how Liem felt about it.

"You don't know him like I do," Liem went on. "You may have the power of higher wisdom, but it's not the same as actually knowing the person yourself. Cameron has great potential, and we both could benefit from him being on our side—alive."

Baine rolled his eyes and exhaled. Then, he remembered the vision he had of him and Liem with Cameron. If it was true, he wanted to make sure that nothing would cause Cameron to change his mind. Baine turned around toward Liem with a smirk on his face, while Liem continued staring at him.

"I want to meet him," said Baine, when Liem smirked at Baine.

Though Isaac stated he wouldn't be using his powers and have a normal life, it didn't stop Jacob and Cameron from their demon hunting. It had been a few days since the last time the three had actually worked together; mostly because Isaac ignored anything that was pertaining to magic. This gave him some peace of mind, but it was detrimental to Jacob and Cameron's impact when fighting off demon attacks.

It was a nice day on a late Friday afternoon, the sun slowly beginning to set over the city. Isaac was driving down the street to meet Valerie for dinner in near Clifton. He was happy about this, since the last two times they had plans, he cancelled due to "unexplainable circumstances." Valerie was slightly suspicious of him, but she ignored her feelings and tried to circumvent the issue. Isaac arrived at a Mediterranean restaurant, pulling into the parking lot. Isaac parked his car and got out, staring at the restaurant. He was dressed to impress, wearing his best white button down shirt with a red tie and his black dress pants and shoes. After a brief pause, Isaac walked on to the front door, entering the restaurant. Once inside, he was greeted by a short blonde haired young woman who was standing near the front desk.

"Hi, welcome to the Mediterranean Cuisine," she said cheerfully.

"Hello," said Isaac. "I have a reservation for two under Blackwood."

"Sure, let me check my list."

The young woman went through the book on her podium and she checked Isaac's name on the list, looking back up at him with a smile.

"Yep, I have you down," she said. "Right this way."

The young woman grabbed two menus and walked toward the seating tables, while Isaac followed behind her. She went over to a table near the wall on the left side and placed the menus on the table.

"Here you go," the young woman exclaimed. "Your waiter will be right with you. Enjoy!"

"Thank you," Isaac said, taking a seat at the table. He glanced around the restaurant, watching customers eat their meals and converse amongst each other, when he started tapping his knee nervously. Isaac looked at his watch and saw that it was five minutes before four o'clock, which was the time Valerie was supposed to meet him at the restaurant. He continued to tap his leg when the utensils on the table suddenly began to shake. Isaac stopped tapping his leg, thinking it was the cause of it, but the utensils continued. Then, Isaac realized he was telekinetically making the utensils move. *Oh God*, Isaac thought, staring at the utensils with widened eyes. *Stop, stop...STOP!!!* Immediately, the utensils stopped shaking on the table. He looked around to see if anyone had noticed, but it appeared they hadn't. He puffed up his cheeks and let out a breath of air, tapping his leg again. Without warning, the utensils began to shake on the table again. Isaac stopped tapping his leg once more and he stared at them angrily.

"Not again," he exclaimed, looking around. Still, no one had noticed the utensils moving on the table, but Isaac wanted to stop them before anyone did.

"Stop...stop it now," he whispered forcefully, but the utensils continued shaking. They started shaking louder, and louder, when finally Isaac spread himself across the table on top of everything, forcing them to stop. Everyone in the area saw this, staring at Isaac in shock and disgust. Isaac sat up slowly and ran his hand through his hair, swallowing nervously and smiling at the other customers. They looked away from Isaac and began to whisper to each other, seeing if anyone else noticed him acting strange. Isaac stared at the table slightly embarrassed, when a tall ivory toned brunette walked over to him, smiling joyfully.

"Hi there, how are you today?" she asked.

"I'm fine, thanks," Isaac replied, with his hand covering his face.

"Well, I'm Leslie," she said. "Can I start you off with any appetizers or something to drink?"

Isaac looked up at the waitress, placing his hands on the table.

"An ice water would be great," he said.

"Okay, I'll be right back with that for you."

Isaac nodded and the waitress walked away from the table. He placed his hands over his face and exhaled, dropping them back down on the table. Isaac looked at his watch again, seeing it was a quarter after four, and Valerie still hadn't arrived. He was beginning to think she wasn't going to show up, since he had cancelled on her twice. Then, the waitress came back to the table with a glass of water for him.

"Here you go," she said, placing the glass on the table in front of him.

"Thank you," he said, grabbing the glass from her. Isaac guzzled the water down quickly, while the waitress widened her eyes in shock. Isaac placed the glass down on the table, exhaling through his nostrils.

"I'll go get you some more," said the waitress, stepping away from the table again. Isaac looked around to see if Valerie had arrived yet, but he didn't see her. He sat back in his chair with a slight frown, when the waitress came back to the table with a pitcher of water.

"Would you like me to fill your glass?" she asked.

"Yeah, that's fine," said Isaac, sitting up. Then, the waitress brought the pitcher near his glass. But before she could fill it, the water slowly began to lift itself from the pitcher into Isaac's glass. Isaac panicked, quickly picked up his glass, and the water filled his cup. Then, he placed it back down.

"Wow, that almost spilled," he joked nervously, while the waitress stared at him confused. "I think I'm okay now; I'll just look at the menu, thanks."

Still confused, the waitress smiled and slowly backed away from the table, walking off. Isaac placed his arms on the table and put his head down on it, sinking into his arms. After Isaac exhaled, he heard a familiar voice behind him and he looked back. He saw Valerie coming toward him with a smile on her face, while he gazed at her beauty. She was wearing a red pencil skirt topped with a sleeveless white blouse, with her hair curled, hanging over her shoulders.

"Oh my gosh...I'm so sorry I'm late," she exclaimed. "I got so twisted around with the directions and I got a little lost."

Isaac wasn't listening to what she was saying; he was too busy admiring her. Valerie stared at Isaac waiting for a response, but he didn't say anything.

"Did you hear me?" Valerie asked. Isaac blinked a couple of times and looked at Valerie, while she flipped her hair over her shoulder.

"Oh yeah, yeah...that's nice," he said. Valerie laughed and stared at Isaac, shaking her head. Then, she looked over at the chair on the other side of the table. Isaac widened his eyes and jumped up to pull out the chair for Valerie, when it moved out from the table before he touched it. *Oh Shoot!* He thought looking at Valerie, who was still smiling at him. *Just play it off Isaac, JUST PLAY IT OFF,* Isaac thought to himself, moving behind the chair quickly. Valerie sat down in the chair and Isaac exhaled deeply, walking back over to his seat. Valerie kept smiling at Isaac, when he sat down again and gazed into her eyes and, placing his hands on the table.

"I almost thought you weren't going to come...since I stood you up so many times," said Isaac.

"You didn't stand me up," Valerie replied, shaking her head. "And I would never do that to you, you're too good of a friend."

Valerie smiled at Isaac and reached out her hand, placing it over his, while Isaac's cheeks turned red.

"Well, I'm glad you came," he said.

At Blackwood Manor, Jacob's phone vibrated on the dining room table. He was on the upstairs level of the house, but sensed it was ringing and rushed down the stairs in a hurry. Jacob ran over to the table and picked up his phone, seeing it was a number he wasn't familiar with. Hesitantly, Jacob answered his phone and stood by the table.

"This is Jacob," he said.

"Hi Jacob, it's Tyler from Paterson Life."

Jacob paused in shock; it had been almost three months since his interview.

"Oh...hi," Jacob replied, a bit nervous.

"Hey listen, I didn't want you to think I had forgotten about you, because hadn't. We've reviewed a lot of candidates for the youth unit...and you're who we want at Paterson Life."

Jacob's heart stopped. He wasn't sure he heard correctly, but it couldn't be true. He stood still in the main hall and swallowed, when

Tyler spoke again.

"Are you there?" he asked. Jacob nodded, as if Tyler could see him, finally responding.

"Yes, yes I'm here," he said.

"Okay, good. So are you still interested?"

Jacob tried to hold in his excitement, calmly replying to Tyler's question.

"Yes, I'm still interested," said Jacob, remaining calm.

"Great! The youth unit isn't quite ready yet though," Tyler told him. "We're planning on launching it after the New Year, so you won't be starting until sometime in December. Is that all right?"

"That's perfectly fine," Jacob said. "I'm in no hurry at all."

"Okay," Tyler said. "By the way, while you're waiting, don't hesitate starting on any material. We're gonna try to get everything up and running pretty fast."

"Okay, I'll get on that."

"All right Jacob, I'll talk with you soon."

"Okay. Thank you so much."

Jacob hung up his phone, jumping up with excitement.

"Oh my God, this is great!" Jacob exclaimed. Then, he started texting Rachel the good news, when a call came through from Cameron. Jacob answered the phone and looked off in the main hall.

"Hello?" he said.

"Hey, can you come get me a little earlier?" Cameron asked. "Class let out sooner than I expected."

"Yeah, I can," Jacob paused, deciding to tell Cameron the good news. "Hey, guess what just happened to me?"

"You got attacked by a demon?" Cameron wondered.

"No," said Jacob, looking confused.

"You fell down the stairs again?" Cameron asked, sounding concerned.

"No...oh wait, yeah. I did this morning...but that's not what I'm talking about!" Jacob exclaimed, as he threw his free hand in the air.

"Okay, chill out," said Cameron. "What is it then?"

"Tyler Donnelly, the head of Paterson Life, called me today and offered me a job for the youth unit."

"Hey, that's awesome," said Cameron. "At least now you can stop job hunting."

"Right," Jacob agreed. "And now we can focus on stopping the dark forces."

"Exactly," said Cameron. "Speaking of that, so has Isaac said when he's gonna be off his 'no magic' kick?"

Jacob stopped for a moment. To his knowledge Isaac had just up and quit the whole thing all together, with no intentions of going back to it anytime soon.

"Not that I know of," said Jacob. "Why?"

"Well, I'm just saying this to you, but he needs to get off his high horse and get back in this with us," said Cameron. "It's been too many times we almost got killed this week because he wasn't there."

"I don't think he cares," Jacob mentioned. "He's banking on us giving up on this before he comes back, but we have to show him up."

"Something needs to knock some sense into him, soon."

"I'm sure it'll happen," said Jacob, "but he has to come back on his own."

"If you say so," said Cameron. "Anyway, I'll be outside when you get here."

"Okay, I'll text you."

"All right, see ya later."

Jacob hung up his phone and took his messenger bag off the table, walking toward the door. He got his jacket off the coat hook and threw it over his shoulders, walking out of the manor. Later at Victor's University, Cameron was standing outside near the classroom buildings, browsing around on his phone. He looked up toward the parking lot, but he still didn't see Jacob's car yet. Exhaling, Cameron saw Liem stepping out of one of the buildings, walking over to him.

"Hey, what are you standing out here for?" Liem asked. Cameron looked up at him and put his phone in his pants pocket.

"I'm just waiting for my ride," he said.

"Well, my brother has my car today," Liem told him. "He's coming to get me if you wanna catch a ride with us."

Cameron looked at Liem and shook his head with a smile.

"No it's cool, I can wait," said Cameron.

"No problem," said Liem. "Hey, walk with me; I want you to meet him."

Liem walked off from Cameron and made his way toward the parking lot. Then, Cameron followed behind him and walked up to Liem's side, looking at him slightly confused. Cameron looked forward and saw Baine walking toward them, wearing a blazer over a t-shirt and dark denim jeans. Cameron stared at Baine, when he and Liem got up to him and stopped.

"Hey Liem," said Baine, looking at Liem and Cameron.

"Hey," said Liem, watching Cameron stare at Baine from the corner of his eye. "Oh, uh…this is Cameron. Cameron, this is my older brother Baine."

Baine looked at Cameron and he glanced at Baine, the two locking eyes. Baine felt Cameron's power running though him, sensing how strong he was. Cameron stared at Baine, when Baine smirked at him.

"It's nice to meet you, Cameron," he said.

"Nice to meet you too," said Cameron with a nod. Then, Cameron looked at the parking lot and saw Jacob pulling in behind them.

"Well um…my ride's here," said Cameron. "I'll catch you later Liem."

"Okay, I'll see you later."

Cameron smiled and attempted to step around Baine, he put his hand out toward him.

"It was really nice to finally meet you," he said with a smile. Cameron stared at Baine and slowly put out his hand. The two shook hands, when Cameron felt a chill run over him. He suddenly began to hear several voices whispering in his head, while he looked at Baine, who was still smiling. Cameron's arm began to slightly shake and the voices getting louder; then, he pulled his hand away from Baine and stared at him.

"So long," said Baine. Cameron stepped away from Baine and Liem slowly, going toward Jacob's car, while Liem looked at Baine.

"What did you just do to him?" Liem asked. Baine looked at Liem and smirk came across his face, while he chuckled under his breath. Cameron got up to Jacob's car quickly and grabbed the handle of the door, pausing briefly. He glanced back at Liem and Baine, watching them speak amongst each other. Then, he opened the door and stepped in the car.

"Hey, you didn't even let me text you," Jacob said, looking at Cameron. He put on his seat belt and exhaled, staring out the front window. Jacob felt something was wrong with Cameron, changing his expression, while he stared at Cameron confused.

"What's wrong?" Jacob asked. Cameron looked at Jacob and shook his head. Since he wasn't sure what he felt moments before, he didn't want to bring it up. He couldn't explain what it was, so to leave it for another to interpret could lead to an unnecessary disagreement.

"Nothing...I'm fine," said Cameron smiled for a few seconds, and then he looked back out the front window. Jacob continued to stare at him, trying to figure out what was wrong, but he couldn't see through him for some reason. Ignoring his feelings, Jacob looked at Cameron with a smile and changed the subject. Jacob looked over at Cameron with weary eyes and a saddened frown, as he put the car in reverse and pulled off from the parking spot.

Back at the restaurant, Isaac and Valerie were laughing and talking, while finishing their meals. The two had been exchanging stories from his wacky experiences at the café, to her times at the art institute she attended in Virginia. For the first time in a while, Isaac actually felt like he had a normal life again. He hadn't had anymore supernatural interferences from his powers that evening and his brothers hadn't called about a demon attack. It all seemed so perfect...too perfect. While they continued to converse, the waitress walked up to them and stood near the side of the table.

"Can I move anything outta the way for you guys?" she asked, when Isaac and Valerie looked at her. Valerie picked up her plate with a smile and handed it to the waitress.

"I'm all done, thanks," she said.

"Not a problem. And you sir?"

"Uh, yeah...I'm done," said Isaac, handing his plate to the waitress. "Thank you."

"I'll be right back with your check," said the waitress, walking away from the table. Isaac looked back at Valerie, who was still smiling at him. Isaac chuckled under his breath, when Valerie rested her hand on her cheek.

"What?" Isaac asked with a smile. Valerie shook her head, lower her hand to the table in front of her.

"Nothing," she said. "I guess I didn't realize how much I would miss you."

Isaac's cheeks turned red, when Valerie laughed and started to blush.

"I missed you too," he said. "It was weird not seeing you every day. I was so used to it…until we graduated."

Valerie paused for a moment. She stared off and cleared her throat, looking back at Isaac.

"And now I'm back," she said.

"And now you're back," he repeated with a smile. Valerie stared into Isaac's eyes and her expression dropped. Noticing this, Isaac stopped smiling and became concerned, when Valerie put her head down.

"What's the matter?" he asked. Valerie looked up at him, seeming to have a little worry in her eyes. He wasn't sure what her concerns were, but he didn't want to pressure her if she didn't want to tell him.

"Just thinking about some things," Valerie replied.

"Like what?" Isaac asked. Valerie stared at Isaac and exhaled, while he stared at her slightly confused. Valerie shook her head again and looked down at the table again.

"Really, it's nothing…I don't want to ruin the mood."

"You won't ruin the mood," Isaac assured her. "What's on your mind?"

Valerie looked back up at Isaac and groaned, placing her hands under her chin.

"Everything is so different now," she started. "I mean, when we were younger, we always told each other our secrets…and now, I feel like I don't really know you anymore."

Isaac swallowed hard and put his hands together in front of him; then, he looked at Valerie nervously. He wasn't sure where she was going with that comment, but he knew it had something to do with all the times he had cancelled on her. He stared at Valerie, while she watched his eyes.

"Wha–what made you bring that up?" he asked honestly. Valerie dropped her hands on the table and placed them together.

"I know it's random, but you cancelled on me twice," said Valerie, "and you haven't even told me why yet."

Isaac stared at Valerie muddled, trying to figure out what to say and how to explain himself. He didn't want to lie to her, but he didn't think she was ready to learn the truth.

"It's more complicated than you think," he said.

"We've never kept secrets from each other Isaac," Valerie went on. "I know over time people grow apart, but I didn't think that would happen to us."

"I didn't think you would just up and leave either...but you did," Isaac commented. Valerie looked at him angrily, not sure how to respond to him. Then, she slammed her hand on the table.

"We're not talking about me," she said. "We're talking about you keeping secrets."

Isaac continued to stare at Valerie. He could see in her eyes it was bothering her for him to keep secret. She was right, they had always been each other's confidant, but Isaac felt this was different. He wasn't telling her for her own protection, and for the protection of their friendship.

"You wouldn't understand anyway," said Isaac.

"Try me," she challenged him. Isaac sat up in his seat and stared at Valerie sternly, while she swallowed and clutched her hands together.

"Have you ever experienced something you can't explain," Isaac started, "something that's beyond normal?"

Valerie looked at Isaac a bit confused, blinking her eyes a few times.

"What do you mean?" she inquired.

"Like, have you ever experienced something that was...I don't know...supernatural?"

Valerie looked around at the others in the restaurant, seeing if they were paying attention to what they were talking about. Then, she looked back at Isaac and shrugged.

"I don't think I know what you're asking Isaac."

"What I'm saying is I've had several situations where something supernatural was involved. That's why I had to cancel on you all those times."

"What does that mean?"

"I can't really explain it." Isaac replied. Valerie placed her left hand on her forehead and shook her head.

"You know what Isaac...I don't speak cryptic language," she said. "So if you really don't want to tell me, I think we're done here."

Valerie grabbed her purse and pushed her chair away from the table. Isaac quickly reached for her hand to stop her, when she stared at him.

"Don't go...I'll show you what I'm talking about," said Isaac. Still disordered but curious, Valerie looked around briefly and sat back in her seat, staring at Isaac sternly.

"Okay, so... I have this...gift," he struggled, while Valerie stared at him.

"Okay, what kind of gift?" she wondered. Isaac puffed up his cheeks and blew out a breath of air, looking around at the other guests. Then, Isaac looked back at Valerie, while she made a gesture with her hands to get him to continue what he was saying. His palms became clammy while he held them together, his heart ponding in his chest.

"I can move things without touching them...using only my mind," Isaac told her. "Those nights I cancelled on you, I was using them to help people who are like me...who are gifted."

Valerie looked at Isaac with her eyebrows raised.

"You expect me to believe that and you have no proof?" Valerie asked.

"No, I don't," said Isaac. "But you wanted me to tell you...so I did."

"Well, I'm not sure I can trust you," Valerie said with a chuckle. Isaac glanced at the table and eyed Valerie's spoon near her glass of water.

"Okay, watch me move that spoon without touching it," he said, while Valerie stared at him in disbelief. Isaac stared at her spoon firmly, focusing on it hard. Soon after, the spoon lifted from the table near the rim of Valerie's glass.

"Oh my God," she exclaimed, when the spoon dropped on the table. Isaac looked at Valerie's face, while she stared at him shocked. Then, the waitress walked over to them, placing the binder with their receipt on the table.

"Okay, here you go," she said. "Would you like to take care of this now or do you need a moment?"

Isaac looked at the waitress briefly, while Valerie got her purse and pushed her chair away from the table. Isaac looked at Valerie, watching her walk away from the table.

"Valerie," he said.

"I can't...I can't do this," she said, walking away from the table. Isaac pulled out his wallet and opened it quickly, fumbling through his money.

"How much is it?" he asked.

"It looks like it's going to be $42.33."

Isaac pulled out a fifty dollar bill, placed it in the binder, and got up from the table.

"Keep the change," he said, rushing after Valerie, while the waitress watched them slightly worried.

"Have a good day," she said, slightly confused.

Outside, Valerie was walking quickly through the parking lot to get to her car, but Isaac caught up to her and grabbed her arm. Valerie jumped and looked back, seeing it was Isaac, snatching her arm away.

"Valerie please, just let me explain?" he said. "You wanted to know what was going on...and I told you."

"What is there to explain? What do you call what you just did?" she wondered, staring at him angrily. Isaac paused, looking into Valerie's eyes. He scratched his head, when Valerie crossed her arms.

"Well, it's called telekinesis," Isaac started again, while Valerie glared at him. "It's like...magic."

Valerie exhaled and shook her head, pulling her keys out of her purse.

"I can't deal with this."

"Valerie please–"

"Isaac just stop! I don't wanna hear it," Valerie screamed. Isaac stood in place, watching Valerie walk away from him and get into her car. She started it and drove out of the parking lot quickly. Isaac turned back and went over to his trunk, balling up his fist and punching the side of the bed. Isaac bent over his truck and put his head down, grunting angrily.

Jacob and Cameron were at the dining room table in the manor later the evening. The crescent shaped moon gleamed through the blinds of the window behind them, while the two stared at a New Jersey map. For the last couple of hours, Jacob and Cameron had been searching and scrying for any suspicious activity connected to the dark forces. So far, they hadn't gotten any leads. Jacob spun a pointed tip crystal between his index finger and thumb over the map, waiting for it to drag itself to a location.

"This isn't making any sense," Cameron said, when the crystal stopped spinning and dropped. "The crystal hasn't made a single connection yet."

"Well, maybe they gave up." Jacob said. Cameron looked over at him with a smirk.

"Really?" he said.

"No, I'm serious. I mean we have stopped them on countless occasions. Maybe they gave up."

"You really think they'd quit…just like that?"

"Possibly."

Cameron exhaled and took his glasses off, when Isaac burst through the front door of the manor. Jacob and Cameron looked at Isaac, watching him slam the door, rushing toward the staircase.

"Uh…Isaac," said Jacob. But he ignored him, running up the stairs. Jacob and Cameron looked at each other and got up, following Isaac. Jacob and Cameron go to the second floor and looked around for Isaac, but they didn't see him anywhere. Then, the two heard a thud come from the attic and looked at the staircase leading to it. Jacob and Cameron walked over to the steps and ran up to the attic. Once they reached the attic, they saw Isaac standing by the podium, flipping through the Book of Magic. Isaac was staring at the Book angrily, still frowning from what had happened earlier. Jacob and Cameron walked over to Isaac, who didn't look up or seem to notice them in the room.

"Um...what are you doing?" Jacob asked, while Isaac continued flipping through the Book.

"None of your business," he snapped. Jacob and Cameron gaped at him, raising their eyebrows.

"I'm sorry, but I believe anything that has to do with that Book...is *all* of our business," Cameron retorted. Isaac slammed his hand down on the Book and stared at Jacob and Cameron. Jacob could see in his eyes that something had gone wrong, though Isaac wouldn't tell them what it was.

"I told Valerie I had powers," Isaac finally told them. "And now she won't talk to me."

"Oh," Jacob said, looking at Cameron.

"What does the Book have to do with that?" Cameron asked.

"I'm looking for a spell to reverse me telling her."

Jacob and Cameron looked at each other again, staring back at Isaac thereafter.

"I don't think that's a good idea." Jacob said.

"Of course you don't," Isaac snapped. "'Cause she isn't your friend she's mine...at least she was."

"Don't you think that's a bad idea?" Cameron chimed in. "Think of the consequences if you did that."

"Why? I want to have a normal life. And I can't even do that with my friends."

"When are you going to get it into your head that your life isn't normal anymore?" Jacob exclaimed. "Your normal life came to an end when we met."

"Fine then," Isaac said, slamming the Book closed and crossed his arms. "I guess I'll just never speak to her again."

Jacob's eyes twitched quickly and he saw Valerie getting out of her car near her apartment complex. She walked down the sidewalk, when a dark fog built up near her feet. Soon it turned into a masculine shadowy like torso, which grabbed her by her neck, choking her. Eventually, it dropped her on the ground and she laid there dead. Jacob's eyes twitched again, realizing he was back in the attic, staring at Isaac and Cameron. Cameron placed his hand on Jacob's back with concern.

"What happened?" Cameron asked, while Jacob stepped back from him.

"I just saw Valerie get attacked…by some shadow-like demon," he said.

Isaac looked at Jacob and swallowed, pretending to show no concern.

"We have to save her," said Jacob.

"Why?" Isaac questioned, while Jacob looked at him shocked.

"What do you mean why?" Jacob exclaimed. "I thought she was your friend?"

"She was, now she isn't," said Isaac. "She doesn't even want to talk to me anymore. And I'm not using my powers for anything else."

"You were about to use 'em for a spell," Cameron pointed out, when Isaac looked at him with a frown.

"Why don't you shut up Cameron," he snapped. "I didn't ask you anything."

"He has a point," Jacob said. "And might I add, you're a pretty worthless friend if you're just gonna let her get killed."

Jacob and Cameron headed toward the attic's exit, when Jacob stopped and looked back at Isaac again.

"You know Isaac," he started, "I'm a little disappointed that you've really taken it this far."

Isaac stared at Jacob angrily, watching him and Cameron leave the attic. Isaac walked over to a chair and flopped down, covering his face with a groan.

It was fairly dark that night; the clouds covered the moon, making the sky look completely black. Jacob and Cameron had arrived at Valerie's apartment complex, waiting in Jacob's car in a parking lot nearby. Jacob looked around the area to see if Valerie pulled into the complex yet, while Cameron watched him silently. Cameron hadn't said much to Jacob since they had left the manor, since he and Isaac had just engaged in a heated discussion. He could tell Jacob was still angry about it, but he knew he was trying not to show it because he had to focus on saving Valerie. Jacob exhaled deeply and Cameron looked away from him and back out the front window.

"She should be showing up here soon," he said, while Cameron continued to stare out the window. Jacob looked at Cameron and saw the sad frown on his face, crossing his arms.

"Look Cameron," Jacob started, "you know we can't control him. If he doesn't want to do this, we can't force him."

"Then, what's the point of doing it? If I recall, we were supposed to do this together," Cameron mentioned, looking at Jacob. Jacob glanced at the dashboard and shook his head, taking another breath.

"I know," he said. Jacob looked back out his window and saw Valerie's car pulling up to the apartment complex gate. Jacob tapped Cameron on his shoulder, when he glanced over and the two watched Valerie reach out of her window, entering the gate code. The gate slowly pulled open, and Valerie slowly pulled into the apartment complex.

"Come on, let's go," Jacob exclaimed. He and Cameron quickly got out of his car ran across the street to the gate. When the gate began to close back, Jacob and Cameron dropped to the ground, rolling past it right, before it shut behind them.

"That was close," said Cameron. Jacob and Cameron stood up and dusted themselves off, looking around. The two looked in front of themselves, seeing the first three apartment buildings in the area, and a path that led to other apartment suites. Jacob and Cameron examined the area, noticing the first two buildings across from each other. There were sidewalks in the middle of them that led to an identical building, where a parking lot could be seen. Jacob and Cameron walked toward the apartment buildings, when they saw Valerie park her car in the parking lot.

"There she is," Cameron said. Jacob looked over, seeing Valerie step out of her car.

"We gotta hurry," he exclaimed. Jacob and Cameron ran toward the sidewalk to reach Valerie, when a dark fog began to build up in front of them. The two stopped and stared at the fog, watching it lift from the ground and turn into a shadow like torso. Jacob and Cameron eyed the shadow creature and it turned its head toward them, revealing its glowing red eyes.

"Oh no," Cameron said, stepping back from it.

"Oh no is right, witch!" the demon exclaimed, with a deep demonic voice. "Prepare to meet your fate at the hands of a Shadow demon."

The Shadow demon thrust its arms out at them, which blew them back on to the ground. The Shadow demon turned toward Valerie and hovered toward her quickly, when Jacob and Cameron stood back up.

"Hey!! Watch out!" Cameron cried out to Valerie. She looked back quickly, seeing the Shadow demon charging toward her.

"Aaahhh!!!" she screamed. The Shadow demon grabbed her, causing her to drop her things. The demon lifted her in the air, while Jacob and Cameron rushed toward them. Then, Cameron saw a large boulder near the edge of the parking lot and ran toward it. He grabbed the boulder and lifted it over his head, staring at the Shadow demon.

"Hey demon," Cameron taunted, "get a loud of this!"

The Shadow demon glanced back at Cameron, when he threw the boulder at it. The boulder went inside of the demon, causing it to drop Valerie. She fell on the ground and she scraped her left arm, while the Shadow demon shook and growled. Jacob grabbed Valerie's arm and helped her up, when she looked up at him.

"Who are you?" she asked, with a fearful look in her eyes.

"A friend of a friend," Jacob replied, while Valerie stared at him confused. The two looked at the Shadow demon and saw the boulder crumbling inside of it. Taking Valerie's by her wrist, Jacob pulled her with him, while Cameron followed them toward the entrance to the apartment complex. But when they reached the middle of the sidewalk, the boulder disintegrated completely inside of the demon, and it stared at them. The Shadow demon flew over to them and knocked them down, grabbing Cameron by his leg.

"Cameron!" Jacob exclaimed. Then, the Shadow demon swung Cameron into the building on the left. Cameron hit the building, falling on the ground with a bleeding gash on his forehead, his glasses broken from the impact. Jacob struggled to his feet and helped Valerie up, when the demon grabbed him and threw him into the building on the right. Jacob hit the back of his head and fell on the grass beneath him, while Valerie covered her mouth in shock.

"Now it's your turn...pretty girl," said the Shadow demon. It moved toward Valerie slowly, while she continued to cover her mouth, stepping away from the demon. The Shadow demon grabbed her by her neck and raised her into the air again, while she tried to release herself.

"It's no use girl...you cannot stop me!" exclaimed the Shadow demon.

Valerie's eyes began to tear up and she gasped for air, kicking her legs around. Valerie closed her eyes knowing her end was coming, when a gust of wind hit her and the Shadow demon, which caused it to release her and she fell to the ground once more. Valerie looked up and Isaac running toward her from the start of the sidewalk. Isaac grabbed her by her hand and waist and he helped her up, as Jacob looked up seeing it was Isaac.

"Are you okay?" he asked her.

"Isaac," she said, with fear in her voice. Jacob got up and looked at Cameron, seeing he wasn't moving. Isaac looked back and saw Cameron, when he and Jacob ran over to him at the same time.

"It's about time you made it," Jacob snapped.

"I had to do some research first," said Isaac, smiling at Jacob. Jacob rolled his eyes at him, grabbing Cameron by his shoulders.

"Cameron...Cameron," he said, shaking him repeatedly. Cameron slowly opened his eyes and looked at Isaac and Jacob. Then, Isaac and Jacob helped him sit up.

"You came," said Cameron, while Isaac and Jacob helped him stand.

"I couldn't let you guys have all the fun," Isaac said, when Jacob and Cameron looked at each other confused. Then, the Shadow demon rose up from the ground and stared at Valerie. Isaac glanced back, seeing the demon charge toward her.

"No!!" Isaac exclaimed, running toward the demon. Jacob reached for Isaac to stop him, but he ran off to quickly toward the Shadow demon.

"Wait!" Jacob hollered, as he and Cameron ran up behind Valerie and stopped. Isaac ran in front of the Shadow demon and put his hand out toward it. Seeing this, the demon stopped in front of Isaac, when a bright white light expelled from his palm and hit the demon.

"Ugh!!!!" the Shadow demon exclaimed, getting knocked back on to the ground. Isaac walked toward the Shadow demon and unzipped his jacket, revealing a small crystal pendant on a black band.

"What did you do to me?" the Shadow demon cried.

"I've ended you," said Isaac. He took off the crystal and threw it into the air, causing it to glow white. The glow lit up the area and swallowed up the Shadow demon.

"Nooo!!!!!" the Shadow demon cried. The demon was absorbed inside the crystal and dropped into Isaac's hand. Isaac dropped the crystal on the ground and it broke to pieces; then, he looked back at Valerie. She walked toward Isaac and held her arm, when he turned around to look at her. Isaac looked at Valerie's arm and saw she was hurt from the attack. Jacob and Cameron watched Isaac swallow and place his hand on Valerie's shoulder near her wound.

"I can help you with your arm inside," he said. "If that's okay with you..."

Valerie nodded, and the two walked toward the apartment building in front of them. Jacob and Cameron looked at each other for a moment, slowly following behind them.

Inside, Isaac and Valerie were in her apartment, standing in the kitchen near her sink. Isaac was running warm water on a towel, while Valerie stared at him silently. Isaac wrung the towel out and turned off the sink, walking over to Valerie.

"Isaac, honestly I'm fine," Valerie told him.

"No you're not," he argued. "You're still bleeding a little bit...that's not fine."

Valerie looked at Isaac and groaned, watching him fold the towel and place it on her arm. Valerie slowly put her head down, while Isaac held the towel on her arm to soothe the wound. She noticed Isaac was avoiding looking directly into her eyes or at her at all. She knew he was upset about earlier, but she didn't want him to be. Valerie lifted her head back up and looked at Isaac, but he still wouldn't look at her.

"Isaac...I'm sorry. I didn't me–"

"Valerie it's okay, you meant what you said," Isaac interrupted. "And I feel the same way about it. You don't have to justify it."

"Could you just shut up for two seconds and let me finish!" Valerie hollered, when Isaac finally looked at her.

"I didn't give you an honest chance to explain anything," she said. "And I'm sorry."

Isaac closed his eyes and cleared his throat. It didn't matter that she was okay with him having powers now. Her initial response was her true feelings...not something fabricated from shock. Isaac didn't want her to accept him now because of what he had done for her; he wanted her to accept him for being him. Isaac opened his eyes and looked at Valerie, shaking his head.

"I appreciate the gesture," Isaac started, "but I don't think you understand that just because you get it now, doesn't make everything all right. You shunned me. And the only reason I even have the chance to explain myself now is because I saved you."

Valerie stared at Isaac, her eyes becoming glassy. He knew she was hurt by what he said, but it was how he felt. Isaac took the towel off Valerie's arm and closed it up, staring at her again.

"Do you have a first aid kit?" he asked, changing the subject. Valerie stared at him, while he looked at her seriously. She cleared her throat to hold back her tears, nodding at him.

"Yeah...it's in the bathroom by the cabinet," Valerie replied. Isaac walked away from her and went toward the bathroom, while tears fell down Valerie's face. Isaac went into the bathroom and stepped over to the cabinet past the sink. He opened it and took the first aid kit from the top shelf. He closed the cabinet and stared at himself in the mirror, having the strangest feeling come over him. Isaac suddenly started to remember how he felt when Valerie first left for college in Virginia. He wasn't sure why that came over him, but to this day, he hadn't gotten any clarity from Valerie to why she left without him. Taking a deep breath, Isaac walked out of the bathroom and went back into the kitchen, seeing Valerie with tears falling down her face. She looked over and saw him staring at her, wiping her them off quickly. Isaac walked back over to Valerie slowly and stopped in front of her, placing the first aid kit on the counter. He took a bandage out of the kit and placed it over Valerie's wound, wrapping her arm up. Then, Isaac stopped and stared at Valerie, when she looked at him again.

"Why did you leave me?" he asked. Valerie looked at Isaac confused, wiping off her tears some more.

"What?" she wondered. Isaac put his hands over his face, stepping away from Valerie and turning his back toward her.

"After we graduated…we were supposed to go away to college together," Isaac started, turning back around. "Why'd you leave without me?"

Valerie froze up. She wasn't sure why of all the things he could bring up that would be it. She stepped away from him, folding her arms together.

"I was scared," she admitted, while Isaac stared at her.

"Scared of what?" he asked, stepping up behind her. Valerie looked over her shoulder at Isaac, turning back toward him.

"Us," said Valerie. "After we graduated, we were crazy about each other. I had never felt that way about anyone before, and it scared me. I was scared of falling for you."

Isaac stared at Valerie, slightly shocked. He had no idea that was why she left. But to be honest, he felt the same way. Isaac and Valerie had known each other for so long that developing feelings for one another seemed imminent. Isaac continued to stare at Valerie, while her eyes became glassy again.

"Why didn't you just tell me?" Isaac wondered. Valerie looked at him, letting tears fall down her face again.

"I don't know," she said. "I didn't know how you felt about me…feel about me."

Isaac gazed at Valerie and placed his hand on her face, wiping her tears from her eyes.

"I'm sorry, I didn't mean to hurt you by what I said earlier," Isaac confessed. "I just don't know what to do. I still have trouble understanding all this myself. But if there was anyone I know I can trust with everything…it would be you."

"Do you really mean that?" Valerie asked, staring into Isaac's eyes.

"Yes…I do," he said. Valerie placed her hand on Isaac's face and smiled at him softly, when the two leaned toward each other slowly. They closed their eyes and they felt the warmth from one another, when their lips touched softly and they kissed. Isaac held Valerie by her waist with his other hand, while she held him behind his back. Then, the front door came open and Jacob and Cameron stepped in on them.

"Oh Lord, soft porn," Jacob exclaimed, startling Isaac and Valerie. He stepped back and covered his eyes, when Isaac and Valerie stopped kissing. The two stared at Jacob and Cameron, while they stared at them slightly embarrassed. Jacob and Cameron slowly walked into the apartment, when Isaac walked over to them.

"What are you guys doing here?" Isaac asked through his teeth nervously. Jacob and Cameron smiled at him awkwardly.

"We were just making sure you guys made it in alright...and stuff," said Jacob, while Isaac stared at him with his nostrils flared. "I didn't see much."

"I didn't see anything; I'm blind without my glasses," said Cameron.

Isaac looked at Cameron and smiled back.

"Really Cameron," Isaac said.

"Okay, I'm not that blind...but still," Cameron went on. Then, Valerie stepped behind Isaac and looked at Jacob and Cameron.

"Isaac, I haven't met these friends of yours yet," she said. Isaac looked back at Valerie, while she smiled at him.

"Uh...well, this is a part of what I hadn't told you yet," he said.

"I'm all ears," said Valerie. "And I promise to be open-minded."

Isaac looked back at Jacob and Cameron briefly; then, he turned back to Valerie.

"Okay, this might seem strange...but these are my brothers Jacob–"

"Hi," Jacob smiled, waving at Valerie.

"–and Cameron," Isaac finished. Cameron looked at Valerie and raised his hand for a stiff wave.

"Hey," said Cameron. Valerie looked at all of them with a smile, waving back at Jacob and Cameron. Then she looked at Isaac and placed her hands together.

"We're half-brothers...we have the same father. We just found each other a few months ago."

"I'm just curious, what are you three exactly?" Valerie asked. Jacob and Cameron stared at each other, while Isaac cleared his throat and looked at Valerie.

"Uh, well...we're kind of like..." Isaac struggled, trying to reveal the whole truth to Valerie.

"You guys are like what?"

"Witches," Isaac answered, when Valerie looked at him with her eyes slightly widened. She exhaled and looked at the three of them, remaining open to the concept.

"We aren't like all witches though," Isaac mentioned. "We're kind of different...I think."

"Yeah, we actually don't really consider ourselves to be witches," Jacob added, when Valerie looked at him. "It's just...that's what our father was."

Valerie took in everything they were telling her. It was hard to believe, but she trusted Isaac, and she wanted to be understanding.

"Wow...that's some secret to keep bottled up inside," she said.

"Yeah...and this isn't the half of it." Isaac agreed, while Valerie laughed. With a smile, Valerie walked up to Isaac and placed her hand on his arm.

"Maybe we can meet tomorrow," Valerie suggested. "Then, you can tell me everything."

"That would be nice," Isaac said, smiling back at Valerie. She kissed him on his cheek and backed away from him, while Jacob and Cameron stepped out of the apartment doorway.

"I'll text you, okay?" she said.

"Okay, I'll see you around."

"Bye...Isaac."

Isaac, Jacob, and Cameron left out of Valerie's apartment, while she placed her hand on her chest and smiled, closing the door thereafter. Outside, the three were walking on the sidewalk, when Cameron looked at Isaac with a smile.

"I'm glad you and Valerie made up," he said. Isaac looked at him and nodded with a smile.

"Yeah...me too," said Isaac. Jacob stopped and looked over at Isaac slightly confused. Isaac and Cameron stopped and looked back at him.

"What is it?" Cameron asked.

"You know what I'd like to know," Jacob started, while Isaac raised his eyebrows. "How did you know what to do to get rid of the Shadow demon?"

Isaac chuckled under his breath, while Jacob and Cameron stared at him.

"Like I said...I did some research," Isaac smiled.

"What does that mean?!" Jacob exclaimed, crossing his arms.

"Well, if you hadn't stormed out of the manor before you looked in the Book, you would have seen that you can't kill a shadow demon with regular powers," Isaac said calmly. "The only way to kill a Shadow demon is to seal it in a crystal and crush it."

Jacob stared at Isaac angrily.

"Considering you haven't been demon fighting with us for like a week now, it's about time you did something useful."

Isaac stared at Jacob, stepping toward him and crossing his arms.

"Hey, hey, hey...guys chill out," said Cameron. "It's late and I think I'm about done with all this arguing."

Isaac put his head down and nodded, looking back up at Jacob and Cameron.

"Actually Cameron, Jacob is right," he said. Jacob glanced over at him.

"Are you sick?" Jacob asked. Isaac chuckled and shook his head.

"No...but I think I owe you and Cameron an apology. I know I put you guys through hell these last few days not helping with all the magical stuff, and you probably almost got killed 'cause of me. I was just being stubborn and stupid...and I'm sorry."

"Would you look at that...Isaac's turning over a new leaf," Jacob joshed, while Isaac stared at him with a smirk. "Apology accepted."

"I forgive you too," said Cameron. Isaac looked at both of them and placed his hand out in front of him, his palm facing down.

"We still partners?" he asked. Jacob and Cameron glanced at each other again, looking back at Isaac.

"Always," Cameron replied, placing his hands on Isaac's. Isaac and Cameron looked at Jacob, when he exhaled and uncrossed his arms.

"To the end," he said, placing his hand on top of Isaac and Cameron's hands.

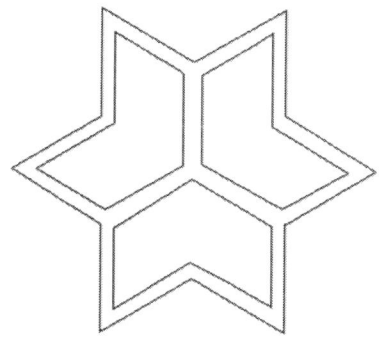

TAKE THEIR POWERS THRICE

THINGS FINALLY STARTED TO CALM DOWN in the brother lives. It had been a couple weeks since their last encounter with the dark forces, which was when Valerie found out their secret. Since that night, Isaac and Valerie finally had a chance to spend more time together. Victor's University took an early fall break, so Cameron was off school for week, which he used to hang out with Liem. Jacob, on the other hand, had begun working on topics for Paterson Life, since he would be starting during the winter season. Jacob was excited about starting work, but for the last couple of days, he hadn't been feeling too bright. He continued having a disturbing sense that something bad was going to happen. He didn't mention anything to Isaac or Cameron, seeing they were preoccupied by their own personal needs; but he knew what he was feeling had to be connected to the dark forces.

It was a quiet morning that Thursday. The sun was shining, and the clouds hovered in the sky over the Manor. Jacob sat in the kitchen near the island, writing in his notebook. He had kept to himself most of the morning, not seeming to be in a good mood. He had a horrible headache, with the awful sense he had been feeling still haunting him. Jacob hadn't mastered his mood yet when it came to his powers. When he felt something was wrong, he couldn't identify it until the last moment. This was frustrating to him, and typically left him with a headache that wouldn't go away. Jacob grunted with a deep sigh, when Cameron rushed down the kitchen staircase and went over to the refrigerator. Feeling his peace and quiet had been compromised, Jacob glared at Cameron and slammed his pen down on the island. Cameron quickly opened the refrigerator and took out a half gallon of milk, popping it open and guzzling it down rapidly.

"Really Cameron?!" Jacob exclaimed, staring at Cameron with disgust. With a loud gulp, Cameron stopped and looked at Jacob, blinking his eyes.

"What?" Cameron asked, wiping off his mouth with his forearm.

"What!?" Jacob snapped. "Having a little common courtesy wouldn't hurt you, would it? Other people use milk in this house."

"I'm sorry; my stomach wasn't feeling too hot," said Cameron. "I needed something to coat it...and quick."

"And you couldn't have gotten a cup to do that?" Jacob questioned. Cameron shrugged and put the milk carton back in the refrigerator, closing the door.

"See, if I would have taken the time to get a cup and pour the milk, I probably would've puked everywhere. Acid reflux doesn't like to wait."

Jacob stared at Cameron sternly, tapping his pen on the island.

"I swear your logic sometimes is unbelievable," said Jacob. Cameron chuckled. He could tell Jacob was in a bad mood, but he wasn't sure why. Jacob shook his head and went back to writing in his notebook. Cameron stepped over to the island and stood next to Jacob, leaning over by him. Jacob put his pen down again, turning his head slowly and staring at Cameron.

"You're in my personal bubble," he fused.

"What's wrong with you this morning? You're all stuffy and tight like Isaac," Cameron joked. He smirked at Jacob and brushed up against his shoulder. Jacob closed his notebook and turned around in his chair, moving back from Cameron slightly.

"Well, you obviously…and I just don't feel like I'm in the mood today."

"Aww Jake, it'll be okay," Cameron said, patting Jacob on his back roughly. Jacob bumped into the island and looked at Cameron angrily.

"I hate you…so much right now," said Jacob. He got up from the island and walked out of the kitchen, while Cameron smirked and laughed under his breath.

"Love you too," Cameron teased. Jacob walked into the main hall and headed toward the steps, when his eyes started twitching. He paused in the hallway and rubbed his eyes, seeing himself in the attic. He looked around in a slight panic, confused to how he had gotten there so quickly. He looked over to his left and saw Cameron standing next by him, looking at him with concern.

"Are you okay?" Cameron asked. Jacob stared at Cameron, feeling as if he had experienced this before. With slight hesitation, Jacob shook his head slowly.

"I don't…think so," he answered. Looking in front of himself, Jacob saw Isaac flipping the Book of Magic, shaking his head.

"He'll be okay…we all will, once this is over," said Isaac. Jacob continued to try and figure out what was going on. Cameron walked over to Isaac and began to look through the pages in the Book with him, while Jacob looked around. Then, Jacob walked over to Isaac and Cameron and looked at the Book, but the entry they were looking at was blurred. Trying to get clarification, Jacob looked up at them confused.

"What do we need this for?" Jacob questioned. Isaac and Cameron looked up at him with their raised eyebrows.

"Are you sure you're all right?" Cameron asked, staring at him. Jacob shrugged his shoulders with a crooked smile, feeling slightly awkward. He tried to play along, but he wanted to figure out what was going on.

"Yeah, I'm fine…I just don't remember what we needed this for," he said. Isaac and Cameron looked at each other again, when Jacob felt a cold breeze come over him. He looked back and a large black fog came charging at him, when Isaac and Cameron looked up in shock.

"Watch out!!" Cameron yelled, when the black fog hit Jacob.

Jacob flew into the living room area of the manor and fell back on the floor, realizing his vision had ended. Cameron came running into the living room and saw Jacob on the floor, struggling to get up. Cameron walked over to Jacob and bent down, grabbing his back and arm, helping him up.

"What the heck happened to you?" Cameron asked.

"Something hit me and knocked me down," Jacob replied. Cameron looked around briefly and shook his head.

"Um...yeah, I don't see anything," he said. Jacob looked at him with a frown, exhaling and brushing himself off.

"I had a vision of something attacking us in the attic," said Jacob. "But I was able to react to what was going on."

"Hmm...that's weird," Cameron said. "You've never been able to do that before, have you?"

"No."

"Maybe your powers are advancing again."

"Maybe...but that's not my main concern."

Cameron stared at Jacob with his eyebrows raised and crossed his arms. Then, the two heard a knock at the door. Jacob looked at the front door confused, looking back at Cameron.

"Who would be knocking on our door at eleven in the morning on a Thursday?" Jacob wondered, placing his hands on his hips. Cameron bucked his eyes, looking over at the door.

"Oops," Cameron exclaimed, walking out of the living room to answer the door. Still confused, Jacob followed after Cameron slowly, when he opened the door and saw Liem standing in front of him.

"Liem, hey what's up?" Cameron said with a nervous smile.

"Hey Cam–" Liem stopped himself, looking at what Cameron was wearing and chuckled. "So...I guess you're one of those chill, sweat pants and tank top kind of guys?"

"Uh no," said Cameron. "I actually just totally forgot that we were hanging out today."

"Oh," Liem paused, seeing Jacob come around the corner. Jacob walked up behind Cameron and crossed his arms, staring at Liem.

"Who's this?" he asked. Cameron glanced back at Jacob and smiled, scratching his head.

"Oh, uh...this is my friend from school, Liem," he said.

"I see," Jacob replied. "Nice to meet you, I'm Jacob."

"Oh okay, you're the nice one," Liem said with a smile.

Jacob looked at Cameron confused, glancing back at Liem.

"I guess," Jacob said with a chuckle.

"Well, nice to meet you too," Liem said, putting his hand out. With a smile, Jacob put out his hand and he and Liem exchanged a handshake. Suddenly, a cold chill rushed through Jacob. He felt a strange dark vibe from Liem, while he stared into his eyes. Noticing this, Liem quickly pulled his hand away from Jacob, still smiling, trying to play him off. Liem looked at Cameron again and crossed his arms.

"So, are you ready to go...or is this a bad time?" Liem wondered, looking at Cameron.

"No, no...I just need to take a quick shower," Cameron replied.

"Where are you going?" Jacob asked, slightly concerned.

"We're just hanging out," said Cameron

"That's cool, but um...Cameron," Jacob started, "keeping in consideration what I just told you, we should probably stay together today."

"Are you guys sure this isn't a bad time?" Liem asked again.

"No, Jacob's just stressing 'cause of a vision he had this morning," Cameron commented. Jacob widened his eyes and hit Cameron on his shoulder, staring at him in disbelief.

"Um...have you lost your mind? Since when is it okay to just blurt out stuff?" Jacob exclaimed, throwing his arms up.

"Relax, Liem already knows about us," Cameron confirmed.

"So, you feel it's okay to just tell anybody our secret?" Jacob asked.

"Isaac did it," Cameron retorted. "Besides, he's a witch too."

"I'm actually a warlock," Liem corrected him, when Jacob looked at him firmly.

"Thanks for sharing," Jacob snapped.

"I mean if you're worried about whatever you're talking about, you're more than welcome to join Cam and I," Liem added. *Cam and me...Really? These two are all buddy buddy?* Jacob thought, slightly disgusted. The last thing he wanted to do was be the third wheel, but he didn't want to seem like he was trying to put a damper on their outing either. But he felt he may need to tag along for Cameron's safety.

"Well, I'm not sure if *Cameron* would mind me going along or not," Jacob replied, trying to talk Cameron out of going tactfully.

"I don't mind," said Cameron, when Jacob looked over at him with a frown. Then, he looked back over at Liem and crossed his arms.

"So, where were you guys going?" Jacob asked. Liem looked at Jacob with a smirk.

"Medallion's Magic Shop," Liem answered.

Jacob and Cameron had never been to a magic shop before, and it wasn't like they had any intentions of going to one anytime soon. Jacob wasn't as excited about it as Cameron; he was more concerned about Liem's motives. Though he was a little skeptical, Jacob knew that he couldn't let Cameron go with Liem alone. He wasn't sure exactly why he was felt that way, but it was similar to the feeling he had been sensing for the last few days.

Pulling into a parking lot in Liem's car, the three arrived near an old brick building. It was the size of a two story stout home, having two large windows on both sides of the lower level, which showed miscellaneous products for sale. Across the top of the building was a border that had **MEDALLION'S MAGIC SHOP** on it. Jacob stared at the shop, not really wanting to go in, when Cameron and Liem got out of the car. Jacob groaned and stepped out of the car, walking up behind Liem and Cameron.

"Well guys, this is Medallion's Magic shop," said Liem, looking back at Cameron and Jacob.

"Wow...this place looks awesome," Cameron exclaimed.

"We haven't even been inside yet," Jacob said, looking at Cameron.

"His anticipation is correct," Liem defended Cameron. "This place is pretty awesome."

Jacob looked at Liem with a frown and rolled his eyes. The three walked up to the shop's door and Liem opened it, stepping aside for Jacob and Cameron.

"After you," he said. Cameron walked inside first, and Jacob followed him. Clearing his throat, Liem walked inside the shop and the door closed behind him.

Inside, Jacob and Cameron looked around, when Liem came up behind them. Walking into the main area of the shop, the three looked over to the right and saw a woman standing behind a counter in the front of the store. She was wearing a long skirt with a shawl over her shoulders, having a purple scarf wrapped around her head and a large topaz jewel around her neck. She looked to be in her mid-fifties, having a medium chocolate skin tone and wide brown eyes.

"Greetings young men, welcome to Medallion's," she said with a smirk. Jacob and Cameron stopped. She continued to stare at them, when Jacob had an eerie feeling come over him.

"Hi," Jacob and Cameron said together. Liem walked up behind Cameron and placed his arm around his upper shoulder.

"Hey Cameron, come with me...I wanna show you something," he suggested.

"Okay," he replied. Cameron and Liem walked over to the left side of the shop. Jacob stood where he was, staring at Liem and Cameron. Then, he looked at the woman behind the counter, who was still staring at him with a smirk. Trying to ignore her awkward behavior, Jacob began to look around at items on the shelves near him. He walked over to a shelf that had skulls on it. Some were slightly grimier and disfigured than others, but they all freaked him out in a way. He peered at the woman behind the counter again, and her eyes were still glued to him like an eagle watching its prey. He slightly widened his eyes and looked back at the shelf near him, moving to the next one, continuing to ignore the strange actions of the shop keeper. On the next shelf, Jacob noticed items that assist those gifted with the power of foresight. He examined the shelf thoroughly, seeing tarot cards, tea leaf tea and fortune telling cups for Tasseography, and various types of Ouija boards. Next to those items was a crystal ball. Jacob became slightly entranced by the crystal ball and he examined its details, down to the ball's precisely cut wooden stand. Jacob moved closer to the crystal ball and placed his left hand over it, when it suddenly started to glow a cloudy blue color. Then, Jacob's eyes twitched and he saw himself with Isaac and Cameron in a dark clouded area. Without warning, darkness came from above the three and consumed them.

"Huuhh!" Jacob gasped, his eyes twitching again, when he realized he was back in the shop. He let go of the crystal ball and took a deep breath, closing his eyes for a moment.

"Future's not so bright?"

Jacob jumped and opened his eyes, catching his breath and holding his chest while his heart began to pound rapidly. He looked to his right and saw the shop keeper standing near him.

"What?" Jacob asked, hoping that she would change the subject or walk away. He had heard what she said, but he didn't want to answer. He tried not to be too obvious when having premonitions, but sometimes it was difficult not to show it. The shop keeper smirked at him again and crossed her arms, and raised her eyebrows.

"All my life I've prided myself on speaking clearly so others could understand," she said back to Jacob. Slightly baffled, Jacob swallowed and stared at the shop keeper, trying to figure out what to say.

"Uh, I was just admiring the crystal ball," Jacob lied. "I've never seen one in person before."

"Ha, ha, ha, ha, ha," the shop keeper cackled and uncrossed her arms, placing her left hand on her hip. "Of course you were."

The shop keeper grabbed Jacob's right hand and turned his palm over, staring at the creases in his hand.

"You're a seer," she said. Jacob widened his eyes and pulled his hand away from the shop keeper quickly. How could she know that? How did she know that? Jacob continued to stare at the shop keeper, while she smirked at him.

"How would you know that?" Jacob asked.

"I'm a seer too...and a palm reader," she said. Jacob stared at her shocked, wondering how to respond at this point.

"I'm Madame Della-Reese, Medallion's founder," she told him with a smile. She took his hand again, examining his palm once more, letting it go shortly afterward.

"And you are...Jacob Blackwood," she said softly. Jacob continued to stare at Madame Della-Reese, while she stared into his eyes.

"Y–yes...I am," he said nervously, stepping back from her.

"Don't worry; your secret is safe with me...I have no intentions of telling others' business."

"That's not what I'm worried about," he said.

"Then, what is it?" Madame Della-Reese inquired. Jacob didn't want to say anything to her about what he saw. He didn't know her, regardless whether she was a fellow seer or not. Jacob shook his head and looked back at Cameron and Liem, watching them look at magician hats and magic cards on the shelf near them.

"Something wrong?" Madame Della-Reese asked once more, staring at Jacob. Jacob looked back over at Madame Della-Reese and exhaled through his nostrils. He put his head down and closed his eyes, glancing back up at her with a stern look on his face.

"Nothing really," he said. "It's just this whole seer thing can be a little overwhelming...especially when you don't fully understand what you've seen."

"Maybe I can assist with that," Madame Della-Reese told him.

"How?" Jacob wondered. Madame Della-Reese smirked and reached on to the shelf, grabbing a deck of tarot cards. Jacob stared at her and crossed his arms, while she looked down and shuffled the deck in her hands. Madame Della-Reese glanced up at Jacob, tilted her head to the side, while he looked at her confused.

"Have you read tarots before?" she asked. He shook his head. That was definitely not on his list of things to do.

"No...and I have no intentions on learning how to read them either," Jacob said, uncrossing his arms.

"Why not?" Madame Della-Reese wondered. "If you're worried about being overwhelmed, this could help you eventually."

Jacob stared at Madame Della-Reese with caution, when she pulled the cards together and spread them out in between her palms.

"Besides, we don't have to look into your future," she said. "We can look into someone else's."

Jacob rolled his eyes, when Madame Della-Reese looked at Liem and Cameron with a smirk.

"Why don't we look into his? Cameron, isn't it?" she asked. Jacob glared at her with his eyes narrowed, while she back away from him toward the front counter. She turned toward the counter and laid the cards face down, while Jacob watched her slowly. Madame Della-Reese looked back at Jacob and made a hand gesture to get him to come near her. Reluctantly, Jacob walked toward Madame Della-Reese and stood by the counter, staring at the tarot cards.

"It's very simple, you'll pull three cards...which will tell you his past, present, and future," she said.

"And what if I don't want to do this?" Jacob asked, glancing back at Madame Della-Reese.

"Then, you want to remain in your current state of prejudice."

Jacob rolled his eyes and looked over at the cards again, letting out an irritated groan.

"Pull the first card from the deck," she told him with a solemn grin, while Jacob stared at her. Then, he placed his hand on top of the cards. Taking a deep breath, Jacob slowly slid a card from the pile and pulled his hand away quickly. Madame Della-Reese touched the card and flipped it over, revealing it to be a "Power" Card.

"In his past...he held power–" she spoke, when Jacob reached toward the deck and pulled another card from it. Madame Della-Reese flipped the card over, revealing the "Betrayal" Card.

"–But in his present...there will be a great betrayal that will lead to–"

Jacob stared at Madame Della-Reese and cleared his throat, taking one last card from the deck. Madame Della-Reese flipped the card over and Jacob glanced down and stared at the card, his eyes widened in shock.

"–Death," she said coldly. Madame Della-Reese looked at Jacob with a serious stare, as he slowly back away from her. Jacob began to shake his head, moving away from Madame Della-Reese, rushing over to Cameron and Liem.

"Where are you going?!" she asked. Liem and Cameron were laughing, still looking at items on the shelf, when Jacob rushed up to them and grabbed Cameron by his arm.

"I think we're done here," Jacob said, tugging on Cameron.

"Hey! What's the matter with you," Cameron snapped, pulling

away from Jacob. Liem put down the deck of cards he held and swallowed, while Jacob and Cameron stared at each other angrily.

"Cameron we need to leave...now," Jacob said. Cameron stared at Jacob, frowning at him with frustration.

"No we don't," said Cameron. "Can't you see Liem and I were having fun over here?"

"It's fine Cameron," Liem chimed in. "I was done anyway."

Cameron looked at Liem, when he pulled out his keys with a smile.

"I'll go start my car," he said. Liem walked out of the shop, and Cameron glared back at Jacob.

"What the heck is your problem?" he snapped.

"I don't have time to explain anything to you...just trust me and let's go."

"Tsk, whatever," Cameron complained, brushing against Jacob and walking toward the shop's exit. Jacob followed closely behind him, when he glanced at Madame Della-Reese, who was still watching him.

"You'll be back," she said, when Jacob and Cameron hesitated and looked back at her.

"What is she talking about?" Cameron wondered.

"Nothing...just go," Jacob said, pushing Cameron out the door. Once they got outside, Cameron stared at Jacob while the two continued toward Liem's car.

"What was that about, Jacob?" Cameron asked, but Jacob ignored him. "Jacob?!"

"Chill out, all right," Jacob snapped. "The shop keeper was a creepy woman...I was ready to leave. Do I have to explain myself all the time?"

Cameron rolled his eyes and walked off toward the car, when Jacob's phone began to ring in his pocket. He took his phone out and saw Isaac calling him. Jacob quickly answered the phone and put it up to his ear with a sigh of relief.

"Saved by the bell," he said, stepping up to Liem's car. Cameron looked back at him angrily and opened the door to the passenger's side, when the two got in the car.

"What?" Isaac said, slightly confused.

"It's nothing," said Jacob. "How was your morning with Valerie?"

"Oh, it was great," Isaac told him. "I'm actually just surprised how open she is to everything. I mean I know it's been two weeks now, but she seems genuine."

"I guess that's a good thing," Jacob said, when Liem pulled out of the parking lot and drove down the street. Jacob exhaled, staring out the front window of the car.

"Where are you at?" Isaac wondered.

"Out with Cameron...and his friend Liem," Jacob mumbled.

"Who's Liem?" Isaac asked, sounding confused.

"Exactly," Jacob replied. Cameron looked back at Jacob with a frown and rolled his eyes.

"So...are you on your way home?" Jacob asked.

"Yeah, I'm headed that way," Isaac said. "You guys too?"

"Yes, we should be home in a little bit," Jacob said. Liem looked at Jacob in the rearview mirror with a smirk.

"Actually, not quite," he said.

"Where are we going?" Cameron asked, while Jacob looked at Liem with his eyebrows raised.

"Well, I wanted you to meet some of the others in my coven...if you are interested?" said Liem.

"Right now?!" Jacob exclaimed, as Liem stared at him in the rearview mirror again. Liem smirked and rolled his eyes, looking back at the road.

"Yeah, we usually hang out at night and train at an old park."

Cameron looked at Liem, nodding in agreement.

"Sure, that would be fun," Cameron replied. Jacob looked at Cameron and swallowed.

"What's going on? Where are you guys going?" Isaac asked, hearing the commotion. Jacob paused for a moment, trying to figure a way to discretely tell Isaac where they were going without being obvious. Jacob inhaled and put on a pseudo smile, glancing up at Liem from the rearview mirror.

"So...where exactly is this training spot?" Jacob asked with false enthusiasm. Liem stared at him, feeling he was up to something, but he wasn't positive. Smiling back at Jacob, Liem looked at him with his eyes squinted.

"It's called Westwick Park," he said. Jacob nodded and leaned over in his seat, returning to his conversation with Isaac.

"Did you here that?" he whispered, trying not to let Liem or Cameron here him.

"Yeah, Westwick Park right? I haven't been there in years," Isaac thought aloud, "I stopped going there when I was like nine."

"That's probably because all the slides and stuff were torn down," Jacob mentioned. After another short pause, Jacob came up with an idea.

"Hey, you should meet us there," he said quietly.

"Wait, what? Why?" Isaac exclaimed.

"Really Isaac, that's enough with the dramatics," Jacob whispered.

"I don't understand why I should meet you all there."

"I don't think I trust this guy Isaac," Jacob said, under his breath. "He seems a little off."

"I don't want to just pop up uninvited," Isaac said. "That won't do us any good in Cameron's eyes."

"Well, if you don't come, I think it'll be worse if something does happen and you're not here."

Isaac sighed and cleared his throat. He felt Jacob was on to something, but he didn't want to aggravate or embarrass Cameron in the process.

"So, is that a yes?" Jacob asked, while Isaac remained silent.

"Yeah…I'll meet you guys there."

"OK, see you later."

Jacob hung up his phone quickly and put it back in his pocket. Cameron looked over his shoulder, staring at Jacob.

"Was that Isaac?" he wondered.

"Yeah, he was just checking on us," Jacob said, glancing out the window. Cameron turned back around in his seat and crossed his arms, staring out the front window.

"Hey, cheer up Cameron," said Liem, when Cameron looked at him. "You're about to meet more of our kind, it's going to be an experience you won't forget."

Though he had his doubts, Isaac had realized by now being skeptical

Jacob's instinct was suicide. He had to trust that what he felt could be a potential threat against them, even if he didn't want to upset Cameron with his unexpected arrival.

In a vacant area, the sun was setting, leaving the sky a reddish-orange hue. Isaac drove down the bumpy road in his truck, looking around the area. Tall trees stood in the distance, while a blend of burnt and green grass was everywhere, shin high. He pulled into what used to be the parking lot of Westwick Park, and stopped his truck near a large tree. Isaac turned off his car and stared at the empty field, where swing sets, slides, monkey bars, and other playground sets used to be. While he continued to stare in the field and reminisce, Liem's car pulled into the area and parked two spaces away from him. Isaac looked over and saw Liem turning off the car, when Jacob and Cameron got out. Once Liem stepped out of the car, he saw Isaac's truck, quickly changing his demeanor. Isaac got out of his truck and stepped around it, catching Jacob and Cameron's eye. Cameron's face was red with anger and his nostrils were flared, while he stared at Isaac angrily. Jacob lit up and walked over to Isaac slowly, while Liem swallowed nervously and stood next to Cameron.

"I'm *so* glad you came," said Jacob lightly, turning toward Cameron and Liem. Liem stared at Isaac, knowing who he was, but to cover it up, he played it off.

"And this is?" he asked, looking at Cameron. Cameron rolled his eyes and crossed his arms, looking off in the field.

"This is Isaac, my eldest brother," he replied, with a dull tone. Isaac raised his right eyebrow and waved at Liem, while he smiled back at him. Liem wasn't expecting all of them to be there, he was only wanting to deal with Cameron first. When Jacob tagged along, he was able to adjust his plan. Now that Isaac was there, he wasn't sure if it would still work. Liem widened his eyes, keeping his composure.

"Hey," he said. "So, did you come to pick up Jacob?" he asked, not really wondering, but suggesting. Isaac shook his head and smirked at Liem.

"No," he said. "I actually came to join you guys for the 'training' you're doing out here."

"Great, the more, the merrier," Liem exclaimed with a smile, quickly turning away from the three and frowning. Cameron watched Liem step away from them. Then, he rushed over to Isaac and Jacob.

"What the heck did you show up for?" he fussed.

"Didn't you hear me earlier? I came for the training," Isaac answered.

"Yeah right," said Cameron. "Like I'd believe that for a second."

Cameron rolled his eyes again and turned away from Isaac and Jacob, catching up to Liem. Jacob turned to Isaac, when he glanced at him with a doubtful look on his face.

"Thanks for coming; now you'll get to see I'm not crazy," Jacob mentioned.

"I never thought you were," Isaac replied. "But that guy does seem a little strange."

"Indeed. I believe a close watch is called for," Jacob proposed. Then, the two followed behind Liem and Cameron, catching up to them in the fields. Isaac and Jacob looked around, slightly confused to where they were headed.

"Uh...where are we going?" Isaac asked.

Still looking straight forward, Liem responded, "The woods, they're not too far from here."

"The woods?" Jacob repeated, when Isaac looked at him. Looking ahead, Isaac and Jacob stared at the tree lines that led to the woods beyond the old park.

"Yes, the woods," Liem responded. "We set up out here and wait for the moon to rise."

"To do what exactly?" Isaac wondered with his eyes squinted, staring at Liem from behind. Liem smirked and continued walking toward the woods, glaring at Isaac over his shoulder.

"You'll see."

Isaac looked at Jacob and the two stared at each other with worried, traveling on through the trees and into the woods. After walking for a couple of minutes, the four arrived in an open area where a few other guys were hanging around. Isaac and Jacob stopped and looked around, while Liem and Cameron continued toward the others. It was five other guys dressed in all black there; two were blonde – one darker than the other – and fair-skinned with green eyes. The other three were brunettes; two were ivory toned with light brown eyes and the other one was caramel toned with dark brown eyes. All of the guys were tall and medium in build.

"These are some of the others in my coven," Liem told Cameron, when they walked up to the guys. The darker blonde walked up to them and crossed his arms, staring at Liem.

"You're late Liem, as usual of course," he said, glancing at Cameron with a smirk, while Isaac and Jacob stared at them from a far.

"So I realized," said Liem, looking at Cameron. Cameron stared at him slightly confused, when the darker blonde uncrossed his arms.

"I see you brought new recruits, I'm impressed," said the darker blonde, staring at Isaac and Jacob. Jacob crossed his arms and started feeling strange vibes from the guys, and even darker vibes from Liem than earlier. What he was feeling seemed similar to how he had been feeling the last few days, but still, he couldn't put his finger on it. Isaac looked at Jacob, seeing the stress in his face while he frowned.

"Is something wrong Jacob?" Isaac wondered. Something was wrong, but for some reason, Jacob wouldn't say anything. Sighing under his breath and looking away from Isaac, Jacob shook his head.

"No, it's nothing," he said quickly. With no more hesitation, Isaac and Jacob continued toward the others, stepping behind Liem and Cameron.

"They actually aren't new recruits; they have their own coven," said Liem. "They're the Blackwoods."

"Hmm…never heard of them before," said the darker blonde, still staring at Isaac and Jacob.

"Our family did a very good job at making sure we remained undiscoverable," Jacob intervened.

"Why is that?" asked the darker blonde. Jacob stared at him, narrowing his eyes and frowning.

"I–I don't know," said Jacob, when the darker blonde squinted his eyes.

"Oh, I guess I should've introduced you guys," Liem jumped in. "This is Cameron, and these are his brothers, Isaac and Jacob."

"Ah, nice to meet you, I'm Simon," he replied, putting his hand out to Cameron. Cameron shook Simon's hand with a smile. Then, Simon looked behind himself at the other guys.

"These guys behind me are from our coven too," said Simon. "The two by the logs are Alex and Allen, the twins; and the ones by the trees are Richard and Felix."

The guys waved at Isaac, Jacob, and Cameron and they waved back at them. Cameron looked at Simon slightly confused, crossing his arms.

"Are you all descendants of the Xaviors?" Cameron wondered. Simon took a deep breath, looking at Liem.

"No, they're not," Liem answered for him. "Baine and I asked them to join our coven."

"And we joined willingly," Simon said with a smile. Then, Simon looked at Liem again.

"Will Baine be joining us tonight?" he asked, when Liem glared at him with a frown. Liem quickly changed his tone, once he realized Jacob was watching him.

"No, not tonight," he said. "He had...a prior engagement that required his attendance."

"I see...well then," Simon started once more, "shall we get ready?"

Liem nodded. Simon turned away from the four and walked over to the others, when they walked off into a wooded area. Liem turned toward Isaac and Jacob, when Cameron turned toward him.

"They're gathering wood together for the fire," said Liem. "It should be night fall shortly. Then we'll start..."

Isaac and Jacob stared at Liem confused.

"Then we'll start what?" Isaac asked. Liem stared at Isaac with a smirk.

"The séance," he said. Liem walked away from the three, when Cameron followed behind him. Isaac and Jacob widened their eyes, looking at each other shocked.

"I thought they were gonna be training," Isaac said.

"Apparently not," said Jacob.

Later that night, the sky was black, the moon was full, and the air was eerie. Isaac and Jacob sat quietly on a couple boulders, while the others prepared for the séance. The two had been on the sidelines for the last few hours, trying to figure out how to deal with everything. Once again, they were doing something that they agreed they wouldn't do, connecting with spirits. Isaac was upset, not wanting to be involved with such foolishness to the point he didn't speak to anyone after finding out. Jacob was fearful. The closer it got to midnight, the more dark vibes he got from everyone, including Cameron. He wanted to say something to Isaac, but he assumed he was overreacting. Cameron, on the other hand, was rather excited about the whole thing; he even helped the others find wood and start the fire. This was the second time the three were divided because of their own beliefs. It seemed they had gotten over that issue, but seemingly they still had some things to deal with.

Isaac and Jacob continued to sit on the boulders, remaining quiet and to themselves. Jacob looked at his watch and saw it was ten minutes until midnight. He dropped his arm down and began to tap his left leg nervously. He sighed and looked up in the sky, staring at the moon. Eventually, Isaac looked at Jacob and groaned.

"We need to leave," Isaac said sternly. "I don't wanna do this stupid séance crap."

"I think it's a little too late to establish that," Jacob mentioned. "'Cause considering we've sat here for like three hours…it would be pointless to up and leave now."

Isaac turned away from Jacob and stared at the others, while they laughed and conversed by the fire. Isaac put his hands together and held them in front of his mouth, breathing through his nostrils.

"This…is…bull," he exclaimed. Jacob closed his eyes, when he sensed Cameron walking over to them. Jacob opened his eyes, sitting up with Isaac. Cameron stood in front of them with a frown on his face and his arms crossed.

"All right," Cameron started, "you guys have been sitting over here pouting for hours. What's the problem?"

"We're party poopers," Jacob said, trying to lighten up the situation.

"That's pretty obvious," Cameron responded. Isaac looked at him with disgust, standing up in Cameron's face. Cameron stared at him with slight shock, though still frowning, looking him up and down for a brief moment.

"You wanna know what the problem is?" Isaac asked. "I'll tell you. We wanna leave, ASAP."

Cameron's nostrils flared, while he uncrossed his arms and dropped them to his sides. He tightened his fists and got up closer to Isaac, standing in his face.

"It's not like I invited you anyway," he snapped. "You should've stayed home."

"Why? So you could come out here for your séance?" Isaac retorted. "Please."

Jacob watched them while they went back and forth, feeling the tension rise. Jacob hopped off the boulder he rested on and stood near the both of them, while they continued arguing.

"You guys wanna go? Fine, go. I'm not holding you back, am I?" Cameron asked sarcastically, throwing his arms out to his sides. Isaac's face turned red, while he began to breathe heavily and look at Cameron. Seeing this, Jacob jumped in.

"Uh guys, can we do this at home and not in public?" he suggested. "I don't think everybody needs to see our brotherly issues."

"Why not? I don't mind showing everyone who's the problem in the family," said Cameron, dropping his hands down again while staring at Isaac. Angered, Isaac pushed Cameron back in his chest, when he stumbled back.

"Hey! Stop that!" Jacob hollered, pushing Isaac away and glaring at him with a frown. In the heat of the moment, Cameron looked at Isaac and swung his right fist toward his face. Jacob grabbed his arm and stopped him.

"Don't touch me!!" Cameron yelled, when Isaac back away and Jacob held him back. The others heard the uproar and looked at them. Then, Liem walked toward them slowly.

"Cameron calm down," Jacob said looking at Cameron. Suddenly, dark auras began to surround Cameron's hands. He lowered his arms down and Jacob stared at them in shock. Cameron felt a strange energy radiating from his palms. Glancing down, Cameron saw the auras around his hands, lifting them up to his face.

"Cameron?" Jacob said. Cameron looked at him, his mouth opened and his eyes widened.

"Is everything all right?" asked Liem. The three looked over and saw Liem standing by them. He saw they were all breathing heavily, since they were fighting. Liem looked around at them and cleared his throat, when Cameron's hands stopped showing off the dark auras and he lowered them to his side.

"It's midnight, we're about to start," he said, glancing over at Cameron. "Are you ready Cam?"

Cameron looked over at Liem and swallowed, not really sure how to respond to him. He opened his mouth to speak, but no words came out. Jacob saw his struggle, seeing that he was still trying to figure out what just happened to him, and interceded.

"Is it okay if we watch?" he wondered, when Liem looked at him slowly. Liem cleared his throat again, smiling at Jacob.

"That's fine," Liem said with regret. "Well, we're starting…so, come on over."

Liem backed away from the three and turned around, changing his smile to an angered frown, walking back near the others. Cameron fixed the collar of his jacket and went in the direction Liem had gone in, while Isaac and Jacob hesitated. The two shared a short stare. Then, Jacob followed after Cameron, while Isaac sighed and walked up behind him. Liem got up to the other guys and they looked at each other, nodding in unison. The six began to gather sticks that hadn't been thrown into the fire and they placed them around the fire in the shape of a pentagram. Cameron walked over by them, watching the six walk around the fire, creating a circle. Cameron backed away from them and stood near a couple of trees, when Jacob walked by him and stopped. Jacob stared at Cameron, while he still had an awkward look of shock on his face. Isaac caught up to them and stood behind Jacob, when Jacob glared back at him. The three looked over at Liem and the others, while they lifted their arms up and out to their sides. Liem tilted his head back, looking up at the moon, and the wind began to blow through the area. Liem closed his eyes and lowered his head back down.

"Powers of the moon…flow through us," Liem began, while Isaac, Jacob, and Cameron watched him closely. Then, the others closed their eyes, as Liem reached out toward the fire with his right hand and touched it. Isaac and Jacob gasped in shock, seeing Liem hadn't felt any pain from the fire. Pulling his hand back, Liem had a small flame on his first finger. He bent down near the sticks formed in the shape of a pentagram and touched them, lighting them on the ground with the flame.

"I don't like the looks of this at all," Isaac whispered to Jacob.

"I don't either, but there isn't much we can do at this point," Jacob replied, watching Liem took a dagger out of his jacket pocket. Liem passed the dagger to Simon, who stood to his right, and he placed the dagger in the fire. Simon pulled the dagger from the fire and brought it to his hand, dragging it across his palm. Simon handed the dagger to Richard on his right, and he repeated the same actions that Simon performed. Liem watched Richard, as he passed the dagger over to Felix.

"My blood is the blood of yours," said Liem, while Felix took the dagger across his palm and passed it to Allen. Allen repeated what the others had done and passed the dagger to Alex, and he did the same.

"And yours, the blood of mine," Liem continued, when Alex passed the dagger to him. Liem took the dagger from Alex, and placed it over his left palm. Then, the others placed their bleeding palms over the flames, and it burned the blood off, sealing their palms closed. Isaac, Jacob, and Cameron continued watching them, not sure what to expect, while Liem continued chanting.

"Seep from thy wounds…in sickened gores," Liem spoke. He took the dagger across his palm and blood seeped out, "when powers rise to be defined."

Liem positioned his bleeding hand over the flames, touching them to his palm. Within moments, the flame burnt out and the entire area went black. Isaac and Jacob looked around slightly confused, while Cameron stood still next to them. Not a sound could be heard – *PHSST!!* A burst of blackish-blue fire shot up from the pit, startling Isaac and Jacob. Liem pulled his hand back from the fire, and the others lifted their arms back out to their sides. Cameron stared at the fire slightly mesmerized, when Liem lifted his head up. Jacob stared at the fire, feeling a strange presence within it, which was odd. Jacob began to analyze the flames, when suddenly he saw faint faces within them, which looked as if they were crying out for help. Jacob started to breathe heavily while he continued to stare at the fire, his heart beating rapidly. Isaac looked at Jacob, wondering what he saw that caused him to change his demeanor. Then, Liem closed his eyes and smirked, beginning another chant.

"Wie wir auf die Dunkelheit nennen," said Liem, "wir senden unsere Kräfte in Abgrund."

Jacob quickly looked at Liem, realizing he was speaking in German, but he wasn't sure what he was saying. Jacob stopped examining the fire and paid more attention to Liem, while he continued.

"Diese drei werden unser Opfer, nehmen Sie jetzt ihre Befugnisse dreimal," Liem finished. He lowered his head back down and opened his eyes, while the guys stared at him.

"Wie wir auf die Dunkelheit nennen, wir senden unsere Kräfte in Abgrund," the all said with Liem, when a dark aura rose from the flames. Isaac stared at this in shock, tapping Jacob on his shoulder.

"Do you see that!?!" he asked, looking at Jacob. But he didn't respond, being too focused on figuring out what they were chanting.

"Diese drei werden unser Opfer, nehmen Sie jetzt ihre Befugnisse dreimal," they finished again, when the dark aura began to swirl around the fire. Isaac looked at Cameron, who still seemed entranced by it all, while Jacob continued to analyze what they said. Eventually, Jacob figured it out, when they repeated the chant for a third time.

"As we call upon the darkness, we send our powers into abyss. These three will be our sacrifice, now take their powers thrice!"

Jacob snapped out of his focus and looked at Liem and the others. The dark aura turned into a shadow figure and rose above the flames.

"NO!!!" Jacob cried. The shadow figure charged at him, knocking him into the tree behind them. When Jacob hit the ground, he began to glow blue, with the glow leaving him and entering the shadow figure shortly afterward. This caught Cameron's attention and he looked back at Jacob, rushing to his aid with Isaac.

"Jacob!!" Cameron hollered, when he and Isaac kneeled by his side.

"You okay?" Cameron asked with concern, while he and Isaac

helped him to his feet. Jacob looked up and gasped, watching the shadow figure go toward Liem. The figure entered Liem's body and he began to glow blue, while he stared at Jacob with a smirk. When Liem stopped glowing, Isaac looked at him with a frown, stepping away from Jacob and tightening his fists.

"Liem!!" he yelled, rushing toward Liem and the others. Liem quickly dashed into the flames and vanished, with the flame burning out in an instant, leaving the area dark. Isaac stopped running toward them abruptly and Richard waved his hand at Isaac, knocking him back into Jacob and Cameron. The three fell over on the ground, and the five guys ran toward them. Cameron got up quickly and pulled Isaac and Jacob to their feet.

"Guys come on," he exclaimed, and the three rushed off into the trees.

"Follow them!" Simon cried. The five ran off after the three into the wooded area. Isaac, Jacob, and Cameron ran through the trees to escape, while the five warlocks chased after them. Simon raised his left hand and electrical shocks began to swirl around his palm. Then, he threw them at a tree in front of the brothers, causing the tree came crashing down. Cameron looked up and balled up his right fist.

"Isaac, Jacob watch out!" he screamed. The two glanced up and saw the tree dropping over them. Reacting hastily, Cameron thrust his fist into the tree and sent a vibrating shock through it, which caused it to explode, shattering to pieces. The three continued running, while Simon frowned at them and grumbled under his breath. Simon raised both his arms, electric shocks appeared in his palms, and he threw them forward at the brothers again. The shocks crossed in front of them rapidly and hit two trees on opposite sides of them, causing them to burst and collapse in front of them. Cameron grabbed Isaac and Jacob by their arms and dashed toward the branches, when the three slid under them. The trees slammed on the ground and the three jumped, rushing off again. Simon became enraged. He and the others leaped over the shattered trees, when he raised his hands again, this time throwing the shocks directly at the brothers. Isaac glanced back, seeing the shocks dashing toward them, when he swung his left hand out and sent the shocks back at Simon. The shocks hit Simon and he stopped abruptly, shaking uncontrollably.

"Ugh!!! Naaaahhhh!!!" he exclaimed. Simon burst into flames and exploded. The impact from the explosion sent a wave through the area, knocking the brothers out of the wooded area and into the open field, while it thrust the warlocks back. Isaac, Jacob, and Cameron flew out into the fields and hit the ground, rolling over on each other. Isaac pulled himself up and looked around, seeing they were near his truck. Isaac moved and pulled on Jacob and Cameron, while they sat up and looked at him.

"Come on guys, let's get outta here," he said. Suddenly, a loud warping noise was heard behind them, when a gust of wind swept through the area. The three looked over at the woods and saw the four remaining warlocks standing there. Isaac helped Jacob and Cameron up, and the three stared back at the warlocks.

"You're not going anywhere," Richard proclaimed. The four charged at them, while the three braced themselves for their attack. Cameron looked at Isaac and Jacob, while they watched the warlocks getting closer.

"Guys go," Cameron shouted. They looked at him with their eyebrows raised.

"What?! Are you crazy?!" Jacob exclaimed.

"Just go start the car, I'll catch up," he said. Isaac and Jacob looked at each other briefly; then, they ran off toward Isaac's truck. Cameron ran toward the warlocks, when Allen and Alex ganged up on him and knocked him down.

"Ugh!" he exclaimed. Jacob looked back and saw Cameron on the ground, while Allen and Alex stood over him. Jacob grabbed Isaac's arm and stopped him, when Isaac looked back at him confused.

"Wait," he said. *WHOOSH!!* Jacob flew off from Isaac and hit the ground. Isaac glanced over and saw Felix and Richard running toward him. Felix waved his hand and Isaac flew away from his truck and near the center of the field, hitting the ground on his back. While Isaac tried to get up, Felix charged at him and kicked him in his side, making Isaac tumbled over. Isaac quickly rebound himself and stood up, while Felix stood in front of him and braced himself.

Jacob got up from the ground, when Richard charged at him and knocked him back down. Richard tried to punch Jacob in his face, but he blocked him and kneed Richard in his stomach.

"Ugh," Richard groaned, when Jacob threw him off and got up. Richard composed himself and stood to his feet, staring at Jacob for a brief moment, only to charge at him quickly again. This time, he swung several punches at Jacob, while Jacob threw up his arms to block himself from Richard's attacks.

Cameron stood up from where he had fallen, when Allen ran toward him. Cameron hit Allen in his stomach, causing him to gag and bend over, while Alex ran up behind Cameron, wrapping his left bicep around his neck. Cameron tried to fight him off, but before he could, Allen regrouped and began to beat Cameron in his stomach and jaw. Seeing this, Jacob got distracted and Richard punched him in his face, knocking him down again. Richard stood over Jacob and took him by his shirt, pulling him up from the ground. Richard held Jacob by his neck and began to choke him, while Jacob grabbed his hands and tried to stop him.

While his brothers struggled, Isaac was dodging fire balls, while Felix continued to throw them at him rapidly. Isaac eventually waved his hand out and one of the fire balls went charging toward Jacob and Richard. Seeing the fire ball coming, Jacob struggled with Richard until it came directly toward him and hit him in his back.

"Ahh!!!" he cried, dropping Jacob on the ground and catching on fire. Jacob jumped up and did a side kick on Richard, which sent him flying away from him on the ground. Allen looked back and saw Richard burning and got sidetracked, giving Cameron an opening to grab Alex from behind his neck. Cameron tightened his arms around Alex's neck and twisted them, snapping Alex neck. Alex eyes rolled back into his head and he lost his grip on Cameron, as he threw him over his shoulders and over Allen. Allen watched in horror, while Alex body fell on top of Richard and he caught on fire.

"Alex!" he cried. Cameron smacked Allen in his left jaw, causing him to fall back on the ground. Cameron grabbed Allen by his shirt and swung him around, throwing him on to the others, catching him on fire.

"Ahhh!!!!" he screamed. Felix glared back for a moment and

realized he was the only one left, dropping his mouth and widening his eyes in fear. Looking back at Isaac, he narrowed his eyes at Felix and sent him flying toward the others using his mind. Felix fell on the others and the all burst into flames, while he screamed.

"Ugh…Ahh!!!!!" he cried. The four ignited and burnt to ashes before the brothers' eyes. The three ran to each other and stared at the burnt spot the warlocks bodies had left on the ground, breathing heavily. After looking at each other briefly, the three ran to Isaac's truck and left the area, driving off into the night.

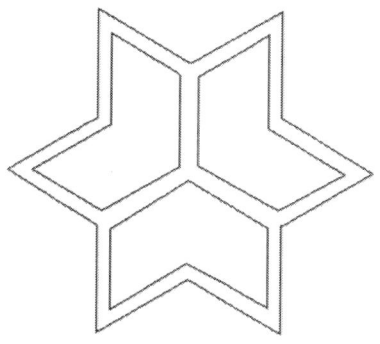

EVIL RISING

"**I KNEW SOMETHING WASN'T RIGHT. I KNEW IT.**" Isaac hollered, when he and Cameron rushed through the doors of the manor and entered the main hall. It was still dark outside, since it was around one o'clock in the morning. The two had been arguing back and forth the entire drive back from Westwick Park.

"Chill out Isaac…it's not like I know he was evil," Cameron said walking up to Isaac. "I didn't think he was going to trick me like that."

Jacob stepped into the manor and closed the front door, hanging his head down. Something felt different, but he couldn't figure out what it was. Jacob looked up at Isaac and Cameron, while they continued to argue in the middle of the hallway.

"Obviously not," Isaac exclaimed. "You need to pay attention to who you're befriending."

"Look, I said I was sorry," Cameron snapped. "How many times do you want me to say it?!"

"That's the point. No matter how many times you say it, it won't change anything. Because of you, we have a coven of warlocks after us!"

"You act like I did this on purpose!"

While the two bickered, Jacob's eyes remained shifty, while he continued to try and identify what had happened. Nothing had changed around him...it was something else. Eventually, Jacob widened his eyes, staring at Isaac and Cameron with an expression of worry on his face. Jacob opened his mouth to speak, but he hesitated, while Isaac and Cameron kept yelling at each other.

This is ridiculous!" Isaac groaned. "Now we have to fight off not only the dark forces, but these warlocks too! As if I didn't have enough to deal with already."

"See, here you go again," Cameron countered. "It isn't about anybody else, it's only about you! You're so selfish!"

"Guys," Jacob tried to interrupt, but his voice couldn't be heard over his brother's screaming.

"I'm selfish?! And this is coming from the one who had his head up his butt, while his evil friend plotted against us!"

"Oh really?! Isaac, the only person who had their head up their butt is you, but that's most of the time."

"Guys," Jacob tried again, this time a little louder. But still, Isaac and Cameron continued to argue amongst each other, not even noticing Jacob trying to get their attention. The two got up in each other's faces, as if they were about to get physical.

"You know me Cameron; you have no idea who you're dealing with," Isaac threatened.

"Please, if you think I'm scared of you, you better think twice, 'cause I'm not," said Cameron. Jacob began to shake angrily, with his tolerance for them decreasing little by little, until he finally snapped.

"GUYS!" Jacob shouted, when Isaac and Cameron looked at him with frowns, their foreheads wrinkled.

"What?!" the two hollered back, throwing their arms up. Jacob stared at them both, breathing heavily.

"My powers are gone," Jacob revealed. Isaac and Cameron dropped their mouths open and widened their eyes in shock. That was impossible. How could that have happened? Isaac and Cameron looked at each other; then, they turned back toward Jacob.

"What?!" Cameron exclaimed.

"Why didn't you say something?" Isaac asked. Jacob huffed and crossed his arms, frowning at Isaac and Cameron.

"I tried," he said. "But maybe if the both of you would've shut up with all that bickering, you would've heard me."

"You can blame that on Isaac, he seems to love hearing himself talk," Cameron said, when Isaac looked over at him with a frown.

"Don't start with me Cameron," Isaac yelled, pushing up on Cameron again. Cameron pushed Isaac back off him, when Isaac quickly retaliated and pushed him back. Black auras appeared around Cameron's hands again and he tightened his fists, charging at Isaac.

"Stop it!" Jacob hollered, rushing in between Isaac and Cameron. Feeling a strange dark presence over himself, Cameron looked down at his hands and saw the dark auras surrounding them again. Cameron stepped away from Isaac and Jacob, staring at his palms with his eyes widened.

"Oh no…not again," he exclaimed, while Isaac and Jacob stared at him. "What's happening to me?"

"Hmm…you've apparently been around the darkness too long," said Isaac, when Jacob looked at him angrily.

"Isaac, would you shut up," Jacob snapped. Isaac looked at Jacob with a frown, and the auras quickly subsided from Cameron's hands.

"First of all," Jacob started again, "this isn't the way we should be treating each other."

Isaac looked off and rolled his eyes, while Cameron put his head down, feeling ashamed.

"Second, we need to be trying to figure out what's going on."

"There's a lot going on," Isaac said, staring at Cameron. "We have warlocks after us, Cameron is developing dark powers, and you've lost yours."

"Yes, but there has to be a logical explanation for all this," Jacob mentioned. Isaac stared at Jacob, confused by where he was going with his thought. Isaac exhaled and crossed his arms, looking at Jacob and Cameron.

"Okay, where do we start?" he asked.

"I'm not exactly sure," Jacob said, placing his hand on his chin. Jacob walked past Isaac and Cameron, making his way to the dining room. He placed his hands on the table's edges and sighed. Isaac and Cameron walked closer to Jacob, when he looked back and turned toward them.

"All I know is whatever happened had something to do with that invocation," Jacob said, looking at Isaac and Cameron.

"What makes you think that?" Cameron wondered. "The only thing that happened was darkness shot out of the fire and attacked you."

Jacob looked at Cameron and remembered the spell the warlocks said, right before the darkness attacked them.

"Yes, but they said a spell…right before it came out."

Isaac tightened his arms – still crossed – and stood up straight, staring at Jacob seriously.

"So what are you saying?" Isaac wondered.

"The spell they said, it was in German. I figured that out by the second time they chanted. But it took me a while to figure out what they were saying."

"Okay, what was it?" Cameron asked. Taking a deep breath, Jacob began to replay the spell over in his mind.

"It was like: wie wir auf – die Dunk-elh-eit nennun," Jacob started, looking up at the ceiling, while Isaac and Cameron stared at him lost. "Wir seden unsere – Kräfte in Abgr–"

"In English, Jacob! In English," Isaac snapped, startling Jacob, when he looked down at him and Cameron.

"Oh, my bad…y'all could tell I was struggling," Jacob said with a smile.

"We know," Isaac and Cameron exclaimed in unison. Jacob looked at the two with a frown, raising his eyebrows.

"Don't do me, okay?" said Jacob.

"Can you finish what you were saying please?" Cameron asked, staring at Jacob. Clearing his throat, Jacob put his hand on his head and closed his eyes, trying to recall the spell after he had translated it in his mind.

"It was on the lines of: we call upon – the darkness, we send our powers into abyss."

Isaac and Cameron looked at Jacob, waiting for him to finish the spell, while he struggled remembering it. Jacob opened his eyes and looked down, repeating the spell.

"Then they finished it with: these three will be our sacrifice, now take their powers thrice."

Isaac and Cameron widened their eyes in shock, staring at Jacob. That was it. The spell was not only to take Jacob's powers, but theirs as well. The two looked at each other, remembering the chant was said three times, once for each of them. Looking back at Jacob, Isaac uncrossed his arms and placed his hand on his forehead.

"This is bad," he said. "This means the spell was read for all of us."

"But we didn't lose our powers though," Cameron brought up, while Isaac shook his head.

"No, we didn't."

"That's because when the spell was finished, the darkness attacked me first," Jacob told them. "I think that's when my powers were taken."

"So how are they doing it...with the darkness?" Cameron asked.

"Possibly, but I was using my power the entire time they were chanting. I'm thinking because of that, my power were vulnerable."

"So we can't use our powers against them?" Cameron questioned.

"I would hold off, at least until we figure out exactly what's going on. Besides, that may be best for you too…at least until figure out why you're exhibiting dark magic."

"What the heck are we supposed to do in the meantime?!" Cameron cried. Isaac and Jacob stared at each other; then, they looked back at Cameron.

"I think we should hit the Book of Magic," Isaac suggested. Jacob nodded in agreement. Then, the three hurried up the stairs to the attic. Once they made it to the attic, the three stepped by the Book of Magic, standing side by side while Isaac flipped through the pages quickly.

"There's gotta be something in here about what we can do," he said, while Jacob and Cameron looked along the pages with him.

"What if there isn't?" Cameron asked. Then, the three reached several blank pages in the Book.

"There's nothing in here," said Jacob. The three stepped back from the Book, while Isaac placed his right hand on his chin, deep in though.

"Great, now the Book can't even help us," Cameron exclaimed, throwing his hands in the air. Then, Jacob widened his eyes, looking at Isaac and Cameron. He had an idea. Isaac noticed his change in mood, staring at him confused.

"What is it?" Isaac wondered. Jacob walked back up to the Book and stared at the blank pages for a moment. Then, he glanced back at his brothers with a smile.

"So…you know how dad has been communicating to us through the Book's blank pages, right?"

"Yeah, so?" said Cameron, staring at Jacob, wondering what his point could be. Jacob turned around toward Isaac and Cameron.

"Obviously he can hear what's going on," Jacob mentioned. "So I'm thinking…maybe we can communicate with him."

"How are we gonna do that?" asked Isaac, when Jacob turned back toward the Book

"Talk to him," said Jacob. Isaac and Cameron stared at each other, stepping beside Jacob, when he placed his hands on the outer sides of the Book.

"Hey um, dad…uh, father," Jacob struggled to find the right words, while Isaac and Cameron stared at him confused.

"Jacob…it's just dad," Cameron mentioned. "No need to talk all cryptic."

Jacob looked at Cameron with a frown.

"You're right; it is our dad…whose spirit lives in a book!" Jacob snapped, surprising Cameron. Isaac stared at him and Cameron, rolling his eyes and placing his hand over his forehead.

"Oh gosh," he said. Jacob blinked his eyes at Isaac, looking back down at the Book, continuing to speak to their father's spirit.

"So, we were just wondering…do you know anything about the Xaviors or the dark forces?" Jacob asked, while the three stared at the blank pages. Five seconds…ten seconds…fifteen seconds passed and they hadn't gotten a response yet.

"I think your theory failed," Cameron said, while Jacob frowned at him. Suddenly, the Book shook on the podium and flipped through a couple of blank pages. Isaac, Jacob, and Cameron gazed at the Book, when their father began to respond to Jacob's question:

> Unfortunately, I don't know much. However, I do believe that the Xaviors are connected to the dark forces. The name Xavior also sounds strangely familiar, but I can't seem to remember where I've heard it.

Jacob looked back at Isaac and Cameron, smirking at them both.

"Ha, I was right," said Jacob. Cameron rolled his eyes, when Isaac stepped closer to the book.

"Does warlocks who steal others' powers ring any bells?" Isaac asked. The previous words their father had written disintegrated into the pages, as other appeared on the pages:

> Yes, that's it! The Xaviors were infamous for stealing magical beings powers. The only thing that is concerning is that they were expunged by a coven of witches they tried to eliminate.

Jacob turned around toward Isaac and Cameron and placed his hand on his chin, frowning up his face.

"Okay, so that helped us somewhat," he said.

"Yeah, but now I'm even more worried," said Isaac. "If dad remembered that the Xaviors were killed off, how did they come back?"

"The same way we did," Cameron jumped in. "No one knew we existed, and they still don't."

Isaac turned away from Jacob and Cameron, shaking his head.

"That still doesn't help us figure out how to fight them off," he said. Jacob and Cameron stared at Isaac, while he paced back and forth. Then, he stopped to glance back at them.

"Well, we can't use our powers against them," Cameron said. "That's most likely how they'll take them."

"We think that's how they'll take them," Jacob interrupted, looking at Cameron.

"Regardless whether we use our powers or not, the spell is already in motion to take ours too," Isaac stated, walking back over to Jacob and Cameron.

"So what do we do?" Cameron asked, raising his eyebrows. Then, the three heard the Book shake on the podium again and they glanced back, seeing their father had written something else:

There is one thing you can do to fight back, but it would require me showing you three how to fabricate molecular manipulation.

Isaac, Jacob, and Cameron stared at the Book, looking back at each other with a nod.

"Okay, how do we do it?" asked Jacob. Without warning, the Book of Magic slammed close and popped back open, flipping through the pages quickly. The Book stopped on the page of a potion recipe.

"All right, so it's a potion," Jacob said.

"This looks like it may be our only option at the moment," Isaac mentioned. Jacob walked around the other side of the Book and stopped, when Cameron twisted up his mouth.

"That's great, but how are we supposed to find these ingredients?" Cameron wondered. Then, the wooden cabinet on the left of the attic flew open, when the three looked at it in shock. Isaac, Jacob, and Cameron stepped to the middle attic, looking back and forth at each other.

"That answers that question," Jacob said.

The three had their work cut out for them. They decided not to use their powers and use an alternative way to fight back. Though the plan seemed scarce, they didn't have any other options. The three had finished setting up to make the potion, after having a few hours of rest. They had pulled out a small round table and placed it in the middle of the floor. They had also laid out different utensils for measuring and containing the potion, with a medium sized cauldron next to it all. Isaac stood near the table, Cameron was stood by the cabinet of ingredients, and Jacob was next to the Book. Jacob stretched out his arms and cracked his knuckles together, titling his head left and right to pop his neck.

"Alright guys, operation first potion is ago," he said. Isaac nodded at him and Cameron gave thumbs up. Jacob stared at the Book and read off the first portion of instructions.

"The first things first, we need a pot of boiling water," said Jacob.

"We have a *cauldron* of boiling water," said Isaac. Jacob looked up at him with his lips puckered and twisted up.

"Great," said Jacob, rolling his eyes. "We also need a candle lighter and measuring spoons."

"All here," Isaac informed him.

"All right then, let's get started," Jacob said, glancing down at the Book.

"Ready when you are," Cameron agreed.

"The first two things we need are: two eagle feathers and a tea spoon of poppy seeds," Jacob said, looking at Cameron. With a nod, he turned toward the cabinet and searched back and forth for the poppy seeds.

"Poppy seeds...poppy seeds...poppy seeds," Cameron said over and over until he, "found 'em!"

Cameron pulled out a small vial of poppy seeds and threw it toward Isaac. Isaac caught the vial and opened it, pouring the seeds on to a teaspoon, dropping them into the cauldron. Cameron turned back toward the cabinet and took out a jar of eagle feathers, holding it out toward Isaac. Isaac took the jar and opened it, taking out two feathers and throwing them into the mixture.

"The next ingredient–" Jacob paused. He read the next ingredient to himself and gagged. Isaac and Cameron stared at him with their eyebrows raised, when Jacob swallowed, trying to keep his composure.

"What?" Isaac and Cameron wondered.

"–A table spoon of troll snot," Jacob exclaimed. Turning toward the cabinet, Cameron looked across the shelf and took out a jar of troll snot, some of dripped on his hand from the lid. Cameron dropped his mouth open and broadened his eyes, slightly gagging.

"Eew, yuck," he exclaimed. "That smells like butt!"

Cameron handed the jar to Isaac and wiped his hand off on a towel from the table, while Isaac took a spoon and scooped out the snot, pouring it into the cauldron.

"Now we need to set the ingredients on fire," Jacob told them. Cameron picked the candle lighter up from the table, standing near the cauldron. Cameron clicked the candle lighter and lit the ingredients on fire, when a burst of flame shot up in his and Isaac's faces.

"Whoa!" the two exclaimed. Isaac and Cameron dropped on the floor away from the cauldron, while Jacob stared at them, blinking his eyes.

"Really guys…really?" said Jacob. The two stood to their feet and walked back toward the cauldron, while Cameron leaned over it. The contents of the mixture were melted into an orange colored liquid.

"What's next?" he asked, looking up at Jacob. Jacob placed his hands on the Book and read on.

"At this point the mixture should be an orange liquid," he said.

"Check," Isaac and Cameron said together.

"Okay, so the last thing we need to add is a bumpy beetle," he said, glancing back up at them. Cameron went back to the cabinet and took out a large bottle of bumpy beetles, handing it to Isaac. Isaac took out a beetle and threw it into the cauldron, which caused a spark and smoke to shoot up from it. Isaac sat the jar down on the table and closed it. Jacob picked up the Book and walked over to his side, when Cameron stepped back over to the table. The three of them stood together, staring at the Book.

"The potion should be done now and have a blood red color," Jacob said. The three leaned over the cauldron, seeing the mixture was still orange. Isaac, Jacob, and Cameron stepped back from the cauldron and looked at the Book, running over the instructions again. Then, Jacob placed the Book down on the edge of the table and crossed his arms.

"What could we have missed?" he wondered.

"It doesn't look like we missed anything," said Isaac. "We put in the poppy seeds, the eagle feathers, the troll snot–"

"Can't forget that troll snot," Cameron interrupted while shaking his head and twisting up his face in disgust. Isaac and Jacob looked at Cameron with a serious stare.

"Then, we melted the ingredients and added the bumpy beetle," Jacob added, glancing back at the Book. "I'm not getting why the potion isn't blood red yet."

Isaac began to skim over the ingredients, when he saw small fine print under the larger portion of the potion materials.

"Oh," he exclaimed.

"What?" said Jacob, raising his eyebrows. Isaac looked at them and pointed to the small print under the main instructions.

"If the potion remains orange, add a hawk of witch spit," Isaac read. Jacob and Cameron stared at him; then, the three stepped back from the table and stared at the cauldron. Isaac and Jacob exhaled in unison, hearing Cameron clearing his throat. Looking to their right, Isaac and Jacob watched Cameron step back toward the table, when he leaned over the cauldron a little.

"Cameron don–" before Jacob could finish, Cameron spit in the cauldron and the potion began to bubble up, when he and Isaac rushed over to the table. Eventually, the bubbling severed and the potion turned blood red. Isaac and Jacob stared at Cameron again, while he nodded his head with a smirk.

"Now that...is some powerful spit," said Cameron, while Isaac and Jacob twisted up their faces.

"Cameron, shut up," Isaac and Jacob said together. Isaac and Jacob walked away from the table and into the middle of the attic, while Cameron started putting the potion into small vials.

"All right, we have the potion," Isaac started, "but how are we supposed to find where the Xaviors are?"

Cameron looked at Isaac and Jacob.

"We could always go back to Westwick Park," Cameron suggested.

"Why would we do that," Isaac countered. "That's suicide."

"Well, if that's how you're looking at it, no matter how we find them will be suicide," Jacob mentioned. Cameron filled up the last vial on the table and looked turned toward Isaac and Jacob. Then, he had a thought.

"Hey, I have an idea," he said, when Isaac and Jacob looked at him. "I think we should go after Liem's older brother, Baine."

"What?!" Isaac and Jacob exclaimed. Cameron let out a heavy sigh, walking over to his brothers.

"If Jacob's theory about them taking our powers is correct, Liem is expecting us to go after him so he can take ours too."

"So…why should we go after his brother?" Isaac wondered.

"Because, he wouldn't see us coming," Cameron said. Jacob looked at Cameron with smile, agreeing with his idea.

"Cameron that's–that's genius!" Jacob exclaimed. Isaac looked at Jacob with his eyebrows raised, when Jacob stood by Cameron's side.

"Okay…I'm obviously the only one who's still lost," said Isaac.

"Don't you get it," Jacob started, "Liem is the one who my powers transferred into. So, Baine wouldn't be able to see us coming."

Isaac stared at the two with a serious stare, nodding in agreement.

"I see what you mean," Isaac said. "Well, let's start scrying then…shall we?"

A quarter past seven that night, the three drove down a dark and deserted road, following where their scrying crystal led them. They were on their way to a cave, where the crystal showed them Baine was residing. They were a little on edge, not knowing what to expect, only hoping that their assumption was accurate. Continuing down the road, they turned off on an exit and drove down another dark road, pulling up near a black lake with several willow trees all around. Isaac parked the car and turned it off, while he and Cameron looked around. Isaac looked at them and groaned, as Jacob looked at him.

"Okay, we're here," Isaac said with a wary tone.

"Don't sound so excited," Cameron commented, when Jacob elbowed him in his side. Isaac and Cameron began to look around the area again, when Jacob let out a groan of annoyance and snatched off his seat belt.

"All right, I'm growing a beard over here...let's go guys," he exclaimed, jumping out of the truck. Isaac and Cameron looked at Jacob, watching him along the dark path near the lake quickly. Isaac and Cameron leaped out of the truck and caught up to Jacob.

"For someone who doesn't have any powers, you sure are rushing into it," said Isaac.

"You know just as well as I do that isn't the reason I'm going so fast," Jacob mentioned.

"Then, why are you," Cameron wondered. Jacob stopped abruptly and turned around toward Isaac and Cameron, when they stopped in front of him.

"Had it not occurred to you that Liem may realize we're going after Baine and inform him of our approach?"

Isaac and Cameron looked at each other, glaring back at Jacob.

"That had been on my mind the entire ride here," Isaac said.

"I think it's best we don't think that way," Cameron suggested. "For all we know he could still know nothing."

"All the more reason to move quickly," said Jacob. The three started walking down the path, moving past the lake, arriving near a dark entrance.

"This looks like the mouth of the cave," said Isaac, while he and Cameron walked closer. Jacob stepped toward the opening and hunched down slightly, peeking inside.

"Yeah, I think this is it," he agreed.

"We should stick together. We don't know what to expect," Isaac said.

"Okay," Cameron said with a nod. He pulled out a flash light and they slowly entered into the cave. It became overwhelmingly cold and the striking scent of mold filled the air, while the three went deep into the cave. The sounds of water dripping echoed through the caverns, like thousands of leaking water faucets. Isaac and Cameron looked back and forth for a path, while Jacob stayed close behind them. After a while, every corner they turned seemed to look the same, like they were going in circles. Eventually, Jacob stopped and exhaled with a loud grunt, when Isaac and Cameron and stared at him in shock.

"Shhh!" they exclaimed. Jacob crossed his arms.

"Oh, excuse me...let me not disturb you two from your train of thought," Jacob remarked.

"No, we could be heard," Isaac said, throwing his arms up. Jacob placed his left hand on his hip and twisted up his mouth, while Cameron continued to look around.

"Well in case you hadn't noticed, no one here," Jacob said. "And I have a feeling if they were, we would've been caught by now."

Suddenly, a flame appeared out of nowhere on a torch, a far off from where they stood. Cameron looked up and tapped Isaac on his shoulder, when the three stared at the burning torch with a sigh of relief.

"Come on," said Cameron. They walked toward the fire, entering a condensed hallway, slightly warmer than the caverns. Making their way up to the torch, Isaac, Jacob, and Cameron looked to their left and saw a large, dark open space. The three walked into the middle of the area and stopped, looking around for a path to follow. Without warning, a circle of torches lit up rapidly around them, and a large white pentagram appeared beneath them. The three stepped back from each other and stared at the ground, hearing a loud crumbling noise to the left of the area. Looking over, they saw a small, door shaped cavity revealing itself. The pentagram vanished from beneath them and they came closer together, staring at the entryway across from them.

"That was weird," said Cameron.

"And I'm sure it's about to get even weirder," Jacob said, while they stayed close and made their way into the next hall. The three moved through the hallway slowly, entering into the throne room of the Xaviors' cave. Stepping in hesitantly, Isaac, Jacob, and Cameron looked around the area seeing two lit torches – several feet apart – on both sides of the room. The three stepped away from each other and examined the room, coming back together in the middle of the floor.

"I don't think anybody's in here," Isaac said.

"Think again," a voice was heard in front of them. The three looked toward the other side of the room, seeing a faint figure within the shadows, sitting at the throne. The figure stood up and stepped out of the shade, revealing he was Baine. Baine stood in front of the three with a smirk, while they stared at him in slight shock.

"Nice to finally meet all of you in person...Isaac, Jacob...and Cameron, again of course," said Baine. They continued to stare at him, while he stood calmly before them, showing no signs of frustration. The three were on edge, not knowing what to expect from Baine's calm demeanor. Isaac, Jacob, and Cameron stepped away from Baine, when Jacob reached into his jacket pocket and held a vial of the molecular potion in his hand. Baine watched him closely, still smirking at them, while they frowned at him.

"You must be Baine," said Isaac.

"In the flesh," Baine said with a short bow. "I'm surprised the three of you showed up here like this. Most covens we go after try to escape us once we've initiate our first attack."

"We're not most covens," Jacob snapped.

"Yes Jacob, I know you're not."

Isaac, Jacob, and Cameron stared at Baine, slightly confused by his comment, while he chuckled under his breath. Their hearts began to beat rapidly, while they braced themselves.

"Too bad no one will ever know," Baine said. Jacob lowered his eyebrows and flared his nostrils.

"We'll see about that!" he exclaimed. Jacob pulled the vial out of his pocket and hurled the potion at Baine, but he managed to catch it in his palm, right before it made contact. Baine lifted the potion up in front of his face and moved it between his index finger and thumb.

"It's amazing what omniscience can do for you...isn't it?" he asked with a sneer. The three stared at him with their mouths dropped and eyes widened. Baine laughed at them and glanced at the potion.

"Hmm...a molecular manipulator," Baine said. "Has the power to rupture molecules, until they combust. Pretty nifty if you ask me."

Baine glanced back at Isaac, Jacob, and Cameron, while they tensed up. Then, Baine tossed the potion at them and it exploded after hitting the ground, knocking the three back into the wall.

"Ugh," they exclaimed, rolling over on each other. Baine laughed again, echoing through the area, while the three struggled to their feet. Standing up, Isaac reached in his pants and grabbed a vial to throw at Baine, but Jacob stopped him. Seeing this, Baine shook his head and waved his first finger in front of himself.

"Tsk, tsk, tsk…I wouldn't try anymore of those if I were you," he said, when Isaac let go of the potion and swallowed. "You see, I know your every move. You can't do anything that I won't be ready for."

"So, Liem did get my power to you," Jacob thought aloud. Baine glared at him.

"Not necessarily," he said. "I already had this power…stole it from a wizard some years ago."

"Then, what did you take my power for?!" Jacob exclaimed. Baine stared at the three with a slight frown, stepping closer to them.

"You really wanna know?" Baine asked. "A few months ago, Liem sensed the connection between three powerful witches. He wasn't sure who you were, but after I had a vision, we got a glimpse of the great power that rests inside you three."

Baine turned his back toward the brothers and exhaled, while they stood still behind him.

"We knew it wasn't going to be easy taking your powers, but what was more interesting to us was why three witches would come into their powers so late in life. Of course, I knew we would eventually figure it out, but my wisdom alone wasn't enough. After Liem acquired Jacob's power, that's when we figured out exactly who you were."

Baine turned back around toward the three with a smirk on his face

"You are descendants of Samuel Blackwood, who referred to himself as Samuel Weltrinch before his death. You three are the abominations of the Weltrinch line."

Isaac, Jacob, and Cameron stared at Baine with their eyes widened in shock. He wasn't supposed to know that. No one was, according to what their father told them. Keeping that secret was crucial to their survival. Baine stared at the three with an evil grin, while they stayed closed to each other.

"Surprised I figured it out?" Baine wondered. "You shouldn't be. I mean, did you really think you would be able to go on your merry way without anyone finding out?"

"It seemed that way," Isaac spoke, breaking his silence. "But what's the point of you telling us that? What are you going to do about it?"

"Oh Isaac, why so eager to die?" Baine commented. Then, he waved his hand and the three flew back into the wall, falling on the ground again. Baine walked up to them and stopped, while the looked up at him from the ground.

"Here's the deal," he started again, "the spell is already in motion to take the rest of your powers, but we can do this the easy way…or the hard way."

The three stood up and stared at Baine.

"Which way is the easy way," Jacob asked, staring at Baine.

"The easy way is actually very simple. Isaac will willingly give his power to us, and Cameron…will join our side, to belong with the darkness."

"What?!" the three exclaimed.

"I will never join you and Liem," Cameron snapped. Baine chuckled and shook his head, putting his head down.

"Uh ah Cameron, you may want to watch what you say," Baine said, lifting his head up. With another rapid thrust of his hand, Isaac and Jacob flew to the other side of the room, rolling over on the floor.

"Guys," Cameron exclaimed, rushing over to them. Before he got to them, Baine grabbed him by his right wrist and held him back. Cameron stopped and stared at Baine angrily.

"You must have already forgotten our handshake," Baine said, staring at Cameron's palm with a smirk. Then, the two main lines furthest from Cameron's thumb turned black, when Baine chuckled under his breath.

"What are you talking about?" said Cameron, as he snatched his hand away from Baine.

"Look at the palm of your hand," said Baine. Cameron stared at his palm, seeing that two of his major hand lines were black. Cameron stared at Baine in shock, when he took Cameron's hand and looked at him sternly.

"I cursed you, giving you three chances to switch sides freely, without any harm being done to you or anyone else. But you've already gotten two strikes against you."

Baine smirked at Cameron again, pointing to the first line on his palm.

"Your heart line turned black first because you weren't emotionally prepared to perform the invocation with Liem as you should have."

Baine moved down Cameron's hand, pointing to his second line.

"Your head line turned black second because you're not mentally ready to join forces with Liem and me."

Baine moved down to the last line on Cameron's palm and stared at him, while Cameron breathed heavily.

"Your last line…is your life line. If you reject us again, your life will end," Baine said quietly, while he stared at Cameron. "Keep that in mind."

Baine grabbed Cameron by his shirt and threw him on the other side of the room with Isaac and Jacob. The three began to get up, when Baine walked back toward the center of the room, sighing deeply.

"Since you three obviously don't like the easy way," Baine said, turning toward the brothers, "I'll disclose the hard way."

Isaac, Jacob, and Cameron finally stood up, when Baine looked grinned at them maliciously.

"We will kill your loved ones, take your powers, and expose you to the Wizards of the Wise."

The three stared at Baine in shock, while laughed at their expressions.

"You wouldn't," Isaac said, staring at Baine.

"Oh…but we would," he said. "You have until midnight to make a decision or else we'll make it for you."

"We'll never give our powers to you," Isaac snapped.

"Just make sure you don't use them against me," Baine said, "or any of my minions."

Baine lifted his arms in front of him, placing his palms close together. Then, a black blob appeared between them, when Baine began to mold it telepathically.

"You wanna know the amazing thing about this power?" he asked, while the brothers stared at him. "I can create anything with it, I call it golem procreation. I mold darkness and clay, and I can create any type of creature I want."

The three continued to watch Baine, while he molded the blob into a long-limbed, skeletal beast. With a smirk, Baine slammed his palms together, and squashed the blob, startling Isaac, Jacob, and Cameron. Abruptly, several long-limbed beasts appeared around them, while Baine smirked and crossed his arms. The three stared at the creatures fearfully, while Baine laughed under his breath.

"I'd love to stay and play...but I have some work to get started on," Baine said, turning away from them. As darkness surrounded him, Baine looked back at the brothers with his hand on his chin.

"Don't forget, you have 'til midnight. Enjoy the Limbers."

Saying nothing more, Baine shimmered off, when the Limbers lifted their heads up and opened their eyes, revealing luminous yellow irides. Without hesitation, Isaac, Jacob, and Cameron ran out of the throne room and entered the hallway, while the Limbers watched them run off.

"EEEEYAAHHH!!!" the Limbers screeched, rushing after them. Once they got back to the pentagram chamber, the three stopped in the middle of the floor, and the Limbers leaped from the hallway, blocking the exits in the area. The brothers moved closer together, staring at the Limbers.

"Guys, we have to fight them in order to get outta here," Jacob said.

"Yeah that's easy for you to say," said Isaac. "You don't have powers that can still be taken."

The Limbers began to walk toward them slowly.

"EEEEEYAAAHHHHH!!!" one of them screamed, stepping toward Jacob. Reaching into his jacket pocket, Jacob took out a vial and tossed it at the Limber. The vial hit the Limber in its face and caused it to stumble back.

"KAAARRGHH!!! KAAARRRGHH!!!" the Limber whined, falling back and bursting into flames. Seeing this, the other Limbers went wild and rushed up on the brothers and knocked them away from each other. Isaac fell back in the center of the room, when two Limbers came toward him. Isaac got up and quickly threw a vial at the closest Limber to him, hitting it directly in its chest, as it burst into flames.

"KAAARRGHH!!!" the Limber cried. Quickly retaliating, the other Limber swung its arm at Isaac and smacked him into the wall. The Limber grabbed Isaac by his neck, slamming him into the wall with its claw. The Limber began to squeeze Isaac by his throat and choke him, while he tried to fight them off.

Jacob hit the ground in the far left corner of the chamber, when two Limbers cornered him. Jacob stood to his feet and stared at the Limbers, taking out his last two potion vials. But one of the Limbers stretched out its arm and knocked them out of his hands, shattering the vials. Jacob stared at the broken vials and glanced back at the Limbers, while they shifted their shoulders to attack. When the Limbers swung at him, Jacob jumped down and rolled on the ground, dodging their attack. Jumping to his feet, Jacob turned around and got hit in the face by one of the Limbers, which knocked him to the ground.

Cameron rolled over on the ground and hopped up, seeing three Limbers gaining up on him. Reacting rapidly, Cameron grabbed three vials from his jacket and threw them at the Limbers, causing all of them to blow up.

"KAAARRRGGHHH!!!" they exclaimed. Cameron glanced over and saw that Isaac and Jacob were both in danger of the Limbers.

"Guys," he cried, rushing over to Jacob to aid him. But before he even made it half way, a Limber's arm grabbed him by his leg, snatching him back on the ground. The Limber slammed down on Cameron and punched him in his stomach.

"Ugh," he groaned, while the Limber continued to hit him and slam him into the ground. Isaac looked over and saw this, though his vision was slightly blurred from his eyes watering.

"Cameron," he muttered, trying harder to break free of the Limbers. Cameron tried to get the Limber off of him, but it over powered him with its strength. Cameron knew if he used his powers against it he would beat it, but he didn't want to lose them. When the Limber punched him in his face, Cameron's glasses flew off and his sight became unclear. Cameron looked were Jacob was, seeing the Limbers lift him up and slam him against the wall.

"No!" he yelled. The Limber grabbed Cameron by his neck and tried to choke him. He looked over again, seeing something blocking his view of Jacob. Glancing up, Cameron realized it was a torch light. While the Limber kept its grasp on him, Cameron hastily grabbed the torch and snatched it out of the ground. Cameron swung the torch at the Limber and burned it in its face.

"KAAARRRGGHHH!!!!" the Limber screeched. Cameron pushed it off of him and rolled over, grabbing his glasses. Cameron jumped up and rushed over to Jacob, thrashing the Limbers, which caused them to drop Jacob. Jacob fell on the ground and the Limbers rolled over, lifting themselves up. The Limbers stared at Cameron, when he spun the torch around himself and burned them.

"KAAARRGHHHH!!!" the Limbers groaned and burst into flames, collapsing on the ground. Isaac finally broke free from the Limbers grasp and kicked them off of him, forcing them over on their backs. Isaac held his throat and panted heavily, when Cameron ran over to him and helped him to his feet. The three remaining Limbers got up and looked at Isaac and Cameron, as the two rushed over to Jacob. Cameron stuck the torch in the ground; then, he and Isaac pulled Jacob up, trying to wake him.

"Jacob, Jacob come on," Cameron exclaimed, staring at Jacob. When Jacob regained consciousness, Isaac looked back and saw the Limbers coming toward them.

"We've got company," he said, tapping Cameron on his shoulder. Cameron let go of Jacob and grabbed the torch again, while Jacob sat up and looked around. Cameron swung the torch at the Limbers, stopping them from coming toward him, fearing they would be burned.

"Guys go, head out," Cameron shouted, when Isaac helped Jacob to his feet. Isaac and Jacob made their way toward the exit caverns, while the Limbers stared at them angrily. When they tried to follow them, Cameron smacked them with the torch, knocking them over into the wall. Then, Cameron ran off with the torch in his hand, following the path to catch up with Isaac and Jacob.

"EEEEYYAAAHHHH!!!" the Limbers growled, jumping up and running after them.

Outside the cave, Isaac and Jacob were running past the lake, when Cameron caught up with them. Cameron tossed the torch into the lake, when they reached Isaac's truck. Cameron looked back and saw the Limbers galloping toward them, widening his eyes in shock.

"Come on guys, let's go!" he exclaimed. The three hopped in the truck and Isaac started it. Pulling the car in reverse, Isaac slammed on his foot on the accelerator, zooming off down the road. The Limbers reached the parking area and stopped, staring at Isaac's truck angrily.

"EEEYAAAHHHHH!!!" the Limbers screamed, dashing off into the night.

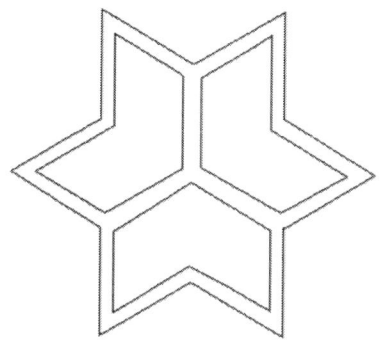

PROTECTION

THINGS HAD JUST GOTTEN WORSE in a matter of hours. Baine revealed that he and Liem knew the brothers true identities, being descendants from the Weltrinch line. On top of that, he threatened to harm their loved ones and expose them if they didn't surrender before midnight. Having one brother short of his powers already, Isaac, Jacob, and Cameron were at a standstill.

The three were speeding down the highway, while the sky darkened above them. Isaac was slightly panicked, while Cameron was gloomy with his head hung down. Jacob sat in between the two, looking back and forth at them while trying not to take on their negative and anxious vibes.

"This is so freakin' crazy!" Isaac exclaimed. "It was already bad enough they're after us. Now, they're saying they'll harm our families and expose us?!"

"Isaac, panicking isn't going to help," said Jacob.

Isaac glared at Jacob and snapped, "Being calm obviously isn't either, is it?"

Jacob stared out the front window of the truck, shaking his head. Jacob glanced over at Cameron, while examined his right hand. Cameron hadn't told them about the curse Baine placed on him, because unfortunately, it had no positive outcomes. Seeing Jacob looking at him from the corner of his eye, Cameron looked at him and dropped his hand down.

"Are you all right, Cameron," Jacob said, while Cameron nodded briefly. Isaac chuckled, tapping his hands on the steering wheel.

"Of course he isn't!" Isaac exclaimed. "Given all that's going on, I'm surprised we all aren't freaking out."

Jacob looked back at Isaac and crossed his arms, twisting up his mouth.

"That's 'cause some of us have a little bit of what they call *self-control*," Jacob muttered. Isaac glared at him with a frown, looking back at the road, rolling his eyes.

"Until somebody can come up with a plan, I'm gonna continue to be on edge."

"That's gonna take some time Isaac," Jacob started again. "We have to plan thoroughly."

"We don't have time for that!" Isaac snapped again. "They are going to be two steps ahead of us now, since you don't have your power anymore."

Jacob stared at Isaac, putting his head down, while Isaac continued to vent.

"It doesn't even matter. Unless we can find a way to fabricate premonitions, we're screwed."

Jacob lifted his head quickly and broadened his eyes, dropping open. He had a plan. What Isaac said struck him with the idea of fabricating a premonition somehow. After considering the circumstances, Jacob felt he had no other choice but to rely on someone he knew could help him with his lost gift...Madame Della-Reese. Looking up at the road, Jacob noticed they were about to pass the exit that led to Medallion's Magic Shop. Jacob looked at Isaac and placed his hand on the dashboard.

"What?" Isaac asked, while Jacob stared at him.

"Take the next exit," said Jacob.

"What? Why?" Isaac argued.

"I have an idea," he said.

Within the next half hour, the three arrived at Medallion's Magic Shop. By now, a thick fog had dropped, covering many areas near Paterson. Isaac parked his truck and looked at Jacob. Jacob stared up at Medallion's, while Cameron glared at him slightly confused. Isaac and Cameron weren't sure why Jacob wanted to come back to the shop; especially since he was so eager to get out before. Jacob took a deep breath and looked at Isaac and Cameron with a serious stare.

"Okay, I'll be right back," he said. Isaac and Cameron stared at him, slightly worried.

"You aren't going in there alone, are you?" Isaac asked. Jacob looked back toward the passenger's door and exhaled.

"Yes, I had planned on it," he said.

"You can't be serious," Cameron broke his silence. Jacob put his head down, thinking of what he was going to say. Jacob lifted his head and sighed, staring out the front window to the truck.

"More than you know," he finally replied, when Cameron crossed his arms.

"Yesterday you were ready to leave this place," Cameron reminded him. "And now you're telling me that you can handle going in alone?"

Jacob looked at Cameron, turning toward the car door.

"There's something I need to take care of."

Without hesitation, Jacob climbed over Cameron and got out of the truck, walking toward the shop. Cameron took off his seat belt and tried to follow him, but Isaac grabbed his arm and stopped him.

"Let him go Cameron," he said. "I'm sure he has a reason for wanting to do this on his own."

Cameron glared at Isaac with worry and sat back in his seat, watching Jacob enter Medallion's and close the door.

Once inside, Jacob looked around briefly. All the lights were off in the shop, which was odd since the front door was still open.

"Hello," Jacob called out, his voice echoing through the shop. He continued to look around in the shadows when he felt someone grab his arm from behind him.

"Gaahh!!!" he cried. Looking back, Jacob realized it was Madame Della-Reese, holding a lit candle. He placed his hand on his chest, his heart skipping a beat.

"I told you you'd return," she said with a smirk, while Jacob stared at her.

"Yes...you did," he agreed. Madame Della-Reese stepped away from him and placed the lit candle on the front counter. Turning back toward Jacob, she smiled and placed her hand on the counter softly.

"What can I help you with?" she asked.

"I thought you would already know," Jacob replied, walking up to Madame Della-Reese.

"Unfortunately, I don't," she replied. Jacob cleared his throat and walked a little closer to her, placing his hands together.

"I actually came to apologize," Jacob started, when Madame Della-Reese raised her left eyebrow. "I didn't mean to rush out so rudely; I knew the tarot reading wasn't your doing...I just didn't agree with what it said."

"Apology accepted," said Madame Della-Reese with a smile. Jacob stared at her, changing his expression to a saddened frown. Noticing this, Madame Della-Reese stared at Jacob confused.

"You seem a lot more open than before," she mentioned.

"I am," he said. "And I need your help."

Madame Della-Reese stopped smirking at Jacob after hearing the seriousness in his tone.

"I'm actually closed for the night; maybe you can come back tomorrow morning around eleven."

"It can't wait that long," Jacob said sternly. Madame Della-Reese continued to stare at him, seeing he was greatly concerned by something.

"What exactly do you need?" she asked him, as he blew out a breath.

"My visions have been...well, stifled," he told her. She crossed her arms and frowned at him, trying to figure out what he was saying.

"I hope you don't want me to lend my power to you or transfer energy," she said with a stern tone. "I do not operate in that manner."

"No, that's not what I'm asking," Jacob told her. "I only need help with seeing a particular event in the near future."

"Ask the tarots again; I'm sure you'll get an answer from them."

Jacob was beginning to get frustrated. He placed both hands on his forehead and exhaled angrily, while Madame Della-Reese stared at him.

"Not the answer you were looking for?" she asked, placing her hands on her hips. Jacob dropped his hands down and stared at Madame Della-Reese with a frown.

"No you don't understand," Jacob said. "I need a vivid premonition of the future."

Madame Della-Reese took her hands off her hips and stared at Jacob, shaking her head.

"I'm afraid there isn't a way to do that," she said. Jacob's eyes locked on hers, with a serious frown. His eyes began to slightly tear up, when turned away from Madame Della-Reese and headed for the exit door. Madame Della-Reese began to feel powerful vibes from Jacob that she hadn't sensed before. It was as if her power showed her he was destined for greatness. Jacob reached for the door, when Madame Della-Reese suddenly put her hand on her chest.

"Wait," she called out, when Jacob turned around. "I believe there is...one way."

Jacob looked at Madame Della-Reese confused, while she began to smile at him again. She placed her hand out toward Jacob, and he walked over to her slowly. Madame Della-Reese took Jacob by his hand, walking him around the front counter, stepping up to a door that was closed. She opened the door, revealing a staircase that led to the basement of the shop. Madame Della-Reese let go of Jacob's hand and glanced back at him with a smirk.

"Follow me," she said. Madame Della-Reese stepped down the stairs, stepping into the shadows. Jacob walked to the edge of the staircase and stopped, looking down hesitantly. Then, he walked down the steps, reaching the bottom level of the shop. Looking around briefly, he saw various items shelves and eyed a several sealed boxes near the right side. Hearing a noise that caught his attention, Jacob looked to his left, seeing Madame Della-Reese standing near a doorway with beaded curtains over it.

"Come on now," she said, stepping through the curtains in a hurry. Jacob stepped around the items in his path and walked over to the doorway, stopping abruptly. Not sure what to expect at this point, Jacob stepped through the beaded curtains cautiously, where he saw Madame Della-Reese sitting near a small round table. The area was a confined space, surrounded by black curtains that made the area even eerier. Madame Della-Reese stared at Jacob, while he stood in the doorway of the room, feeling out of place.

"Have a seat," she said. Jacob walked over to the table and sat down across from Madame Della-Reese, while she continued to smirk at him.

"Have you ever practiced divination before?" she asked him, pulling a large bowl from under the table and setting it in the center. Jacob stared at her slightly confused, clearing his throat and blinking his eyes.

"No, I haven't," he replied. Madame Della-Reese took a small vial of water out of her skirt pocket. She put it on the table and looked at Jacob, placing her hands on its edges.

"The way most diviners work is usually based on their cultures' religious beliefs and rituals. But there are other *secret* ways of performing divination that are particularly grounded by a more supernatural connection."

Jacob looked at Madame Della-Reese with one eyebrow raised.

"So, which way are we gonna to use?" Jacob asked, staring at Madame Della-Reese. She picked up the vial of water and opened it, holding it over the bowl.

"The supernatural way, of course," she said. Madame Della-Reese poured the vial of water into the bowl and placed it down on the table. Jacob watched her closely, as she moved her hands over the bowl facedown and closed her eyes. She swiftly turned her hands over and lifted them up, when the water in the bowl began to expand, filling the bowl to its rim. Madame Della-Reese put her hands down on the table and opened her eyes.

"Are you ready?" she asked him. Jacob stared at Madame Della-Reese, nodding to assure her he was ready. Madame Della-Reese reached her hands out to Jacob, placing his hands over hers.

"Close your eyes," she said, "and think of what you want to know."

Doing like she said, Jacob closed his eyes and thought over what he wanted to see. Then, he thought about his mother and Isaac's mother, thinking they would most likely be Baine and Liem's first targets to get to them.

"Now, open your eyes," said Madame Della-Reese. Jacob opened his eyes and Madame Della-Reese let go of his hands.

"Are you ready to see what you asked for?" she asked him. Jacob blinked at Madame Della-Reese a few times before responding to her question, putting his head down. He could feel his heart ponding in his chest, screaming anxiously. Jacob looked up at Madame Della-Reese and nodded again, while she smiled at him.

"Yes, I am," he said.

"All right," she said. "Place your first finger on your left hand into the bowl…and you will see what you have asked for."

Jacob sat up in his seat, placing his hand over the bowl of water. With hesitation, Jacob dipped his finger into the water, watching it ripple from his touch. Jacob lifted his finger from the water, while the ripples subsided and a faint image gradually began to appear. Shocked, Jacob stood up and stared into the bowl, seeing Fiona leaving her seamstress shop near the outer parts of downtown Paterson. She held two bags of materials in her arms and walked toward her car, when something rushed by her and knocked her down. Fiona looked around in a panic, picking her things up quickly. Then, a dark shadow came behind her and grabbed her, slamming her into her car, while it held her by the neck. Soon after, the dark shadow crushed Fiona's neck and dropped her on the ground.

"No," Jacob exclaimed, while Madame Della-Reese stared at him with concern. Watching the water ripple again, Jacob saw Rachel leaving her office. She walked toward her car swiftly, when a dark shadow came over her. The dark shadow knocked her over and she stumbled to regain her balance, rushing to her car. After getting in her vehicle, the dark shadow picked it up and tossed it into a nearby building, crushing it and killing Rachel on impact.

"Nooo!" Jacob cried, when the water evaporated from the bowl. Madame Della-Reese stood up and stared at Jacob, while he panted continuously.

"What's the matter?" she asked. "What did you see?"

"I saw...my mother and my brother's mother being attacked by the darkness."

Madame Della-Reese gasped and widened her eyes. Jacob pushed his chair in and turned away from Madame Della-Reese, when she put her hand out toward him.

"Wait," she said. "I just want you to know...even though a tarot reading shows us the future, it's never what it seems."

Jacob stared at Madame Della-Reese, grasping she was referring to the tarot reading he had gotten for Cameron. Jacob didn't realize that was still on his mind. But with all that was going on, there was no way that he could keep himself from not thinking of it. Jacob smiled at Madame Della-Reese, while she smiled back at him.

"Thank you Madame Della-Reese, for everything," he said, running out of the room. Madame Della-Reese sat back down and closed her eyes, still smiling.

"He is going to be a very powerful seer someday," she said to herself.

Back outside the shop, Isaac and Cameron were beginning to get worried, waiting for Jacob to return. He had been inside the shop for almost an hour.

"Come on Jacob...come on," Cameron said, staring at the shop door. Then, the door opened and Jacob came running out of the shop, when Isaac and Cameron sat up in their seats. Jacob got to the car and got in quickly, moving Cameron over to the middle seat.

"We gotta go! Our mothers are in trouble!" Jacob exclaimed. Isaac and Cameron stared at Jacob in shock.

"What?!" the two said, when Jacob put on his seat belt.

"I don't have time to explain, just go!" Jacob hollered. Isaac started the car up and they drove out of the parking lot of Medallion's Magic Shop.

Driving down the road, Isaac looked at Jacob with concern, slightly shaky.

"Are you gonna tell us what you're talking about?" he asked. Jacob looked at Isaac and turned toward him in his seat.

"Remember what you said about fabricating a premonition?" Jacob asked.

"Yeah," said Isaac.

"The shop keeper at Medallion's is a seer like me, and I asked her for help. She showed me how to see into the future using an enhanced form of divination."

"Like what diviners do?" Cameron asked.

"Yes, like that," said Jacob.

"Okay, get to the part about our mothers please," Isaac demanded.

"The water showed our mothers being attacked downtown by some dark creatures, but I could see them clearly."

"I don't think it matters what it was that attacked them," said Isaac. "We have to save them before they're attacked."

"Yeah, but the only problem is…they were being attacked around the same time," Jacob revealed. Isaac glared at Jacob with a frown.

"So you're saying we have to choose which one we're gonna save?!" Isaac cried, while Jacob looked at him. He opened his mouth to comment, but he didn't say a word.

"You've gotta be out of your mind if you think I'm doing that!!" Isaac exclaimed.

"I didn't say that was what we were going to do," said Jacob. "But we really don't have a choice."

Cameron looked at Isaac and Jacob, figuring out an alternative way to save his brothers' mothers.

"I can save one of them while you two save the other one," he suggested. Isaac and Jacob looked at Cameron with their mouths dropped open.

"What?!" Isaac and Jacob shouted together.

"No, we aren't splitting up!" Isaac snapped. "That's exactly what the Xaviors want us to do, so we'll be forced to use our powers against them."

"Look, I don't want you guys to have to choose whose mother you want to save, cause that's not fair. And I won't have to use my powers against the enemy; I can take potions with me."

Isaac stared at the road, shaking his head, when Jacob looked at him.

"Isaac he has a point," Jacob said. "What do we have to lose?"

"A lot if this goes wrong," said Isaac.

"Yeah, but everything has already gone wrong," Cameron mentioned. "There's no sense in waiting for it to get worse."

Isaac stared at Jacob and Cameron for a moment; then, he turned back toward the road and blew out a deep breath.

"Okay, fine...I guess we have no choice."

Cameron looked at Jacob and climbed over him toward the passenger's door.

"All right, where were your mothers at?" Cameron asked.

"Well, my mom was leaving her office; it's right by your eye doctor," Jacob said. "Maybe you should go after her."

With a nod, Cameron opened the passenger door and looked back at Isaac and Jacob.

"Meet up with me after you save Isaac's mom," he said.

"We will," Jacob agreed. In a quick second, Cameron jumped out of the truck and dashed off down the highway. Isaac stared at Cameron, as he left his sight and zoomed off down the road.

"Really?" said Isaac.

"Yep, that's Cameron for you," said Jacob. The two had a moment of silence, realizing if they saved their mothers in time, they would have to explain everything to them. Jacob looked out the front window again and exhaled, while Isaac eyed him from the corner of his eye.

"You know we're gonna have to tell them about all this," Jacob mentioned. Isaac cleared his throat and swallowed, still staring at the road.

"Yeah, unfortunately," he said.

"Are you ready for that?"

Isaac looked at Jacob briefly, groaning under his breath.

"I have to be."

The wind whistled through the trees, while the night got cooler outside of Fiona's shop. Fiona was inside, bent down near the safe under the front counter. She locked the safe and turned on its alarm. Fiona stood to her feet and walked to the back office, turning off the lights and setting the alarm. She grabbed her purse and two bags from the front counter, heading for the front door. Fiona opened the door and turned the lock, leaving out of the shop and closing the door tightly. She glanced down at her watch and saw it was ten minutes before ten. Taking a breath, Fiona turned toward the parking lot and made her way to her car. While she continued walking, she heard a strange growling noise behind her, which caused her to stop. Fiona glanced back and looked around briefly, not seeing a thing in sight. She turned back around and started walking toward her car faster, when she was knocked over by a dark shadow.

"Ugh!" she exclaimed. She plunged to the ground, dropping her purse and bags. Fiona sat up and looked around herself terrified, while she started gathering her things together hastily. Then, a dark shadow came over her, when she stared at the ground with widened eyes and began to quiver. She could fell her heart rate increasing when she looked behind herself, seeing one of the Limbers the brothers had been fighting.

"EEEYAAAHHHHH!!!" the Limber screeched. Fiona fell to the ground.

"Aaaahhh!!!! Get away from me," she cried. Fiona stumbled to her feet and ran for her car, while the Limber followed after her. She reached the driver's side of her car, but before she could get in, the Limber slammed her into the back of the car and held her tightly by her neck.

"Let–go of–me," she choked, grabbing the Limber's claw, trying to pull it off her. The Limber stretched its arms out while it stood in the middle of the parking lot, still keeping a tight grasp on Fiona.

"EEEEEEEYYYAAAAHHHHH!!!" the Limber screamed. Suddenly, Fiona heard a car horn faintly. She glanced to her left and saw a truck speeding down the road toward the parking lot. While the horn got louder, the Limber looked in its direction, staring at the truck with worry.

"ERR," the Limber expressed. The truck slammed into the Limber and it went flying across the parking lot, when Fiona dropped to her knees. The truck slid across the parking lot and left large skid marks, stopping in the middle of the area. Fiona held her neck and looked over at the truck, when the passenger's door flew opened and Isaac hopped out. Fiona's face lit up and Isaac ran over to her, helping her up.

"Mom, are you okay?" he asked, helping Fiona to her feet. Fiona stared at Isaac for a moment. Then, she grabbed him and held him tightly in her arms.

"Uh...uh, mom," Isaac said. Fiona let go of him and kissed his forehead.

"I'm so glad you c–" before she could finish, the truck revved its engine, and the two looked at Isaac's truck. The truck pulled forward and backed up near them, when Fiona saw Jacob sitting in the driver's seat.

"Hi, I hate to interrupt this beautiful moment, but our friend is getting up," said Jacob. Isaac looked over and saw the Limber regaining its balance.

"Right, come on mom," Isaac said, pushing Fiona from behind into the truck. Isaac looked back at the Limber, when it locked eyes with him and began to shake angrily.

"EEEEEYAAAHHHH!!!!" it screamed, when Isaac jumped into the truck and closed the door. Jacob put the car in reverse and pulled off, speeding off on the road. The Limber growled under its breath and began to chase after them, following the path they took. The three rode down the street, while Jacob moved from around other cars to get away from the Limber. The other drivers panicked at the sight of the Limber and pulled over. Jacob continued driving and the Limber followed behind him. Fiona was staring at Jacob the entire time, while Isaac watched behind them, keeping his eye on the Limber.

"At least everybody is moving outta the way," Isaac said. Jacob smirked and looked at Isaac, while Fiona stared at him awkwardly. Jacob cleared his throat and smiled, continuing to look at Fiona.

"I'm sorry...I didn't introduce myself. I'm Jacob," he said. Fiona sat back in her seat and stared straight out the front window. Isaac looked at Jacob and shook his head, while Jacob glanced back at the road.

"I think introductions can wait 'til a little later," Isaac suggested.

Hearing a loud thud noise, the three were startled, feeling something hit the car. Seeing a shadow over the back window, Isaac and Jacob looked back and saw the Limber in the truck bed, arching its claw back.

"Jacob!" Isaac exclaimed, as Jacob turned back toward the road. "You gotta turn!"

Jacob looked up at the next intersection and saw that the light was yellow. Jacob sped up and turned to the left, when the light turned red quickly. Then, a loud truck horn sounded, when Isaac looked to the right and saw a semi-truck driving through the light.

"Watch out!!" he cried. Jacob jerked the car around in a circle. While they spun around, the Limber flew out of the truck bed and into the semi-truck, which caused it to burst from the impact. The semi-truck came to an abrupt stop in the middle of the intersection, and Jacob stopped the truck on the side of the road. Jacob and Isaac were panting heavily, while Fiona swayed back and forth. The two stared out the front window and saw the Limber exploded on the front of the semi-truck. Isaac looked over at her and held her, catching his breath.

"Mom," Isaac said, staring at Fiona. Fiona's eyes rolled into the back of her head and she passed out in her seat. Isaac gasped, when Jacob looked at her and widened his eyes.

"Oh no," he said.

"I think she's okay," Isaac told him. "My mom can't really handle a lot of unusual stuff."

"Clearly," said Jacob, when Isaac looked at him with a frown. Then, the driver got out of the truck, while Isaac and Jacob watched him try to wipe off the Limber goo.

"Well...one down, two to go," said Isaac. The truck driver looked over at them and threw up his arms, mouthing "Really?"

"Yep, that's our queue," Jacob exclaimed putting the truck in reverse and whipped back quickly. Isaac held on to Fiona and the dashboard, staring at Jacob.

"Do you always drive like this?" he asked with his eyebrows raised.

"Nope, today was a first," Jacob said with a smile. "Still glad we switched?"

"No."

"Too bad!"

Switching gears, Jacob zoomed off down the road, in route to his mother and Cameron's location.

Near Rachel's office, she was stepping out of her building, and after locking up, making her way toward her car. It had been another long and busy day at the office, which was why she had stayed so late. Slightly overwhelmed with dozens of messages from her patients and others that came in demanding to be seen, Rachel was ready to get a good night's rest when she arrived home. She began to walk down the street, until she got to the back alley parking lot and felt her phone vibrating in her pocket. Rachel took her phone out and saw it was Jacob calling her. Being so tired, Rachel didn't feel like talking at the moment and figured she would call him when she got home. Rachel declined the call and sent him back an auto reply, telling him she would call him later. Placing phone back in her pocket, Rachel continued walking toward her car, when a Limber rushed up on her and pushed her over.

"Ngh," Rachel exclaimed. She tumbled to the ground and dropped her purse.

"EEEEYYYAAHHHH!!!" the Limber cried. Rachel sat up and looked back, seeing the Limber charging toward her. She grabbed her purse and stood to her feet, and began to hit the Limber in its face with her purse, while it flinched and backed away from her.

"You–better–leave–me–alone," Rachel shouted, every word following a hit. The Limber eventually fell on its side. Rachel ran to her car and got in. Rachel started up the car and put it in reverse, turning the car around, facing the Limber. When the Limber stood up, Rachel drove toward it to smash into it, but the Limber grabbed the car from the bottom and held it in the air.

"Put me down! Put me down!" Rachel screamed, when the Limber tossed the car at a nearby building.

"Aaaahhh!!" Rachel cried. She covered her eyes, while she went flying toward the building. Suddenly, Rachel felt something hit the car from the bottom of it and was startled. She opened her eye, realizing she was floating in the middle of the air. Rachel looked around her car in a panic, watching the car lower to the ground, seeing Cameron place the car on the ground. Rachel stared at Cameron shocked, when he waved at her with a smile. She continued to stare at him, watching him look over her car. Rachel looked back and saw the Limber running toward her, when she started fumbling through her things, trying to figure out what to do. A revving engine broke Rachel's thought process and she looked back again, seeing Isaac's truck zoom into the area and slam into the Limber. The Limber flew across the lot and the truck came to a complete stop. The driver's side door flew open and Jacob hopped out, when Isaac moved over and took the wheel again. Fiona by now had regained consciousness, but was still overwhelmed from everything, while watching on in fear. Cameron ran over to Jacob and they met half way, looking over at the Limber.

"I figured you might need this," Jacob said, handing Cameron a potion vial.

"Thanks," Cameron responded. The two looked back over at the Limber, while it stumbled to its feet, staring at them angrily. Cameron gripped the vial tightly in his hand.

"EEEEYYAAAHHHH!!!" the Limber screeched, charging toward Jacob and Cameron. Reacting rapidly, Cameron tossed the potion vial at the Limber and it hit its chest, causing the Limber to fall back on the ground.

"KAAARRGH! KAAARRRGGHHH!!!" the Limber hollered. It disintegrated and turned into a black puddle on the ground. Rachel powered off her car and got out, staring at the puddle and looking at Jacob. Jacob glanced back at her, when she walked over to him and Cameron. Isaac looked out his window and stared at the puddle, when Cameron looked at Jacob.

"How many was that?" he asked.

"That was two," said Jacob. Rachel stared at them confused.

"Then, where's the last one?" Cameron wondered. They all began to hear a growling noise above them. Jacob, Cameron, and Rachel looked up at the building in front of them and saw the last Limber perched on the edge, with its bottom claws clapping the siding.

"EEEEYYYAAAHHH!!!" the Limber yelled. It lifted its head up and arched its back. Without warning, the Limber jumped down and smacked Jacob, Cameron, and Rachel, knocking them from where they stood. Rachel and Jacob fell back on the ground, while Cameron flew into the side of a building and slammed into the wall.

"Ugh!" he cried, falling to the ground. Jacob and Rachel looked over at Cameron, while the Limber charged toward them.

"Mom, get to your car!" Jacob demanded. Rachel jumped up and ran for her car, but the Limber stretched out its arm and hit her, knocking her back down.

"No!!" Jacob yelled angrily. He got up and rushed over to the Limber and jumped on its arm. The Limber shook Jacob off and hit him in his side, throwing Jacob away from it. Cameron looked up from where he lay in shock, while Isaac stared on from his truck, seeing Jacob hit the ground.

"Jacob!" Isaac cried. He watched the Limber pick up Jacob, while Jacob kicked and swung at the Limber, trying to get it off him. Isaac reached into the glove compartment and took out another vial of the potion. Isaac jumped out of the truck and threw the potion at the Limbers back, which immediately caught on fire, causing it drop Jacob on the ground.

"KAAAARRRGHHHH!!!" the Limber cried, melting on to the ground. Jacob sat up and looked at Rachel, as he hopped up and ran toward her. Isaac followed Jacob and helped him lift Rachel from the ground. Cameron stood up slowly, holding his arm, walking toward his brothers and Rachel. Cameron got up to the three and they walked back toward Isaac's truck. Fiona stepped out, letting Isaac and Jacob sit Rachel down on the edge of the seat, while she held her slightly bleeding forehead. Isaac, Jacob, and Cameron stepped back and looked at her.

"Mom," Jacob said, "are you okay?"

Rachel stared at Jacob, frowning up her face and groaning under her breath.

"Am I okay...am I okay?!" Rachel exclaimed. Isaac and Cameron flinched, not used to Rachel's flustered behavior.

"Yeah, are you okay?" Jacob asked again, while Isaac and Cameron stepped back from him. Still staring at them, Rachel dropped her hand from her head and crossed her arms.

"Well, I don't know," she started again. "I've been chased by a demonic looking creature, had my life flash before my eyes several times, and I was saved by a boy who looks strikingly familiar, but I don't know why…you tell me."

Isaac, Jacob, and Cameron looked at each other. Then, Fiona began to stare at Cameron. She too felt that he looked unusually familiar, but like Rachel, she couldn't explain why. She moved closer to Cameron and placed her hand on his face, when he staring at her in shock.

"Uh…hi," he said. Fiona continued to stare at him, while Isaac and Jacob widened their eyes and raised their eyebrows.

"Umm mom…what are doing?" Isaac asked.

"So strange," she said. Fiona eventually took Cameron's glasses off and stared at him even harder.

"Uh, I can't see without those in the dark," he mentioned. Fiona grabbed Cameron by his chin, suddenly realizing his resemblance to Samuel.

"Oh my God," she exclaimed, stepping away from him. Fiona looked at Isaac and gasped, glancing back at Cameron.

"You look…just like my ex-husband, Samuel," she said. Rachel shot a quick look at Cameron, realizing the same thing.

"Okay, can I have my glasses back now?" Cameron asked.

"That's who you look like!" Rachel exclaimed. Then, Fiona and Rachel looked at each other, slightly confused.

"Wait," Rachel thought, "*my* ex-husbands name was Samuel…and that's how I recognize him."

"That's impossible," said Fiona. "There's no way we both could've been with Samuel."

"Can I have my glasses back?" Cameron asked again, while Fiona ignored him, arguing with Rachel.

"We weren't, he was with me," Rachel snapped. Seeing a slight tension building between Fiona and Rachel, Jacob chimed in.

"Okay, before any of us jump to conclusions, let us explain," Jacob suggested, when Rachel glared at him.

"Start talking then," Rachel snapped.

"Uh, hi…blind guy over here," said Cameron, waving his hand.

"Mom, could you give him his glasses?!" Isaac exclaimed, staring at Fiona. Fiona had a double take, realizing she was still gripping

Cameron's glasses in her palm. She handed the back to him swiftly and he put them back on.

"Okay...talk," Rachel demanded. The three looked at each other, trying to figure out where to start. Then, Isaac looked at Fiona and Rachel nervously, taking a deep breath.

"Well, mom, um..." Isaac struggled. "There's something that you didn't know about dad when you married him."

"What do you mean?" Fiona wondered.

"He wasn't completely honest with you," he replied.

Shaking her head at Isaac, Fiona asked, "What does that mean?"

Isaac looked at Jacob for help, when he cleared his throat and looked at Rachel.

"There were a lot of secrets that dad kept," Jacob said.

"Like what? That he had another wife and a brother?" Rachel said sarcastically, staring at them.

"No mom, this isn't dad's brother...this is his youngest son," Jacob replied. Fiona and Rachel stared at Jacob in shock. Then, they looked at each other.

"And I'm his eldest son," Isaac told them. "Jacob is his second son."

"What?!" Fiona and Rachel exclaimed together, glaring at the three of them.

"So not only did he leave me, he was messing around with two other women?!" Rachel snapped, while Isaac shook his head.

"No, it's a little more complex than that," he said. Rachel's face turned red, while Fiona's eyes became slightly glassy.

"Then, what the heck is going on?!" cried Fiona, braking into tears. Seeing that Isaac and Jacob were still struggling with telling their mothers their secret, Cameron jumped in.

"Our dad had a secret his whole life he didn't tell anyone," he started. "He married Fiona first. But because of his secret that forbade him from marrying you and having a child, he left you to protect you."

"And he did the same thing with you mom," Jacob added. Fiona and Rachel looked at him. Fiona regained her composure and looked at Cameron.

"What about your mother? What happened with her?" she asked.

Cameron exhaled and looked off, shaking his head.

"I don't know," he said hastily with a shrug. Rachel got out of the truck and looked at the three of them with her arms crossed.

"So what was his secret?" Rachel wondered. Isaac, Jacob, and Cameron looked at each other again. This was the moment they dreaded. It was time to tell them what they had been trying to hold back for the longest. After the three nodded in agreement, they looked back at Fiona and Rachel, and Isaac revealed their father's secret.

"His secret...was that he was a witch," he said. Fiona and Rachel stepped back from the three of them briefly, staring at them. They were shocked. That wasn't what they were expecting. Rachel swallowed and she looked at Jacob, her mind racing.

"So if he was a witch...and we're not, what does that make you?" she wondered.

"Half witch, half mortal," Isaac said. Fiona and Rachel looked at him, when Jacob clarified his statement.

"Well, actually, dad was half witch, half mortal...so were mostly mortal and a quarter of a witch," he said. "But when we completely advance in our abilities, we'll be half witches."

Fiona and Rachel looked at each other again. Realizing they both had the same husband, that he was a witch, and that their sons were witches was a lot to take in at once. Fiona placed her hand on her chest, thinking of Samuel. Then, she looked up at Isaac.

"Where is he?" she asked, "Your father that is."

Isaac looked down, blowing out a breath. Then, Jacob looked at Fiona with a saddened expression.

"He...he was killed," he answered, when Fiona's eyes became glassy again.

"Why?" she asked. Jacob stared at Fiona, while tears fell down her face.

"Like Cameron said earlier, it was forbidden for him to be with you and my mother...and Cameron's, because he was witch."

Rachel shook her head, staring at Jacob, uncrossing her arms.

"I don't understand," Rachel said, still shaking her head. Jacob looked at Rachel, when Isaac looked back up to explain.

"Mortals have a power within themselves they cannot reach," Isaac started. "If a magical being or a witch had this power within them and activated it, they would be all powerful. This is considered a threat in the magical world; therefore, a law was created that magical beings couldn't mate with mortals. If the law was broken, it was punishable by death."

Rachel and Fiona paused for a moment, sinking everything in. Jacob looked at Isaac and Cameron, while Isaac finished.

"That's why dad left both of you, to protect you from that penalty."

Rachel looked up at them, staring at each of them one at a time. Then, she closed her eyes and exhaled.

"How long have you all known all this?" she asked. The three looked at each other; then, Jacob looked back at Rachel.

"For about three or four months…give or take," Jacob said, shrugging his shoulders.

"You've known all that time…AND YOU'RE JUST NOW TELLING US?!" Rachel exclaimed, startling Isaac, Jacob, and Cameron.

"Your mom's scary," Cameron whispered.

"Who you telling," Jacob said under his breath, when Rachel crossed her arms.

"Is this what you didn't want to tell me that night?" she asked him.

Jacob began to scratch the back of his head, while Isaac and Cameron looked over at him.

"…Yeah," he said hesitantly, when Rachel put her hand on her forehead.

"I just don't understand why you didn't tell me," she went on.

"You can be pretty critical at the worst times," Jacob mentioned.

"I'm your mother, I'm supposed to be critical," Rachel countered. "There was no reason you should've kept this a secret so long."

"I agree," said Fiona, looking over at Isaac. "You should've said something."

"So glad I'm not getting badgered," Cameron commented. Isaac and Jacob glared at him and crossed their arms, while he widened his eyes and stepped back from them.

"We can take care of that," said Jacob. Rachel shook her head at them, still upset that they hadn't told them everything sooner.

"Oh trust me, when I'm done…all of you are gonna feel badgered," she said. "What did you think we would do if you told us? Disown you?"

"Yeah, kind of," said Isaac. Fiona and Rachel glared at him. "Witchcraft goes against what you thought me, but it's a part of who we are."

"If that's how you three feel, why didn't you think we'd feel the same way?" Fiona wondered.

"We were scared," said Jacob. "It took us a long time to accept everything ourselves."

"We're your mothers," said Rachel. "You shouldn't feel that there's anything you can't tell us."

"Okay, from now on…no more secrets," Jacob said. Isaac and Cameron nodded, agreeing with him.

"Good," said Rachel. "Now for starters, what the heck was all this about?"

"Yeah, about this," Isaac said, looking at Jacob and Cameron for help explaining.

"Um, well…it started after we first found out we were witches," Jacob told them. "We were asked to join the fight against the dark forces,"

"The 'dark forces?'" Rachel wondered.

"Yes, but we just realized they're being orchestrated by two warlocks known as the Xaviors," said Cameron.

"They're power thieves that steal other magical beings abilities," Isaac added. "We aren't sure what they're plotting, but they've already taken Jacob's power."

Fiona and Rachel stared at the three, confused by what they were telling them.

"What does that have to do with us?" Fiona wondered. "We don't have anything they want do we?"

"No," Jacob answered. "But they threatened us that if we didn't give up our powers, they would kill you…and expose us to the wizards over the magical world that killed our father."

Rachel closed her eyes and slightly tensed up, exhaling deeply.

"So, what do we do now?" she wondered. Jacob looked at Isaac, and he looked at Rachel.

"The plan was to take you both to my apartment outside of the city," Isaac suggested. "I've never been attacked out there, so I figured it'd be a safe haven…until we get this situation under control."

"Wait, what about James…and Jay J?!" Rachel exclaimed, looking at Jacob.

"I don't think they go that far," Jacob said. "As long as we end this tonight."

"Then, why can't we just go there?" Rachel wondered, while Cameron cleared his throat.

"If we take you guys out there, that'll put us all at risk," he said.

Rachel stared at Cameron and crossed her arms again. Isaac looked at his watch, seeing that it was 10:30pm.

"Unfortunately, we don't have time to explain everything," Isaac stressed. "We have to get you there now."

Isaac looked at his mother and she got into his truck cautiously. Rachel continued to stare at the three, when Jacob held out his hand to her.

"I'll drive your car and follow Isaac," he said. "You and Cameron can ride with me."

Rachel handed Jacob her keys and he and Cameron walked over to her car. She followed behind them, while Isaac watched them and hopped in his truck. After getting settled in their vehicles, they left the area and headed for Isaac's apartment.

Even after their drive to Isaac's apartment, Fiona and Rachel still weren't very happy with the idea. They continued to ask questions the entire ride, trying to get closure with everything. The three were able to give Fiona and Rachel more information about Samuel, mainly how he had been communicating with them and all that he had told them about the magical world. Eventually, the two realized they had to trust that Isaac, Jacob, and Cameron knew what they were doing. After leaving their mothers at Isaac's apartment, the three returned to the manor in Isaac's truck, entering with haste. Isaac and Cameron rushed in and Jacob followed behind them. Once they all enter the manor and shut the door, Liem appeared in the front yard, when thunder and lightning struck in the night.

"It's only a matter of time," he said, staring up at the top of the manor. Liem lifted his hands in the air and looked up, while darkness built up in his palms. The darkness swirled around his arms and surrounded his body, and he looked back down at the manor with a smirk. Liem closed his eyes and could see what was going on inside the manor, as if he were inside with them.

Isaac and Cameron walked toward the staircase in the hall and glanced back at Jacob, seeing a look of worry in his eyes. He began to feel like something was about to go wrong, though he wasn't sure how. He didn't have his power anymore, but he couldn't stop what he felt.

"What's wrong Jake?" Cameron asked. Jacob looked up and saw Isaac and Cameron staring at him with concern.

"Nothing, just thinking," he replied, shaking his head.

"Well, I think we should check the Book and see what dad thinks we should do," Isaac suggested.

"Okay," Jacob agreed with a nod. The three made their way up the stairs, heading for upper level of the manor. After reaching the attic, Isaac rushed over to the book and began to flip through it, looking for what they could do next. Jacob and Cameron walked into the middle of the floor, staring at Isaac, while he searched the book diligently. Then, the strange feeling Jacob felt moments before returned. Cameron looked at Jacob, while he stared off into space.

"Jacob," Cameron started, when he looked up at him. "Are you okay?"

Jacob stared at Cameron, remembering this moment, having experienced it several times before. Jacob stepped back from Cameron slightly and began to take deep breaths, and Cameron looked over at Isaac.

"He'll be okay," said Isaac. "We all will, once this is over."

Jacob glared at Isaac, when Cameron walked over to Isaac and the two continued flipping through the book. While Jacob looked around the attic, what was going on suddenly hit him. He was experiencing déjà vu. Though he had technically seen this event three times before, he had never lived through it. Within moments, a chill rushed over him and he glanced back at the attic entrance.

Outside, Liem opened his eyes. Liem held his arms out toward the front door and the darkness created a large dark aura between his palms. Then, the aura shot from his hands toward the manor rapidly.

BOOM! Isaac and Cameron looked up at the attic entrance, while Jacob began to pant nervously.

"We gotta move guys! We gotta move!" Jacob exclaimed.

"What are you talking about?!" Isaac exclaimed. Jacob ran up to the podium and the darkness shot into the attic toward them. Isaac and Cameron stared at the darkness in shock, while Jacob leaped in front of them.

"Watch out!" Cameron exclaimed. The darkness hit the three and knocked the back, pushing them out the attic window. Isaac, Jacob, and Cameron fell down toward the front yard, when a dark vortex appeared below them and swallowed them up.

"Aaaaahhh!!!" the three cried, as the vortex vanished.

Cameron gradually regained consciousness, after a thunderous crackle echoed over him. His eyes shot open and he placed his hand over his forehead. Cameron sat up hesitantly and looked around the area, realizing he had lost his glasses. After patting his hands around on the ground for a couple of moments, Cameron grabbed his glasses and wiped them off on his shirt, putting them back on. He looked behind himself and saw Isaac and Jacob lying on the ground. Cameron crawled over to them and placed his hands over their backs, shaking the repeatedly.

"Guys...guys!" he exclaimed, when Isaac and Jacob opened their eyes slowly. The two sat up and looked around the area. Jacob looked behind Cameron and widened his eyes, when Isaac glared at him.

"What? What is it?" he asked. Isaac and Cameron looked behind themselves, realizing what Jacob was gawking at. A tall, black mansion stood far off from them, while trees stretched over a dark path of gravel. The three stood up and looked around, trying to figure out where the vortex had taken them.

"Where the heck are we?" Isaac asked. Jacob and Cameron looked at Isaac; then, Jacob looked forward at the mansion.

"I don't know," he said. "But I'm sure that mansion is our only option at this point."

Isaac and Cameron glared at Jacob, when he started walking down the path toward the mansion. After exchanging a quick look at each other, Isaac and Cameron followed behind Jacob slowly. The three eventually reached the tall brass doors that led to the inside and stopped, feeling eerie about entering.

"I really don't think this is the best idea," Cameron mentioned, when Jacob grabbed a hold of the door handles.

"We don't have a choice," he said. Jacob pushed the doors open and the three stepped in, gazing around at the mansion's main hall. Black marble flooring covered the entire area, travelling from the foyer to the upper level of the mansion. A dual staircase stood in front of them, while a dark lit chandelier hung over them. The three stepped closer to the staircase, when the front doors slammed shut. They jumped in shock and glared back at the door, breathing heavily. After moments of silence, a familiar voice echoed through the mansion.

"Ha, ha, ha, ha, ha...welcome boys," the voice laughed. Cameron looked toward the second floor, recognizing the voice immediately.

"Liem," he grumbled with a frown, dashing up the stairs.

"Cameron, wait!" Isaac exclaimed. Isaac and Jacob rushed after Cameron, following him up the stairs. Once he made it to the second floor, Cameron looked around the wide spaced hall. Eventually, he glanced to his right and saw Liem standing in the middle of the floor. Liem smirked at Cameron with his arms crossed, while Cameron stared at him angrily.

"You," Cameron growled and charged at Liem, grabbing him by his shirt.

"Whoa, whoa, whoa...Cameron, what's your deal?" Liem asked with a laugh.

"I trusted you...I trusted you!" Cameron screamed at Liem.

Isaac and Jacob rushed up the stairs and saw Cameron holding Liem up in the air.

"Cameron stop, he'll take your powers," Jacob warned him.

"I don't need to use my powers on a pathetic being like him," said Cameron. Liem stared at Cameron and began to laugh loudly, grabbing a hold of his hands.

"Oh Cameron…I'd think again," Liem countered. Then, shocks penetrated from Liem's palms and electrocuted Cameron, when Liem thrust him back.

"Ugh!" Cameron cried, falling back on the floor. Isaac and Jacob ran over to Cameron and helped him up, when Liem walked closer to them.

"What the heck is this place?" Isaac asked, while Liem stared at him.

"In the early seventeenth century, this land was founded by the first Xavior, a German native named Louis Xavior. When he tried to claim this land for our family, a coven of witches came against him to take the land and kill him. As a last resort, he cast a spell over them: Ich appelliere an die Dunkelheit, Senden Sie meine Kräfte in Abgrund. Sie werden das Opfer, nehmen Sie ihre Kräfte für den Preis."

Liem smirked at the brothers, while they stared at him confused.

"If you can hear a resemblance, the spell we used on you three was derived from that spell our ancestor created. After the spell was cast, all of the witches used their powers against him, and lost them immediately. Louis Xavior took advantage of the witches' shock, and killed them with their own abilities. Thus began the greatest legacy…of power thievery."

Liem placed his hand on his chin, still smiling at the three, while they stared at him angrily.

"And if it wasn't for Jacob's omniscience combined with ours, we would have never found it."

"Thanks for the unnecessary history of the Xaviors," said Isaac. "But if you two think you're going get away with this, you're not."

Liem laughed again and shook his head.

"We already have," he said. "And now, it's time to claim what belongs to us…power."

"How can others' power belong to you?" Jacob wondered. "What kind of twisted perception is that?"

"It's a perception like that one that keeps you alive this world," said Liem.

"You're insane," said Cameron. Liem glared at him.

"Cameron," Liem started, "you know are way is the way you've always wanted."

Cameron stared at Liem confused.

"You've wanted nothing more than to be free with your powers like, Baine and me," Liem said. "You can have a life of *true* magical freedom."

Liem stopped a few feet away from Cameron and held his hand out toward him with a smirk.

"Join us...take the path to freedom," said Liem. Isaac and Jacob stared at Liem with worry, while Cameron stood still. This was the moment Cameron was dreading. He had to decide whether to deny them or join them; to live...or to die. Cameron looked down at his right palm, staring at the lines on his hands, while Jacob stared at him in fear. He couldn't stop thinking of the tarot reading he had gotten, and if this was what it had foretold. Jacob watched Cameron, when him closed up his hand and held it tightly, glaring back up at Liem.

"You're right...that's what I want," Cameron started, while Liem stared at him. "But I don't want that anymore."

Liem's eyes widened in shock and his smirk departed, while he lowered his hand to his side. Then, Cameron felt a sharp stinging pain shooting from his palm.

"Ugh!" he exclaimed, turning his hand over. Darkness built up in his hand, when the last major line turned black, and a straining pain shot up his arm to his heart. Cameron held his chest and looked at Liem, while he stared at him angrily.

"That was the wrong choice, Cameron," he snapped, holding held up his right hand. Shocks appeared around Liem's hand, while Isaac and Jacob stared at him.

"Let me put you out of your misery," Liem growled.

"No!!" Isaac hollered, waving his hand at Liem. Liem jerked back a little and stopped, when the shocks vanished from his palm and Isaac stared at him confused. Isaac waved his hand at Liem again, but nothing happened.

"Oh no," Isaac said, realizing what he had just done. Dark blue lights left out of Isaac and went inside of Liem's hand. Seeing this, Isaac and Jacob stepped back with fear in their eyes, when Liem looked at his hand. With a laugh, Liem turned stared the three and smirked.

"Oh...I'm sorry," he said, "were you trying to do...this?!"

Liem waved his hand at Isaac, Jacob, and Cameron, which tossed them down the hallway into the wall.

"Ngh!" they cried, tumbling to the floor. Liem lifted himself into the air and raised his arms up, while the mansion rumbled like there was an earthquake.

"You wanna play boys...let's play!!" he exclaimed, while the three struggled to get up. Jacob looked at Liem, while he searched himself for a potion. Finding one in his pants pocket, Jacob hopped up and ran toward Liem, tossing the vial at him. Liem put out his hand and sent the vial flying back at Jacob. It hit the ground and knocked Jacob into glass case. The case shattered over Jacob and hit the floor, stabbing the palm of his hand with a piece of glass.

"Aah!" he cried, moving himself away from the casing and pulling the glass out of his hand. Liem put his hand out toward Jacob, when Cameron looked up at him and pushed himself up. Cameron charged at Liem and jumped him, knocked him down on the ground. Isaac rushed over to Jacob and tore off the bottom of his shirt, wrapping his wound quickly. The two looked over at Cameron and Liem, while they rolled over on the ground and Cameron pinned Liem down. He began to punch Liem in the face, when he grabbed Cameron's hand.

"Come on Cameron, beat me to a pulp," said Liem. "You know you want to."

Angered, Cameron stood to his feet and lifted Liem up, arching back his left fist to punch him in the face with his full strength.

"Cameron, No! He's trying to get you to use your powers on him!" Isaac yelled, when Cameron paused. Out of nowhere, the pain in Cameron's chest came back, which caused him to drop Liem on the ground. Reacting quickly, Liem stood up and grabbed Cameron in his chest and caused him more pain, while he smirked at him.

"You know what's really funny, Cameron?" he said. "You're the pathetic one."

Liem hit Cameron in the face and knocked him back on the floor. Isaac got up and ran toward Liem, but he waved his hand and knocked Isaac away from him. Isaac flew back and hit the balcony over the staircase and flipped over it, when Jacob rushed over to him.

"Isaac!" Jacob cried. He got up to Isaac and grabbed him by his arm. Isaac hung from the balcony, while Jacob kept a tight grip on him. Liem watched the two and stepped around Cameron, walking toward them slowly. While Jacob pulled Isaac up, Liem put his arm out toward them and shock waves started extruding from his hands.

"And this is where you die," he exclaimed. Jacob looked back at Liem, when Cameron sat up, watching Liem prepare to attack his brothers.

"No!!" Cameron groaned, grabbing Liem by his leg and pulling him down. When Liem hit the ground, Cameron pulled him toward him and punched him in the face again. Liem grabbed Cameron and threw him off of him, standing up quickly. Cameron rolled over and bounced back up, staring at his brothers, when Jacob finally helped Isaac over the balcony safely. While Cameron wasn't looking, Liem charged at him and knocked him down. Liem raised his right hand in the air and an Athamé appeared in his clutches.

"Time to end you," he said, coming down on Cameron with the Athamé. Cameron grabbed Liem's hand and stopped him, thrusting him off rapidly. Cameron flipped over and jumped up, when Liem rolled over and leaped to his feet. He charged at Cameron and the two collided, with Liem holding the Athamé near Cameron's chest. Cameron and Liem struggled back and forth, while Cameron tried to stop Liem from stabbing him. Cameron felt the sharp pain in his chest again, which caused him to lose some of his strength. He got closer to Cameron's chest with the Athamé and Cameron continued to get weaker. He knew that in a matter of moments Liem would stab him in the heart with the Athamé. The only way for him to stop him was to use his powers against him one last time. Glaring at Liem, Cameron grabbed Liem's hand, forcing his hand away from him. With a quick thrust, Cameron shoved the Athamé into Liem's chest.

"Ugh!" he groaned, staring at Cameron. Suddenly, light blue lights began to leave Cameron and went inside of Liem, while Cameron felt his strength draining. Liem stared at Cameron angrily and shaking repeated.

"You–will–die!" he exclaimed, shoved Cameron away from him.

Cameron flew down the hall and hit the wall, getting punctured in his back to through stomach by a large iron hook.

"Cameron!!!" Isaac and Jacob cried, rushing over to Cameron. Cameron fell on to the floor, when Isaac and Jacob got up to him.

"Stay with us buddy…stay with us," Isaac panicked. Liem enjoyed a soft laugh, dropping to his knees and panting.

"He's going to die–a painful–and slow death," Liem said, pulling the Athamé out of his chest and dropping it on the ground. "Good luck–dragging him back–to the vortex–before it closes."

The doors to the mansion flew open and the vortex that swallowed the brothers up reappeared at the end of the gravel path. Isaac and Jacob looked back at Liem, when he slowly vanished from the mansion. Isaac and Jacob stared at each other with worry and picked up Cameron, holding him over their shoulders and dragging him out of the mansion. Once they got outside, the vortex began to slowly disappear, while they drug Cameron along the dirt road.

"Come on Cameron, we gotta get you home," Isaac said. Right before it closed, the three were in range for the vortex to catch them in its rift, and they were swallowed up once more.

In the Xavior's cave, Baine stood still in the throne room with his eyes closed, replaying the previous events over in his head. Suddenly, Baine's eyes sprung open, when a look of worry came over his face. He sensed that Liem was mortally wounded, and there was a strong possibility that he wouldn't survive the stab wound from his cursed Athamé. Baine's eyes filled with tears and he balled up his fists, staring off in the cave. He began to panic.

"Liem…LIEM!!!" he screamed. Without warning, Liem appeared before Baine and dropped to his knees. Baine rushed over to him and bent down, lifting his face up to look at him.

"Liem, are you all right?" he asked with a shaky tone. Liem stared at Baine with a slight smirk.

"I have all of their powers Baine," Liem said. Baine stared at him and shook his head.

"I don't care about that right now," Baine snapped. "I need to know if you're all right."

Liem laughed lightly again and shook his head.

"You have to take their powers from me before I die," said Liem. "It's the only way you can kill them."

"No, no, no!!" Baine shouted, while he shook Liem in his grasp. "Stop talking like that, you hear me?! You're not going anywhere."

"Baine, it's over. I screwed up…I didn't go according to our plan."

"It's fine Liem, it's all right" said Baine. Liem shook his head at Baine again. He was in denial. Liem knew the cursed Athamé was killing him slowly, but Baine wouldn't accept it. Liem took Baine's hand and placed it over his chest, while Baine stared at him.

"Take the powers form me now Baine," said Liem, "Before it's too late."

Baine stared at Liem, while tears fell down his brother's face. Doing as Liem said, Baine closed his eyes, and lights came out of Liem in three different shades of blue. Once the lights entered Baine, he opened his eyes and stared at Liem.

"I'm–so sorry…Baine," Liem said. His eyes closed and he fell into Baine's arms. Baine held Liem tightly in his arms, while he started shaking angrily.

"Noooooo!!!!!" Baine cried, laying his head down on Liem's lifeless body.

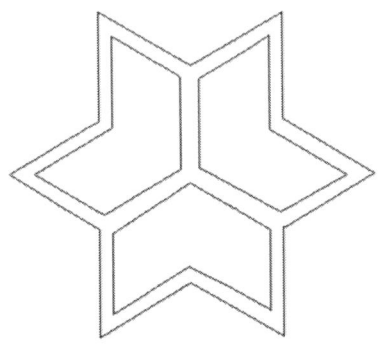

THE LAST STAND

ISAAC AND JACOB BURST INTO THE ATTIC, carrying a severely wounded Cameron to the center of the room. They placed Cameron on the floor, while he continued to shiver and look at them. Isaac and Jacob bent down near him, staring at his bleeding wound. They lifted Cameron up and took off his jacket, laying him back on the floor gently. Jacob began to unbutton Cameron's shirt, staring at the whole in his stomach while shaking nervously. Upon seeing the wound uncovered, Isaac gasped and leaned back.

"Oh God," he groaned, covering his mouth. Isaac began to look around the room, when Jacob looked at him.

"What are you looking for?" Jacob asked.

"A pillow to elevate his head," said Isaac, still looking around frantically. Jacob got up from the floor and ran out of the attic. Isaac moved closer to Cameron and he lifted him into his lap and held him in his arms.

"It's gonna be okay buddy…just hold on," he said while Cameron stared at him, his eyes closing slowly. Cameron's forehead and chest became clammy, his temperature dropping rapidly. Isaac wiped his tears off and grabbed on to Cameron's hand, seeing how much strength he had left. His grip was gradually getting weaker, but he held on while his vision became blurred and hazy.

"Don't let go Cameron, don't let go," Isaac whimpered, his eyes becoming glassy. Then, Jacob ran back into the attic with a small pillow, bending down by Isaac and Cameron. He placed the pillow on the floor under Cameron. Isaac put him back down on the floor. Tears fell down Isaac's face and he began to look around frantically again. Jacob looked up at Isaac with teary eyes, while Isaac wept.

"Where's a–a towel or something," he cried.

"For what," Jacob wondered, staring at Isaac.

"We gotta stop him from bleeding," he answered. Jacob shook his head at Isaac, glancing over at him.

"Isaac, a towel isn't gonna stop him front bleeding."

"Well, we gotta do something!"

"He has a whole in his stomach through his back Isaac!" Jacob snapped.

"Then what the heck are we supposed to do?!" Isaac exclaimed.

A loud thud startled the two and they glanced back at the podium, seeing that the Book of Magic had popped open. Then, the Book started flipping itself through several pages. Isaac stood to his feet and wiped his eyes, walking over to the Book, when it stopped on a page for a healing remedy.

"What is this?" he asked himself out loud, while Jacob stared at him.

"Jacob, there's a tonic in here that we can use to heal his wound," Isaac exclaimed.

"Do you think it'll work?" Jacob wondered.

"I'm not sure," he said. Jacob looked down at Cameron again, checking his pulse, which continued to drop rapidly.

"I don't think we have time to be making tonics," said Jacob, shaking his head. "His pulse is dropping too fast."

"That's where faith comes in," Isaac declared. He picked up the Book and placed it on the table next to the cauldron. He ran over to the cabinet and grabbed various ingredients needed for the remedy. Isaac went back over to the table and began to put the ingredients in a small bowl quickly, while Jacob held on to Cameron's hand. Cameron began to gradually close his eyes, which caused Jacob to panic.

"Come on with the tonic Isaac, we're losing him," Jacob exclaimed.

"I'm making it as fast as I can," Isaac countered, picking up a spoon and mixing the contents together, until it was a light yellow paste. Placing the spoon back on the table, Isaac rushed over to Cameron with the bowl and bent down near him. He put his hand in the bowl and grabbed a handful of the remedy, moving toward Cameron's stomach. Seeing him, Jacob grabbed his wrist and stopped him.

"Wait a second," said Jacob. "You can't just touch bloody wounds with your bare hands. We need gloves."

"Screw gloves!" Isaac snapped, pulling his hand from Jacob's grasp. "Cameron's our brother, and I'm not about to waste another second to save him just to put on some gloves."

Isaac began to place the paste on Cameron's wound, while Jacob stared at him, seeing the determination in his eyes. With little hesitation, Jacob reached into the bowl and joined Isaac, rubbing the tonic over Cameron's stomach. When the two finished, Isaac placed the bowl down on the floor beside them and stared at Cameron. The wound wasn't healing. Isaac leaped up and looked at the Book, reading over the recipe for the remedy several times. Shaking his head, Isaac ran back over to Cameron and bent over him.

"Cameron wake up buddy, wake up," he said, staring at Cameron. Then, their amulets began to glow their respective shades of blue, while Isaac and Jacob continued watching Cameron. Isaac held Cameron's hand, when his hands began to glow bright white. Jacob looked at Isaac and saw this, widening his eyes in awe.

"Isaac," said Jacob, "your hands."

Isaac looked at his hands and saw them glowing. Then, Jacob glanced down and saw his hands were also glowing. The two stared at each other, feeling they knew what to do now. Jacob held Cameron's other hand, as the two moved their free hands over Cameron's stomach. Cameron's wound started healing, while Isaac and Jacob continued holding on to him. Suddenly, darkness came out of Cameron's body, breaking the curse that Baine put him under. Then, he started glowing white, when the wound healed on his stomach completely. Cameron stopped glowing and shot up from the floor, gasping for air. Isaac and Jacob stared at Cameron with joy, and their hands and amulet's stopped glowing.

"Cameron!" Isaac exclaimed, grabbing Cameron.

"Hey…what…what happened?" Cameron asked. Jacob placed his hand over his back.

"You almost died," he said, "but we saved you, somehow."

Isaac let go of Cameron and stood up, looking over at Jacob, while Cameron held his forehead.

"Man…I have the worst headache," said Cameron.

"Come on Jacob, let's help Cameron get cleaned up," Isaac suggested. Jacob nodded in agreement and the two helped Cameron to his feet, walking out of the attic.

About ten minutes after eleven, Cameron was lying down on the couch in the living room, while Jacob sat next to him. Isaac paced back and forth, staring at the Book of Magic while it sat on the table. The three had all lost their powers, but somehow could still use magic if they connected. Their issue now was figuring out how to take out Baine before midnight. Isaac stopped pacing and stared at the Book, while Jacob looked at him.

"So, we've obviously established that we can still use magic, but only if we connect," Isaac said, looking over at Jacob and Cameron. "But I don't think that's enough to keep ourselves from getting killed."

Jacob cleared his throat and stared off in the room, trying to think of an idea.

"Maybe we should try and make a potion that'll blow him up," Cameron suggested, holding a cold towel over his forehead.

"That's too risking," Isaac shot down the idea.

"Why?!" Cameron exclaimed, sitting up quickly from where he laid. Jacob placed his hand on Cameron's shoulder and pushed him back on the couch, shaking his head.

"Number one: he has our powers, and the last thing we need to do is make a potion that he can throw back and kill us with. Number two: you don't need to be sitting up that fast yet; you did almost die."

Cameron rolled his eyes, leaned back on the couch, and blew out a deep breath, staring at the ceiling.

"Well, there has to be something we can do," he argued.

"Like what?" Isaac asked. Cameron shook his head and closed his eyes.

"I don't know...cast a spell or something," he said. Jacob glared at Cameron. What Cameron said sparked something. He began to recall his vision of them in the attic before the darkness attacked them. There was a spell in the Book they found, though the darkness attacked them in reality sooner than in his vision. Whatever the spell was, he knew it would help them deal with Baine. Jacob stood up from the couch and walked around the coffee table, picking up the Book and flipping through its pages. Isaac stared at Jacob confused, while Jacob stared at the Book firmly.

"What are you looking for?" Isaac asked. Jacob stopped and placed the Book down on the table.

"This," he said. Isaac looked at the Book and saw that Jacob had found an astral projection spell. Isaac looked at the Book with his eyebrows raised, glancing back at Jacob.

"An astral projection spell?" he wondered. "What are we supposed to do with that?"

"I had a vision yesterday that we were in the attic, and you and Cameron were flipping through the Book...much like how we were before the darkness attacked us and sent us through that vortex. There was a spell in the Book that you guys found, but I couldn't see what it was clearly. I only saw a few words."

"And this was what we found?" Isaac asked.

"Yes," Jacob replied. "I just trusted my instinct to find it, but I know for sure this is it."

Cameron sat up slowly and looked over at Isaac and Jacob.

"Okay, that still doesn't tell us how to defeat Baine," Cameron mentioned. Isaac nodded in agreement with Cameron.

"It's simpler than you think," Jacob started again. "In astral form, our spirits will separate from our bodies, which will bide us so time."

"To do what exactly?" Isaac asked.

"Distract Baine," Jacob answered. Isaac and Cameron stared at Jacob, skeptical of his idea. They weren't sure the plan would be necessary or efficient. Seeing their doubt, Jacob reiterated.

"Look, I know you guys don't think this will do us any good, but I feel that if we weren't meant to use this spell, I wouldn't have seen in in my vision."

"We get that," said Isaac. "But the concern is what do we do after that?"

"We can set a trap for him," said Jacob. "This house is our stronghold; and I think if we lure him back here, we'll be able to defeat him."

Isaac and Cameron glared at each other for a moment. Then, they looked back at Jacob.

"All right," Isaac said, walking over by Cameron. "What's the plan?"

"I'm assuming Baine is waiting for us to surrender to him before midnight," Jacob started.

"Okay…so?" Isaac wondered.

"I think he's in the cave we met him in earlier."

"So we go and pretend like we're surrendering–"said Cameron.

"–And trick him into following us back here," Isaac finished.

"Exactly," Jacob agreed. Isaac crossed his arms and looked off, thinking everything over. Then, he turned back toward Jacob and Cameron and nodded.

"Okay, this will be a challenge," Isaac started, "but if we think we can do it, we better give it our all."

"Right," said Jacob. "Let's do this."

Midnight was closing in on them quicker than the last few hours had passed. They were determined not to give up hope, though the odds were clearly not in their favor. The three arrived in the area outside of the Xavior's cave in Isaac's truck, hesitantly stepping out. They waited for each other, not moving faster than the other, continuing like that until they reached the large willow tree by the lake. Jacob looked around the area briefly.

"So is this our happy medium?" Cameron asked, still looking off.

"Yes," Jacob replied. "If anything goes wrong, we make sure we meet up here."

"Sounds easy enough," said Isaac. Cameron looked back at them and put his hands in his pockets, while Isaac stared at him. Jacob began to reach into his jacket pockets, pulling out three pieces of paper.

"Here's the spell," he said, handing the papers to Isaac and Cameron. "Now, when we came here the first time, I saw a few different entrances to the cave."

"We went through the main one?" Cameron wondered, staring at Jacob.

"Yeah, but I think we should split up," said Jacob. "He won't be able to sense us casting the spell if we're not together."

"He'll still see us coming," Isaac mentioned.

"Yes...but he won't sense us if we're separated," Jacob added. Isaac shrugged, staring off into the area, when Cameron looked at Jacob.

"So, where exactly are these *other entrances*?" Cameron asked.

"I wrote out maps on the back of the spell," Jacob informed them. "Isaac can use the entrance we took before."

Jacob looked at his watch, realizing it was 11:30 PM. Jacob exhaled, looking back at Isaac and Cameron.

"All right, let's go," said Jacob, when he and Cameron walked away from the willow tree. Isaac watched them go their separate ways, while he stood still. Isaac closed his eyes to clear his head of any doubt; then, he opened them back.

"Isaac, you can do this," he told himself. He walked off from the tree and headed for the cave's entrance.

Jacob reached the other side of the black lake, near one of the other entryways to the cave. He walked aside the lake slowly, glaring around at the dark trees and bushes that surrounded him. *I know it's around here somewhere*, he thought, staring at the paper and continuing along the path past the lake. Once he turned the next corner, Jacob looked to his right and saw the entrance to the cave.

"Great," he said, walking toward the cave. Stopping near the cave,

Jacob flipped the paper over on the opposite side and stared at the spell, clearing his throat.

Meanwhile, Cameron walked along a dark path near a swamp, when he reached another cave entrance. Cameron stared at the cave, stopping in front of it. He flipped the paper over to the spell, shaking nervously.

"Okay…get it together. It's just a spell Cameron," he reassured himself with a sigh. Cameron held the paper in front of himself, staring at the spell.

Near the main entrance, Isaac walked toward the cave and stared at it firmly, second guessing their plan. He knew there were several things that could go wrong, the main one being that Baine could figure them out early on and attack their true bodies while they were in astral form. Isaac closed his eyes and took a deep breath, saying a prayer to himself.

"Please help us," he said. "Shield and protect us from the darkness…guide us by your light."

Opening his eyes, Isaac lifted the paper up, and the three began to read the spell simultaneously from where they were.

"Depart from thy body–" Isaac started.

"–Depart from thy soul," Jacob continued.

"Once this is done–" said Cameron.

"–Return to us whole," the three finished together. Isaac, Jacob, and Cameron closed their eyes and white transparent figures left their bodies. They dropped their heads down and stood in place, while the bodily figures hovered into the cave, from their respectable entrances.

Inside the cave, their white bodily figures hovered into the center area of the cave, lowering to the ground. Then, they turned into Isaac, Jacob, and Cameron. The three looked at each other surprised, while glancing around in the cave.

"It worked," Cameron exclaimed.

"Shhh!!" Isaac and Jacob said, as Cameron covered his mouth. Jacob looked around, seeing if anything was lurking nearby that could've heard them. Nothing was in sight, and the cave was quiet.

"It doesn't look like anything is around," said Isaac.

"That doesn't mean anything," Jacob mentioned. "We have to keep our guards up at all times."

Cameron uncovered his mouth and looked over at the hall that led to the pentagram chamber. He looked at Isaac and Jacob with a nod and the three walked into the chamber. Once they entered, the three stepped into the center of the pentagram seal, and it lit up immediately. They looked to the left and saw the hallway leading to the throne room.

"Come on," said Isaac. He began to walk toward the hallway, while Jacob and Cameron followed close behind him. The three walked through the hallway and got up to a large brass door. This was odd, because they hadn't remembered that being there before. Isaac stepped forward and grabbed on to the door knob, turning it slowly and opening the door.

The area was dark and dimly lit, but it didn't seem to be like a cave anymore. The three looked around, seeing several red stained glass windows along the walls, with the flooring being changed to marble. The three looked onward and saw a large black throne, seeing a dark figure sitting in the seat. The three stopped and stared at the figure, watching it stand from the throne. Suddenly, candles lit up along the walls, revealing the figure was Baine, who was draped in a cascading cloak of darkness. The three continued to look at Baine, while he frowned at them. Eventually, Isaac cleared his throat and crossed his arms, staring at Baine firmly.

"What's this about? Preparing for your proposed victory by remodeling your cave?" Isaac instigated, while Baine looked at him angrily.

"You three have some nerve…entering my cave like this," said Baine, watching Cameron tightened his fists. "And no, Xavior's mansion is merging with the cave."

Isaac, Jacob, and Cameron stared at each other briefly, looking back at Baine shortly after.

"The mansion has always been the core of the Xavior's power. But when we lost it, we lost the core of our *true* power. Now that it's been relocated, I will be more powerful than many may have expected."

"Are we supposed to be scared?" said Cameron, crossing his arms. Baine began to walk toward them again, stopping in the middle of the room.

"I'm going to assume you three have come to surrender before midnight," Baine said. Jacob laughed under his breath, as Baine turned to him.

"Well, we kind of assumed you would've known that," Jacob commented.

"Hmm," Baine grunted, staring off in the room. "No matter what you've come for…I have control over what happens next."

"So you're backing down on your own word?" Isaac wondered.

"No, what I'm doing is following through with my original plan, before you three even connected."

"Which was what?" Jacob asked. Baine dropped his frown and smirked at the three.

"To kill you three and take every ounce of magic that flows through you."

The three widened their eyes and stepped back from Baine.

"All I wanted from the beginning was to take your powers and destroy you, so my brother and I could take over the magical community and rule it together. Of course, Liem had to grow fond of a certain someone who he felt would be a good addition to our brotherhood, which triggered a vision I saw that Cameron would join us. But it was just a fabricated illusion of what Liem wanted, and my powers channeled his feelings…before he even had them."

Isaac, Jacob, and Cameron stared at Baine, when he frowned at them again.

"Now that he's been killed, I can start fresh with my original plan and avenge him…by getting rid of our enemies!"

"What makes you think you'll be able to over throw the entire magical community?" Isaac asked. "Do you really think that one warlock can do that?"

"With the power of you three…I can do anything," Baine said with a smirk. Without warning, Baine waved his hand and the three flew out of the throne room. They slide across the hallway floor and rolled into the pentagram chamber. When the three struggled to get up, Baine rushed up to them and thrust an electric shock at them, knocking them back into the walls. Cameron stood up and stared at Baine angrily, while Isaac and Jacob looked at him. Then, Cameron charged at Baine, while Isaac and Jacob stared on in shock.

"Cameron don't!" Jacob exclaimed. Baine smirked at Cameron and held his right hand out. Suddenly, a knife appeared in Baine's grasp and he stabbed Cameron in his stomach.

"Ugh," Cameron cried, looking at Baine. Baine dug the knife deeper into Cameron's stomach and twisted it to the side, causing him to gag. Baine pulled the knife out of Cameron abruptly and he dropped to the ground. Baine looked at the knife with a smirk, but changed his expression to shock, realizing there was no blood on the knife. He stared down at Cameron, seeing no blood coming from his stab wound.

"Impossible," he muttered through his teeth. Baine glared at Isaac and Jacob and he began to breathe deeply with anger.

"Uh oh," Jacob exclaimed, scrambling to his feet with Isaac.

"Let's go Jake," Isaac shouted, grabbing a hold of Jacob and running deep into the caverns. Baine followed after them, while the two ran off to escape him. Then, darkness appeared around Baine and he merged with it, turning into shadows and dashing toward them. Baine charged directly into Isaac and Jacob, knocking them away from each other. Baine grabbed a hold of Jacob and slammed him against the wall, turning back into himself. Baine held Jacob by his neck, when the knife appeared in his hand. Baine stabbed Jacob in his lower back and pulled the knife out, seeing that there was no blood. Baine dropped Jacob on the ground and stared back at Isaac, watching him jump up and run off. Then, Baine's eyes twitched and he began to see the three brothers looking through the Book of magic and finding the astral projection spell. Shortly after that, he saw the three in the woods near the cave, casting the spell on themselves at the same time. Baine's vision cleared and he began to shake with rage.

"You can't escape me!" he exclaimed, returning to his shadow form and rushing after Isaac.

Meanwhile, outside the cave, Cameron's body remained motionless, when suddenly his spirit returned. Cameron gasped and dropped to his knees, grabbing his stomach. The piercing pain from the stab wound his astral self received was present, but it gradually lessened when he stood to his feet. He assumed by now, the spell had worn off and Baine had figured them out. Cameron began to looked for Baine, but there was no sign of him anywhere.

"I gotta find the others," he said to himself. Cameron ran away from the cave, while he looked side to side for Isaac and Jacob. He rushed past the swamp and ran through the trees, until he reached the lake. Cameron stopped and stared at the lake, looking back and forth. Then, he heard someone calling out to him.

"Cameron, Cameron," a familiar voice cried out. He looked behind himself and saw Jacob running toward him. Jacob caught up to him and stopped, panting heavily while he tried to catch his breath.

"I–I found you," Jacob panted, hanging over his knees. Blowing out a breath, Jacob stood up straight and cleared his throat.

"Where's Isaac?" Cameron wondered. Jacob looked around for a brief second, glancing back at Cameron and shaking his head.

"I don't know," he said, "I've been looking for him too, but I didn't see him anywhere."

Jacob and Cameron paused. Then, the two rushed off toward the main entrance of the cave, where they saw Isaac's body frozen in place.

"Oh no," Jacob exclaimed, while he and Cameron walked over to Isaac. "He hasn't awakened yet."

Jacob and Cameron stared at each other with their eyebrows raised, looking back at Isaac worried.

Back inside the cave, Isaac continued to run from Baine through the caverns, while he shot darkness around him. Debris dropped from the ceiling around Isaac and he dodged it as fast as he could, eventually getting knocked down.

"Ngh!" Isaac exclaimed, falling over on his side. Baine caught up to him and turned back into himself. Baine bent down over Isaac and grabbed him by his shirt, slamming him on the ground repeatedly. Then, Baine lifted Isaac up in the air and stared at him furiously.

"You thought you could fool me…ME!?!" he exclaimed, slamming Isaac into the wall. Isaac began to choke, while Baine pressed his hand up against his throat. Baine held out his right hand again, when an Athamé with a pentagram on the handle appeared in his grasp.

"Well guess what? I'll be the one with the last laugh this time," said Baine. Baine stabbed Isaac in his stomach and twisted the Athamé to its side, when a dark aura appeared around it. Baine smirked at Isaac and began to say a spell.

"With these wounds thou shall not hide, return his soul like a raging tide. Now the blood his soul will shed…shall leave his body cold and dead."

Isaac stared at Baine, feeling his pain becoming gradually worse. Suddenly, Isaac felt something moving down the back of his head and his neck. He looked down and saw blood dripping from his shoulder. Isaac looked back at Baine, realizing he was turning his astral self into his whole self. Isaac's vision became blurred, feeling himself slipping away into death.

Back outside the cave, Jacob and Cameron watched Isaac's body, when wounds began appearing on him that weren't bleeding.

"What's going on?" Cameron exclaimed, while they stared at Isaac in shock. Then, Jacob and Cameron's amulets began to glow, but Isaac's didn't. The two stared at Isaac's body confused, when a strong sense came over them abruptly. They could feel the pain that Baine was inflicting on Isaac's body from inside the cave, realizing that the body that stood before them had been transformed into Isaac's astral self.

"This can't be," said Jacob. Cameron ran up to Isaac's body and shook him repeatedly, trying to wake him.

"Isaac, Isaac wake up!!! Come back to your body now!!" he exclaimed, while Jacob shook his head.

"That's not gonna work," said Jacob. Cameron looked back at Jacob, his mouth dropped open.

"Well what the heck do we do!?! Baine's killing him!"

"I know. I'm trying to figure that out."

"There's gotta be a way we can reverse the spell."

Jacob stared at Cameron, searching his pockets for the astral projection spell. Pulling out the piece of paper, Jacob started rewording the spell in his head to bring Isaac's soul back.

"Okay," said Jacob. "Um…return to his body, bring back his soul. His spirit is done…now make him whole."

Staring at Isaac's body, the two gazed at him in amazement, watching his amulet glow along with theirs.

Inside the cave, Baine held the knife inside of Isaac's stomach, until he heard him take his very last breath. Baine snatched the Athamé out of Isaac's stomach and stared at him. Suddenly, Isaac's eyes turned white and his body dropped.

"What!?!" Baine exclaimed in shock. Then, the white bodily spirit came out of Isaac's body and hovered out of the cave, while Baine watched angrily.

"NOOOOOOOOOOOOOOOOOOO!!!!!!!" Baine screamed. He picked up Isaac's lifeless astral body and threw it across the room. Baine placed his hands on his head and began to breathe heavily, when his eyes twitched and he saw Jacob and Cameron by Isaac's body. Then, he heard Jacob casting the spell, realizing that was what stopped Isaac from dying. His eyes twitched again and he shook furiously, as the cave began to vibrate like there was an earthquake.

"AAAAAAAAAAHHHHH!!!!!!" Baine screamed again, staring up at the ceiling of the cave.

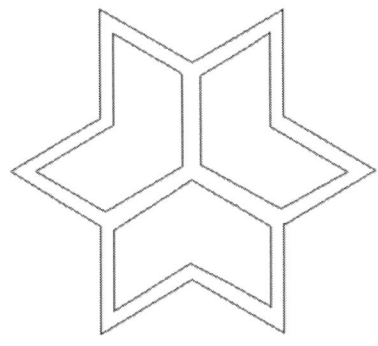

THE FINALE

ISAAC OPENED HIS EYES and dropped to the ground, panting heavily and catching his breath. Jacob and Cameron bent down near Isaac and helped him to his feet, as their amulets stopped glowing.

"Oh my God! Isaac, are you okay?" Jacob asked. Isaac looked up at him and nodded, still panting. Jacob looked around for a moment; then, he looked over at Cameron.

"We need to keep moving," he suggested. Jacob and Cameron helped Isaac continue on, making their way back to Isaac's truck. By the time the three made it to the large willow tree, they began to feel the area shaking and stopped. They looked around frantically, trying to see if Baine was in sight. Isaac looked up and saw dark clouds coming together in the sky, while the wind brushed through the area with force.

"What the heck is going on?" Cameron wondered. Suddenly, the three heard Baine's holler echoing through the area. The three looked back toward the cave and lightning struck above them.

"Baine's coming," Isaac said. Jacob and Cameron looked over at him with worry in their eyes.

"Come on guys we gotta go," Jacob suggested. The three rushed from under the willow tree and ran off through the woods.

Back at the entrance of the cave, shadows swirled together and turned into Baine. He walked out into the woods and looked around. His nostrils were flared and his face was swollen with anger, while he tightened his fists and shook anxiously.

"I WILL KILL YOU THREE–IF IT'S THE LAST THING I DO!!!!" Baine screamed. Baine raised his left arm into the air and electric bolts surrounded it quickly. After a rapid thrust of his wrist, a bolt of lightning shot out of Baine's hand and into the sky, which caused the lightning to strike faster and harder than earlier. With a slight spin, Baine turned back into the shadows and dashed off into the sky.

Isaac, Jacob, and Cameron continued running through the woods, when Baine caught up to them and knocked them all over. Cameron rolled over on the ground and Baine leaped on top of him, grabbing him by his neck. Baine grasped him tightly, while Cameron tried to force him off.

"You three are such fools! You think you can stop me without you powers!?!" Baine taunted.

"Stop!" cried Jacob. He and Isaac stood to their feet and the two ran toward Baine to get him off Cameron, but Baine sent them flying back away from him.

"Ugh!!" they exclaimed, hitting the ground on their backs. Then, all three of their amulets began to glow again and a force field shot out of Cameron's amulet, knocking Baine away from him. Isaac and Jacob rushed over to Cameron and helped him up, running away from that area shortly afterward. Baine lifted himself up and growled under his breath. The darkness swallowed him up and he shot up into the air.

Continuing to run off, Isaac ran a little faster than Jacob and Cameron to make it to his truck.

"Isaac, slow down!" Jacob shouted. Isaac got to the parking area outside the woods and ran over to his truck. He opened the door on the driver's side and hopped in quickly. Isaac started the truck and turned on the windshield wipers, when he looked out his window and saw Jacob and Cameron running out of the woods. Jacob and Cameron jumped into the truck and began to put on their seat belts, while Jacob stared at Isaac angrily.

"Thanks for running off like that!" Jacob fussed. Isaac put the truck in reverse.

"Well, we can't waste any more time," Isaac responded. "We have to get out of here."

Isaac backed out of the spot and put the car in drive, pulling off from the area. Soon after, Baine's shadows rushed through the air over the parking lot. The wind blew through the trees, and Baine's shadows shot off in the direction the brothers had gone in.

On a dark road, the three were going through the storm, making their way back to the manor before Baine caught them. Isaac was staring straight down the road, while Jacob and Cameron looked around the area.

"Still think this was such a good idea Jacob?" Isaac asked.

"It got him to follow us, didn't it?" Jacob asked

"Yeah, but it almost got us killed," Isaac snapped.

"It wasn't like we knew that was going to happen," Cameron jumped in.

"Right, but we did know that we were going into this powerless didn't we?"

Jacob and Cameron sat back in their seats, ignoring Isaac's comment. Jacob felt they were going too fast and looked over at the speed meter, seeing that Isaac was driving 90 MPH.

"Isaac, you're going too fast," he said.

"Would you rather me go too fast, or go the speed limit and get caught?" Isaac asked. "Besides, it's not like the police will see us out here."

Jacob and Cameron glanced over at Isaac, while rain came pouring down. Isaac turned the wipers up and they brushed across the window rapidly, but the road was still unclear from the heavy rain fall. Suddenly, a faint siren sounded off in the distance, as Jacob and Cameron looked around.

"What the heck is that?" Cameron asked. Jacob sat still and listened through the strong winds and rain, realizing what the sound was.

"It's a tornado siren," said Jacob. Jacob and Cameron looked out the back window of the truck and saw debris swirling around in a circular motion in the middle of the road. The siren got louder. Soon the debris got caught up in the wind, when a loud rushing noise like a train could be heard. Without warning, a tornado touched down on the road behind them.

"Holy crap! It's headed this way!" Cameron exclaimed with widened eyes.

"Isaac! Isaac you need to pull into a ditch or something!" Jacob cried.

"I'm not pulling over," said Isaac. "This could be Baine's way of trapping us. We have to try to escape!"

Ignoring Jacob's plea, Isaac floored the accelerator and the truck pulled forward quickly. Jacob looked over at the speed meter, seeing Isaac was over 110 MPH. The truck began to sway back and forth on the road, while tree branches and debris flew toward it.

"Isaac, watch out!" Jacob hollered. Isaac began to swerve on the road, dodging the wreckage that came at them. He managed to dodge some of it, but eventually the front widow was struck by a tree branch, which created a large crack in the front window.

"Isaac, pull the car over now!" Jacob cried. Isaac continued driving down the road, while the storm worsened and the tornado got closer.

"I'm not stopping! We can't let him win!" Isaac retorted. Jacob stared at Isaac with disbelief. Jacob's facial expression converted to a frown and an angered stare, due to Isaac being so irrational. Cameron looked back at the tornado again, seeing that it was closer than before.

"Can we please stop!?!" Cameron said anxiously.

"No! Chill out, I've got this under control!" Isaac exclaimed.

"No you don't Isaac! This is not having it under control!!" Jacob snapped. Cameron began to shake nervously and began to breathe heavily.

"Oh God…we're gonna die, we're gonna die!" he cried.

"Would you just stop the car before it's too late?" Jacob pleaded again. "We might be able to let the tornado pass!"

"LOOK!! IF YOU BOTH WOULD SHUT UP I COULD FOCUS AND WE WILL GET OUT OF THIS JUST FINE!!!" Isaac yelled, his throat becoming slightly hoarse.

"ISAAC STOP BEING STUBBORN AND PULL THE STUPID CAR OVER!!!"

CRASH! A large tree branch collided with the truck on the passenger's side and shattered the window, knocking the truck into the center of the tornado. The truck spun around rapidly, while Isaac, Jacob, and Cameron clung to the truck desperately.

"Aaaahhh!!!" the three cried together. Debris and other wreckage constantly smashed into the truck, bouncing them around like a Ping-Pong ball.

"Guys, hold on!!" Isaac shouted.

"We aren't gonna make it!!" Cameron cried.

SCHREECH! CLUNK! The passenger's door ripped off its hinges and Cameron's seat belt snapped off. A gust of wind rushed through the truck and pulled Cameron out of the truck.

"Aah!!!" he screamed, grabbing on to the top of the seat.

"Cameron!!!" Jacob hollered, taking Cameron's arm to prevent him from flying out. Isaac looked over and saw Jacob struggling to save Cameron, when he reached from behind him and grabbed Cameron's other arm. Isaac and Jacob held on to Cameron tightly, pulling him back in the truck. Then, another tree branch crashed into the truck from the driver's side, which spun the car around in a circle. Isaac, Jacob, and Cameron held on to each other, when a large piece of debris smashed into the front window and shattered it, as they covered themselves and the glass fell on them. The three looked out the front window, seeing an image of Baine's face appear within the tornado.

"Baine!" Isaac exclaimed.

"THIS IS THE END FOR YOU THREE!!!" he exclaimed. With a sudden charge, Baine dashed toward the truck, and sent it hurling back.

"Aaaahhh!" they wailed. The truck began to fly out of the tornado, everything seeming to go in slow motion. Isaac, Jacob, and Cameron gripped each other tightly, their lives flashing before them. This was the end of the line. Right before the truck flew out of the tornado, the spirit of their father appeared above them, as they glanced up slowly.

"My sons...you have done well," he said softly, "It's time to come home."

Samuel's spirit reached his hand out to them and smiled.

"Take my hand," he said to them. Isaac, Jacob, and Cameron reached for his hand and held on to it, becoming immersed in a bright white light. The truck flew out of the tornado and hit on to the ground several feet away. It flipped over a couple of times, right before crashing upside down, crushing the roof of the truck. The tornado lifted itself in the air and vanished into the clouds, when Baine's shadows came charging toward the truck. Once they touched the ground, the shadows turned back into Baine. He gripped his fists tight, approaching the truck with haste. Reaching the driver's side, Baine grabbed the door and snatched it off, with lightning and thunder roaring above him. Baine bent down to observe the scene, seeing that Isaac, Jacob, and Cameron's bodies were gone. Baine stood back up slowly, while he widened his eyes and shook with fury.

"NAAAAAAAAAAAAAHHHHHHHH!!!!!!!" Baine exclaimed, his face turning red. Baine lifted into the air, turning into shadows once more, and he dashed off into the stormy sky.

Jacob opened his eyes. Rain fell on his face, while he stared up into the sky. He turned over and lifted himself on all fours, realizing he was in the front yard of the manor. Jacob stared up at the house in shock. He was certain after they had flown out of the tornado they were dead, but the spirit of their father must have pulled them out in time. Jacob looked back and saw Isaac and Cameron, still lying unconscious on the lawn. He got up and ran over to them, shaking them to wake them from their comatose state.

"Isaac, Cameron! Wake up, wake up!" Jacob cried, placing his hands over their backs. Isaac and Cameron struggled to lift themselves up, looking up at him. With a brief smile, Jacob grabbed Isaac and Cameron by the hand and helped them to their feet.

"I can't believe were alive," said Isaac. Thunder roared loudly and lightning struck in the sky. Isaac, Jacob, and Cameron looked up and felt a strong gust of wind come over them. The three quickly ran up to the door of the manor and went inside, locking the door behind them.

Isaac and Jacob walked into the main hall and stopped near the staircase to catch their breath, while they exhaled deeply.

"Are you all right?" Isaac asked, looking at Jacob. Jacob nodded and sighed, looking at Cameron. He had his head hung down, suddenly dropping to his knees. Tears fell down Cameron's face and he whimpered under his breath. Seeing this, Isaac and Jacob walked over to him and Jacob bent near him.

"Cameron, what's wrong?" Jacob asked. Cameron looked up at Jacob and Isaac.

"We're going to die," said Cameron. "We should've just died in the storm; we can't stop Baine."

"Cameron, don't talk like that," said Jacob, while Isaac stared at Cameron slightly worried. He felt like he agreed with Cameron. They had no powers to against Baine, and at this point, his wrath would probably enhance his abilities. But deep down Isaac knew if they stayed together, they would make it through. Isaac bent down near Cameron and placed his hand on his back.

"Cameron, you're wrong," Isaac started, shaking his head. "We made it out alive because we were meant to. And we can beat Baine, as long as we stick together."

Cameron lifted his head up and wiped his face, sniffling continuously. "You think so?"

"I know so," Isaac replied. Isaac placed his hand over Cameron's with a smile.

"You're right," Jacob chimed in, as Isaac glanced over at him. "We have something Baine will never have…a bond, a bond that ties us together."

Jacob placed his hand over Cameron's other hand and Isaac looked at them with a smile. Jacob glanced back at Isaac, placing his hand over his.

"We have an unbreakable bond," Jacob said. Isaac and Cameron looked at him and nodded in agreement.

"Exactly," Isaac agreed. Then, their amulets began to glow and a bright white light shone under them. The three saw looked down and saw the divided six-pointed star appear under them, flashing three different shades of blue. Suddenly, the symbol stopped flashing and the divided lines vanished, creating a whole six-pointed star. Isaac, Jacob, and Cameron looked up at each other and realized what had happened. They had reached their full potential.

Like their father's spirit stated, they would not reach this point until they developed a strong brotherly bond. With the sudden change of events, the three had to depend on each other in a way that brought them closer. Isaac, Jacob, and Cameron stood up and looked at each other in slight shock. Their amulets stopped glowing and the six-pointed star disappeared from underneath them.

"We've done it," Isaac exclaimed, looking over at Jacob and Cameron. "We've reached our full potential!"

"How?" Cameron wondered.

"I think we finally realized that being together is our true strength," Jacob mentioned. "We trust in each other, not our powers."

"It all makes sense now," Isaac added. "Dad wanted us to realize that our power was in our bond...we were trying to rely on ourselves...our powers. But in the end, we had to put our lives in each other's hands."

Outside the manor, Baine's shadows hit the ground in the front yard, while lightning struck down and the shadows turned back into him. He exhaled heavily, staring at the manor furiously.

"This is your end," he groaned with a deep sigh. Baine dashed toward the door of the manor and his shadows consumed him again. He burst into the manor, knocking Isaac, Jacob, and Cameron back into the table in the dining area. The three hit the table and it collapsed on to the floor. Isaac, Jacob, and Cameron struggled to sit up, seeing the shadows turn back to Baine, while he stood at the end of the hall. Baine waved his left hand and the front door shut behind him. The three stood to their feet and Baine stopped near the staircase, tightening his fists. He stared at them angrily, and the three stood close by each other, waiting for Baine to make a move.

"You thought you would be able to escape me, didn't you?" he sneered. Jacob and Cameron swallowed, staring back at him fearfully.

"We did get away," Isaac retorted. "And we're obviously still alive...aren't we?"

Baine stared at Isaac with a frown. He looked at the three of them for a moment; then, a smirk came up on his face.

"Ah, ha, ha, ha, ha, ha," Baine laughed. "Boy, you sure know how to be cocky for someone who has no power."

"We have more power than you think," Jacob jumped in. Baine looked over at him, his eyes narrowed.

"Hmm...I beg to differ," Baine said, thrusting his left palm out, which caused the three to fly back into the wall. After they dropped to the floor, Baine lowered his hand to his side and smirked at them maliciously, letting out another cackle.

"You know, it's a shame I'm going to have to kill you three. What a waste of power, which will soon be MINE!"

Isaac, Jacob, and Cameron grabbed each other's hands and lifted themselves from the floor.

"You can't have our true power," said Cameron, staring at Baine. "Because you'll never understand what it is."

Baine looked at Cameron and laughed under his breath, raising his left hand into the air.

"We'll see about that," Baine said with a smirk. Darkness shot out of his palm and dashed through the air, shattering all the lights throughout the manor, which darkened it immediately. Without warning, Baine was consumed by the shadows and charged at the three, but they ran off into the kitchen. Once they made it to the kitchen, they looked over to the right at the back staircase to the second floor.

"Come on!" Isaac exclaimed, rushing toward the staircase. Jacob and Cameron began to follow behind him, when Baine's shadows burst through the kitchen door and grabbed Cameron's legs.

"Aaaahhh!!" Cameron cried, as Baine's shadows pulled him down the stairs. Isaac and Jacob looked back and saw the shadows swallowing Cameron, running back and to save him. The two grabbed Cameron's hands, holding him tightly.

"Don't let go Cameron!" Jacob exclaimed, while he and Isaac continued to pull him from the shadows. Then, a bright white light expelled from their hands and hit Baine, shocking him as he fell back into the kitchen.

"Naaaahhhh!" he exclaimed. Cameron stumbled on the staircase, when Isaac and Jacob lifted him up and made their way up the stairs quickly. Reaching the second floor, Isaac closed the door to the stairs. Baine got up and charged up the staircase, returning to his shadow form. Baine burst through the door and knocked Isaac, Jacob, and Cameron into the middle of the hallway. Jacob looked up and saw Baine's shadows coming over him. The shadows grabbed Jacob's neck and lifted him against the wall, Baine's face becoming clearly visible while he tried to choke Jacob. Isaac and Cameron got up and rushed over to aid Jacob, when darkness shot out of Baine toward them. Isaac and Cameron placed their palms out in front of them, stopping the darkness from attacking them and pushing it back. Then, a bright light shot out of their hands and knocked Baine off of Jacob.

"Ngh!!" he cried, flying into the wall and dropping Jacob on the floor. Isaac and Cameron grabbed Jacob and the three ran toward the steps to the attic. Baine lifted himself up and stood in place, watching the three rush up the stairs.

"You can't escape me…it's already over!" Baine yelled. Isaac, Jacob, and Cameron made their way into the attic, Isaac closed the entrance door, and they rushed over to the Book of Magic.

"I don't think closing the door is really helping," Cameron mentioned.

"It's stalling him for a second though," Isaac replied. "He has to use more force to get through."

"Okay, we need to focus on how to stop him," Jacob intervened. Without warning, the Book of Magic popped open, flipping itself through the pages quickly.

"Uh, what's going on?!" Cameron exclaimed. Suddenly, they saw their father's handwriting appear when the Book opened on a blank page. The three watched the writings diligently, seeing the words of a spell appeared one by one:

We call upon all power, from darkness to light

Shine your forces through the skies moonlight

Darkness we now banish thee

As you feel the power of Trinity

Isaac, Jacob, and Cameron stared at the Book in shock. Then, Baine crashed through the attic door. The three looked up at him and he walked toward them slowly.

"Hmm, hmm, hmm, hmm, hmm...It's over now boys," he laughed. "Too bad you have to die this way. It will be the biggest disgrace to your ancestors."

The Book of Magic shook on the podium. The three glanced back down at it and looked at the page to the right of the spell:

READ IT NOW!!!

The three looked at each other and nodded, looking back down at the Book.

"We call upon all power, from darkness to light," Isaac started with a shaky tone, when Baine's smirk turned to a frown. He charged at them rapidly and they flinched, but he was knocked back by a transparent force field that appeared when he got close to them. Isaac, Jacob, and Cameron looked up and saw Baine on the floor, while the force field subsided. The three glanced back down at the Book and Jacob began to read the next line.

"Shine your forces...through the skies moonlight," Jacob read. Baine stood up and stared at them, when turbulent winds began to swirl around him. Then, Cameron looked down at the Book and read on.

"Darkness we now banish thee," Cameron said nervously, looking up at Baine. Baine suddenly began to feel a strange burning sensation in his chest, placing his hand over his heart.

"Stop this...NOW!!!" he demanded. The three looked back down at the Book and read the final line of the spell together.

"As you feel the power of Trinity," they declared. Bright white auras come down from the ceiling and swirled around Baine quickly. Then, the six-pointed star appeared under them, glowing bright blue.

The winds that spun around Baine closed in on him and the darkness became consumed by the light. The burning in his chest worsened, when Baine shot his last look at the brothers.

"NOOOOOOOOOOOOOO!!!!" Without warning, a burst of red light shot from Baine's chest and he vanished. The winds stopped and the white auras dimmed, while Isaac, Jacob, and Cameron stood still behind the podium, realizing they had defeated Baine.

"We did it...we did it!" Cameron exclaimed. The three shared a brief embrace, seeing three blue auras appear where Baine was vanquished. They walked around the podium and stood in the middle of the attic, when their amulets began to glow. The three looked at each other confused and the auras flew toward them, entering them. The three began to feel tingling sensations flowing through them and began to glow different shades of blue.

"Are powers are coming back," Jacob realized. The three stopped glowing and looked at their amulets, seeing the glow dimming slowly.

"Our bond will keep us strong," Isaac said with a smile.

"We just can't forget that," said Cameron, Jacob laughed under his breath.

"I know we won't forget," said Jacob. "I'm sure of it."

BANG! BANG! BANG! A continuous knocking was heard at the front door of Isaac's apartment later that morning. Fiona woke from her sleep and sat up quickly on the couch. Rachel opened her eyes and stared at the door firmly, sitting up in the recliner. Fiona and Rachel stared at each other. Then, they both stood to their feet and crept over to the door. Fiona stayed behind Rachel, watching her reach for the door knob, while the knocking continued. Pulling the door open, the two gasped in awe, seeing Jacob and Cameron standing before them.

"My goodness, we thought something got you," Cameron said.

"Oh thank the Lord!" Rachel exclaimed, grabbing Jacob and Cameron tightly.

"Ugh! Uh, mom...I'm suffocating here," said Jacob.

"Oh," Rachel stepped back from them with a smile, "I'm sorry."

Jacob stared at Rachel and shook his head.

"Actually, no I'm not!" Rachel exclaimed, grabbing Jacob again for another brief bear hug.

"Mom, you have to remember, I'm only a hundred and thirty-five pounds...with clothes on," said Jacob. Cameron chuckled under his breath and Jacob stared at him with a frown. Fiona stepped around them and peeked down the hall, seeing Isaac walking up to them from the right.

"Isaac!" she exclaimed, rushing out to him. Fiona grabbed Isaac and held him, as he widened his eyes in shock.

"Hi mom," he said, patting her on the back.

"Is everything okay?" Fiona wondered, staring into Isaac's eyes. Isaac nodded at her with a smile.

"Yeah, we got our powers back...and the dark forces have been stopped," he said. Fiona smiled at Isaac and held him again, kissing him on his cheek. Cameron smiled at Isaac and Jacob, seeing they were happy to be reunited with their mothers. Then, Rachel cleared her throat and Cameron looked over at her.

"I never got to thank you for saving me," she said to Cameron, her arms wide open. With a smile, Cameron hugged Rachel and she held him tight, like he was her son.

"Thank you," she said. Cameron's eyes became glassy, while Jacob watched them with a smile. Isaac and Fiona stepped over to them, when Rachel let go of Cameron and he wiped his eyes.

"So, is it over?" Fiona asked. Isaac looked at her and nodded again.

"Yes, it is," he said. "But I don't think this is our last fight."

"What are you going to do?" Rachel worried, looking at Jacob. Taking a deep breath, Jacob stared at his mother and crossed his arms.

"We're gonna keep fighting, for our freedom," he said. "And for a better world."

Fiona and Rachel looked at each other, not sure what Jacob meant.

"But that doesn't matter right now," said Isaac. "We've got plenty of time to prepare for all that."

"So, what are we going to do about telling James and Jay J?" Rachel asked Jacob. Jacob paused for a moment, and then he looked at her and slightly twisted his mouth.

"I think that can wait for another day," he said.

"So we're not going to tell them?!"

"Yes mom. Just not right now," Jacob replied. Isaac looked at his watch, realizing it was ten minutes until nine. With a smile, he looked at Jacob and Cameron, when they glanced back at him.

"Let's get outta here shall we?" he asked.

"Yes, 'cause I am starving. Let's stop at a breakfast café or something," Rachel suggested, as the five walked out of Isaac's apartment and closed the door.

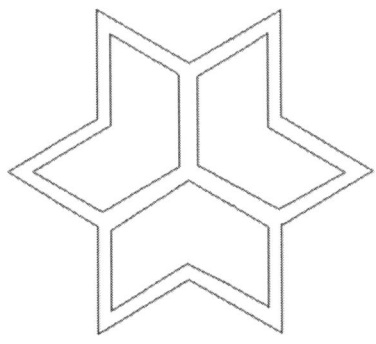

A MAGICAL LIFE

THE MOON WAS FULL THAT NIGHT, while the stars sparkled brightly in the skies. Cameron sat on the grassy hill at the end of Manor Avenue, staring up at the stars. Several thoughts were running through his mind. So much had happened over the last few months: he found out he had brothers, found out he was a witch, battled countless demonic creatures, and stopped the dark forces. To be honest, he was surprised to be alive. Even after all that had happened, he didn't know what would be next.

Cameron exhaled, still staring at the sky, when he heard a noise behind him. Looking back, Cameron saw Isaac and Jacob walking over to him.

"Hey," said Isaac.

"What's up," Cameron asked. Isaac and Jacob sat down on the ground, their backs facing each other.

"What are you doing out here?" Jacob asked, peering over his shoulder. Cameron shook his head, looking back at Jacob.

"Nothing...just thinking," he said.

"About?" Isaac wondered. With a chuckle, Cameron turned his upper body toward Isaac and Jacob.

"Everything," said Cameron, when Isaac and Jacob turned toward him. "So much has changed in my life recently...some things I wouldn't have ever expected."

"Yeah," Isaac agreed, "in mine too."

Jacob stared at Isaac and Cameron, turned back around, and took a deep breath.

"At least some were good ones," Jacob started. "But we've all learned how to deal with them."

"Yeah," Cameron said with a sigh, turning away from them. Isaac glanced at Cameron, raising his eyebrows.

"What's wrong Cameron?" he asked. Cameron paused for a moment, staring up in the sky again.

"I just keep wondering...what happens next?" he said. "I mean, I know we still have things to do, but how do we know where to start?"

Isaac and Jacob looked at each other. They hadn't thought about that yet. Their main focus for so long had been to stop the dark forces and the Xaviors. Now, with them defeated, their next move was up in the air. Jacob and Isaac turned back away from each other, staring into the stars as Cameron was, taking in the cool breeze that brushed across them.

"I think we'll figure all that out in due time," said Jacob firmly. "We just have to wait and see what's in store for us."

Isaac nodded in agreement. "I think Jacob's right. We'll know exactly what to do when it's time. So for now–"

Isaac leaned back, lying flat on the grass with a smile.

"–we should try to relax and enjoy our break."

Jacob and Cameron looked at Isaac, smirking at him. Then, the two leaned back on the grass, gazing at the stars. Suddenly, some of the stars began to glow brighter than others, forming a six-pointed star, similar to the symbol that appeared under the brothers the night before. The three stared on in awe, watching the symbol glow in the sky.

"You know what else I thought about?" Cameron asked.

"What?" Isaac and Jacob responded together. Cameron grinned, closing his eyes.

"Yesterday was Friday the thirteenth," he said. Isaac and Jacob paused.

"Wow, that is crazy," Isaac replied. Cameron chuckled under his breath, opening his eyes.

"I think that was the best bad luck I've ever had," Cameron joked. Isaac and Jacob laughed with Cameron, shaking their heads.

"I agree," said Jacob.

"Me too," said Isaac.

Made in the USA
Charleston, SC
04 January 2014